EX L

VINTAGE CLASSICS

THE BACHELOR

Stella Gibbons was born in London in 1902. She went to the North London Collegiate School and studied journalism at University College London. She then spent ten years working for various newspapers, including the *Evening Standard*. Stella Gibbons is the author of twenty-five novels, three volumes of short stories and four volumes of poetry. Her first publication was a book of poems, *The Mountain Beast* (1930), and her first novel *Cold Comfort Farm* (1932) won the Femina Vie Heureuse Prize in 1933. Amongst her works are *Christmas at Cold Comfort Farm* (1940), *Westwood* (1946), *Conference at Cold Comfort Farm* (1959) and *Starlight* (1967). She was elected a Fellow of the Royal Society of Literature in 1950. In 1933 she married the actor and singer Allan Webb. They had one daughter. Stella Gibbons died in 1989.

ALSO BY STELLA GIBBONS

Cold Comfort Farm
Bassett
Enbury Heath
Nightingale Wood
My American
Christmas at Cold Comfort Farm
The Rich House
Ticky
Westwood
The Matchmaker
Conference at Cold Comfort Farm
Here Be Dragons
White Sand and Grey Sand
The Charmers
Starlight

STELLA GIBBONS

The Bachelor

VINTAGE BOOKS
London

Published by Vintage 2012

2 4 6 8 10 9 7 5 3 1

First published in Great Britain by Longmans, Green & Co. Ltd in 1944

Vintage
Random House, 20 Vauxhall Bridge Road,
London SW1V 2SA

www.vintage-classics.info

Addresses for companies within The Random House Group
Limited can be found at: www.randomhouse.co.uk/offices.htm

The Random House Group Limited Reg. No. 954009

A CIP catalogue record for this book
is available from the British Library

ISBN 9780099529323

The Random House Group Limited supports The Forest Stewardship
Council (FSC®), the leading international forest certification organisation.
Our books carrying the FSC label are printed on FSC® certified paper. FSC is
the only forest certification scheme endorsed by the leading environmental
organisations, including Greenpeace. Our paper procurement policy can be
found at www.randomhouse.co.uk/environment

Typeset in Bembo by Palimpsest Book Production Limited,
Falkirk, Stirlingshire
Printed and bound by CPI Group (UK) Ltd, Croydon, CR0 4YY

To
Brenda Bennett and Stella Crow

1917

1944

'. . . and we have no right to cut people
out for old bachelors'
Leonora, Maria Edgeworth

'An admirable German writer—you shall see,
my dear, that I have no prejudices against good
German writers . . . says that "Love is like the
morning shadows, which diminish as the day
advances; but friendship is like the shadows of
evening, which increase even till the setting of the sun"'
Leonora, Maria Edgeworth

1

In spring, the mountains that isolate the tiny country of Bairamia from the rest of Europe look down upon an expanse of rose-colour, ethereal and pale, that fills a wide valley. It seems too solid to be cloud, yet when there is a high wind it moves with a slow dreamy motion, disclosing narrow green paths winding through the delicate pink. A delicious smell, fresh yet luxurious, comes up on the wind to soften the brown rocks and brilliant little flowers of the heights, and the tourist says with satisfaction—*That must be the blossom in the Vale of Apricots.*

The fruit farms in this valley are made of massive white-washed stones with slits cut in them to take a rifle, and are built around a central courtyard. The inner walls are covered with espaliered peaches or apricots, for the Bairamians, whose only hobbies used to be fruit-growing and fighting, liked to have the one near at hand while they were engaged in the other, and in the old days they used to be buried in those courtyards, just as they fell, with the fruit blossom that had been shaken down in the battle scattered over their thick white linen clothes and fair heads.

But after the First World War things gradually got quieter, even in a remote little country that has no communication with the rest of the world except through the mountain passes by which it sends fruit down into Turkey and Greece; and Bairamia began to progress. It bought some rolling-stock and other commodities from Great Britain, and shortly afterwards the most famous newspaper in the world patted it on the head in a second leader, recalling that its sons had ever espoused the cause of Liberty and quoting that stanza dubiously attributed to Lord

Byron by the small part of the British public whose reaction to
Bairamia was something more than 'Apricots':

> *Farewell, Bairamia, land of smiling maids*
> *Shapely and small, yet valiant as their sires,*
> *Farewell, ye snowy heights and fruitful glades*
> *Where Nature smiles on all Man's soft desires!*
> *Fair Freedom lies in chains in wider lands*
> *But on thy rocks unconquered yet she stands.*
> *Far o'er the darkling wave though I may be*
> *Thy vales, Bairamia, keep some part of me!*

The leader reminded its readers that relations between Great
Britain and Bairamia (population, 700,000) had never been interrupted by their going to war with each other, and that on more
than one historic occasion Great Britain had been of some assistance
to Bairamia when her national liberties were threatened. After a
reference to the increased prosperity which the establishment of
the British naval base on the island of Santa Cipriana had inevitably
brought to the easterly mountain hamlets of Bairamia, the leader
concluded by expressing the hope that relations between Great
Britain and Bairamia would continue to be as happy in the future
as they had been in the past. And Bairamia, for twenty years or so,
continued to get better.

But the worst of a rich little country getting better is that
other countries, which are neither little nor rich and are getting
worse, begin to notice it; and so it came about that on a fine
morning in the late nineteen-thirties Bairamia, which had just
concluded a most satisfactory trade agreement with the British
Government, and had nearly decided to buy two more aeroplanes
for its air force, and was making up its mind that this time it
really *would* bring in a Bill making education both compulsory
and free—Bairamia, before it had time to ask anyone for help,
woke up one morning to find itself taken over.

A lovely day was beginning in the Vale of Apricots, and the chickens were walking round the whitewashed walls of one of the biggest fruit farms, pecking the ground for grains and lamenting quietly to themselves. At first they had been frightened by the noise of the tanks and lorries full of soldiers going by, but they had got used to it after a while, and their breakfast had been scattered for them as usual, and a minute ago one of the girls had come out with the carpet and arranged it in the sunniest place, just as it was arranged every morning; and so, although the tanks were still grinding past (they used to be great fighters, these 700,000 Bairamians and you never knew) the chickens were comforted.

Presently an old man came quickly and lightly out into the sunshine, and took off his shoes and knelt down on the carpet and lifted his face, with closed eyes, to the east. The sunlight warmed his brown skin and made his thin silver beard glitter and the red and blue and yellow embroideries on his white tunic glow again. He waited. The faint smell of dewy petals, mixed with the smell of hot petrol, blew into his nose. He was listening, trying to hear the sound of the prayer bell above the rattling of the tanks and the loud slow roaring of forty aeroplanes that were now crossing the valley at a great height in the white blue sky; but he could hear nothing save these sounds and, underneath them, the talking of the chickens, and after a little while he bowed towards the east, opened his eyes, and began to put on his shoes.

At once there came an excited chattering, rather like that of the chickens but fiercer, from the gate of the farmhouse, and he turned quickly round.

Seven or eight females, some of them hardly more than infants and others wearing the box-like linen hat of a Bairamian grandmother, were clustered just inside the massive stone gateway, peering at him. Their small slender bodies and white clothes sewn thickly with patterns in brilliant cotton, their little brown faces and ashen fair hair, gave them all a look of belonging to one family that was increased by their angry, excited expression. The smallest girl, aged about six, was clasping to her heart a tin labelled *Carter's Finest Home-grown Peas.*

'The prayer bell has not sounded!'

'The dogs have shot the holy man!'

'Shall we go to the mountains, father?'

'Death to the Italian dogs!'

'Where are the English?'

The last question (which was to be asked a good many times in varying tones throughout the length and breadth of Europe during the next few years) was ignored by the old man, who got up from the mat and advanced upon his womenfolk.

'No, we shall not go to the mountains. We shall stay here and work as usual. Thou, Yania, and Djura and Yilg, return into the house and spin and make the curd cakes, and you others, go out and slay the useless young buds on the peaches as though nothing had happened. And thou, granddaughter Medora, put away that thing with the sharp edges that may wound thine inexperienced hands. Have I not forbidden thee to take presents from the English sailors?'

'I have taken no present from the English sailors, dear and venerable grandfather Gyges,' retorted Medora in a sturdy pipe, stepping out from the group in her full white trousers and little jacket sewn with yellow thread, 'I *bought* this beautiful silver thing. I found it among the grass where English sailors had been making a feast, and I asked (I was alone, for thou and the dear and venerable grandmother Fayet were sleeping and Aunt Yania was, as ever, making a letter to Aunt Vartouhi) and I asked and said, 'Brave and respected English sailors, is it permitted that I have this beautiful thing?' and one of the sailors made signs' (she began to gabble, as the old man made an impatient movement as if to dismiss her) 'that if I would kiss him I might have it. So, he having shown me a shiny picture of one of my own age and sex wearing the clothes of the English, I consented to kiss him and he gave me——'

'Peace, peace. Thou hast done no wrong. Go with Yania now. Yilg, bring the pipe.'

'—this beautiful thing, all stained with green, which I washed——' She had only time to make the bow that Bairamian children make to their elders with hands upon the heart, before Yania, a plump girl with plaited hair decorated with coins, whisked her away through the gate.

A woman slowly detached herself from the group and came forward and seated herself upon the carpets, and presently the old man sat down beside her, resting his arm on one that had been rolled into a pillow.

They watched the passing lorries in silence. One or two of the soldiers waved to them and they raised their hands in salute, smiling politely. Only when a truck went by full of soldiers who shouted and waved branches of peach blossom the old man clenched his hands and muttered.

'Peace. They have worked in factories and they do not know,' said the woman calmly, but her eyes were not calm.

'A kiss is *not* a present,' suddenly said Medora's clear little voice from a window just above their heads; she was continuing the argument with her mother in the house. 'And I hold the English sailors in my heart, as do all our people.'

'Eat thy porridge and be silent, kisser of the English.'

'Gyges, my husband, what will happen to our country now?' asked the woman presently. She had been beautiful, and now the severe national cap with its white embroidery seemed a part of her face (where beauty was changed, not destroyed), rather than an extraneous head dress.

'The English will drive them out,' answered the old man, beginning to draw at the Turkish pipe the girl Yilg had arranged for him. 'They came in 1742, and the English drove them out.

They came in 1813, and the English drove them out. They did not come in 1914 because in those days they and the English were fighting on the same side, but now they have come again and, as it happened before, the English will drive them out.'

'But the English are not at war with them.'

'Who can tell what is in the heart of that strange race? Perhaps even now they prepare in secret. And as long as our country lies opposite to the great place of ships at Santa Cipriana, so long will the English smile upon us. That is not the kindness of their hearts, for, as I have said, who knows what is in the hearts of the English? No, it is geography, and geography, unlike the heart of man, does not change.'

She nodded, and they continued to sit in silence, watching the sunlight growing in strength and radiance along the avenues of black trees with pink and white petals. The paths had tiny red anemones growing in their brilliant green grass.

'We could poison the crop?' she suggested presently. 'They did that in 1813.'

He shook his head.

'The enemy were not so strong in those days, and it was easier to take to the mountains and live there: there were no aeroplanes then to search out the smoke of our fires. No, we can do nothing until the English come.'

The last of the tanks was grinding along the road to Ser, the capital town. Somewhere up among the mountains there was gunfire, and presently five aeroplanes raced across the sky towards the sound.

The woman was muttering angrily.

'I have five strong daughters, and one has married and become a coward, and one you have sent away, and you say 'wait—wait till the English come'! In the old days I would have led them up into the mountains, the three who are left, and crept down at night to stab the Italian dogs. It was better in the old days.'

'In the old days there was no music from Istanbul. Thou lovest thy music that dances along the air.'

She nodded, smiling suddenly. Bairamians smile often and are the politest race in Europe.

'Truly, I love that. It is like magic. I remember the Feast of the Fruit when I was a little maid, younger than Medora, and as thou knowest, there was magic at that time. But it was poor magic beside that music that dances along the air, like a witch set free from her peach stone and singing.'

Three single heavy thuds came from the mountains, and the echoes rolled.

The old man nodded. 'Now, honoured queen of my bed and mother of my daughters, the heavy days are upon us and our country. We must smile, and work, and the Christian dog with the corrupt heart will take the fruit from our trees and the joy from our hearts. But God is good. Blessed be His Name. Will He not send the English at last to save us? and did He not put the thought in my heart, a moon ago, to send Vartouhi to England?'

2

Charity begins at home, but it is often more convenient to exercise it upon foreigners.

Miss Constance Fielding, of Sunglades, Treme, near St Alberics, in Hertfordshire, found that it was one thing to keep open house for any educated and internationally minded Indian or European who might care to stay there before the Nazi War, but quite another thing to give hospitality to a mother and two little girls who had been bombed out of Hackney.

'And I cannot do it again, Kenneth,' she said to her brother as they sat together at dinner on the first evening after the Rigbys (the raids on London having practically ceased) had gone back to Hackney. 'It was a grave mistake ever to undertake it. I should have followed my intuition.'

Kenneth Fielding, a tall red-faced man in the late forties wearing Home Guard uniform, instantly thought of somebody else who had an intuition, but he did not laugh, nor did he want to. It was as if jokes at his sister's expense came up silently into his mind like that race of fishes which has lived for so long in the dark that it is blind. Up they came, met the barrier of his admiration for his sister, and down they sank again.

'It was not a mere distaste for the task, which some short-sighted people might have called selfish,' pursued Miss Fielding, carefully packing a fork with Spam, lettuce, beetroot and watercress. 'It was a definite *warning*; exactly the feeling I have when someone in the house is going to be ill.'

'I thought at the time it would be too much for you, old girl, with all your other work and everything.'

Miss Fielding finished packing the fork and insinuated it into her mouth before she answered, and then she said: 'As it is, one thing and one thing only emerges clearly from the experiment. *It must never happen again.*'

'We must see that it doesn't,' he said vigorously. He smiled at her, then glanced round the room. 'Gosh, isn't it quiet!'

Miss Fielding's eyelids trembled, but she nodded. 'Very pleasantly so.'

It was quiet; and the room looked pretty, with the reflections of crystal glasses and jugs dancing on the ceiling, and the summer evening sunlight, and the sudden vividness of the reds and blues and feathery green in many vases of flowers. It had light green paint and yellow walls and the furniture was of pale oak. Miss Fielding would not have dark colours in the house, holding that they encouraged the Evil Principle and dust. There were some pictures on the walls of people swirling about in bluey-green draperies with circles of stars round their heads. The window at the end of the long room looked over a very large and perfectly kept lawn and some beds blazing with all the proper flowers for the time of year, which was late July.

And all round the porcelain handle on the pale green door were the marks of small dirty fingers.

'Ha! ha! young Deirdre got a last one in before she left, I see!' said Kenneth, pushing his chair back and holding up his cigarette case with an inquiring look at his sister and indicating the door.

'Yes, naughty little thing. (You may smoke, Kenneth, if you want to.) I only noticed that after Mrs Archer had gone home this afternoon.'

'I'll get the coffee, shall I?'

'Please, if you will.'

He went out of the room and across the octagonal hall about which the rooms were grouped, and into the kitchen. White and gold coffee cups were arranged with a patent machine on a tray, and he carried it back to the dining-room.

'Is Frankie coming down or shall I take it up to her?'

'She said she would come down.'

'How is she?'

'Oh, better, I think. As long as we don't get another alert to-night——'

'Ah, here she is! And how's Frankie this evening?' Kenneth, who had just sat down with his cigarette, got up again as the door opened and a small elderly woman in a pale grey dress came slowly in. She trailed across to Miss Fielding and gave her a peck, then trailed over to Kenneth and gave him a peck, and at last sat down, and gazed out of the window.

'What an exquisite evening,' she observed at last, in a low voice. 'It is almost too much.'

'Ha! ha! only hope it keeps like it, I've got to sleep out to-night,' said Kenneth with his loud laugh.

'Did you get any rest this afternoon, Frankie?' inquired Miss Fielding.

'A little, thank you, Constance. But the house! So hushed, so quiet!'

'Delightfully quiet, Kenneth and I were just saying so.'

'I miss them,' said the lady in grey dreamily. 'While they were here their presence and their laughter constantly jarred on me, but now they are gone there is a gap.'

'Well, do you know, I rather feel that, too,' said Kenneth, drinking coffee. 'They were a confounded nuisance, but that little beggar Deirdre was cute. Full of gu—pep, I thought.'

Miss Fielding's eyelids shuddered again.

'Well, I have *quite* made up my mind,' she said. 'What emerges quite clearly from the past few months is that my special gifts must *never again* be wasted on dealing with the Rigbys of this world. We all have special gifts; I have mine; you have yours——'

'I *did* have mine . . . once,' the lady named Frankie corrected her.

'And you gave it to the world; it is there in black and white for all to see. But for the present *my* special gift, my talent for furthering international brotherhood by personal contact, must lie fallow. When one cannot even send a letter out of the country without its being read by coarse eyes, when there are barriers of hurtful wire (surely symbolic!) about our shores, when every mind is darkened and poisoned by hatred and suspicion and fear—how can my work go on? And it all seems so futile. Was that the warning?'

'No; only a car going up the hill,' said Kenneth. 'But Con, you know, we can't have those swine getting away with everything. I mean to say, I don't want to contradict you or hurt your feelings——'

'We won't discuss it again, dear old boy. We have argued so often before. We will just agree to differ. But if everybody would only *love* enough——'

'Ah, yes!' put in Frankie.

'——there would be no problems and the war would end to-morrow.'

'Well, as it doesn't look like ending to-morrow and old Arkwright will be on my tail if I'm not on parade at 8 pip emma sharp, I'd better beat it,' said Kenneth cheerfully, getting up and patting the shoulder of Frankie, who looked up with a watery smile.

He went to the door, but just as he was opening it he turned round.

'Con, I was thinking—if you really don't want the place overrun with evacuees again, how about filling it up ourselves? Getting some decent people of our own sort down to live here, I mean? You were talking the other day about having a refugee to help with the housework, and it ought to be easy enough nowadays to find someone else who'd come and fill up a bedroom. How's about it? Good-bye, girls, I'll be home to breakfast.'

He did not wait for her answer but went out.

They were watching him with an indulgent smile (mitigated

in Miss Fielding's case by the eyelid-flicker at 'How's about it?') but no sooner had the door closed upon him than the smile vanished and the manner of both ladies changed completely.

Miss Fielding shut her large blue-grey eyes that ought to have been beautiful and were not, and said, 'I can only hope that he does not know how the sight of him, in a uniform, in these rooms, where Our Mother spent her last years, makes me feel.'

'Yes, I often think of how grieved poor Aunt Eleanor would be if she could see him dressed like that,' replied Miss Burton in the same subdued voice, but with a noticeably more animated manner.

'I have no doubt that she *does* see him, Frankie. And that is my constant sorrow,' said Miss Fielding, opening the eyes again.

'He has nothing of that feeling, of course.'

'No. He is a very young soul.'

She got up and crossed over to the window and looked out. The sun was still shining strongly, and there were richly coloured caverns between the heads of pink phlox and love-in-a-mist and roses and pansies, and darker caverns full of sun rays and gauzy summer insects between the branches of the elms at the far end of the lawn. The air smelled hot and sweet.

'And all those expressions,' said Miss Fielding suddenly, 'those cheerios and O.K.s and rippings—every one of them is like——'

'A drop of red-hot lead,' put in her cousin neatly, as she hesitated. '*I* know. Dear old Ken has no feeling for words, has he?'

'None.'

'To me, they are mosaic,' announced Miss Burton.

'But with all his limitations, one cares for him,' said Miss Fielding turning away from the window. 'Shall we go into the drawing-room? Oh no—I forgot—we had better stay here, I think.'

The Rigbys had insisted upon sleeping for six months in the drawing-room, because they felt safer there. No one can sleep in the drawing-room for six months without its becoming obvious that they have done so, and that morning, as soon as the Rigbys had gone, Miss Fielding had entered and taken a good look round and pronounced it unfit for Fielding habitation until it had been done up, or, if that should prove impossible, spring-cleaned by Mrs Archer.

The two ladies now drew chairs up to the window and sat down. Presently they would put away the bread and the remains of the salad and Spam, because they must not be wasted, but they would not clear away the dirty plates and wash up, because it did not occur to them to. Miss Burton was not strong, and her mind was occupied by Art, and the mind of Miss Fielding was occupied by even higher things.

Until the Nazi War came, Miss Fielding, who was fifty-three years old, had taken it for granted that there should be three maids—a cook, a housemaid and a parlourmaid—at Sunglades. It had been regarded by her as a natural law, like water finding its own level, and even now, after two years of increasing domestic experiment and difficulty, the remnants of that attitude of mind lingered on. Life being as unfair as it is, this calm assumption helped Miss Fielding to get domestic help where other women, less assured and less feudally minded, failed. Domestic helpers were usually willing to employ themselves with this prosperous, reliable-looking lady with her greying hair parted in the middle and her neat conventional clothes (Miss Fielding's unusual theories did not extend so far as dress), but in spite of this she had no Treasures; servants who had been with the family for twenty-five years and identified their interests with those of the family, and this lack of Treasures was rather strange, because she seemed just the sort of mistress who ought to have had a Treasure or two.

3

After they had said a few more things about Kenneth which lacked no interest to both of them because they had said them so many times before, Miss Fielding and Miss Burton were quiet for a little while, enjoying the calm of the evening, and the sunrays which were now long and sparkling and almost out of sight behind the elms.

'Do we want the news?' said Miss Fielding at last, glancing at the clock. 'No, I don't think we do, do we?'

'Oh, I don't. Only this morning I opened the paper, and then I thought no. It is an exquisite morning; why should I spoil things for myself? And I shut it up again.'

'Ah, I wish I could do that. But I have to realize it all, and suffer. All this hate like a black cloud everywhere.'

And Miss Fielding waved her hand round and round in front of her face, rather as if she were a pussy washing it.

'Frankie,' said Miss Fielding, presently, 'I want to ask your advice about something.'

'Of course, Connie. I shall be only too pleased.' Miss Burton leaned forward in her chair, looking immediately rejuvenated and important.

'Well, I shall appreciate it if you can help me, because I'm really undecided. Usually I am quite—luminous is the word I want, I think—about problems of this sort, but in this case I can't'—Miss Fielding made more gestures in front of her face, as of one brushing away gnats—'quite see my way.'

Miss Burton nodded. 'I know just how you feel. I get like that sometimes about my——'

She swallowed the last word just in time.

14

It had been 'knitting.'

Miss Fielding knew, and Miss Burton knew that she knew, that upstairs at the bottom of Miss Burton's chest of drawers was about fifteen pounds' worth of Scotch Fourply, Paton and Baldwin's Fingering, Angora, Peri-lusta, Fairydown and all the rest of them, with patterns for vests and jumpers and gloves, and scores of knitting needles, all tangled together in an inextricable and Laocoön-like embrace from which only Miss Burton's demise or a direct hit could release them. And further down still in this woolly Record of the Rocks were half-finished stool-covers and chair-backs and firescreens in gros-point with their accompanying twelve skeins of wool to each piece and their needles and frames. Miss Burton bought a new design or pattern for a jumper every time she went up to London but she always got in a muddle or bored with them and not one, except a muffler for Kenneth ten years ago, had ever been finished. She was far from indifferent to their plight; the thought of it often came upon her, as a painful contrast, when she was looking at some particularly peaceful landscape or tidy room and she made up her mind for the hundredth time to tidy that drawer up, and take out just *one* piece of knitting or gros-point work and finish it. But somehow she never got further than beginning to make a ball out of one of the wild tangles of wool and then lunch was ready, or it was time to go out in the car or (since the war) there was an alert and they all had to go down the garden to the shelter; and when she came back her fervour had ebbed. And the drawer remained as before.

Miss Fielding, who abhorred disorder of mind, body or drawer, knew of this lazar-house under her roof and deplored it. She seldom spoke frankly of it to Miss Burton, for although she often tackled people about their faults for their own good there were occasions when she thought it best to let the Good Principle work on people in its own way and this was one of them. But sometimes when she was a little longer than usual in getting to sleep at night she lay in bed breathing deeply and sending out thought-waves to Frankie about tidying that wool drawer. It was all good practice and in time, no doubt, it would work.

She now felt in her handbag and brought out a letter.

'It was really very strange Kenneth saying what he did about having someone to live here,' she said. 'This came this afternoon.' She handed the letter, which was addressed in an unusually pretty writing, to Miss Burton.

Miss Burton glanced at it, then across at her cousin, with eyes widened in surprise.

'Betty,' she said.

'Betty,' answered Miss Fielding, nodding.

Miss Burton unfolded the letter.

Dear Connie,

I do feel awful for not having written for such ages, but you know how things are nowadays. How are you all? I hope you haven't been having too many raids. It's been pretty quiet in London lately and we don't want any more.

Isn't it fun; I've got a job at last with the Ministry of Applications who've been evacuated to St Alberics, as I expect you know, and I've got to find somewhere to live near there. Do you think I could come and live with you?—as a p.g., of course. It would be divine if I could. How are Frankie and Ken? Give them both my love. Richard is still out on tour with the Dove Players, they're doing *Comus* at Burslem this week. He seems to like it though of course he'd rather be doing his own job. He's still rather seedy, too.

Do let me know if I can come. My lease of this flat is up next month so it all fits in rather well.

With love,

Yours ever,

BETTY.

Miss Burton carefully replaced the letter, and then the cousins exchanged a long look.

'Just the same,' said Miss Burton at last. 'How long is it since you heard from her?'

'Oh, it must be over a year. She and Richard were on holiday in France and just got back before it fell.'

'Let me see, she must be—what? Forty-three?'

'Forty-five. She is eight years younger than I am.' (Miss Fielding never attempted to conceal her age, which she regarded—in the light of things eternal—as non-existent.) 'But she doesn't look it, or didn't the last time I saw her. Nothing *like* forty-five.'

Miss Burton looked out of the window for a minute or two, and Miss Fielding waited for her to speak.

Miss Burton was tacitly accepted at Sunglades as the authority on Love. Miss Fielding was deferred to in any doubt about the age of people's souls, Kenneth was allowed the last word on all aspects of vegetable-growing, and Miss Burton, so to speak, held the keys of Cupid's garden. This was because she had once been jilted. She was not often consulted, because at Sunglades they rarely spoke of Love, but the thing will crop up sometimes, however conscientious you may be with the decontaminating, and when it did Miss Burton was always called in.

'He never mentions that affair, of course?' she said now, after a long pause.

'Oh, never. Well, I have heard him joke about her being an old flame, and that sort of thing you know, but never anything serious.'

'That may be bluff,' said Miss Burton knowingly.

'I don't think so for a moment.' Miss Fielding's tone was decided. 'I flatter myself that if there is one human being I do know inside and out, it is Kenneth.' And she put back a bit of honeysuckle that was coming in at the window and smilingly pushed up her lips into her nose in the way she used to when she was a little girl and had triumphed over somebody.

Miss Burton looked at her. Ah, but Love has a way of lingering on in our poor human hearts, strive to dislodge him how we will, Connie, thought Miss Burton. And what do you know about Love, anyway? thought Miss Burton. *You* were never engaged to anyone for two years and got all your trousseau together and everything. Nobody ever told *you* that you had eyes like wallflowers. And as she was trying to memorize that bit about Love lingering on in our poor, etc., in order to write it in her Journal when she went upstairs to her own rooms, and also feeling curiously annoyed with Miss Fielding, as if she would like to take her down a peg or two, her tone when next she spoke was slightly absent-minded.

'I shouldn't worry about it if I were you,' she said. 'Have you shown the letter to Ken?'

'No, I thought it wiser not to. And I'm not really *worried*, of course. I'm sure Ken hasn't thought about her in that way for years; certainly not since Our Mother died. But you know what Betty is.'

'A flirt.' Miss Burton's tone made the pretty word seem to open in the air, as though a fan had clicked.

'Not consciously, Frankie. I used to think she was, but now I really believe she can't help attracting people. I have seen her very upset about it.'

'She always seemed very cheerful to me,' said Miss Burton.

'Besides, she *is* forty-five and I haven't seen her for two years. She may have Gone Off,' went on Miss Fielding hopefully. 'People do.'

Not people like Betty, thought Miss Burton.

'And when it comes to actually having her in the house——'

'Well, you can always say you're sorry, but you've half-arranged to have someone else here, and haven't got room. I wouldn't have her at all if you feel uneasy.'

'I am *not* uneasy, Frankie. It's just that——' Miss Fielding did not finish her sentence, because there was no need to. She went on smoothly: 'After all, it would be much nicer to have an old friend like Betty, who knew Our Mother, in the house than a stranger.'

'Aunt Eleanor never liked her,' said Miss Burton rather maliciously.

'Our Mother found her frivolous, which she certainly is,' retorted Miss Fielding. 'I gave up years ago trying to get Betty to take an interest in anything except Richard and hats. That was why Our Mother was so thankful when she jil—decided not to have Kenneth after all.'

'I suppose that means Richard will be coming here too, to see her,' said Miss Burton despondently.

'We can't refuse him house-room if she's here, Frankie—her own son.'

'He upsets me, I admit it. He *is* so rude and he doesn't seem interested in anything except Spain.'

'I think he has the makings of a charming man.'

'The last time he was here he told me that his mother was not a type that appealed to him sexually,' said Miss Burton, looking down and smoothing her skirt, but speaking distinctly, 'I don't call that very charming.'

Miss Fielding gazed at her helplessly, then slowly blushed.

'He must have been funning,' she said at last. 'These young things love to tease us oldsters.'

'Then I don't like being teased—not like that, anyway,' said Miss Burton, still distinctly and with downcast eyes, and smoothing her skirt.

'Oh, he *must* have been funning,' said Miss Fielding again. 'Anyway—you think it safe, then, to tell Betty that she can come?'

Why are you asking me, since you wouldn't have mentioned it at all if you hadn't made up your mind to let her come? thought Miss Burton, suddenly irritable. And why do you take it for granted that I agree with you about Kenneth? I'm sorry for Kenneth. He and I have been in the same boat.

These little gusts of irritation and malice occasionally swept

19

over Miss Burton, and when they did Someone Else looked for a second out of her eyes; a witty and imperious Usurper who got her own way and was not afraid of people. Miss Fielding did not like this Usurper, whose mocking gaze she met when Miss Burton glanced up.

'If Kenneth is such a confirmed old bachelor as you are always saying he is, Connie, it won't hurt him to be exposed to Betty's charms,' Miss Burton said, drawling the long sentence without stumbling. 'And personally I've always thought that she'll never marry again. Dick was one of the nicest men I've ever known and I think she'll stay faithful to his memory.'

'So morbid, I've always thought. After all, there is no death.'

No death, isn't there? thought Miss Burton, studying her as she again pushed back the spray of honeysuckle. What a donkey you can be, and how you do need taking down that peg or two.

'Well, I should ask her if I were you, Connie,' she said in a final tone, and standing up, 'I suppose you'll discuss it first with Kenneth?'

'Oh, not necessarily,' interrupted Miss Fielding airily, swinging the letter in time with one large foot, 'We might just spring it on him as a surprise. I think it would be rather a lark.'

Ass, thought Miss Burton, feeling crosser every minute, but she only said, 'Well, I suppose you'll have to decide how much you're going to ask, won't you, and you'll have to talk to Kenneth about that? I think I shall go to bed; I'm very tired after last night.'

'Yes, do; I will too, an early night will do us both good. I *would* have her for nothing, of course, only the cost of living has gone up so appallingly and I expect she would feel more comfortable if she paid something, don't you?'

'Oh, yes, however small,' said Miss Burton.

Kenneth Fielding and his two sisters, children of a solicitor owning an old-established firm in St Alberics, had inherited in 1920 a comfortable fortune, left to them by three very wealthy old aunts. It was invested in sound undertakings in the western parts of the British Empire, and since the war, despite crushing income tax, the Fieldings had not found themselves noticeably less comfortable. Kenneth continued to attend the offices and nominally direct the firm that his grandfather had founded but as the years went on he tended more and more to lead the life of a retired soldier of independent means, and to leave the active management of Fielding, Fielding and Gaunt to Mr Gaunt, who was capable and ambitious.

Betty, or Mrs Richard Kenway Marten, was at this time living in two rooms in Chelsea. She had a post as secretary to a women's club in Woburn Square that brought her in four pounds a week and her lunches and teas. She had also the pension paid to her on behalf of her husband, Captain R. K. Marten, D.S.O. (posthumously awarded), who had been killed at Landrecies in 1918.

'Two and a half guineas a week?' called Miss Fielding over her shoulder as she strode into the kitchen to find Pony, the cat, and put him out. 'Would you like some lemon and barley? I shall. I wonder how much she will be getting from the Ministry of Applications?'

'No, thank you. Yes, I should think that would be all right. Connie, I'm going up to bed; my shoulder is rather painful. You won't trouble to black out, will you? I don't know, I'm sure, what do they usually pay?'

'Oh, no, it isn't dark until nearly twelve.' Miss Fielding blew some biscuit crumbs out of her mouth and then sucked some of them in again; she was standing at the kitchen window eating, staring out at the darkening garden, and enjoying the perfume of the tobacco flowers. 'How delicious not to have to put up those symbolic black cloths at nightfall! Not very much, I believe, but she has Dick's pension.'

'So she has, of course. Good night.'

'Good night. I hope we shall get a quiet night.'

'Oh, so do I. Good night.'

'Good night.'

As Miss Burton was going slowly upstairs Miss Fielding, crossing the hall with Pony under her arm, called up to her, 'It will be quite pleasant having Betty in the house, you know, she is good company although she is so frivolous.'

Probably because of it, thought Miss Burton, but did not think it necessary to make any answer except 'N-n-n' as she went slowly up the stairs. *A bad bad woman, but good good companee*, was the line that had come irrelevantly into her head. That was what that girl, Alicia Arkwright, who came to lunch had said, the one who had been mixed up in a divorce case and been away for months and had now come back to live at the house down the road. She had grinned as she said it. She had beautiful blue eyes, cool and tired, and a long pale face like—like a handsome young horse. (Miss Burton was pleased with this; it sounded modern. She would put it in her Journal with the bit about Love having a way, etc.)

Her rooms were on the top floor of the large pleasant house. She had had them converted into a self-contained flat as soon as she had made up her mind to spend the rest of her life with her cousins. She had her piano, and photographs of her friends, shelves of minor poetry and her favourite books, *The Road Mender, The Wood Carver of 'Lympus, The Little Flowers of Saint Francis*, and all the novels of 'Ouida' and 'Saki,' and a late Victorian writer named Mrs Hungerford in whose stories of love in English and Irish society she took great pleasure.

She sat down by the open window, and gazed out into the evening.

The moon was rising above the gentle hills. The western sky was still light, and the elm trees were dark against the large pale field of oats, cultivated this summer for the first time, that Miss Burton loved to look at. Before the Nazi War it had been possible to see the lights of St Alberics, four miles away, sparkling through a dip in the fields, and in the daytime the tower of the cathedral could be seen rising out of the ploughed land. Miss Burton liked to imagine it there throughout the centuries that the town of St Alberics, which had begun as a settlement of Christian monks under the Romans, had stood on the hillside. That tower, rising out of the dark fields, was the first glimpse of the town that travellers coming down from the North would see; centurions on leave from Hadrian's Wall, monks on pilgrimage, knights on their way to join their feudal lord, ordinary country people out marketing, cavaliers, and high-waymen, and the coaches of Dickens's day, and the cyclists of the early nineteen-hundreds, and now the American and Canadian soldiers rattling down the road in their tanks—and it was always the same fields and tower. That thought fascinated Miss Burton, she never grew tired of playing with it, but she never mentioned it to Miss Fielding, who would have said something about Old Souls and New Souls, which always made Miss Burton think of a card game and irritated her very much.

The world won't be nearly such an interesting place when Connie and her sort have persuaded us all to love each other and Richard Marten and his sort have tidied us all up, thought Miss Burton. Thank God I shall be dead by then.

She got up and went to the piano.

The soft summer dusk was too far advanced for her to make out the notes on the single sheet of music that stood there, but she began to play.

The words were passionate and tragic——

> *My Love had a silver ring*
> *Wrought by a jeweller in an Eastern land*
> *A rare and a lovely thing,*
> *Fit for an Empress's white hand!*

and the music followed them with a simple throbbing air in a minor key. Miss Burton had evidently been trained by good masters for she played accurately and with feeling and her voice, though worn, was true and without mannerisms. The song rose to a thrilling climax——

Wasted like water in the desert sand!

then ended on some soft pseudo-Eastern chords, and Miss Burton dropped her hands onto her lap and sat for a moment thinking.

How strange it is——Reggie has been dead for twenty years and I suppose I'm the only person left alive who ever thinks of him now, and here's the song I wrote because of him, all those years ago, still alive and still being played on the wireless and in the cinemas——and I suppose it will go on after I'm dead too. In a way it's like our child.

My Love had a Silver Ring, Words and Music by Frances Burton, had been a firm favourite with the larger and simpler audiences all over Great Britain since 1908. The coming of the wireless had only widened its appeal; a day seldom passed without *Until, I Hear You Calling Me*, or *My Love had a Silver Ring* being heard over the air; and unlike many popular favourites composed at the end of the last century, the song had earned a small fortune for its writer and she was now living comfortably in the house of her cousins on the remains of it.

Except Reginald Farquharson and *My Love had a Silver Ring*, nothing had ever happened to Miss Burton. After the publication of *My Love had a Silver Ring* had made her famous in a small way, she had lived with her mother in Kensington, among a little circle of admiring and artistic friends and occasionally contributing some verses or a story to *The Lady*, *The Queen* and *The Girl's Own Paper*, or going on a sketching holiday with a woman friend to Norway or Greece. No one else had ever proposed to her, because, in those years immediately after her jilting, it was The Usurper who was most often in command of her temper and tongue, and The Usurper did not have the luck to meet a man who was not afraid of her. And then the Other War came and after that the century began to race like a mad tank and Miss Burton had given up trying to keep pace with it. She drifted into a backwater and stayed there, a little affected or bitter sometimes, but usually moderately content with what she did and was. Sometimes she thought about her lost lover, but she only remembered her memories; they were no longer real.

She was not completely ineffectual and pathetic, and occasionally that Usurper who was both witty and self-willed looked out of her large fading brown eyes; and she had written *My Love had a Silver Ring*. If a person has created a song that has given pleasure for forty years to millions of people, she must have a little of what it takes, and it was this, doubtless, that sustained Miss Burton throughout her nights and days.

What a shame it is about Ken, she suddenly thought, as she got up from the piano with a yawn. Of course he'll never marry now, he's too comfortable and set in his habits, but Connie is too bad, keeping all the attractive women away from him and getting so worried if he ever looks at one. And Joan is as bad (Joan was the other Fielding sister, who lived in London). Poor Ken, why shouldn't he enjoy a little flutter? I'm glad I advised her to let Betty come.

The Usurper looked out of her eyes for a moment in the summer dusk. And it may be rather amusing, thought The Usurper.

Downstairs in the blacked-out bathroom Miss Fielding was cleaning her excellent teeth and thinking: And I must get a refugee, too.

4

About a fortnight later Alicia Arkwright was in the train returning to Treme after a day in London, and she was rather tight.

It was not easy to attain to this condition in London during the latter period of the Nazi War, when the West End is best described as *Americans, Americans, everywhere, nor any drop to drink*, but Alicia knew the barman who was waiting to be called up for the Navy at a little place at the back of the Green Park Hotel which still had two storeys standing, and she had run into some fighter-boys she knew who were on leave and between them they had managed to find something and had enjoyed a cheerful time, only Alicia had had to come away early because she was on a night shift.

Her head sang in time to the wheels of the train, and the hard core of anger and pain that was always inside her had dissolved, and although she knew it would come back again, it was grand to be without it for the time being. Before that affair with H. she used to get a kick out of things, and now she didn't any more. So what?

Outside the window, rows of little houses and gardens went past, with occasionally one of those little ruins that may be seen all up and down the railway lines of Greater London since the autumn of 1940, and in the blue sky the balloon barrage was anchored low above the roofs and gleamed pure silver in the evening light. The train was just leaving the suburbs and the barrage and entering the unprotected country. Shame, thought Alicia, who, like many other people, was rather fond of the balloons; and she looked benevolently at other occupants of the carriage without seeing them.

In the Royal Ordnance factory where she worked, she wore on the arm of her overalls a device of two crossed shells above the motto *Front Line Service*, and she felt that this, the badge designed by Lord Beaverbrook for the workers who came into the munition factories immediately after Dunkirk, gave her certain privileges about clothes coupons. So this evening she had on a black suit from Simpson's with a black jersey turban adorned by a yellow jewel and people on the platform in London had been staring at her shoes and stockings, and none of those clothes, with the exception of the jewel, were older than three weeks. In the factory she was one of the very few women who always wore the regulation cap, and she looked like one of those photographs printed by *Vogue* to show the rest of us the Smart Munition Worker, in clothes as stylized and correct and becoming as those for hunting.

There was someone else in the carriage wearing a black suit, only it was not a suit when seen beside what Alicia was wearing; it was a coat and skirt, and there is a difference. It was also shiny, and underneath the coat its wearer had on a white silk blouse fastened by a little gilt badge with some device upon it. The girl had no hat and the last rays of sunlight came through the window and made her milky-gold hair sparkle.

Alicia looked benevolently at them all; two men reading their evening papers, three prosperous women who had been shopping in town, the thin mother with three stout dirty little girls climbing over her and banging their gasmasks against each other, and the baby in her arms who was trying to push its fingers into the plaited coronet of hair wound round the head of the girl in the corner.

'Don't, Sylvia,' muttered the mother tiredly in a minute. 'Leave the young lady's hair alone, can't you?'

The baby strained away out of her arms and earnestly offered the girl in the corner a wet biscuit.

'Do give over, Sylvia,' the mother murmured once more, glancing at the girl with a faint smile.

It was at once politely returned, and the girl inclined her head towards the child so that her hair was within its reach. Soon the tiny fingers were moving experimentally about in her plaits, while the other three girls looked on, giggling.

Alicia watched for a little while; then turned away, bored, and looked out of the window. She did not find brats amusing, though she supposed it was different if they were your own. Presently, through the haze of alcohol that still pleasantly dulled her senses, she heard the mother say:

'Don't let her worry you.'

'I am varry glad to please her,' answered a fresh young voice with a foreign accent that all the English people in the carriage found attractive, though not so attractive as they would have some years ago. 'The other three children are girls too also?' it went on, with a respectful inflection.

'Oh yes, worse luck,' said the mother with a rueful smile. She seemed undecided what to call the girl and finally, with the new simplicity that has come to England since the war, went on talking without using any mode of address at all.

'I'd have liked a boy and so would Dad (he's in Egypt, been there since this lot started, almost), but you don't always get what you want in this world, do you?'

'Some do get it,' said the girl cheerfully. Little Sunshine, thought Alicia.

'You aren't English, are you?' the mother went on.

The girl shook her head and Alicia slowly turned to look at her again.

'Polish? There's a lot of Poles up in Scotland where my sister is. Lovely dancers they are, she says.'

'My country is Bairamia,' said the girl, smilingly but with pride.

The woman stared, uncomprehending and not wanting to seem 'ignorant' (which to her meant rude, not ill-informed).

'There's such a lot of these places since the war,' she said at last in excuse.

'You will know if I say—Bairamia—Apricots!' said the girl, and laughed.

At once the woman laughed too and so did the three children, glad of the excuse.

'Of course! Eightpence a tin they used to be in the old days. Apricot Valley Brand—that was it.'

'Wish we could have some now, don't you, Shirley?' said one of the little girls.

'I wish we could have a quarter of the fruit we used to,' said the mother reminiscently, letting the baby jump with bare brown feet on her faded dress, 'Pineapple—quite turned up my nose at pineapple, I used to, anything less than peaches I wouldn't touch. Sickening to think of those Nazis eating your apricots. I suppose it's them, as usual?'

'It is the Italians.'

'Oh—the Eyeties! They're a joke, my Dad says. Fourpence a packet they are, out where he is. Are all your people still out there, then?'

The girl nodded.

'Must be awful for you. Do you hear from them regular?'

'Since more than a year I am not hearing.'

'Won't the Nazis let them write?'

'The letters did come through Greece. Now the Germans have Greece so I am not hearing.'

'Fancy. Must be awful. Are you one of a big family?'

Can't you pipe down, thought Alicia irritably; you *must* see she doesn't want to talk about it. How these people do stew in horrors; and she leant forward and offered the mother her cigarette-case.

'Oh—that's ever so kind of you, but sure you can spare it?'

'Quite. I've got some more at home.' The mother took a cigarette which Alicia lit, and then she offered her case to the girl with the plaits.

'I have cigarettes too also.' The smile grew wider on her

round sallow little face as she took from her shabby handbag an exquisite case of hammered silver, flat and ancient, with delicate scrolls outlined in turquoise-coloured enamel. She held out the case to Alicia, who laughed and shook her head.

'No thank you. Too strong. Make my head go——' she waved her finger round and round and shut her eyes.

'You know Bairamian tobacco?' asked the girl, laughing too.

'Oh, yes, I know Bairamian tobacco. I've had some.'

'You smoke tobacco in Bairamia?' she asked eagerly, leaning forward.

'No. In the Dorchester Hotel in London.'

Alicia then said no more because the conversation was beginning to bore her, and the girl began to smoke in a way that fascinated the children, who sat and stared at her graceful movements and absorbed face in silence. The quick gestures and the blue smoke winding up from the little dark yellow cigarette made them think vaguely of a dance.

The train was drawing into a station, and the mother stood up to collect her parcels from the rack. With the help of the Bairamian girl (Alicia never joined in such communal manifestations of goodwill, and old ladies might die of heart failure wrestling with obdurate windows before she would say, 'Let me do that') she got them all down just as the train stopped. Alicia watched them climbing out, and thought what a circus the children were, with gas-masks, and pieces of wet biscuit, and grubby panties showing under their shabby little dresses. She yawned, and looked down at her wicked shoes.

The Bairamian girl was helping out the last of the children.

'Come on, Joy—be careful now, Shirley. Thank you! Hope you hear from your family soon. Good-bye!'

'Good-bye.' And then the Bairamian girl, standing at the window, made a deep respectful bow and said clearly, as the train began to move away, *'Hail to you, honoured mother of four daughters, peace and joy be yours.'*

Suffering cats, thought Alicia, staring hard and wondering if this was an old Bairamian custom or if the gin was making her hear things. But she was certainly not going to ask, for in her opinion there was too much asking and discussing in the world; too much chewing and not enough doing; and she sometimes amused herself by seeing how few sentences she could get through the day on. She shut her eyes, hoping that the girl in the corner would not talk to her, and dozed until the train began to draw into the next station, which was St Alberics. Doors opened and soldiers began to crowd in. Alicia stood up and pushed her way out, wondering if the little number with the plaits would try to string along too, but the little number had competently saddled herself with an enormous rucksack and showed no signs of stringing along beyond catching Alicia's eye and giving her a smile and a polite little bow. Alicia returned it with a reluctant grin, and then the girl disappeared in the crowd of commuting business men, noisy young girls from the new munition factories outside the town, and Service people.

Alicia went upstairs to find her bicycle and the sheepskin boots she would pull on over her lovely stockings, while her shoes rode in the carrier. Just outside the station she ran into Mr Fielding, wearing civilian dress for once, and looking thoroughly browned off.

5

She had known him since she was nine, and so she continued to think of him as 'Mr Fielding,' although the more natural mode of thought now that she was twenty-seven would have been 'Kenneth Fielding.' He used to pull her bobbed hair and make jokes that, even at nine years old, she had thought silly; and now of course he was just an old thing; in fact he was a year younger than that H. who had done all the damage, but whereas no one could possibly have thought of that man-of-the-world as an old thing, Mr Fielding had probably seemed one to the more discerning among his contemporaries when he too had been nine years old.

He's had a few, too, she thought as he came towards her. At first he did not see her, for he was looking moodily down at the pavement, and she hoped that she might slip past without having to speak to him, but suddenly he stopped and glanced at her uncertainly, then smiled and took off his hat.

'Hallo, Alicia. How are you? Lovely afternoon, isn't it? Been shopping?' His glassy gaze slowly wandered down to her feet. 'I say, I say! What stunning shoes!'

'They are rather nice, aren't they?' she said, bored. 'Are you lost or something?' she went on, in the impertinent tone she had always used with him.

'Ha! ha! No, I happened to get away from the office early this afternoon and I just blew along to see if a wild and hairy Austrian that Connie's expecting had come on this train. The buses are so crowded nowadays, I thought I might drive her home. Got twopennyworth of petrol; may as well use it, you know. Suppose I can't give you a lift too?'

'No, thanks very much. I've got the bike here.'

'Mind my bike!' laughed Mr Fielding. 'Oh, come now. No nice ride home?'

(He'll be saying 'La!' in a minute, she thought.)

'No, really not, thanks.'

'I'd like to, Alicia,' he said, and looked down sentimentally at her with his head on one side.

'I'm sure you would,' she said coolly, 'but I can't hang about while you find your Austrian. Good-bye.'

'No—but look here—Alicia——'

She smiled slightly and shook her head and was turning away from him when a pretty voice said 'Hallo, Kenneth!' and a tallish slender woman in fashionable grey tweeds came up to them and took Mr Fielding's arm and gave it an affectionate squeeze.

'Betty!' cried Mr Fielding, and his red face went redder with pleasure. 'What luck! We didn't expect you until to-morrow. How are you?'

'I'm very well, thanks. Yes, I came on this train. Didn't Connie get my wire? No, of course she didn't; as if anyone ever got wires in time nowadays. How are you, Kenneth?'

'Oh, I'm flourishing, thanks. Being a Happy Warrior suits me down to the ground—literally sometimes, ha! ha! Now this is really great luck, I can drive you home. Is this all you've got?' picking up a shabby pigskin suit-case.

'My other stuff's coming later. Kenneth, it is nice to see you again and you haven't changed a bit, you don't look a scrap older——'

That's right. You get on with your bits and your scraps and I'll get home, thought Alicia who was now striding to the bicycle shed. A shout came after her——

'Alicia! Don't run away! Come and talk to Mrs Marten while I go and get the car.'

Curse, thought Alicia. 'How do you do?' she called, smiling and half-turning. 'I really can't, Mr Fielding, I shall be late and the foreman charge-hand will knout me.'

'We've met before—years ago,' said Betty Marten, coming towards her smiling, with the sun on her face. She had a clear skin and sparkling grey-green eyes and delicate impertinent features; a very pretty woman, but so charming that her prettiness was only a secondary charm. Vintage 1914, too sweet; I like mine drier, thought Alicia. In a few minutes she decided that she had better go by car, and after she had arranged about her bicycle, they waited for Kenneth together.

Betty Marten was thinking that the affair with H., of which she had heard details from Miss Burton, had spoiled Alicia almost completely. She remembered her as a striking twenty-three-year-old, elegant and dowered with personality, who had kept a younger brother and sister and a father who had divorced her mother amused and in order. Now, four years later, she was still elegant and striking but her personality was dimmed in some way; and she was so plainly unhappy that she made Betty feel uncomfortable.

'Mr Fielding has to collect an Austrian or something,' Alicia observed, after a pause.

'Oh, yes, Miss Fielding said something in her letter about getting a refugee to help with the housework. Of course that's a huge house for the two of them to run with only a daily woman.'

Betty was a completely civilized person, as perhaps only people who grew up before 1914 know how to be, and the details and difficulties and plans of daily living among her friends were interesting to her. Her power of deep feeling had been destroyed twenty-five years ago, when her husband had been killed, but what had grown up in the ruins were the flowers of affection, and gaiety, and courage, and the little joys of every day. She only differed from most people in her indifference to the thought of death.

Alicia said nothing. She did not give a damn if it was a huge house, for she considered Mr Fielding a bore and Miss Fielding and Miss Burton asses. Our Mother, whom she had also known, she had at the age of twelve dismissed as a beast. The late Mrs Fielding had been handsome, energetic, virtuous, clever, and active in promoting the good of her fellow beings; nevertheless, whenever Alicia recalled her nowadays she only modified her twelve-year-old verdict so far as to think of Mrs Fielding as an old witch.

'Would it be down on the platform, should you think?' suggested Betty, at last, as Kenneth did not return. 'The Austrian, I mean.'

'Heaven knows. I expect so. They're all ropey anyway.'

'Oh, do you think so? I met some rather nice ones in London.'

'Yes, the men have got what it takes,' said Alicia maliciously.

Poor little thing, she's like a cat with a scalded tail, thought Betty, and wondered if Alicia would later on confide in her, as girls very often did. No, I shouldn't think so, she decided, studying the shape of Alicia's chin, and felt slightly relieved. Then she said:

'Do you think this might be it?'

Alicia looked. A small hatless figure in a black coat and skirt, laden with an enormous rucksack, was coming towards them, with hair sparkling in the evening light. She was accompanied by an old porter who looked stunned. She was saying cheerfully——

'So if you find my hat you post it to me by the postman. At the house of Miss Constance M. Fielding, Sunglades, Treme, near St Alberics, Hertfordshire.'

'Yes, miss. Only I can't quite make out what you say. If you could just write it down on a piece of paper——'

'I have not any paper.'

'Well——' and the old porter fumbled desperately in his bosom—'p'raps I've got a bit. Your name's a bit of a mouthful, too.'

'I do not understand.'

'Your name. Hard to make out. See?'

'Still I do not, too also.'

The old porter stood still, and said quietly: 'Strewth. (Beg your pardon.) The 6.15'll be down in three minutes. Look here. If I find your hat on the line——'

'Can I help?' asked Betty, laughing and going up; she had heard Miss Fielding's name. Alicia sat down on Betty's case, determined not to be drawn into yet another funny refugee story, and at that moment Kenneth drove up in the car.

'No use, girls. I can't find her. Sorry to have kept you waiting,' he said.

'I think that's her,' said Alicia, nodding towards the group.

He went up to them at once, thinking in a fuddled way that such a little thing ought not to scrub floors and hoping Con would not ask her to. He had had two or three double whiskies at the George, and he had come down to the station in the grip of one of those ghastly fits of depression he got sometimes; no reason for them; liver, probably. The double whiskies did not always succeed in banishing the depression; they had not done so this afternoon, but the prospect of driving two attractive women—and the little thing was rather taking, too—did cheer him up, and as he addressed Mrs Marten he was jovial.

'Sorry to have kept you hanging about, Betty. How do you do, Miss——'

'Miss Annamatta,' said Betty, 'has lost her hat, and we're just arranging to have it sent on if they find it.'

'It blow off,' confirmed Miss Annamatta, nodding.

'How do you do, Miss Matta?' said Kenneth carefully, and he smiled down at her and held out his big hand. To his incredulous horror she at once made him a low curtsy, sinking down on her heel and smiling politely up into his face.

'Good God—here—I say, you mustn't do that!' exclaimed Kenneth, turning crimson and glancing at Betty, who was looking amused. 'You mustn't really, you know. Here, let me——' and he began to take the rucksack from her shoulders. After he had put it, and Betty's suit-case, into the car, Alicia sauntered up (having resigned herself to going without dinner, for she never ate much after a pub crawl anyway) and got into the driver's seat beside him.

'That girl has lost her manners, too,' thought Betty, as she settled herself next to Miss Annamatta and felt a natural irritation because she was not sitting next to her old friend. However, her sweet temper soon recovered itself and she began to enjoy the familiar sight of the long hill leading from the station up into the town.

This evening the High Street was crowded, but crowded with people, instead of the lengthy procession of cars coming out from London that would have been passing through it at this time three years ago. Women were wheeling perambulators down the middle of the road and there were many horse-drawn vehicles, including a graceful dog-cart driven by a girl in a sweater and trousers. The scene was softly coloured and cheerful and pleasing to the eye, although there was not a single completely beautiful object in sight except the evening sky. The pale old houses were marred by huge advertisements sprawling across them, shouting at the people to Dig for Victory and Save Fuel, and the newer shop-fronts were either in the Diluted Gothic style of the early nineteen-hundreds or copies of brick Regency fronts that looked flat and mean; yet the ancient shapes of the streets were charming. They were like the beds of old streams: the weeds on the bank vary in thickness or type and trees are cut down or new ones grow, but the path of the water remains much the same, and so the line of these irregular, winding, steep streets had not changed much in the last thousand years. Every now and again there were alleys leading into paved courtyards where geraniums and pansies and beans grew in window boxes outside ancient little houses, or a flight of worn steps led down to a smooth lawn. And sometimes, framed in a stone archway against the blue sky, as those of us who are lucky enough to have seen Italy remember that her towers and palaces and churches are so often framed, there was a glimpse of the cathedral.

Betty was looking expectantly out of the window as the car began to go down the other long hill leading out of the town. It is nice to get out of London, she thought, even though it is such a little way out. (She had been born in Devonshire and kept her love of the country.) In a minute we shall pass the cathedral. Suddenly there was open space instead of houses on the left, and there were the lawns going down in their gentle slopes to the river, with the evening light shining on them and the big shadows of trees lying long on their grass, and there was the river reflecting the blue sky between the green and yellow water-iris plants and the flowering rush, with the hills and scattered woods beyond; and there at last, with flower-sprinkled grass sweeping up to its mighty walls, was the cathedral.

The tall square tower is made of tiny Roman bricks, in colour neither rosy nor ginger but a happy marriage of the two, and it is a thousand years old. Behind it, as if protected by it, lies the long mass of the cathedral itself; a huge shell with high, pale, bare walls on which groups of apostles and saints wearing dim yellow haloes or faded red cloaks sometimes make a faint flush of colour. Through the windows of the clerestory, set at an immense height, pours the light, the first created thing, in an endless flood. On the large pale stones that form the floor there is ranged such a richness of sculptured tombs and broken statues, gilded wooden carvings and grilles of wrought iron work, images with hands clasped in prayer and tablets commemorating the dead of a thousand years, that the mind reels beneath the impact of the Past; and nothing seems to matter except the making of beauty and the loving of God.

'What a mercy they didn't hit it,' said Betty, leaning back after watching the cathedral out of sight and saying what everybody, except Miss Annamatta, was in their different way thinking.

'They did have one in the Close but it was only a hundred-pounder and it was a bit of luck, it fell in the Dean's garden and did in his perpetual spinach, ha! ha!' said Kenneth. 'Oh, and a couple of incendiaries on the roof but they soon put those out. About eighteen months ago the blighters used to come over and pop at it with machine-guns but they don't do that now, oh, no!' and he glanced cheerfully up at the sky where a couple of Spitfires were playing about.

His depression had disappeared, for it was a lovely evening and the air had smelled sweet of hay, he was full of good whisky, and he was driving home three attractive women. His revived gaiety communicated itself to Betty, who was always ready to laugh and had one of those delightful helpless laughs that is not quite a giggle but is a collateral of the giggle family and seems to gush out almost against its lucky owner's will. Miss Annamatta smiled with a politeness that was partly Bairamian and partly because she was twenty years old and riding in a luxurious car with a big kind man, and once or twice even Alicia put in a wisecrack. So they were all cheerful, and gaily Mr Fielding drove his harem on towards Treme.

6

It happened that Miss Fielding had endured a trying day. She was in the habit of telling her intimate women friends (she had no men friends, unless we count one Dr Stocke, with whom she had for many years corresponded upon international matters of interest to them both) that although her *appearance* might be robust she was in fact far from strong. And she Gave Out, too; if you are far from strong, and Give Out, milk, as is well realized nowadays, is very good for you; so are port and beef broth and chicken, of course, but whereas it would be merely silly, as well as wicked, to try to get hold of *them*, surely it ought to be possible to obtain some extra milk? It was not as if the time were the depths of winter when the milk is strictly rationed, or even as if the Fieldings obtained their milk from one of the large combines which are helpless in the grip of the Government and cannot give you an extra drip even in summer without your milkman being flung into the Tower; the Fieldings had dealt for the last fifteen years with Soanes's Farm, a small farm upon the hill which before the war had been exceedingly dirty (and lovely to look at and exciting to play in and smell) and was rapidly, as the saying is, falling into desuetude. But since the Nazi War Soanes's Farm had perked up no end, and ploughed a lot of ground that had not been ploughed for twenty years, and it had got in a lot more cows, and some pigs, and a tractor too, and Mr Wilkins the farmer (for of course no Soanes had been there for thirty years and more) had got a bit above himself and inclined to be up-stage about the milk; disobliging, Miss Fielding called it to Miss Burton, who was also not strong and required to be soothed by the sight of five pints of milk sitting in the refrigerator in addition to a jug on the dresser. After all, he had been on cap-touching terms with Our Mother, and Miss Fielding considered that this should have made him their admiring serf for life.

And after this disagreeable interview with Soanes's milk boy, Miss Fielding, descending to the kitchen to tell Mrs Archer about the morning's duties and break to her the news that a young foreign girl was coming to live in the house and help with those duties, had (*most* unwisely, she admitted) allowed herself to be drawn into a discussion with Mrs Archer about the wars; both of them, the Nazi one *and* the Other One.

Mrs Archer was sixty-two, and she was the wife of Mr Archer, aged sixty-five, who used to be an agricultural labourer before the Other War; had been all through it in France; and was now employed at Mayflower's Nurseries in St Alberics where they were at present growing tomatoes. Mr and Mrs Archer had Sid, aged twenty-two, in the Tanks in Libya; Clive, aged twenty-one, in the K.O.Y.L.I. in Egypt; and George, aged twenty, in the Commandos, his family did not know where. In addition to these, Jessie, aged twenty-three, was working in the munition factory just outside the town, and Mrs Archer had had a young nephew taken prisoner in Crete. That was in this war. Then, as has already been recorded, Mr Archer had been in France all through the Other One, and two of his brothers had been killed in it. So taking them all round the Archers were quite a military family, and if they had been German they would have had a Certificate of Honour or something all over red seals hanging in the front parlour. Naturally the views of Mrs Archer and Miss Fielding upon the wars were divergent, but then, as W. E. H. Lecky truthfully observes in his *History of European Morals*, 'the opinions of learned men never faithfully reflect those of the vulgar.'

Mrs Archer was small and inconspicuous and neat, with a reserved expression. Her mind and body had never been completely at ease since she was four years old and free to wander about picking cowslips in the meadows, still too small to be put in charge of her smaller brothers and sisters; but she took life for granted, and had prosaically borne and brought up the four superbly healthy, ordinary children who were now in the Tanks and the Commandos and making shells.

Miss Fielding considered it her duty never to lose an opportunity of gently pressing the cause of the Brotherhood of Man, especially among the working classes, but Mrs Archer seldom gave her the chance, for she did not often mention the war. Very occasionally she observed that Sid's tank had been having a go at that General Rommel again and it did seem a ding-dong sort of business, or said that George was going out on another of those Commando raids come Tuesday (she always seemed to know when he was) and she did hope he wouldn't do anything silly, only he always was one for showing off, but mostly she got on with her work without talking.

She was a country woman, of course, and therefore her mind worked more slowly and she felt herself to be more of a person than a London 'char,' who has to work no harder than the country woman but who works under worse conditions and has fewer, less conscious traditions. Mrs Archer had been born at a labourer's cottage a few miles from Treme, and could remember when it was a day's excursion into St Alberics and back, and the local children had gone to the village school hungry, and in fantastic, cut-down adults' clothes. That was fifty years ago, and Mrs Archer firmly maintained (in spite of the wars) that things were much better now and don't you talk nonsense.

Because St Alberics was only twenty miles from London, none of the villages within five miles of it had a traditional, full village life. Improved communications, death duties, and the decline in agricultural industries, together with the building of many large handsome houses by wealthy people who had no inherited interest in their nearest village, had reduced Treme, Cowater,

Blentley and the rest to shells of villages; not deserted or decaying, but flourishing (especially since the war) with a mock-suburban life, watched over in each case by a lovely ancient church that suggested a museum and was in fact still alive and doing its duty. Miss Fielding was one of these builders of handsome houses who had only lived in Treme for eighteen years or so, and Mrs Archer (who had been a kitchenmaid at Treme Hall for a few months before old Miss Manderbie died and the house began its many years of standing empty) did not respect Miss Fielding. She saw no qualities in her to respect. She always called her 'Miss Fielding' and was perfectly polite, but to Mr Archer in the privacy of the Archer kitchen she said that Miss Fielding was silly and Didn't Believe In The War.

On this particular morning Miss Fielding had happened to remark to Miss Burton, who had come trailing down into the kitchen to get her elevenses, that she feared Dr Stocke's last letter must have been torpedoed, for it was so late. Miss Burton, whose taste in men had been formed once and for ever upon Reggie Farquharson and who considered Dr Stocke very dull, said oh dear, she was sorry, was it really too late to expect it now? and went out into the grey but warm garden with *The Times* and her elevenses. At that moment the postman's knock sounded through the hall and Mrs Archer, in response to a glance from Miss Fielding, who was getting her own elevenses, went to get the letters.

'No—oh, dear, too bad. It isn't here,' said Miss Fielding, examining them and shaking her head. 'No. I sadly fear the fishes must have got it, Mrs Archer.'

'Fishes! Huns, more likely, Miss Fielding,' said Mrs Archer.

'Now, now, Mrs Archer!' said Miss Fielding playfully. 'What good does it do us to call the German people Huns?'

'No good, I s'pose, Miss Fielding, but it's what they are.'

'Not all of them,' said Miss Fielding, smiling steadily and sweetly. 'Some—the Leaders of the people—have strayed so far

43

away from the true path that it is difficult to see how they can ever be persuaded to return. Others—the great mass of the people—are misled. Simply misled, and it does them, and us, no good to call them evil names——'

'I didn't call them bad names, begging your pardon, Miss Fielding. I said they were Huns. So they are Huns. Mr Archer he calls them Jerries, that was what they used to call them over in France in the Other War, but me and Jessie and Sid (only he doesn't often write about them) we always call them Huns. My Clive, now, he's a great reader and he's all for the Russians and always has been, and he calls them Fasheests. But me and Sid and Jessie we always call them Huns. We were only saying the other day when we heard Mr Churchill——'

Miss Fielding shut her eyes.

'——on the wireless calling them Narzis in that way he does, how *we* always call them Huns. It seems to come more natural, somehow.'

'The German people,' said Miss Fielding, opening her eyes, 'have suffered very deeply. For twenty-five years they have been the dupes of men themselves duped by the Evil Principle. They have allowed themselves to be led astray——'

'Well, why are they always led into other people's countries, that's what I'd like to know, Miss Fielding,' said Mrs Archer, wiping up a cup rather hard. She had gone red.

'That is part of their punishment and ours,' said Miss Fielding rather sharply. 'We all share the responsibility for the Treaty of Versailles.'

'I read in the *Daily Mirror* the German officers were all taking frocks for their wives in Paris and Hitler's stolen a lot of French pictures from some famous museum out there. That can't be right, say what you like, Miss Fielding. Taking other people's things away. You can't say you like that *Goring*, Miss Fielding. The things he's done! And that old Kaiser! Dying twenty-five years too late, the old misery, after he'd done all the mischief!'

'But Goering and the late Kaiser are only individuals, Mrs Archer, and what they do or did not do has no permanent bearing upon the whole situation,' said Miss Fielding very patiently.

'Well, Miss Fielding, I s'pose at least you'll admit Hitler made this war? and the old Kaiser the Other War?'

'Certainly I do not admit it, Mrs Archer. This war arose out of the deep dissatisfaction of the German people with the over-harsh treatment meted out to them after the last war, which in its turn arose out of Great Britain's desire for economic domination of the Continent and the natural, though deplorable, resentment of the already misled German people at that fact.'

She stopped, aware that her voice was more heated than she liked it to be. Mrs Archer was now trembling, as well as red. Her feelings were all mixed up with thinking about Sid all those miles away, and hating the noise of the sirens, and the sight of the ruins in the High Street, and some pictures she had seen of Greek children starving, and not quite knowing what 'economic domination' meant, and, underneath the whole confusion, a deep contempt for Miss Fielding as one who 'didn't know anything about anything.'

Suddenly she remembered what Miss Manderbie's housekeeper used to tell her to do when she was kitchenmaid at Treme Hall and was threatened with the loss of her naturally quick young temper. *Say the first line of the Lord's Prayer, Annie, it's better and quicker than counting ten.*

Our Father, Which art in Heaven, she thought. A moment later she said quietly:

'Shall I do the salad now, Miss Fielding?'

'Please,' said Miss Fielding with dignity, and withdrew to join Miss Burton in the garden until lunch-time.

Well, that, and the milk incident, and Dr Stocke's letter not coming, and the fact that Miss Burton was in her most unresponsive mood all the afternoon, refusing to be drawn into a chat about Dr Stocke and the possible fate of his letter; and the arrival at half-past five of a telegram from Betty Marten saying that she would be coming that evening instead of the following one, contrived to ruffle Miss Fielding's tranquillity considerably.

'Of course, I do not wish to say anything against Betty, she is a very young soul and allowances must be made,' said Miss Fielding at six o'clock, flinging open the spare bedroom window so violently that showers of rust fell off the catch, 'but I do think she might have sent her wire earlier. Now this room is not blacked out——'

'She can undress in the bathroom,' suggested Miss Burton, who was negligently making the bed and looking forward to hearing Betty laugh.

'Just for this evening, she will have to.'

'Is Miss Ann—whatever her name is's—room blacked out?'

'Miss Annamatta's room is quite ready,' replied Miss Fielding, to whom many years of addressing Stockes and Mukerjis had given a most un-English competence with foreign names. 'Except for some flowers. I thought that perhaps you would like to do that, when you have made the bed.'

'I'll do it now,' and Miss Burton hurried away, leaving bits of sheet hanging out and thinking remorsefully that Constance really had a good heart; most people would not have bothered to put flowers in a mother's help's room.

Indeed, if Miss Annamatta had not been a refugee Miss Fielding would not have bothered, but it was so much a habit with her to be nicer to foreigners than she was to English people that her gesture was automatic.

But the picking of a bunch of pink phlox and white cosmos, and the artistic arranging of them in the small but light and pleasant room at the top of the house, and the preparing of Betty's room, all took time; and then there was supper for five people to lay, and to prepare. 'I WILL NOT COOK' announced Miss Fielding, standing in the middle of the kitchen with her eyes shut and trying to recall what tins there were in the store cupboard. 'Where is the tin-opener?'

'In its usual place, I presume,' answered The Usurper, for Miss Burton.

'Was there any Spam left from lunch?' pursued Miss Fielding.

'There does not seem to be any,' retorted Miss Burton's voice from inside the refrigerator, and went on to murmur that perhaps Mrs Archer had taken it.

'Oh, surely not,' said Miss Fielding decisively. 'In peace time I allow perks, of course, but in war time it is *quite* different. That would be really dishonest.'

'Well, it isn't here.'

'Oh, it must be. I was Relying on it.'

'Come and look for yourself. I'll go and get some lettuces,' and before Miss Fielding could prevent her, Miss Burton had drifted off again, pulling a piece of sweetbrier to smell as she went out of the door and looking forward to wandering about by herself in the big kitchen garden.

Left alone, Miss Fielding found the tin-opener, methodically opened three tins, placed plates and knives and glasses on a trolley, and wheeled them into the dining-room and began to set the table. But she was very cross and the drawing-room just across the hall looked so cool and quiet, and on a side table was the new number of *The Aryan Path*. *There* is where I ought to be, developing my special talents, instead of doing *this*, which *any* fool could do, thought Miss Fielding, and she so far allowed the Evil Principle to invade her personality as to bang down a glass. *Oh*, what a relief it will be to have someone to get these *everlasting meals*!

It was at this unpropitious moment that a loud, a drunken (that was the word that instantly leapt into Miss Fielding's outraged mind) hooting was heard outside. A little tune was even played on the hooter, and then Miss Fielding, coming out of the dining-room with slightly greasy fingers and a set smile of welcome, saw through the open front door her brother sitting in the car, roaring with laughter and surrounded by women.

'Ha, ha! Connie, little surprise!' he said, the laughter fading from his face as he saw his sister's expression.

Miss Fielding came majestically forward.

'Not such a surprise, Kenneth; Betty's wire arrived in time for us to get her room ready, an hour ago. How are you, my dear? and Miss Annamatta, too; how do you do? and Alicia——'

Alicia made an impudent little gesture of greeting. Kenneth was busy getting out the rucksack and suit-case, having opened the door for Betty and Miss Annamatta, who got out and greeted Miss Fielding—Betty with a peck on the cheek and Miss Annamatta with a bob-curtsy. The quiet evening air was full of the noise of women's voices. Miss Fielding said something kind and welcoming to Miss Annamatta, and then shooed the flock into the house, where Miss Burton came across the hall to welcome them all over again.

God protect me from ever living in a hen-coop, thought Alicia.

Betty was enjoying the ample sweep of the lawn in front of the house and the brilliant faces of the flowers. The mere absence of ruins and vegetable plots and strips of paper on the windows was as pleasant to her as a drink or a sweet scent. Miss Annamatta kept her brown eyes fixed respectfully and politely upon her new employer.

'I'll just run you home, Alicia,' said Kenneth, coming out of the house after taking the suit-case and rucksack up to their owners' rooms.

'Thanks,' she said, and he got in beside her and drove off.

Miss Fielding took Betty upstairs, chatting all the way about Richard and mutual acquaintances, and Miss Burton, obeying a meaning nod from Miss Fielding, was left to escort Miss Annamatta.

'I will take you to your room,' said Miss Burton, advancing upon Miss Annamatta and receiving in her turn the smile and bob-curtsy. She rather liked them. An elderly woman may know that her years deserve respect from the young, but what a surprising little glow of warmth when she unexpectedly gets it!

'Thank you. You are Miss Burton,' stated Miss Annamatta.

'Er—yes. Yes, I am.' Miss Burton looked round as she trailed (her dress of course showed her ankles but her movement was traily) upstairs. 'How did you know?'

'Miss Constance Fielding say in her letter to me, "The household consist of myself, my brother Mr Kenneth Fielding, and my cousin Miss Burton. There is help for the rug-h."' Miss Annamatta, looking neither to the left nor the right, followed Miss Burton up the rich dark green carpet.

'The rug-h?' repeated Miss Burton, bewildered. 'Oh, the rough. The rough work. Yes, Mrs Archer comes in from the village every day. How well you speak English.'

'Thank you. But I say "rug-h." You say "ruff."'

'Yes. The "g" isn't sounded. Foreigners always find that so puzzling. This is your room,' and she opened a door and stood aside to let the girl see in.

Miss Annamatta stood looking about her, while the sunlight shining through curtains of yellow spot muslin showed up the shabbiness of her coat and skirt and her bare tanned legs and a patch on one of her shoes. There was a bed-cover that matched the curtains, and Miss Burton had really spread herself over the pink and white flowers, and done her best with them in a glass vase like a big rainbow ball that displayed their delicate green stems. The bedroom walls were pale green, and all round the window twined the little dark leaves and white flowers of a climbing jasmine and the room was full of its delicious scent.

After a moment the girl said:

'There is one bed.'

'Yes,' encouraged Miss Burton, who had been trying without success to guess from her expression what she was feeling.

'I sleep in the bed with another?'

'Oh, no, by yourself,' answered Miss Burton, amused.

Miss Annamatta was silent again for a moment; then she said, 'Thank you,' and bobbed another curtsy and smile. Miss Burton, having shown her the rest of the rooms on the floor and told her that dinner would be ready almost immediately, went downstairs.

In a little while, having washed her face and feet and put on a crumpled art silk dress out of the rucksack, Miss Annamatta went over to the window to look out. But first she smiled with pleasure at the jasmine, as if at the sight of an old friend, and turned one of its flowers about to see the clear pink of the underleaves, and put it up to her nose and inhaled its fragrance; but then she gently put back the spray without picking it, and gazed out between the flowers over the calm and pretty country-side, where the sun was setting. The low blue hills and the gentle rise of a distant field of silver barley attracted her attention, and she listened intently to the evening cries of birds hidden in the elms; she slowly moved the window to and fro to work its catch, and caught up a fold of the curtain and smelt its faint clean odour. The beautiful evening light, the stillness, the song of the birds and the scent of the jasmine made a world that was, for the moment, perfect.

Miss Annamatta turned away from the window, and after some delvings into the rucksack brought out a small scarf woven in brilliant colours. This she spread on the floor in front of the window. Then she took off her shoes and knelt down on the scarf, and prostrated herself three times towards the setting sun.

'O God,' she began in the Bairamian tongue, 'following the custom of our country after the Proclamation of Ser in the year 1922, I, though at that time but a child in arms, in common with all others of my race forswore the faith of my fathers and denied the fact of Thine existence. Nevertheless, O God, when I look upon this beautiful little room which is to be mine alone, my heart is so filled with gratitude——'

The musical clanging of an elephant bell wielded very vigorously by Miss Fielding below in the hall interrupted her. She got up, pulled on her shoes again, stuffed the scarf back into the rucksack, and ran downstairs.

7

The household of four women and a man soon settled into a routine. At seven o'clock Miss Annamatta got up and replenished the almost extinct fire in the boiler and took everyone up a cup of tea, and laid and prepared the breakfast. Sometimes Miss Burton or Miss Fielding, if slightly indisposed, partook of this meal in bed. About a quarter to nine, which just gave the two of them time for a cigarette that led to a certain amount of eye-shutting on the part of Miss Fielding, Kenneth drove Betty into St Alberics and dropped her at the Ministry of Applications (which was housed in Parkwood School for Girls, the latter having been evacuated to Penzance), before he went on to the elegant house in the High Street, built in 1783, which was the offices of Fielding, Fielding & Gaunt, Solicitors. About ten o'clock, having washed up the breakfast things, made all the beds and dusted the bedrooms, Miss Annamatta went into St Alberics on a bicycle to do the shopping. There she got the rations every Wednesday, which was the day that all the rations seemed to arrive in St Alberics, and sometimes stood in queues for fish, which caused Miss Fielding to shut her eyes but did not prevent her from eating the fish after Miss Annamatta had cooked it. After Miss Annamatta had prepared lunch for Miss Burton, Miss Fielding and herself, she mended holes torn in the household linen by the laundry, or tidied any cupboards that might be in disorder or performed any other small tasks that Miss Fielding might find for her to do. At half-past four Miss Burton and Miss Fielding, if neither of them had gone up to London or into St Alberics, liked to drink their tea on a stone terrace at one side of the house which overlooked the rock garden, the tables and chairs being arranged and the tea prepared and carried out to the two ladies by Miss Annamatta who, it was tacitly understood, drank her own tea somewhere in secret, Miss Fielding indulgently making no attempt to find out where. Then Miss Annamatta was absent, presumably upon her own affairs, until six o'clock or so, when the house awoke from its afternoon hush and Kenneth returned from the office and just before seven or sometimes not until after eight, Betty came back from the Ministry of Applications. Dinner was prepared, set and dished up by Miss Annamatta, whose name Kenneth had now mastered and who dined with her employers. After Miss Annamatta had prepared coffee and carried it into the freshly purified drawing-room, the three older women sat chatting while Miss Annamatta washed up and tidied the kitchen and Kenneth worked in the vegetable garden, and at about half-past ten there began that brewing of Bengers or Horlicks or Ovaltine without which some people cannot get through the night: Kenneth and Betty usually had a drink, hoarded or obtained legally enough but with immense cunning and dash, and over it they made jokes; rather milder jokes than most people make over drinks nowadays because they were both what Miss Elizabeth Bowen might call 'people of 1914.' Then, Miss Annamatta having put up such few black-outs as were necessary on these lingering summer evenings, everyone went to bed except Kenneth, who on most nights was out with the Home Guard. Miss Annamatta was paid a pound a week and all found.

The immunity from any form of war work enjoyed by Miss Fielding and Miss Burton will have struck the Gentle Reader. It had not been achieved without a struggle: not a struggle with the local authorities or those hortatory posters which make you feel a social outcast every time you go to the pictures, but a struggle with their own consciences. Miss Burton's struggle was not a hard one; she was soon defiantly taking the line 'Why should I? I'm sixty and I rolled miles of bandages for

53

four years in the Other War and one war in a lifetime is enough for anyone.' But Miss Fielding's conscience was of quite another calibre; it went deeply into the question: it pointed out that not only must Miss Fielding, if she truly abode by her principles, refuse to join the W.V.S., she must also refuse to collect her salvage or watch for fires. In short, if Miss Fielding truly abode by her principles, she must try to behave exactly as if there were no war. She had had her worst struggle over the black-out, which, had she followed her principles to their logical limit, should never have darkened her windows at all. She had explained and defended her views to Kenneth and Miss Burton for the whole week immediately before war broke out, and the matter was only settled by the most unexpected action of Kenneth, who drove without her permission into St Alberics on the final Saturday afternoon of peace, and bought up the last fifty yards of black-out material in the town. Miss Fielding had been solemnly angered with her brother and Miss Burton had never been so relieved in her life. If only Ken would do things like that more often! had been one of her reflections at the time.

As for the salvage, it would have remained shamelessly uncollected (for this was in the days before it was officially reckoned a crime to abandon a piece of string) had not Mrs Archer, who was conscientious about salvage, felt compelled to take the Sunglades salvage under her wing. It may be imagined that this did not increase Mrs Archer's respect for Miss Fielding, who, though she shut her eyes whenever she saw Mrs Archer smoothing out a sugar bag, did nothing to check her activities. If other people chose to notice the war, Miss Fielding did not propose to dissipate her energies by pointing out to them how misguided they were.

The fact was, whereas Miss Fielding's mother had been large, handsome and clever, Miss Fielding was only large and handsome. None of her children had inherited Mrs Fielding's outstandingly good memory, grasp of the machinery of public affairs and capacity for putting her own plans into successful action; and her eldest daughter's Work (consisting chiefly of organizing tea and sherry parties for influential foreigners who were interested in the preservation of world peace), while doing no harm and giving pleasure to many harmless persons, was easy and vague compared with the many years of hard personal toil put in by Mrs Fielding in aid of local health and educational services in St Alberics, whereby many helpless and unfortunate persons secured solid, lasting benefits.

Mrs Fielding had been the possessor of one of those personalities like an enormous old-fashioned battlepiece, all over rearing horses and hussars hauling cannon out of the mud and soldiers expiring in the arms of their comrades with Napoleon or somebody of that sort in the middle of it; no one can ignore it, although it exhausts everybody to tears, and weaker spirits simply avoid the room where it hangs. Constance, Joan and Kenneth had of course been subjected to the full pressure of this personality from babyhood, and their mother had been unscrupulous in the extent to which she had moulded their minds. The girls had inherited much of their mother's overwhelming personality without her brains, and in their teens they had already strikingly resembled her, with their ringing voices and vigorous movements, their air of completely knowing their own minds and being patient with other people's, their handsome profiles and fine full figures and quantities of strong brown hair.

But Mrs Fielding's eyes had had a deeper blue than most women's and her hair had curled at the tips and her neck and bosom had been unusually beautiful. Misled by these properties, the young and warm-hearted Mr Eustace Fielding had made what was on his side at least a love-match with her; and Kenneth's nature resembled that of his father rather than that of his mother. This had been a source of disappointment to Mrs Fielding, and she had never scrupled to say as much. There was no trace of a lifelong grief in the handsome earnest face that looked out from so many silver frames in the drawing-room and bedrooms at Sunglades; yet Kenneth never encountered the gaze of his dead mother's eyes without an uneasy sensation. And he never wondered why he had a lowish opinion of himself as a solicitor, a brother and a man. He only venerated the memory of his clever mother and admired his handsome, energetic sisters, to whose views and wills he had deferred ever since he could remember.

There were many photographs of Constance and Joan, as well as those of their mother, at Sunglades; those large faces with their powerful noses and confident eyes looked out at the visitor from the piano and the mantelpiece or suddenly stared up at you from behind a bowl of sweet peas, but there were no photographs of Mr Eustace Fielding at Sunglades.

As soon as it became apparent that Miss Annamatta was strong enough to do the work at Sunglades and that her cooking, though exotic, was palatable, and that she was willing and intelligent, Miss Fielding relaxed; and proceeded to enjoy what was left of the summer and to take up, so far as it was possible to do, her interrupted work. Of course, Miss Annamatta could not run the house; Miss Fielding had to assist her by suggestions for the meals (especially for puddings, of which both she and Kenneth were fond and of which Miss Annamatta seemed never to have heard), and this meant more preoccupation with domestic affairs than Miss Fielding had suffered in the pre-war days when there had been Cook and Nancy and May. But, on the whole, her life was much pleasanter since Miss Annamatta had come, and on a certain afternoon when it was pouring with rain, and the girl had been there nearly three weeks, she remarked as much to Miss Burton. They were sitting in the drawing-room. Miss Fielding, who played the piano accurately if noisily, had been regaling Miss Burton with a long Beethoven. Miss Burton had been asleep.

'Dear me, it's almost cold enough for a fire and I want my

tea. It's nearly four o'clock,' said Miss Fielding, blundering up off the piano stool and slamming Beethoven together. 'Vartouhi—Vartouhi—!' she shouted, going out into the hall, 'we'll have tea now, please.'

Miss Fielding had decided that 'Vartouhi' sounded prettier than 'Miss Annamatta.'

'Please. In a moment I bring it,' answered the polite tones from the kitchen, and immediately there began that faint clashing of china that has sounded amid the battle's fury in Libya and Crete and is the signature-tune of civilization.

'Ask her to have it with us,' suggested Miss Burton, yawning and looking out of the window. The garden was brilliantly green under the dashing rain and petals were blowing in showers off a bush of yellow roses. The chilly air was faintly perfumed with wood smoke.

'Oh, all right, if you like.' Miss Fielding looked at once surprised and rather mysterious. 'But she's a strange little person. I don't expect she will.'

'Why not?'

'Well, I don't know if you have noticed, but she is very difficult to get *at*.'

'I can't say that I have. She seems a nice little thing, rather quiet, but always very polite.'

'Oh, well, Bairamians are, of course. That's nothing to go by. She might be hating us with all her heart but she would still be perfectly polite.'

'Like the Japanese. How unpleasant.'

'Bairamians are Orientals,' pronounced Miss Fielding. 'One tends to forget that, because they are so independent and lead such active lives.'

'Like the Japanese, again.' Miss Burton yawned.

'And therefore their way of looking at things—their picture of life—is the reverse of our way,' elaborated Miss Fielding. 'Now, if Vartouhi had been an English girl in a similar situation,

57

alone in a foreign country with her own family and country in the hands of an—an invading power, she would have confided in me. She would have recognized my special gift for furthering sympathy between members of different races and poured out all her anxiety and grief. But she hasn't said a word. Not one word. She has not even asked me if I could get news of her family through the Greek Red Cross, and she must know that I have useful connections of that sort.'

'Perhaps she doesn't get on with her family,' suggested Miss Burton.

'Quite impossible. Bairamians have a strong family sense and lead a devoted family life,' said Miss Fielding decidedly, as though quoting from a book on spiders. 'No, it is just that she is a funny little thing. Not exactly sly. No, I hesitate to use that word. But what does she do with herself from four o'clock to six every afternoon up in her bedroom? That is what I should like to know.'

'Goes to sleep, I expect. And often she has a bath.'

'Does she?' exclaimed Miss Fielding.

'Very often,' nodded Miss Burton, deciding not to relate that Vartouhi had one every afternoon.

'Well, Bairamians are among the cleaner Oriental races,' conceded Miss Fielding, still quoting from the spider book.

'And she writes letters,' went on Miss Burton, rearranging a rug over her feet, which were up on the chesterfield.

'Does she!' said Miss Fielding, much interested. 'Funny little thing! I wonder who to? The Bairamian alphabet, of course, is based on the Roman lettering nowadays; they adopted it on the same day that Kemal Ataturk introduced it in Turkey. But I am surprised that she writes fluently enough to write *letters*. How do you know she writes letters?'

'I see her carrying them off to the post every morning. Don't you know anything about her people?'

'Nothing at all. I got her from Tekla House. They simply said that she spoke English and had been in England for about three years and had been employed at a café in Portsbourne, which she left because the hours were too long.'

Miss Burton raised her eyebrows and remarked, 'That can't have been much fun,' which was an expression she had picked up from Betty.

'Oh, I feel certain it was a good-class place,' said Miss Fielding. 'Probably one of those home-made cake places where they do light lunches, run by ladies. I am sure Vartouhi has never been employed at a low-class place. Such experiences always leave their mark.'

'Still—Portsbourne, Connie. It's up north and very rough, so one hears; full of wild Irish even before the war; goodness knows what it must be like now. But she is hardly the type to suit a rough sort of eating-house.'

'I don't know *what* type she is, to tell you the truth.' Miss Fielding's voice was a little sharper than usual. 'I must say I prefer people to be a little less reserved. In these days of horror and hatred, surely it behoves us all, of whatever nationality, to open our hearts to each other freely and generously. I don't know quite where I *am* with her.'

'Well, I shouldn't worry about it——'

'I am not worrying about it, Frances.'

'——she isn't at all a bad cook and she seems to have settled down very nicely,' soothed Miss Fielding, who in pre-Nazi-War days had suffered from foreigners coming to the house and freely and generously opening their hearts to anyone who would listen; and who did not wish Vartouhi encouraged to do likewise; and at that moment Vartouhi came in and began to arrange a low table for tea.

She seemed to have only two outer garments; the coat and skirt worn on her arrival, and the bright rayon dress whose crumpled condition had brought an offer of the use of the electric iron from Miss Fielding on her first evening there. This afternoon, as the weather was chilly, she wore the coat and skirt. Miss Burton and Miss Fielding made some remarks about the rain and then sat indolently watching her while she spread a delicate cloth and arranged the cups, her small sallow hands contrasting with the rich gold and crimson and blue of the Crown Derby service.

'Do stay and have it with us, won't you?' suddenly invited The Usurper, looking out of Miss Burton's faded brown eyes with imperious charm, just as Vartouhi had set down the teapot and was going out of the room.

'Yes, do, Vartouhi,' seconded Miss Fielding graciously. 'It is so lonely all by yourself in the—all by yourself,' she ended, not being quite sure where Vartouhi usually did have her tea.

'In this room with you, too also?' asked Vartouhi, pausing at the door.

Miss Fielding smilingly nodded.

'Thank you.' Vartouhi came back to the table and sat down upright on the edge of a chair, and Miss Burton studied her face, wondering if she were pleased to be there or not, but it was impossible to tell.

Miss Fielding vigorously dispensed tea, talking all the time to Vartouhi about shopping and cooking and queues, and Vartouhi sipped, with her eyes fixed upon Miss Fielding's face. She's as unselfconscious and mysterious as a cat, thought Miss Burton, and suddenly became filled with curiosity about her.

'Do you have tea in Bairamia, Vartouhi?' she inquired, in a lull while Miss Fielding's mouth was full.

Vartouhi shook her head, but before she could answer Miss Fielding said cheerfully:

'Oh, no, Bairamians are great coffee drinkers, aren't they, Vartouhi? Not coffee as we know it, Frankie, but thick as syrup and very sweet and black. I had to show Vartouhi how to make coffee in the English way.'

Miss Burton thought this a pity but did not say so.

60

'And one of the traditional duties of the eldest daughter is to prepare her father's coffee at sunset, isn't it, Vartouhi?'

Vartouhi smiled and nodded.

'I expect you often used to do that for your father, didn't you? or perhaps you are not the eldest?' pursued Miss Fielding, who, to tell the truth, loved knowing everything about people and unconsciously used the Brotherhood of Man as a lever for prising their family skeletons out of foreigners' cupboards.

'I am not the oldest, no. I am the three.'

'The three?' repeated Miss Burton, puzzled.

'She means the third sister, I expect. You have two elder sisters, is that it, Vartouhi? Two older than you?'

Vartouhi nodded. Her expression became if possible even more polite.

'How nice.' Miss Fielding took a piece of cake. '*I* have only *one* sister, Joan. She is married and lives in London. Are any of your sisters married?'

Vartouhi nodded.

'Both of them, or only one?' Miss Fielding's tone was playful, even as the elephant sports with the tree he is tearing down and eating.

'One,' said Vartouhi.

'How nice,' said Miss Fielding again. Miss Burton looked at her with respect. She herself was very interested in these facts about Vartouhi's family but could never have persevered in the face of such silent, smiling, polite reluctance.

'And has she any children?'

'I have one nice,' said Vartouhi. 'I may eat one of those small biscuit, please?'

'What did you say, my dear?' demanded Miss Fielding, startled. 'You have one——?'

'One of the small biscuit, please?'

'Yes, of course.' Miss Fielding confusedly held out the plate. Miss Burton was less surprised, for she was fairly sure that it would turn out to be another case of international misunderstanding due to differences in language and the next moment it did, for Miss Fielding suddenly nodded and said vehemently:

'Oh, a *niece*, a little girl. Your married sister has a little girl and she is your *niece* (not *nice*).'

Vartouhi nodded.

'And what is her name?'

'I am not remembering what is her name. Is three year since I am seeing her. Miss Fielding, I go and get more boiling water, I forget it, and now tea is almost cool and here is Mr Fielding coming for tea.'

She got up and bobbed her curtsy and went quickly out of the room just as Kenneth drove the car past the french windows on the way to the garage, with a wave of his hand for the occupants of the drawing-room as he went by.

'How early Kenneth is! Really, he does less and less at the office every week,' said Miss Fielding discontentedly. Then, lowering her voice, 'You noticed? She obviously doesn't want to talk about her family. That's quite absurd, saying she didn't remember her niece's name.'

'Perhaps her sister lives miles away or something and they didn't see much of each other,' said Miss Burton, who felt a little ashamed for them both. 'I expect she just can't bear to talk about them. After all, they may all be dead.'

'Nonsense; even if they are, it never does any good to bottle things up. Morbid. Well, Kenneth,' as her brother came into the room smiling and rubbing his hands, 'how very early you are! and what weather you've brought with you!'

8

The wet weather lasted for a few more days and then it became fine more once and Kenneth could spend his evenings in the kitchen garden without getting soaked through.

The kitchen garden at Sunglades was at the back of the house, and it was the most unusual one for miles around, for it had been for two hundred years the kitchen garden of Treme Hall. The Hall had been pulled down in 1924 but the wall surrounding the kitchen garden was still standing when the Fieldings, newly come into their money, had bought the plot of land backing onto it. The building company proposed that another house should be built upon the garden's site, but Kenneth Fielding had taken such a fancy to the neglected, sheltered place that he had gone behind his sisters' backs, in one of his fits of self-will, and bought the land on which it stood.

Miss Constance Fielding had been much annoyed. Their old relations' money was divided equally between herself, Kenneth, and her sister Joan, and she resented any independent financial actions by the other two because, in her eyes, such actions imperilled the whole monetary structure of the family. Where one could live in modest comfort, three could unite their incomes and live in considerable comfort, and for one of the three to spend a large sum on an old kitchen garden without consulting his co-heirs was, said Miss Fielding, as senseless as it was selfish. 'But if I'd told you, Con, I'd never have got the place,' Kenneth had said sulkily. It was one of those retorts to which there is no answer; nevertheless, Miss Fielding lectured him on his action for weeks, and even after Sunglades was built and a handsome flower garden laid out to her own wishes she showed her displeasure by seldom visiting the kitchen garden and by publicly deprecating, as if it were a disreputable habit, Kenneth's hobby of growing vegetables. Vegetables, to Miss Fielding, were commonplace and dull. She was not one of your natural green-fingers and even her own flower gardens never saw her grubbing on her knees, though she could wear a shady hat and cut roses into a trug with the best.

Kenneth had told himself frequently at that time how sorry he was that Con had been rubbed up the wrong way, but somehow his sister's anger did not impair the pleasure he took in his garden, which increased with every year.

A door with a rounded top, once painted green and now much faded by weather, led through the wall into the garden, which covered nearly half an acre and had pear and apple and plum trees scattered up and down its length, as well as the vegetable beds. When once the door was shut, no one could come in unexpectedly to trouble Kenneth, for there was no other entrance.

The high wall of dark red brick, worn with age, was by itself enough to make the place memorable, but inside it there were two other striking features.

The first was an ancient greenhouse built of small elongated panes in the shape of a half-circle, that bulged like a huge, fragile, glittering bubble from the wall immediately facing the door. Seen across the sober brown of the vegetable beds and the unremarkable shapes and colours of their contents it had a fairylike charm, irresistible because entirely unexpected. Inside there was much confusion, with broken flowerpots and bundles of dried pea and bean supports and tangles of bast lying about, for the place was too dilapidated for Kenneth to entrust any seedlings to its care except in the windless days of high summer, and on every blowy night he would awaken at intervals throughout the dark hours and listen for the crash that should tell him the old greenhouse was down at last. But so far, sheltered by the wall, it had survived, and on cold days, if he had any small jobs that could be done under shelter, he would take them into the greenhouse and sit there in the hush and faint warmth of the winter sun, working and whistling softly to himself.

The other wonder of the kitchen garden was its peaches, which were espaliered against the south wall and made in the height of summer a long, sumptuous trellis of dark leaves and dusky red fruit almost identical in colour with the bricks to which they clung. Visitors invariably exclaimed aloud on seeing these delicate things growing in such profusion; three hundred of them, in a good year, smouldering coolly among their leaves.

Late one cloudy evening at the end of September, Kenneth had put in an hour or so's digging and was finishing his work by making a bonfire of potato haulm and other rubbish at the far end of the garden. The light pearly smoke wavered up into the still air and spread out among the bronze-coloured pears and reddening apples, and all the rest of the garden was beginning to lose colour as dusk approached. The evening was so dim and Kenneth was so absorbed in the care of his fire, which must be extinguished before black-out, that he did not see the door in the wall open, and Betty coming along the path towards him, until she called:

'Hallo, Ken, are you making a bonfire? What fun! I'll come and help you.'

'In that dress? Ha! ha! Do you mind sitting on this—it's quite clean.' He spread a new sack on an upturned wheelbarrow, near enough to the fire to let the faint light fall on her face but not so near that the smoke would drift into her eyes, and she sat down. He was not in his talkative mood, and went on raking the fire and feeding it in the silence that he had preserved throughout dinner, and Betty watched the flames and thought how pleasant it was to get away from Connie and Frankie for a little while.

All through dinner the two had argued about contemporary art. Miss Fielding had never seen any of Salvator Dali's paintings but did not like the sound of him or them even though he was a foreigner, and Miss Burton had once seen a reproduction of a painting by him in *Vogue* and defended him, partly because she posed as a person knowledgeable in painting and partly out of perversity and the wish to annoy Miss Fielding, while the ignorance of both parties naturally reduced them to those generalizations which so easily become heated (not that an argument is necessarily less heated because the combatants are well informed on their subject). Miss Fielding enjoyed arguing, though she had a habit of suddenly ending the battle at its height by remembering the Good Principle and saying with a smile, 'But of course, Truth is a jewel with a million facets, as the Jains say, so why dim those facets by arguing?' and leaving her opponent maddened but helpless.

Betty, Kenneth and Vartouhi had played a passive part in the struggle by all three bolting their food in order to get away from the table as soon as possible.

'That old thing!' said Betty suddenly, smiling, rousing herself and finding that she was moving her foot in time to the tune Kenneth was whistling.

> *If you were the only girl in the world*
> *And I were the only boy*——

'It's a good tune. This war hasn't produced any good tunes so far, someone was saying in the *Telegraph* the other day,' said Kenneth.

'Oh, I don't know. *Boum—why does my Heart go boum*—do you remember? the last tune out of France. That was a good tune. And *Run, Rabbit, Run.*'

'Not like the old ones, though. It's a different kind of war.' He lifted a forkful of dried greenstuff and dropped it onto the low mound of glowing ashes, and the smoke and crackling noise and flames began again.

'Perhaps,' said Betty, a little absently. She had almost broken herself of that habit of going off into memories, but the tune, and the quietness of the garden, and the witchlike flare and crackle of the flames among the slow rolling of the smoke, had made her thoughtful for a moment. However, she had made it a practice for over twenty years to banish painful thoughts by cheerful speech, so she continued immediately:

'Nice smell of things burning. Kenneth, I had a letter from Richard this morning. He wondered if Con would mind if he stayed here from the twentieth to the twenty-seventh; he's got a week out.'

(Thus did Richard's mother paraphrase Richard's request, which had read, 'I suppose the Fielding woman won't object to my putting in a week with you if I pay her?')

'Of course; very pleased to have him. And how is Richard these days?'

'Well, he always has his lung, you know, but he seems to like being with these Dove people. They're more or less his sort.'

'Bolshies and conchies,' said Kenneth as if to himself.

'Richard isn't a C.O. He would have fought in Spain if the doctors would have let him,' Betty said quickly. 'But he doesn't take quite the ordinary view of the war; he says it might never have happened if we'd all stood by Spain in the beginning—you know who I mean, the Republicans, wasn't it?—and naturally he likes to be with people who have the same views as he has.'

'And what does Richard's mother think about it?'

'Good heavens, Ken!' said Betty with her delightful laugh, 'I haven't any politics.'

'Richard's friends and their views, I meant.'

'Oh, they're all cranks, of course, but they're all such infants too, and some of them are sweeties. I'm afraid I don't take their views very seriously. They're *still* going on about the Men of

Munich and poor dear old Chamberlain and Non-intervention, and they're all rather bitter, poor little things.'

'How long ago all that seems. Yet it's only three years.'

'Doesn't it? Absolutely another life.' She pulled her cardigan, which hung over her shoulders, closer about herself and went on gaily:

'But I don't see much of his crowd unless he asks me to lunch at the Arts Theatre Club to look over his girl friends.'

'So he gets you to vet. his lady-loves, does he?'

'He never *says* so; he's a mighty independent young man, you know. But I've noticed I usually get invited to meet the latest.'

'The latest! It's like that, is it?'

'Oh, very much so!' The elders laughed indulgently.

'Doesn't show any signs of wanting to settle down yet, eh?'

'Far from it.'

'And how do you feel about it?'

'I really don't know,' said Betty, after a pause. 'He doesn't look after himself properly when he's not living with me and of course I can't always be fussing round after him. A nice girl would be rather fun; I liked the last one, Marion Somebody, a little thing with yards of black hair. But he said she had a shocking temper.'

Kenneth lifted another load of rubbish onto the fire and the flames lit up his large Fielding nose that was not quite Roman and his blue eyes and nondescript mouth. His features are much better than Richard's, and yet Richard's face is charming and no one could call Ken good-looking, thought Betty. But it is strange that he has never married; I wonder why. For she was not a vain woman and it did not seriously occur to her that he might still be pining after herself.

'Oh, the pretty *pretty* bonfire!' cried Miss Burton's voice at this moment, and down the path she came, wrapped in a Libertyish scarf and other draperies. '*Look* at the shadows on the trees. Truly fairylike! I should have been down here long ago if

I had known you were having such fun,' and she sat down upon another seat which Kenneth had been silently assembling for her and glanced mischievously from him to Betty.

'Trying to get all this stuff burnt before black-out,' said Kenneth.

'Isn't there rather a lot of green there?' suggested Miss Burton, 'of course I don't pretend to know anything about gardening but I always supposed that everything possible should go on to the compost heap, especially nowadays. But I expect I'm quite mistaken, I usually am about everything, as Constance pointed out to me at dinner this evening,' and her face became doleful.

'It's mostly potato tops,' said Kenneth after a slight awkward pause. 'I do put most of the stuff onto the compost heap.'

'Oh, that's all right then, I only mentioned it, I thought you might not have noticed,' said Miss Burton and hurried on, 'Kenneth, I don't want to trouble you with my little worries, and I am sure Betty doesn't want to hear anything about them— no, you don't, my dear, of course not; why should you, you have your own life to live—but I just wondered if you could drop a hint to Constance about being a little less dictatorial and unkind. Really, she is *unkind*. She doesn't seem to think that one has any feelings, and if I even so much as hint that she has upset me (which she often does, I assure you), she says I'm morbid.'

'Oh, come now, Frankie, I don't think she means it; her bark is worse than her bite, you know.'

'That's all very well, Kenneth, you are out all day and can get away from it.' Miss Burton had now brought out a little hand-kerchief. 'You don't know what she's like sometimes when it's raining and she hasn't heard from that old Stocke of hers.'

'Is he hers? I always thought there was a Mrs Stocke,' said Betty, who was very willing to change the subject. 'However long have he and Connie been writing to each other? It must be getting on for ten years.'

'His wife died last year. Yes, nearly eleven years; eleven years this Christmas. After all, I have a perfect right to my opinions even if they aren't the same as Constance's. Why *should* I say I think Dali's pictures are morbid if I don't?'

'Of course not, Frankie. But Connie doesn't mean it, you know, she has a heart of gold, kindness itself——'

'Oh, yes, to any *foreigner* who likes to turn up,' sniffed Miss Burton, 'but she isn't kind to her relations. She is *not*, Kenneth, nor to her servants.'

'I say, it's getting rather chilly, I think I'll go in,' said Betty, at this point, but Miss Burton detained her with an outstretched hand.

'No, you needn't go away because of me, I've just finished and then I'll cheer up and won't say another word. Constance never could keep servants, Betty, as you know, because she bullied them and overworked them with all these parties for foreigners and the house always full of Indians and people who must have special food or their religion gets all upset. I don't wonder they wouldn't stand it. *I* wouldn't have. Mother and I had our dear Emily for twenty-eight years and then she only left us to go into a Home for Incurables. Constance has never had an Emily!'

'Frances!' called Miss Fielding, striding down the path through the dusk with her fur coat flying open, 'are you there? Very silly of you, with your rheumatism. You'd better go in at once. You'll never get all that stuff burnt before black-out, Kenneth; better damp it down and relight it to-morrow night. Frances, that sack is damp. Get up at once now, don't be tiresome, there's a dear woman, and go indoors. An early night would do you no harm; I've mixed your Horlicks.'

'I am not going to bed for hours, Constance,' said Miss Burton with dignity but getting up from the sack. 'It is kind of you to have mixed my Horlicks but you need not have troubled. I will heat it upstairs. Good night, Betty. Good night, Kenneth. I hope you are not offended at what I said about the bonfire; I admit I was in the wrong, I often am. Good night, Constance.'

And Miss Burton, amid murmured farewells from Kenneth and Betty and a hearty 'Sleep well, Frances, and don't be so touchy,' from Miss Fielding, slowly retired into the shades of evening.

'You ought to give Frances a talking-to about being touchy, Kenneth,' pronounced his sister, when Miss Burton had vanished through the gate in the wall. 'She wouldn't resent it from you, because you're a man.'

'Really, Connie——'

'She will take anything from a man, where she would get into a ridiculous tantrum if Betty or I tried to tell her, don't you agree, Betty?'

'Probably,' said Betty, who was amused but also a little dismayed for Kenneth's sake. They're all getting old, she thought, and in a few years this will be a most depressing household; far from festive, as Richard's friends would say.

'And of course that's why you always take her part,' went on Miss Fielding; to their dismay she had seated herself in Miss Burton's place and seemed prepared to make a night of it, 'because she flatters you.'

'Oh, I say, Con! Really. And I don't take her part.'

'You are very vain.' Miss Fielding wagged a finger at him with a playful glance at Betty for approval. 'You always have been. When you were a tiny thing you used to look at yourself in the glass for hours.'

'Funny little spook,' said Betty.

'Even now you go as red as a beetroot every time Vartouhi does that ridiculous curtsy to you.'

'Well, hang it, Connie, who wouldn't? I wish you'd—er—drop her a hint—without hurting her feelings, of course.'

'I am used to handling young people: I shan't be likely to hurt her feelings and I am sure Vartouhi is not the morbid over-sensitive type, anyway. As a matter of fact I *have* dropped her a hint but I am not sure that she understood quite what I meant. I shall mention the matter again. Have you seen her since dinner, by the way? I want to make sure she has practised her typing to-day.'

'Are you teaching her typing, Connie? That's very kind of you,' said Betty, surprised and remorseful.

'It will be an advantage to her when she wants to get another post,' said Miss Fielding, getting up. 'The more accomplishments she has, the better.'

'But I say, you aren't thinking of sacking her, are you?' Kenneth's tone was dismayed and he stopped in his task of stamping out the last ashes of the bonfire and gazed at his sister's massive form in the near-dusk. 'I thought things were going so well.'

'Of course not. Never entered my head. But I don't suppose she wants to stay here for the rest of her life.'

'Oh, as you were, then; I was afraid she'd been a naughty girl. There!' The bonfire was now a darker patch on the ground with faint wreaths of acrid smoke winding over it. 'And it's just on black-out,' he ended in a satisfied tone.

'I will go and turn on the wireless; I don't want to miss the news,' said Miss Fielding, striding away. She shouted over her shoulder just as she reached the wall, 'Don't be long, Betty, you'll get eaten alive with midges if you hang about there.' Then came the slam of the door as she passed through.

She walked briskly up the dim paths towards the dark house, between the beds now filled with red and amber chrysanthemums breathing out their cold scent into the evening. Her thoughts were playing vaguely about the two people she had just left, and suddenly a disturbing and alarming thought struck her. How pretty Betty had looked with the firelight on her face, how well she and Kenneth seemed to be getting on together, and why had Betty lingered on with Kenneth, instead of accompanying her, Miss Fielding, back to the house? Could there be anything in it?

Miss Fielding compressed her lips. I will not have it, she thought. If necessary, I shall tell Betty that I must have her room for another refugee, and she must go. I thought he had got over all that nonsense since the affair with the Palgrave girl. I suppose men are never too old to make asses of themselves in that way. But I am not going to have it. I shall watch, and make sure, and if it is so, then she must go.

She went into the house and banged the door.

It was now nearly dark in the kitchen garden. Betty had been looking idly across the dim beds of brussels sprouts and winter spinach, and suddenly she gave an exclamation.

'Kenneth! There's someone down by the peach trees!'

He was gathering some scattered tools together and did not trouble to look up at the small, dark figure that was pacing slowly along the twilit path under the espaliers.

'That's all right, it's only Vartouhi.'

'How do you know? You can't see any better than I can, it may be a parachutist!'

'She comes down here almost every night and walks about for a bit—has done, ever since she discovered the peaches. I suppose they remind her of home. She asked if I minded, and of course I said I was delighted—poor little girl.'

'Poor *Ken*—all your womenfolk pursuing you into your retreat to ask you favours and bring you their grizzles.'

'I don't mind—much,' said Kenneth, his voice betraying that he was smiling. Betty laughed too and said, 'I'm going in, it's chilly.'

'Yes, you run along, I won't be a moment now, I've nearly finished.'

As she passed the peach espaliers Betty glanced curiously towards the fruit bushes that had concealed Vartouhi while Miss Fielding was in the garden, but there was no dark little figure there now; Vartouhi had slipped away.

Kenneth lingered for a little while longer, unwilling, though it was nearly dark, to leave the garden. He was still whistling *If You were the Only Girl in the World* as he put away the rake and hoe and other tools in the shed and locked its door and put the key in his pocket.

At last all was tidy. He took a last look round in the dusk in case there was anything he had overlooked, and flashed his torch once or twice over the bonfire to make sure it would not burst into renewed flames. The trees were black shapes against the motionless clouds that hung low in the dark blue air, and the sweet cold smell of dew, mingled with the strong odour of cabbage leaves, came up from the damp vegetable beds. A murmuring noise began to sound in the sky, and Kenneth looked up and waited. Presently the thundering drone passed over his head, growing fainter as the hidden squadron went on its way, and finally fading into the silence. He went across the garden, found the door in the wall and passed through, locking it after him. He was still whistling softly but now the tune had changed to *Tipperary*.

9

The news was broken to Miss Fielding that Richard Marten was coming to stay for a week and was amiably received by her, for she flattered herself upon her capacity for understanding what she called the wayward moods of youth and dealing with them and she hoped that Richard might give her opportunities. She also welcomed the prospect of some masculine society, to which she was not averse, and finally she trusted that the sight of her twenty-five-year-old son would banish from Betty's head any unsuitable ideas that might have got into it.

So a room was prepared for Richard by Vartouhi, and Miss Fielding herself wrote to him about the Bus, trusting to no one else to convey with necessary clarity its times and eccentricities. Drunk with sight of power, the Bus which covered the four miles between St Alberics and Treme had become since the Nazi War a moody and incalculable tyrant running the gamut of temperament, from being ten minutes late in starting to going round by another route to save wear on the tyres, and generally behaving more like a medieval baron than a bus. Miss Fielding covered two sheets of note-paper with neat instructions and warnings about the Bus and Richard put it down on a chair and never saw it again.

The afternoon of his arrival was of course a Sunday; he was decanted onto the platform at St Alberics, down which a slight east wind was blowing, with the fish; and stood there for a moment under the gloomy sky, looking abstractedly about him, and sniffing the sweet air. He was hatless and his fair hair blew about and in one hand he dangled a large half-empty rucksack that seemed a long way down because he was six feet two inches tall. He was thinking about Mimas, one of the moons that revolve around the planet Saturn, and although his thoughts had been momentarily interrupted by the pushing of himself out onto the platform by the friendly hands of the people in his compartment, with whom he had shared his lunch and talked about Spain, remnants of reflection were still clinging to him like shreds of the Milky Way.

'Yes. Ticket,' he muttered energetically, and took it out of his trousers pocket and dropped it, and picked it up again. He strode along the platform, a striking figure in clothes unusually shabby even for the third year of a war, with a Greek nose and an absent expression.

The streets outside the station were almost empty of people and looked squalid and ugly under the grey clouds broken here and there by livid light. He walked up the hill in the middle of the road, not thinking about Mimas now, but looking at the mean little shops (one in every three was to let) with their displays of dummy chocolates and empty cigarette cartons, and thinking about them: his thoughts were uncoloured by emotion, and were stiffened by that accurate and extensive knowledge of economics and the mechanics of the social structure possessed by well-educated Leftists, which makes it difficult for generous but lazy Liberals to argue with them. How hideous it is, he thought; and his mind presented him at once with all the historical and sociological reasons for the hideousness; the rise of the joint stock companies in the reign of Charles the Second and the consequent transferring of responsibility from the wealthy individual to the wealthy company; the resultant decline among the cultured *rentiers* of a sense of personal responsibility for the social structure; their gradual retreat from political life and their replacement by uneducated but able men completely unfamiliar with the tradition of *noblesse oblige*; the ruthless construction of ugly ill-built towns to house the cheap labour employed in such men's factories; the displacing of beauty as a natural ideal among the architects by the ideals of utility and comfort for their wealthy but ignorant patrons; the spread of these latter ideals, mingled with a debased conception of rural domestic architecture, among——

At this point in his thoughts Richard's ankle turned over, and he fell sprawling in the road in front of a car which was slowly approaching him, driven by a young woman beside whom was seated his mother. The latter was loudly hailing him, 'Richard! Richard! Coo-ee!' but he did not hear her until it was too late, and then he came out of his fit of amnesia to find himself lying in the road, to hear confused exclamations above him, and then to feel the wheel of the car go slowly, agonizingly, with a horrible crunch, over his right ankle.

'I'm frightfully sorry,' said Alicia Arkwright, leaning back in her seat, white-faced and shaking but calm.

'His head——' stammered Betty, struggling to get the door open, and Richard, hearing what she said through the faintness brought on by pain, called as loudly as he could:

'I'm all right but get the wheel off my ankle,' and moved aimlessly about with his arms in an attempt to shake off the agony by feeling for his rucksack.

'The wheel—it's on his ankle! Back the car!' cried Betty, kneeling in the road beside him, in the middle of a crowd that had begun to collect. Alicia did as she was told and then sat still again, angry with herself for feeling sick.

'Is there a doctor anywhere near here?' asked Betty, turning round and appealing to the little crowd, and out of the doubtful murmurs and shakings of heads finally someone said, 'Dr Macintosh, just up the road.'

'I'm going for a doctor, it isn't far,' said Betty, bending over her son's greenish face. 'I'm afraid it's very bad, isn't it, darling?'

'Excruciating, thanks,' he answered calmly, not lifting his head from his arms. 'That's you, isn't it, Betty? Could someone light me a cigarette? In my left-hand coat pocket.'

'Here you are, chum.' A soldier put a lighted one between

his lips. 'Keep smiling. The lady's run for the doctor. Only just up the road.'

'Only they're mostly out of a Sunday afternoon,' pessimistically muttered someone.

'I'm all right. Thanks,' said Richard and shut his eyes and lay still, thinking how hard the road felt and remembering Alec Tankerton who had been killed in Spain.

Alicia got out of the car and walked as steadily as she could for the shaking of her legs round to the place where he lay. She pushed her way past the Sunday school children and elderly women and Air Cadets and knelt beside him.

'I'm frightfully sorry,' was all she could say. 'Your mother and I were coming in to meet you because—that is—I did hoot, but you didn't seem to hear.'

'I didn't hear,' he answered crossly. 'It was entirely my fault but that doesn't make it any easier to bear. Do you mind if I don't talk?'

'Of course not. I'm most awfully sorry.'

Here Betty arrived with the doctor, who had just been setting out for a well-earned game of golf and was inclined to be terse. With the help of the soldier they got Richard into the car, and Alicia drove to the surgery and he was carried in by the Army and the R.A.F., who afterwards expressed opinions favourable to his fortitude.

The ankle was pronounced to have a number of bones injured but not so seriously as to make an X-ray necessary, and the doctor gave it treatment and gave Richard something to lessen the pain. There then arose the question of where he should be taken to, for it was obvious that he would have to remain at wherever he was going to for many weeks, and that expert massage would be needed. Three nursing-homes and the Cottage Hospital were telephoned without a vacant bed being found, and then Betty, who had been glancing anxiously at her son's face, said decidedly:

'You must come back to Sunglades, darling. Your room's all ready and I'll telephone Connie now—if I may?' to the doctor.

While she was answering as briefly as possible the staccato exclamations and questions from the other end of the line, Richard was helped out to the car again by the doctor and Alicia with an arm about the neck of each. He was no light weight, and Alicia reflected how much difference there was in having a personable young man's arm around your neck for his pleasure and having it there for his support.

Then, the party being settled and their address being given to the doctor, she drove them quickly homewards past the fields of stubble and yellowing hedges, and the oaks and elms with here and there a great branch already fading into gold. There was relief and pleasure to Betty and to Richard, even in his pain, as the car left St Alberics behind and they drove on, deeper into the open country; but Alicia's spirits drooped still further, as they always did when she found herself surrounded by hills or the silent fields. It was not that she was still affectionately pining after that H. who had caused all the trouble; indeed, she had now reached the stage when she wondered how she could ever have cared for him, but although she no longer found his qualities attractive even in memory, the anger and humiliation that she had experienced when, having permitted herself to be cited as co-respondent, he became reconciled with his wife, remained with her in their first painful strength; and therefore, as fields and hills were conducive to a reflective mood, she preferred streets and cinemas, which were not.

Unrelieved pain is very tiring, and by the time the car drove up to the front door of Sunglades, Richard, whose health was never good, felt completely exhausted. He sat without moving, staring in front of him, and observed to his mother:

'I'll make the effort in a minute, Betty.'

'Take your time, darling,' she said, trying to be casual. She leant forward and asked Alicia for a cigarette.

At this point in the proceedings a kind of distant cackling and chattering, suggestive of the Parrot House on a sunny afternoon, was heard approaching across the hall of Sunglades, and the next moment the door was flung open and out into the porch hurried Miss Fielding—'Well, Richard, you *are* unlucky! The last time you were here you fell out of the cedar-tree!' Miss Burton—'Poor dear, *poor* dear, *what* a beginning for your visit, what *bad* luck!' Vartouhi (the only silent member of the party, who at once made her way to Richard's rucksack), and Kenneth—'Hallo, Richard, glad to see you but sorry to see you like this, just lean on me and take it easy.'

Richard could make no response to all this kindness except to smile as they crowded round the car; but then, noticing a pair of small sallow hands that he at first took to be a child's tugging at his rucksack, he roused himself enough to turn slightly and look down upon a head crowned with plaits of fair hair.

'Don't bother with that, it's full of books and extremely heavy,' he said faintly.

She looked up and curtsied and smiled. He saw a face that seemed to him delightful, round and dimpled, with long brown eyes. Just the sight of it made him forget his pain.

'Gently does it,' said Kenneth, helping him out of the car. 'That's right—arm round my neck.' Alicia moved forward to help once more, as Miss Fielding and Miss Burton had fallen into that state of interested staring which comes so easily to most of us when there are pathetic and interesting doings afoot, and Betty was helping Vartouhi with the rucksack. 'Other arm round me,' suggested Alicia without coquetry.

'Oh no, you've done your stuff already and I'm so heavy,' he protested, not too much in pain to try to secure the neck that he wanted, and even as he glanced helplessly round, Vartouhi came forward and lifted his arm and arranged it over her shoulders. The contrast in their respective heights was ludicrous and she saw it as soon as he did and laughed up at him, gently removing his arm from her neck.

'You put your hand on me—*so*,' she commanded, pressing his hand down upon her shoulder. 'Better like that.'

'Much too heavy for you,' he smiled, shaking his head.

'I am varry strong!' she answered proudly, and indeed he could feel, in the easy way she had lifted his relaxed arm, that she was. The unexpectedness of this added to her charm, and he was not grateful to Miss Fielding when she bore down upon them and upon Kenneth, who was waiting to see what they were going to do, exclaiming authoritatively:

'No, no, Vartouhi, you will strain yourself. See, *I* will help Mr Marten' (in the voice of one about to demonstrate their watch-spring to a three-year-old), and she grabbed Richard's arm and festooned it about her neck. 'There! That is right. Now—up we go!'

Bother, thought Richard, who conserved much energy by never swearing even in thought, but she's right, the little love with the plaits would only have strained herself. And he made a moderately comfortable journey up the stairs with an arm about each of the broad Fieldings.

Betty followed them, and Alicia went into the drawing-room after Miss Burton, whom of course she knew slightly. It was by now nearly six o'clock, and she hoped that there might be a drink, which she felt she deserved.

The drawing-room was one of those long, dark rooms with a low ceiling and diamond window panes and much sombre wood panelling which are found in houses of the pseudo-Tudor type, such as Sunglades was. Miss Fielding had not been able to indulge her belief in light walls here, and she had refrained from having the panels painted over because it had been Our Mother's favourite room, but she had done her best with curtains of yellow glazed chintz patterned with large birds in claret and turquoise, and the latter colour was repeated in the beautiful Chinese carpet on a rust ground. There were some flower paintings and one or two portraits, including one of Our Mother in grey chiffon and pearls above the mantel-piece, and many Chinese bowls and vases which were always kept filled, even in January and February, with large handsome flowers. The windows overlooked the terrace where Miss Fielding and Miss Burton liked to drink their tea in fine weather, and immediately beyond it was the bed of amber and red chrysanthemums now glowing in the light of a stormy sunset. It was remarkable, considering how many beautiful objects were assembled in the drawing-room and that a pleasing outlook from its windows was included, that the complete picture made by room and garden was not beautiful, but Richard supposed he was the only person who had ever noticed the fact and he explained it to himself, when musing upon his dislike of the room, by the one word Proportions; and recalled a room in a house of 1780 at Regent's Park which was furnished with undistinguished objects, and yet was beautiful.

'I *think* there is some sherry!' said Miss Burton brightly to Alicia. 'Do sit down. You must be quite worn out; such a horrid experience for you.'

'Oh, no, I'm not, thanks,' said Alicia, sitting down before the fire and taking out her case and lighting up. 'I'm all right.' What a lot of old things there were about, she reflected. Almost every-where you went that wasn't a bar or a factory absolutely crept with them, and they would talk.

'Kenneth will be down in a minute and then we can have our sherry,' pursued Miss Burton, from whom The Usurper was absent this evening, and who therefore could not convey to Alicia her interest in her as the heroine of a scandal; even such a heroine as Miss Burton had been in 1908, but of course a less innocent one. Alicia wondered why they had to sit with their tongues hanging out waiting for Kenneth to descend and dispense the sherry; and at that moment Betty came in, followed by Miss Fielding.

'We all want some sherry,' announced Miss Fielding, sitting down all over a large chair, 'but we will wait until Kenneth comes down; he won't be long. He is getting Richard into bed.'

Why will we wait? thought Alicia. Hell, why should we wait? And she thought with some envy of Kenneth's task; she was susceptible to masculine attractions, as men were to her own, and Richard, despite his shabbiness, had for some reason passed her rather exacting standards. The trouble is, she thought, there are too many old things about; talking, and waiting for their sherry.

'I feel quite limp,' went on Miss Fielding. 'It is strange how exhausting the spectacle of another's suffering is to some natures.'

'Vartouhi's getting Richard some tea,' said Betty, resting her dark head with its one lock of silver hair against the brilliant birds and flowers of a cushion.

'There will be some sherry in a minute,' murmured Miss Burton.

I don't believe it, you're having me on, thought Alicia.

'We must hear *all* about it presently, Betty,' said Miss Fielding. 'I took in nothing on the telephone, but *nothing*. I never do on these occasions; nothing except the bare Fact.'

While Betty and Alicia were taking this hint and putting their separate versions together to make a story out of the afternoon's events, Kenneth came in. Something appeared to have irritated him and he splashed out sherry and busied himself with filling glasses and handing cigarettes in silence.

'——So as Miss Arkwright happened to be going in to St Alberics she very kindly offered to give me a lift and meet Richard and drive us both back,' explained Betty. 'I was sure he would have lost your instructions, anyway, Connie.'

Miss Fielding, drinking her sherry in a manner not conveyable in words, which seemed to make it sort of *solid* like soup, shook her head indulgently as if to say, 'Youth will be served,' and Betty went on with her story, appealing every now and then to Alicia for confirmation.

She's pretty, but they aren't in the least alike to look at, thought Alicia, staring at her. The sherry was soothing, and she suddenly remembered a rather pleasant afternoon, on another Sunday, that she had passed in this room seven years or so ago: some young foreigners had been staying with Miss Fielding and she had invited the young English people of the neighbourhood to meet them and play tennis. There had been no unusual attractions or events during that afternoon of broken English and laughter and polite conversation, but there had been a young Norwegian who had obviously liked Alicia and whom she had liked in return, and her dress had been unusually becoming, and at the end of the afternoon the long summer months, and her whole future life, had seemed to stretch before her, full of gaiety and promise. She had been twenty years old. On this autumn evening seven years later she was again sitting in the Fieldings' drawing-room, and thinking about a young man who mildly attracted her: and the contrast between her mood now and the mood of her twenty-year-old self was painful.

I'm getting into a sourpuss, she thought. I wasn't a bad kid, seven years ago. If Mother hadn't gone off; and then H.—oh, well. By the time *I'm* forty (she was still watching Betty), if I go on as I am now, I shan't be like that.

Upstairs, Richard was lying on his side and watching the sunset reflected on the windows, while muttering over to himself a poem of Dylan Thomas's in the hope that it might act as counter-irritant to the agony in his ankle. At the same time his mind was busy in an idle feverish way with how he should approach Vartouhi, whose exotic name, even as spoken by Miss Fielding's unlovely voice, had added another strand to the net of charm in which he was caught. When he recalled the frankness of the smile she had given him downstairs he was inclined to think that a completely straightforward 'You are very lovely and I want to kiss you' would be the best method.

The room was already beginning to settle into the dusk of

evening and was illuminated only by the glow from the stove, and the house, the large gardens surrounding it and the autumnal countryside spreading away to the low hills were all silent. Richard could just hear the faint sound of voices downstairs, and by a certain sustained impersonal note which shortly intruded itself he thought that the six o'clock news was being listened to. He was nearly asleep, in spite of the pain, when there was a slight sound at the door, and he opened his eyes languidly and saw Vartouhi coming in, with the last light of the fading sunset illuminating her face and hair.

'I bring you tea,' she announced, smiling and setting down a tray on the bedside table, 'with toast, too also.'

'Thank you,' he answered quietly.

I could never get tired of looking at her, he thought, watching as she poured out the tea. How strange it is (he moved restlessly, for he felt very hot and the pain was increasing), one's read about this sort of thing so often in Proust and other people's novels; Albertine asleep, and Maurice Guest watching Louise at the piano, and it's never happened to me before, and now it has. I suppose one just happens to be allergic to certain concatenations of colour and shape and the proportions between bone and bone, and when one finds them all in one face——

'Is it bad, dear?' asked his mother, standing beside his bed and remembering as she looked down at him how she had had to suffer the anxiety of his baby illnesses alone, because his father had been killed in France.

'It is rather but I'm divinely comfortable here,' he answered, thinking, she's gone out of the room.

She had, shutting the door after her with another polite curtsy that he had not seen because he was taking care to keep his eyes on his mother's face. He suddenly felt very ill and wretched.

'I'll feed you,' said his mother, taking up the cup and a piece of toast.

Absurd, a little thing like that trying to help a man upstairs,

STELLA GIBBONS

thought Kenneth irritably, leaning against the mantelpiece and silently listening to the talk of the women as he drank his sherry. Might have injured herself for life. Good thing Connie stepped in when she did.

10

Most of Richard Marten's friends had that dislike of their fellow creatures which accompanies the reformer's temperament, but he himself had inherited his mother's pleasure in company and talk; even ordinary company and commonplace talk was to him better than isolation (unless he was thinking out some problem to a conclusion) for both fed his appetite for the social history always unfolding beneath his eyes: he was a natural, as well as a trained Mass Observer. On the fifth day after his accident, therefore, he suggested that he should come downstairs and lie on a couch 'somewhere.' It would save stairwork (and Vartouhi would pop in and out oftener).

Miss Fielding agreed without argument. He must be her guest until Christmas at least, the surgeon said, and letters had been exchanged which severed his connection with the Dove Players, and the arrangement would certainly mean less work. So one morning before breakfast Kenneth helped him down to a couch in a small room opening off the hall which had been Mrs Fielding's work room, and he lay there reading the newspaper and thinking how deplorable it was, and how necessary a free press was, and eating his breakfast and half-listening to the talk going on in the dining-room across the hall, whose door was ajar.

He heard Miss Fielding give a pleased exclamation.

'How delightful! Dr Stocke has sent me a copy of *Little Frimdl and the Peace Reindeer* from New York!' followed by much rustling of wrappings.

'Is it a fairy story?' inquired Miss Burton languidly.

'Not a story; a fairy play with a message of international peace.'

I obscenity in the milk of Little Frimdl and in the milk of the Peace Reindeer too also, thought Richard, putting down his paper and looking across at the drawing-room door. He could just see Kenneth eating bacon; Vartouhi was out of sight.

'How nice of him. How is he?' asked Betty.

'He is fairly well, but his digestion is troubling him; American food is too rich for him,' answered Miss Fielding, evidently reading a letter, 'but he says his work is so singularly worth-while that he does not allow himself to become discouraged by trifles.'

'With real cream, ha! ha! May I have some more tea, Connie, when you're ready?' from Kenneth.

'——And he hopes I may see my way to having some readings from *Little Frimdl and the Peace Reindeer* here, and asking anyone who might be interested. But what a splendid idea! And why only *readings*? Why not the play itself?' Miss Fielding rustled the letter with excitement and Richard guessed that she was looking round the table at the faces of her household, and could imagine the expression on every face but Vartouhi's, who would not realize all the implications of what had just been said.

'Splendid idea,' said Kenneth loyally at last, 'but isn't it going to be a bit difficult, in the circumstances?'

'Difficulties are only Put Here for us to deal with them! We won't admit there *are* difficulties! We will *brush* them away!' cried Miss Fielding, gaily making brushing movements. 'Betty, don't you think it's a splendid idea? You can bring some young people from the office to be Spirits of Mutual Mistrust, can't you?'

'Well, Constance, I'd love to, only it's the black-out. Their mothers do hate them being out in it in the winter. And there would have to be rehearsals——'

'We will wait till there is a moooon!' promised Miss Fielding in a luring tone. 'There are the Spirits of Mutual Co-operation too, and a Very Old Man who afterwards turns out to be History.'

Richard, listening with his mouth full of toast, shook his head.

He was more of a realist than the other Dove Players, and had a truer sense of the theatre, and although he continued to believe that the ordinary public *ought* to like plays of the *Little Frimdl* type, experience had taught him that what they did like, especially in the middle of a war, was jokes, religion, sentiment, beauty and legs. He doubted if *Little Frimdl*, with a text well decontaminated of all these ingredients, would have much box office appeal. No doubt the Spirits will chant, too, he thought; and sure enough in a moment Miss Fielding, who had apparently been studying the play, exclaimed again:

'Oh *yes*! we *must* do it. It's *such* fun—it ends with the Spirits of Mutual Co-operation and the Spirits of Mutual Mistrust grouped together at the back of the stage, chanting a Hymn to Peace while History (the Very Old Man, you know, he turns out to be History; Dr Stocke's plays always have a sly little joke in them, he has a great sense of fun), the Very Old Man writes down their names and records in a Big Book. Oh, yes, we *must* do it!'

'I do really think it's rather an ambitious scheme, in the circumstances, Connie, as Kenneth says,' said Betty, gathering her strength to crush the infant idea at once. 'Everybody's so appallingly busy just now, it's almost impossible to get hold of people to do anything. And with the winter coming on and everything——'

'It will mean so much extra work for Vartouhi, too,' put in Miss Burton, smiling kindly towards Vartouhi, who was placidly eating porridge with her eyes fixed on the bowl and taking no part or interest in the discussion.

'Nonsense, we can get Mrs Archer in to help, she will love it,' said Miss Fielding optimistically. 'And she has a small grandson, too; he could do Little Frimdl. Now who else is there? Frimdl's Father—you could do that, Kenneth, unless you'd rather do the Very Old Man; Frimdl's Mother, that will do for you, Betty, and then there's the Spirit of Peace, she only has a very small part, I could fit that in. With all the producing as well, I'd better not undertake too much——'

'We're going to be very busy round about Christmas in the Home Guard, Connie,' said Kenneth, desperately but without conviction. 'I really don't see how I can fit it in, honestly. And I don't think people will want to see a play about peace, either. It isn't quite the moment, if you see what I mean.'

'I think no, too also!' suddenly said Vartouhi, looking up from her porridge, and causing Richard to start. 'I think no one will come.'

'How can you possibly know anything about it, Vartouhi?' Miss Fielding's tone was impatient rather than cross. 'There is a deep-seated longing for peace in every heart and this play will call to that hidden longing.'

'If it doesn't call to good old 18B,' muttered Kenneth. 'No, really, Constance, if you insist on doing it, I do think you'd be wiser to just call it 'Little So-and-so and the Reindeer,' and then everybody'll think it's a play for children. Don't want to get up people's noses, you know.'

Miss Fielding shut her eyes for a moment.

'Very well, Kenneth, if you make such a point of it,' she said at last, opening them again, 'we will have the posters printed——'

'Goodness, are we going to have posters?' said Betty faintly.

'Oh yes, Constance always does these things in style,' said Miss Burton, who was offended at being left out of the casting. 'And what am I to be, Connie? The reindeer?'

Everyone laughed, which restored her good humour.

'Oh, we will hire a reindeer-mask from Clarkson's——'

'I thought Clarkson's was blitzed?' put in Betty.

'Well, from Hamley's, then—there are lots of places,' said Miss Fielding impatiently. 'No, Frankie, you can be one of the Spirits, if you like. I propose to make each Spirit represent a Nation— perhaps you would like to be Greece?'

'Yes, indeed I would,' answered Miss Burton heartily; her cheque book and her thoughts were very often at the disposal of that country.

'And I shall ask Alicia Arkwright to be in it,' pursued Miss Fielding, 'and of course *Richard*! Richard with his stage experience will be a great help to us!'

'Excuse if I go to see if Mr Marten wants more to eat,' said Vartouhi at this point, and a minute later she came into the room where Richard lay.

'What are they all talking about?' he asked her, smiling.

'A plaaay,' she said, smiling teasingly back at him. 'Someone send a plaaay to Miss Fielding from America and she is going to plaaay it, with them all.'

'Are you going to be in it?'

She moved her shoulders. 'If I am ask. You want more toast, Mr Marten?'

'No, thank you. Do you want to be in it?'

She made the same movement of her shoulders.

'If I am ask, I shall.' A change of expression came over her face but he could not tell of what she was thinking, as he watched her. Her fingers moved absently towards her throat, and then she frowned.

'No, you haven't got your little badge on this morning. What is it? The League of Free Bairamians in England?'

She nodded. 'I forget it when I dress in a hurry.'

Richard sighed. The gulf between the forces shaping world politics and the instinct that made her wear the little badge seemed to him utterly pathetic, and he could not begin to explain to her why.

'You want more tea?' she asked, pausing at the door.

He shook his head. 'No, thank you. Vartouhi, don't go just yet.' He held out his cigarette case. 'Come and sit down and let us talk.'

'I do not like to talk, Mr Marten.'

'So I have observed. I never thought to find a girl who didn't. Do you talk much in your own country? or is it just that you dislike to talk in English to English people?'

'I like to talk in Bairamia, yes. Now I go to finish my breakfast, Mr Marten.'

'I'm sorry; I didn't know you hadn't finished it. Please call me Richard, will you?'

'If you want. Rich-ard. Richard.' To his great pleasure she went out of the room murmuring his name, but he was disconcerted to observe a dimple come into her cheek as she turned away.

He lay still for a little while, staring at the distant blue winter sky visible through the low windows, and hoping she was not a flirt. To the sly yet innocent gaiety of approach to him that he occasionally detected in her, the only word applicable was 'flirt.' His mother had that manner too, and he was disturbed to find it in Vartouhi, for he was a young man who did not like his love affairs to upset his mental programmes and his bodily plans. Already she was making him unhappier than he reckoned to be when he was in love, for there was no real exchange of conversation between them both to enable him to discover what her nature was like, and so he was forced to love as the very young or the very simple must love, ravished by the curve of a cheek or the fluting of an upper lip.

I suppose, he thought, that she has that picture of *Home* in her head that they all carry. They sit in the Corner House in London and in the cafés and milk-bars all over England, sometimes together and sometimes alone, and the English battle-dress makes them look all alike and yet brings out their differentness, their swarthiness or blondeness, the width of their cheekbones and the tilt of their eyes. The young women are gaudily dressed and get on your nerves with their unceasing vivacity and the older ones creep about Hampstead in trousers and peasant handkerchiefs looking stunned, only rousing themselves to make scenes in the food shops. One gets sick of the sight of them, and then one remembers those pictures they carry in their heads, so different, but all a picture of Home. For one it's the neat wooden houses above the water among pines and rocks; for another the canals between the tulip fields; for others the shabby white plaster houses and old towers and plains of Poland, or the broad grey streets and gentle shabbiness of Vienna; for Vartouhi I suppose it's fruit trees in flower. For all of them it's the smells of their own food, the sounds of their own streets, the incommunicable light of their own skies. And then we ask them if they like England, and some of us feel offended when they let us see that they don't.

Here Miss Fielding came in with *Little Frimdl* and sat down beside him in a dreadfully solid manner and began to tell him her plans for the play.

Little Frimdl, once launched, sailed remorselessly on, and no notice was taken of anybody's excuses or disinclination to perform. Betty was now so busy at the Ministry of Applications that she had to bring home every evening the work that she had been unable to finish during the day, and when she remembered her gay idle hours in a Government Office during the Other War, she smiled and sighed, and it struck her that if the Nazi War were better organized, at least from the civilian point of view, than the Other War had been, this was chiefly due to what she had sometimes heard discussed by Richard and his friends as a sinister figure——the contemporary civil servant. But the consciousness that she herself was doing her duty did not make her more willing to be a Spirit of Mutual Co-operation in *Little Frimdl*, and she grew to dislike the rehearsals, which took place three times a week. Her severest condemnation of any event was to call it a bore, and she called *Little Frimdl* a bore to Kenneth and Richard very very often.

In the course of years Miss Fielding had acquired a collection of alleged national costumes which she had used in other *Little Frimdls* in the past, and she now so far conceded to Kenneth's and public opinion as to suggest that three Spirits of Mutual Mistrust should be dressed as Italy, Germany and Japan, while the Spirits of Mutual Co-operation should be dressed as the United Nations. She herself was feeling most amiable just now, for she was never more content than when there was some plan for a party or play afoot, with furniture and people to be moved about. She kept an observant eye upon Kenneth and Betty, despite her many preoccupations, and although her fears were not completely set at rest, she felt that at least matters had gone *no further*; just as she had hoped, Betty's attention was now chiefly absorbed by her son, and Miss Fielding congratulated herself upon her sagacity in having said that he might come on the visit; and really, that ankle had been quite providential!

She had telephoned to Alicia one evening, disturbing her as she lingered over her late and solitary dinner after nine hours spent in the factory, and informed her that she had got to be a Spirit of Mutual Mistrust in *Little Frimdl*. Alicia was just about to refuse vigorously when she recollected that Richard Marten was still at Sunglades and realized that if she accepted a part in *Little Frimdl* she was bound to see something of him. The prospect seemed to her more attractive than most prospects she came across nowadays, so she altered her reply to, 'Oh, have I? All right, I expect I can fit it in. Who have I got to be? I don't mind doing Italy if you've got one of those square peasant head-dresses but I do draw the line at Japan.'

'The costumes are accurate in every detail,' replied Miss Fielding repressively, 'and the Japanese, Alicia, should at least be given the benefit of the doubt. They have done nothing so far.'

'Do you call what they've been doing to the Chinese for the last five years nothing?'

Miss Fielding was understood to mutter that it was all very unfortunate, and then went on in a louder voice to arrange that Alicia should come over on the following Tuesday evening to look at the play and the costumes and fix up dates for rehearsals.

What a bore, thought Alicia as she carried her brandy into the drawing-room. She lay down on a couch and put up her feet, in lovely little brocade sandals, on the cushions among the pages of the *Evening Standard* which her father always brought down with him from the City, while the voluminous skirts of her green house-coat, most graceful of contemporary garments, fell in folds to the floor. She slowly turned the brandy round and round in its big glass, occasionally taking a sip and thinking how good it tasted and congratulating herself on having told her father that she wanted a bottle put aside, from their dwindling stock, for her personal use when she was unusually tired. She shut her eyes.

For nine hours she had been manoeuvring a crane, attached to a cabin, to and fro under the roof of the factory; hauling the barrels of the big guns into position with the crane as the men and women working on them below needed the angle changed. She rather liked the work, which isolated her from the other workers and gave her a not unattractive bird's-eye view of the enormous long, low, airy shed in which the guns were shaped, but it was very tiring and she was glad to lie still. The softness of the couch, the warmth, the silence broken only by a murmur of dance music from the wireless, and the fiery bite of the brandy, were all so pleasant that she began to think vaguely about her own comfort, and to wonder what the other girls and women who had shared her journey homewards in the crowded bus were doing; some of them, she knew, went back to shabby Council houses on the outskirts of St Alberics and cooked supper for a family; others hurried home to look after a delicate sister or invalid mother or a brood of little children in some picturesque but inconvenient cottage in Cowater or Blentley; others again lived in one room in the back streets of the town, or were one of a family crowded into some small house, patched up after being damaged by blast, in the High Street or out towards the London road. A few of them, but only a very few, went home to houses where there was domestic help, talk about books and music, and some sense of social and financial security in spite of the war, and she was fairly sure that she was the only one who went home to lie on a couch in 75s. brocade sandals and sip 1890 brandy. So she was very lucky, and she told herself that she ought to realize it.

She slowly opened her eyes, and let them wander round the cream, dark brown and fawn drawing-room, which had been decorated by Heals', when their arrangements were the height of fashion, at her mother's wish. It's like a room in an hotel, she thought, and I'm bored here, in spite of being so comfortable and so lucky. There were only herself and her father at home now, for her youngest brother was at a boarding-school, her sister had joined the W.R.N.S., and her elder brother was a prisoner in Italy. Her mother was with her new husband somewhere and Alicia had not heard from her since last Christmas when a card had come saying, 'All my thoughts, sweetie. Mums.' The establishment was too comfortable, however, for Alicia seriously to consider setting up a less luxurious one of her own, in spite of her boredom when she was at home. Mr Arkwright ranked technically as a widower in the eyes of domestics, and as his daughter never interfered with the management of the household, perfect service was secured at a very high cost that troubled nobody, and everybody concerned was satisfied.

Yes, it's comfortable, Alicia thought as she sipped her brandy, but I *can* do without comfort. I don't really mind getting tired at the works or smothered in oil or going without sleep on a night shift. If I could live the kind of life that would make me happy, I could, honestly, do without comfort—only I don't know what kind of life that would be. It will be amusing seeing him again.

11

After lunch on the following Saturday afternoon, Vartouhi wheeled her bicycle out onto the road, and stood looking about her with a pleased smile.

It was just half-past two. The sunlight, silvery rather than golden for there was as yet no mist in the air, glistened along the twigs and branches of the willows, the elms, the beeches that were now all bare of their leaves, and showing their dark delicate shapes against the pale green hills of winter grass and the long rolling pale brown fields. The cold air smelled chiefly of freshness, but every now and again a breath of distant smoke, or damp leaves, or scent from hawthorn and yew and bryony berries would drift along on the general coldness and make Vartouhi, whose sense of smell was keener than that of a fully civilized person, sniff with pleasure. To her, the ivy growing over a wall that she slowly cycled past had a faint bitter perfume, and the bank of moss at the edge of the wood smelt of damp, while there was a keen woody scent, not so strong as that of freshly cut logs, from the bark of the trees. A blending of the damp smell and the bitter smell came from a long rampart of rhododendrons growing above the wall of some private estate, and when she dismounted at a bridge and leant over it to watch the winter stream swirling silently past with its long bright green weeds weaving and flowing, she breathed the marshy odour of mud and water plants. The silver sunlight glittered on the little stream, the red and yellow branches of naked willows hung down into it and were swept sideways, with sunlight silvering them too, and the water made a low sweeping rippling sound, hardly audible in the stillness.

She cycled slowly on, the faint pleased smile always on her

face. There was no need for her to hurry, for Miss Fielding had taken Richard out for his first drive in the car, and had announced that they would not be home until dark. She looked at the birds flying above the ploughed fields or walking in the grass, the distant hills with their little black trees, the near wood where a few solitary yellow leaves lingered on the oaks, and all the time she was climbing up into the low hills. The lane passed between ploughed fields and was lonely; in half an hour she passed only two cottages. The slope continued gently upwards and at length brought her out into a village where old cottages made one long straggling street ending in a church with rich dark yews. The sun was now sinking towards the west and the mists were beginning to rise, and the stones of the church tower looked golden in the thickening light. She rode on past a few children coming out of the village school, and left the village with its pale houses and dark trees behind her. The air began to grow intensely cold.

This part of the country had become very lonely since the war. The villages were still crowded with evacuees from the London raids, but much of the countryside had been taken over by the Army, and at one stroke silence and peace had been reimposed upon lanes and fields that had not known them for forty years. There were roads that climbed between fields, dancing in summer with the blue and purple vetch, that were abruptly barred to the walker by notices: 'No entry. W.D.'; and the village, the fabled view or the brass tablet had to be reached by some old, faint track that no one but poachers and badgers had used for years. Here, if Vartouhi had known it, the hedges and fields were like those of an older England. The spirit of a place is changed if many people go to it; it can no longer be itself. Since the solitude enforced by the war had come over these tracts of land, they had been able to be themselves once more. Their flowers had budded, blossomed and faded unpicked, their blackberries had slowly ripened and then rotted richly on the bushes, weeds grew with furious speed and strength over the footpaths and against the hedges and stiles. Only the aeroplanes passed over these woods and fields, and left no trace of their ominous shadows. Loneliness could do what it would with such places, and fortunate were the few people who saw what it made of them.

At last Vartouhi dismounted at the top of a hill.

Open country rolled away before her, with its low grey hills and meadows wreathed in mist, and the red sun sinking coldly below shreds of gold and scarlet cloud. Not a light shone from the little houses on the far hillsides; it was nearly time to pull the curtains against the enemy and the coming night; the island was preparing for its sixteen hours of darkness. So far away that it made no sound, an aeroplane was moving across the sky. Vartouhi looked long about her; observed the aeroplane and gazed at the fiery fragments of vapour above the sinking sun until she was dazzled, and breathed with delight the icy air of evening. Her eyes were used to great distances, to following the slow sail of the eagle across sunny miles of light ending in broad summits of snow, and her ears had been accustomed from childhood to a very few musical sounds; the crowing of a cock and the splashing of water, the prolonged call to prayer, the chatter of familiar voices in a quiet place and the rustling of the wind through the fruit trees. Here, on this little hill above an alien landscape, where trees and soil and sounds were so different from the ones where she had been born, she nevertheless felt for the moment no longer a stranger. The openness, the solitude and the peace were the same.

Suddenly a pleasant young voice addressed her, and she quickly turned and confronted a cheerful hatless parson, one of the new kind, who was slowly cycling past.

'I am sorry—I do not hear,' said Vartouhi.

'*I'm* sorry to butt in—I only said that if you *are* going on down the road to Treme, don't be alarmed at the two tough-looking gents, working in the fields; they're only Italian prisoners.'

'So?' said Vartouhi, with her polite little smile.

'Quite harmless. Good scouts, really,' said the young parson, much taken with that smile, and smiling himself as he cycled slowly away down the lane. 'Just thought I'd tell you. Good night.'

'You are varry kind and good. Thank you.' She stood on tiptoe to call after him.

Then she turned to mount her bicycle, with a very changed expression. Her lips were pressed together and she frowned. 'But I,' she muttered, as she began to cycle away down the road which he had indicated, 'I am not kind—nor good, too also,' and she increased her pace.

The lane led back to the main road from which she had come. She rode through a small wood, where there was a thin violet mist among the darkest trees and a red light hovering in the open glades, and came out between grassy fields. Then she saw two men who were working in a ditch on the left, wearing a peculiar striped dress. As she approached they both glanced up.

They were small men with dark complexions and long drooping noses, and so alike that she thought they might be brothers. They stared at her unsmilingly but not sulkily; they looked tired and indifferent.

Vartouhi stopped, and dismounted. Leaning on the bicycle at a distance of about twenty feet from them, she called clearly in Bairamian:

'Italian dogs!'

The men stared, ceasing to move their small dark hands among the bleached grass and thorn stems. Then one of them called something back to her that sounded polite and inquiring.

'I am not here to talk to you, dog and murderer, breaker of oaths!' she shouted. 'I come to mock at you in your misery, you slaves and prisoners of the English!'

They stared at each other, shaking their heads. Then one climbed out of the ditch and began to come towards her, with a doubtful smile. The other leant on his spade, staring.

The first man spoke again in the same polite tone. He had nearly come up to the bicycle when Vartouhi stamped on the ground, and spat.

'Do not dare to approach nearer to me, dog. Go back to your ditch in the ground. May it be your grave!'

The Italians were already numb with cold and confused by the misty winter twilight that was so different from the clear dusk of their own land, and this furious little woman in a red cap and unbecoming trousers who shrieked at them in yet another unknown tongue completed their bewilderment and unhappiness. The dreary cold! and her angry, bitter voice! Their soft romantic natures, that could so easily turn to boastfulness and thence to bullying, seemed to curdle inside them with a misery they felt to be undeserved, and the one who had come out of the ditch stopped short, staring at her in horror.

'Yes, I spit at you! I spit for my father, whose farm you have doubtless taken away, for my mother whose old age you have ruined, for my sisters whose youth you have ravished, especially for my niece Medora who because of you is banished to Turkey and my sister Yania who is banished to New York in the United States of America. I spit at you for all my country of Bairamia——'

The man in the ditch, unable to endure the hatred in her voice, uttered a loud jeering laugh as he heard the one word he could recognize and said something to his companion, who, after a moment, began to laugh too. Vartouhi was now beside herself with rage, and none of the three noticed a man making his way quickly towards them across the freezing meadow. As he reached the ditch and called angrily 'What's going on here?' a car came round the corner behind Vartouhi and was pulled up sharply by its driver. The next instant he exclaimed, 'Vartouhi! What on earth are you doing?' It was Kenneth Fielding, and behind him were the surprised faces of his sister, Betty and Richard.

12

As Vartouhi took no notice but went on shouting, Kenneth got out of the car and went up to her and shook her gently by the arm.

'Vartouhi! steady on! What on earth's the matter?'

She gasped, stopped short in the middle of an abusive sentence, and turned and stared up at him as if she did not know him.

'What's the matter? Did these fellows—er—annoy you?' jerking his head at the Italians.

'No.' She shook her head and seemed to come to herself. 'I annoy them. I stop on my bike and tell them how I hate them, dogs and pigs and sons of she-dogs!'

'I say—I say! Steady on, you know!' said Kenneth, but his voice was gentle and an admiring smile was beginning in his eyes. 'Can't have a little girl like you going for two men, you know— hit one your own size is the rule in England!'

'Kenneth,' called Miss Fielding authoritatively, 'what is the matter?' And she began to descend from the car, at the same time calling to the Italians, '*Cosa è seccesso? Parlare lentamente.*' (What's the matter? Talk slowly.)

The two burst forth together, not talking at all slowly, and Miss Fielding's small knowledge of Italian was completely swamped. She was on the point of repeating her question, this time to Vartouhi, when the man who had been hurrying over the meadow jumped across the ditch onto the road, and said roughly:

'You're not supposed to talk to these men, madam. They're prisoners of war employed on Hallett's Farm and I'm in charge of them. The young lady started it; I saw the whole thing.' He turned to the two men, who were still explaining, and said slowly

102

with gestures, 'All right; go back to work. Non far nienty,' then went over to them and said something in a lower tone, and Miss Fielding caught the words *donna* and *la follia*. The men laughed again and returned to the ditch but did not take up their work; they rested on their spades and watched the group in the road, on which the last light of the sunset lingered.

'This young lady is a refugee, and does not yet understand our ways,' explained Miss Fielding winningly. She shook her head at Vartouhi, who was looking from one embarrassed face to the other with her usual polite smile, now touched with defiance. Richard and Betty, who were taking no part in the affair, both thought that the scene looked like one on the stage, with a backcloth of dark trees against blue mist.

'She is in my employ,' continued Miss Fielding, 'and I can promise you that this will not happen again. She is a Bairamian— and as you know, the—the relations between Italy and Bairamia are temporarily most unhappy.'

'Took it in 1938, didn't they?' said the labourer, nodding.

'Er—yes, if you like to put it that way. And I suppose our little friend here,' Miss Fielding put her arm kindly about Vartouhi's rigid shoulders, 'was carried away by the—er—the sadness of it all and unfortunately said more than she meant.'

'I mean it all,' put in Vartouhi, smiling more politely than ever, while Kenneth shook his head at her with a delighted frown.

'Well, I don't know anything about that. All I know is she went for Tony and Jessuppy here, and the public isn't supposed to talk to the prisoners. It's lucky for her these two are good-tempered, she might have had a nasty time. It's time for them to knock off now, anyway.' He turned to the two Italians, whose jeering expression had quite vanished and who were gazing yearningly at the hand-some car and the generally prosperous appearance of the English group. 'Come on, Tony, Jessuppy. Good night, madam; good night, sir,' and with a touch of his forehead that included the silent two in the car, he tramped away across the misty fields. The Italians shouldered their spades and followed him, but first one of them turned and made a sweeping bow to Vartouhi in which was all the mockery of Punchinello. In return, Vartouhi silently made the gesture of one who spits, but Miss Fielding was conferring with Kenneth and fortunately did not see.

Richard was breathing the frosty, smoky scents of the evening, and watching the delicate red light shining on Vartouhi's face. His senses were charmed but his conscience, the judging power, was uneasy and disturbed. How enchanting she seemed, among the brown branches and the grass already white with frost and the blue and grey mists—but *was* she enchanting, herself, her spirit? He simply did not know. He loved her with pain and enchantment, but he had never been able to love anyone so deeply that his reason went to sleep, and it was not asleep now. He had just heard her screaming with fury, and had seen her spit to express her hatred; and then she had become silent, and once more she was lovely to him, and mysterious as a leaf or a stream. Yet she *had* screamed; she *had* made that ugly gesture; and he knew that he would not be able to forget it.

His extremely sensitive face was not so fully under his control as he supposed it to be, and although his mother was far too wise a woman to make the boast that she could 'read him like a book,' she could read his face with far more intelligence and interest than she bestowed on most books, and she read it now.

Let's hope that will cure him of fancying her, she thought. She's a charming little thing, but there's something about her that gives me the shivers. I should think she could be very unkind. It was Betty's strongest term of disapprobation.

'Well, Vartouhi, I'm afraid you'll have to ride home after us,' said Miss Fielding heartily, turning away from her colloquy with Kenneth, 'we can't fix the bicycle on the car, Mr Fielding says. But we'll go quite slowly, we're only about eight miles from home and we shall be back before it's quite dark.' She gave her a pleasant smile and returned to the car, which Kenneth was already starting up, and Vartouhi slowly mounted the bicycle and set off down the road through the deepening dusk.

'Deplorable,' began Miss Fielding, leaning back comfortably and addressing herself to Betty. 'She must be a very young soul——'

'A very plucky soul,' put in Kenneth unexpectedly, who was frowning over his negotiation of the downward road, obscure in the twilight. 'It isn't every girl who would have gone for a couple of great louts like that. All alone, too.'

'They were unusually small even for Italians, didn't you think?' put in Richard mildly. 'They are a small race, of course, chiefly because of their farinaceous diet.'

'Ugly-looking pair of toughs, I thought,' retorted Kenneth. 'Damned plucky of her to speak up like that. Shows patriotism. I know patriotism isn't the thing with your friends, of course.'

'No; it is "not enough,"' murmured Richard.

'But I like to see it myself,' concluded Kenneth, sweeping the car out into the main road.

'It is the root of all evil,' put in Miss Fielding solemnly.

This stopped the conversation, as Miss Fielding's remarks had a way of doing, and in this case it was just as well. Betty felt relieved as the car passed Vartouhi, slowly cycling at the side of the road, and nothing more was said. The absence of emphasis in Richard's tone had been insolent, and Kenneth's voice had been heated, and she had feared that a disagreeable argument might ensue. She disliked arguments, and could never see why human speech should not be confined to the expression of innocent requests, the recital of amusing incidents, and endearments.

Unfortunately, Miss Fielding reopened the subject.

'I was not at all surprised to see Vartouhi attacking those men,' she announced. 'Bairamians are a revengeful race with a long history of bloodshed and warfare behind them.'

'Who hasn't?' said Richard absently, staring at the misty fields gliding past.

'And all that politeness of hers is only the custom of her country,' Miss Fielding went on firmly, 'it means nothing. I should never be surprised to find out that she hates us all.'

'They must be a delightful people to live among, if their manners are all as pleasant as hers.' Richard was displeased by the turn the conversation had taken and resolved to end it. 'I think it was Dr Johnson—or was it Bacon?—who said that *cheerfulness is the least regarded and the most necessary of the virtues of daily life.* When we consider how much worse the world would be if no one were ever cheerful, and how much pleasanter it would be if everybody were cheerful, we see how true that observation is. Cheerfulness is taken for granted where chastity' (Miss Fielding and his mother both stiffened slightly) 'is constantly suspect, as if it were more important. Cheerfulness—though you accuse Vartouhi's of being assumed—cannot be suspect because it cannot, according to Bacon—or it may be Dr Johnson—be successfully counterfeited. A man is either cheerful or he is not——'

'I'm not,' said Kenneth. 'It's damned cold and I want a drink.'

But the subject of Vartouhi's behaviour and character was not returned to, for Richard's homily and the increasing chill and discomfort of the party quelled any desire to talk. All were glad to enter the house in search of warmth and tea; and when they entered the drawing-room (Richard most reluctantly supported by Kenneth) they were so dismayed to find Miss Burton dreamily playing *My Love had a Silver Ring* with the fire almost out and no signs of tea that they were momentarily incapable of speech.

'Frances! No tea?' cried Miss Fielding, advancing upon her cousin, 'and what a fire? We are all frozen!'

'Yes, it *is* cold.' Miss Burton slowly turned her head and smiled upon her, while continuing to play. 'I had to put on this little jacket. Did you have a nice drive? I haven't blacked out upstairs; perhaps Ken had better do it at once; they're so fussy in the winter.'

Richard was lowered onto a sofa by Kenneth and sat there shivering while his host sped away in search of alcohol. Can't let the fellow get a chill even if he is a squirt; he's bound to have been pulled down by this foot, thought Kenneth.

'Well really, Frances, I do think you might have had tea ready for us!' exclaimed Miss Fielding; in many ways life with her was the simpler because she always spoke out her indignations. 'Here we come in frozen and starving and the fire nearly out and you strumming away as if nothing mattered!'

'Isn't Vartouhi back yet?' inquired Miss Burton.

'Of course not; we passed her on the road and she won't be home for hours. And what do you think——' Miss Fielding was about to embark upon a recital of the afternoon's adventure, when there were sounds in the hall, the front door opened and they heard Vartouhi saying prettily, 'You are so good and kind to ride me all this way home——' and then a deep Canadian voice said earnestly, 'You're welcome,' and 'good nights' were exchanged, and the door slammed. While Betty and Richard were still exchanging interrogative glances, and Miss Burton had turned away from the piano and was gazing at the door, it opened, and Kenneth came in grinning and carrying sherry, followed by Vartouhi.

'I get tea raddy?' she asked placidly.

'Yes, please, Vartouhi. How did you——' began Miss Fielding.

'Picked up a Canadian in a lorry, by George, and he drove her home!' burst out Kenneth, roaring with laughter.

'My wheel break and I am not knowing how to mend it,' explained Vartouhi.

'How very kind of him; how much goodness there is in human nature!' said Miss Fielding, frowning at Kenneth. 'You might not have been home for hours, Vartouhi.'

'She mightn't have anyway, and it's strictly against regulations,' murmured Kenneth, giving sherry to Richard, who was chilled, and in pain with his ankle, and angry because it was not he who had driven her home, listening to her voice and catching glimpses of her long eyes and her smile in the winter dusk. He thanked Kenneth in a cold tone, for he did not find his remark amusing.

Betty was amused and also rather pleased. There was no harm in the incident, of course, but it was not the kind of conduct Richard's usual young women indulged in: they might be free with their favours in their own social circle (Betty suspected that some of them were), but they did not allow themselves to be picked up on twilit roads by soldiers, and she thought that Richard's disillusionment with Vartouhi would now be complete.

Richard sipped his drink and watched Kenneth carrying in logs for the fire (to which Miss Fielding at once extended her stout legs), and then pensively turned his gaze on Vartouhi as she wheeled in the trolley laden with the tea equipage. He was jealous of the friendliness and gaiety that had been wasted on that Canadian soldier. The soldier had called out, 'Hallo, gorgeous!' or 'H'ya, baby!' (Richard's training as a Mass Observer had given him a familiarity with the current proletarian vocabulary and he knew precisely the phrases that Mass-men were likely to use in Mass-situations), and then he had slowed down the lorry, and Vartouhi had said something unguessable—her use of English could never be predicted—and been so friendly and childishly confiding that the Canadian's better heart had been completely won, and Richard, realist as he was, felt sure that every word and gesture passing between the two might have been repeated without offence to Miss Fielding in the drawing-room. How unrestrained in some respects, how complicated and calculating in others, now seemed the young women whose company he used to frequent! She is like the Noble Savage of the eighteenth-century writers, he thought, watching her and forgetting to pass other people their tea until briskly reminded by Miss Fielding; and he imagined her in Turkish trousers and brilliant zouave and cap, working among the fruit trees in spring below the bald savage mountains of her own land, where life was simple and satisfying and nobody talked too much.

13

On the following Tuesday Alicia set out to walk the quarter-mile through the bright moonlight to the Fieldings' house to attend the first rehearsal of *Little Frimdl*. She was tired after her day's work, as usual, but the cold air and the beauty of the night revived her. The moon's radiance slightly dimmed the brightness of the stars and the frost glittered on the grass and the sky was lofty and purple above the grey fields. Her footsteps rang on the road with a challenge; she felt that she could have walked for miles with that motionless icy air going past her face.

Miss Burton opened the door.

'Do come in; isn't it cold. I wonder if we shall get them to-night?' she murmured, peeping up at the remote sky before she shut the door. 'Everybody is out. So tiresome—the first rehearsal.'

'Who? Oh—the Luftwaffe.' Alicia threw her fur coat on a chair and followed her into the drawing-room. 'Too busy round Moscow, I should think. How do you do,' to Richard, who looked up from his book with a smile. Miss Fielding was sitting by the fire with the typed parts of *Little Frimdl* strewn about her, and glanced up over her glasses.

'Oh, there you are, Alicia. Come in, do. Isn't it a nuisance, everybody is out. Kenneth has had to go to something at the Home Guard, *or so he says*, and Mrs Marten is working late at the Ministry this week and Vartouhi has gone to the *cinema*. Slipped away on the bicycle, if you please, before I could prevent her; so annoying. It *is* her free evening, I know, but I do think she might have stayed in for the first reading; it isn't even a silly symphony; it's that man Gable—obviously a very young soul and I should say a low physical type, though of course allowances must be made for the distorting effect of the camera.'

She returned to her sorting of the parts, muttering, and Alicia, who always planned her campaigns as carefully as any German general, coolly sat down by Richard, leant back, folded her arms and smiled at him. Her long hands were faintly stained and scarred; all the preparations of Elizabeth Arden could not completely remove these signs of her daily toil.

'Is your ankle nearly well?' she inquired.

'It's better, thank you, but it still gives me considerable pain and I shan't be able to walk in comfort, so I am told, for at least another six weeks,' he answered, making no attempt to disguise the extent of his injury and his impatience with it.

Alicia studied her cigarette before replying. He's the sort of charming ass who falls down in the road and I'm the sort of ass who can't drive a crane without driving everything else like one. I shan't say anything about it, she decided.

'What a bore; I'm so sorry,' she said. 'What's happened to the repertory company you were with? Acting isn't really your job, is it?'

'I suppose they are managing as best they can. No. I'm an economist. I took a degree at the London School of Economics in 1938 and I was just going to get my first job when the war broke out. I knew these people, the Dove Players, very well and they wanted someone to produce and stage-manage so I went out with them.'

Alicia knew from his mother that he had first been refused for all three Services, and warned that he would be more trouble than use in Civil Defence.

'Did you like it?'

'Moderately well, so long as I didn't have to act. I generally find the technicalities of any art more interesting than its intangibilities.'

'I knew a girl at the School of Economics, Marion Fabian,'

Alicia said after a pause. 'Did you ever come across her? I should think she would have been there in your time.'

'I knew her very well,' he answered, indifferently, but not meeting her eyes, and as Miss Fabian was not a girl of whom young men usually spoke with indifference, Alicia immediately thought *Ho-ho! I hope you enjoyed her nasty temper, that's all.*

'There!' exclaimed Miss Fielding, suddenly appearing in front of them and slamming down two parts on the sofa. 'Alicia, you haven't got much to do as Italy. Richard, you've *got* to do the Very Old Man, I've decided.'

'I shall have to sit down, Miss Fielding. I shan't be well enough by Christmas to stand.'

'Oh, that will be all right, you can have a big chair and your Big Book on a table in front of you; it will be great fun!'

'Will it?' smiled Richard. 'Very well. I will do the Very Old Man.'

You disagreeable so-and-so, thought Alicia. But I like you, all the same, and you must have got what it takes or you wouldn't have known choosey little Marion 'very well'! I particularly like the back of your neck.

'S'sh!' said Miss Burton, suddenly holding up one hand. 'Listen.'

'It's a car going up the hill,' said Miss Fielding.

But it was the familiar unpleasant sound.

'I had a *feeling* they'd come tonight,' said Miss Burton, discontentedly, huddling herself and her knitting together. 'As soon as I saw that moon getting up.'

'What shall we do?' demanded Miss Fielding of Richard and Alicia, rising from her chair.

'Stay here, of course. May as well be blown up in comfort,' said Alicia, who had worked in the factory throughout the Battle of Britain without taking shelter. 'It probably won't be much.'

'Richard?' asked Miss Fielding, standing with Miss Burton, who was trembling, by the door.

'I can't walk,' he said irritably, 'so of course I'll stay here.'

'I will settle Frances in the shelter,' announced Miss Fielding, going out of the door as the guns which defended the aerodrome three miles away went off deafeningly loudly in the country silence.

The ladies disappeared. Alicia so far forgot her role of a *femme fatale* as to glance across at Richard with a grin, but when she saw his expression, the grin vanished. Gosh, he's scared, she thought disgustedly. Even the back of his neck doesn't make up for that. As she stared at him, he glanced up and said still irritably, 'It's all right, I'm not frightened. I just happen to be gun-shy. I detest the hideous noise incidental to air attack.'

'Oh, well, let's put on the wireless, shall we?' She could see by his eyes that he was telling the truth. She switched on the wireless but after a few moments during which a loud voice talked about bombs, the station went off the air. 'Oh well, that's that,' murmured Alicia. 'Have they got the Warsaw Concerto? I'll bet they haven't,' and she wandered over to the gramophone.

'Yes, they have. Kenneth admires it greatly,' said Richard stiffly. 'Do you really wish to hear it?'

'I adore it,' she said, and found it and put it on.

Richard was silent. The gunfire was heavy now and they could hear aeroplanes going over. Slowly the romantic strains of the Warsaw Concerto filled the room. Alicia sat staring into the fire and Richard endured the noise of the guns and sweated.

'Mind if we have it again?' she asked, after the final quick drum-beats had sounded.

'If you really desire it.'

'I do really desire it,' said Alicia, attending to the gramophone and not looking at him and feeling sorry for him. This dislike of heavy noise was the first weakness she had detected in him, and it was endearing, as a weakness often is.

'Do you hate it all that much?' she inquired, after the drum beats had sounded again.

'I've been gun-shy from birth.'

'The Concerto, I meant.'

'I don't consider that I know the meaning, personally, of the word "hate." I dislike the Warsaw Concerto because it is an inadequate and falsely romantic piece of programme music professing to express the suffering of the Polish nation. As a piece of restaurant music—or so I am told by people who understand music—it is not without merit.'

'*I went out last night with a lovely Pole,*' murmured Alicia.

'What?'

She repeated the sentence, adding, 'It's all the girls ever talk about at my factory.'

To her pleasure, Richard gave a reluctant laugh. The gunfire was getting less frequent.

'Who's your favourite composer?' she asked presently.

'Mozart. And I admire William Walton among the moderns.'

'I think Duke Ellington's wizard, don't you?'

'No.'

'I adore swing.'

Richard shook his head. 'I can see its merits but it gives me no pleasure.'

'What does?' asked Alicia, getting up and coming over to the sofa.

'What gives me pleasure?' repeated Richard, looking up at the tall blue-eyed girl in the black siren suit. 'Reading. Music. Astronomy.'

'Is that all?'

'And making love,' ended Richard, with a sudden smile. She smiled too.

'What do you like?' he asked.

'Oh—dancing and swing, and messy jobs and really divine shoes and drink and the other thing. What you said.'

He laughed again.

'You seem fairly pleased with life,' she said suddenly.

113

'If you mean that I seem happy, yes, I am.'

'That makes a nice change,' she said dryly.

'Because most people aren't? I agree; but then, you see, my circumstances have been unusually fortunate.'

'Have they? From something Miss Fielding once said I thought you must have had a ropey time.'

'I agree that the situation does not sound propitious,' began Richard judicially, offering her his cigarette-case. 'My father was killed in the First World War, and I am not strong; I have inherited what is called in our family the Barfield Lung. My mother has only my father's pension and her own earnings to live on, and I am an only child; her sexual life ended with my father's death, and in these circumstances you would expect her emotions to have centred morbidly upon myself.'

'No I shouldn't,' interrupted Alicia. 'That sort of thing only happens in highbrow books.'

'Indeed it doesn't; it is quite a common situation, I assure you. But in my case there were other factors which more than counterbalanced the unfortunate ones. To begin with, my parents were passionately in love with one another, and they both wanted me. That was an admirable start. And my mother had always maintained friendly and affectionate relations with her own family, which is large and clever. After my father's death she went to live with me at her old home in Devonshire, where the conditions for bringing up a delicate only child were perfect; a beautiful house built in 1680 surrounded by large gardens and paddocks and woods, streams to play in and ponies to fall off, and seven cousins of both sexes aged from eighteen months to ten years who constantly came to the house on long visits; some of them, indeed, lived there and provided me with all the companionship I needed. The only unmarried aunt's sexual instincts had been sublimated with unusual success into gardening, so there was no unfortunate influence there, and finally there were my two clever uncles, both of whom were happily married, whose influence was strongly masculine and offset any tendency there might have been for my upbringing to become too influenced by my women relations. My grandparents were cheerful and healthy old people and I have most affectionate memories of them both. What amuses you?'

'You've got it all so beautifully taped, like a card index or something,' said Alicia, composing her face.

'You illustrate Bergson's theory that we laugh when we see a living thing behaving like a mechanical one,' he retorted. 'My uncles soon found that I was clever, and it was they who began, and afterwards supervised, my education. One of the valuable things I learned from them as a boy was the difference between shallow brilliance, mere intelligence, and that solid cleverness which achieves, and which varies little in quality from century to century. The example of my uncles led me to rule my life chiefly by reason, but the example of my mother led me to include tenderness as well.' He paused, thinking, while she watched him curiously.

'I was unusually fortunate,' he went on at last, 'the atmosphere of my childhood home was aristocratic rather than *bourgeois*.'

'It sounds swell,' she murmured, and indeed the picture he had painted attracted her very strongly. Her own childhood had been marred by the quarrelling of her parents, and she had always vaguely wanted a different kind of home.

'What are you going to do after the war?' she went on.

'Teach economics in South America, I hope.'

'Not in Russia?' she asked, smiling. The few intellectuals she had met had all had a thing about Russia and, so far as she classified Richard at all, she put him among the intellectuals.

'Not in Russia,' he answered, unsmiling. 'And I shall marry and have four children, and live a life without the inessentials but with all the essentials.'

'Such as?'

'Bare beautiful rooms, a piece of ground to grow things on, music, hundreds of books—all the things I like.'

Alicia thought this over. Evidently love and a good time and interesting people and a car and a nice home and a steady income were not regarded by this odd young man as essentials.

'Where will you get the money from?' she asked.

'Earn it.'

'You'll have to earn a whale of a lot if you want to educate four children decently.'

'I shan't want to educate them "decently"; I shall only want to educate them. Most people who are "decently" educated are not educated at all.'

'If you have boys it isn't fair to make them into cranks,' said Alicia.

'I shan't do that. I dislike cranks as much as I'm sure you do. I was at Radley, and enjoyed every minute I spent there. The fact that I didn't emerge as a typical public-school specimen is due to the influence of my home. I shall send my sons and daughters to conventional schools and trust to the strong influences of home to keep them from turning into types.'

'They won't do that!' she assured him, and then went on, 'It's odd to meet someone who's got everything taped; most of the men I know are just keen on their job or want a good time or shoot a line about every girl they meet falling for them, but you seem to have worked out a—a—sort of blue-print for your whole future!'

'That's an admirable simile,' he said with his charming smile. 'If more educated people made blue-prints for their lives the world would be much tidier.'

She appeared to be considering this, but was actually thinking how silly and cheap now seemed the plans for his subjugation with which she had entered the drawing-room. It was not a pleasing reflection, and she gave expression to a little of her annoyance by exclaiming:

'I suppose feelings don't come into your blue-print?'

'You mean love, I suppose. Naturally it does.'

'You sound very calm about it.'

'That is deceptive,' he answered coolly, but for the second time not meeting her eyes, 'Actually, I am rather susceptible to certain combinations of line and colour, and I have to exert my reason to prevent their gaining more power over me than I like.'

'You mean you fall for people easily?'

There was a pause before he answered. There had been no gunfire now for some time.

'Sexually, yes; romantically, no; and I haven't yet met any woman whom I would consider making my wife,' he said at last.

No woman could have listened to such a remark without irritation, and Alicia was more annoyed than ever that he showed no signs of being attracted to herself: she would have enjoyed taking her revenge.

'What sort of a person will you want?' she murmured, so lullingly that even the Mass Observer observed nothing in her voice but polite interest.

'I should require a strong maternal instinct of the best type and a well-developed capacity for friendship.'

'And must she be awfully highbrow?'

'Not necessarily. She must be completely without bad temper, jealousy, over-emotionalism and spite, of course.'

'Of course,' said Alicia, who was naturally checking off the enumerated qualities in herself and had arrived at the depressing conclusion that she possessed none of them. She stood up, and looked round the room. 'How about some more gramophone?' Glancing down at him she found his grey eyes fixed upon the roll of dark hair that encircled her head.

'What's the matter—am I coming to pieces?'

'I was thinking that your head is a good shape,' he said indifferently. 'Will you see if you can find some Bach, please?'

14

Meanwhile, Miss Fielding and Miss Burton were sitting on camp stools in the air-raid shelter.

This situation will be familiar to many of our readers, and those of them to whom it is not familiar and who desire a vivid pen-picture of people sitting on camp stools in an air-raid shelter can go elsewhere for it. Those who are surprised that anyone holding Miss Fielding's opinions should have a shelter at all will hazard the guess, and rightly, that Kenneth had insisted upon getting one because Miss Burton was very afraid in the raids and felt slightly better when she was sitting in a thing prescribed by the Government for her protection. Kenneth could not endure the spectacle of an elderly lady, endeared to him by chivalry and family ties and habits, in a state of terror without wanting to strangle Germans by the score; he went out into the garden and swore foully in solitude after the first bombs had fallen near Sunglades, and as there were no Germans handy to strangle, he relieved his feelings by buying a shelter for Miss Burton and furnishing it with every luxury that a cheque book could provide and a shelter could contain.

Miss Fielding, of course, would have preferred to take no notice of the raids. She was without imagination and was not afraid of bombs. She thought of the Luftwaffe as Misguided, like the rest of the German nation, but felt no personal rancour towards it: she ignored it; she mentally brushed it aside like a tiresome fly and looked vaguely forward to the day when English and Germans alike would enjoy a hearty laugh together over the time when they were silly enough to bomb each other's towns. Pending this happy occasion, she always accompanied

Miss Burton into the shelter because it made Miss Burton less nervous to have her there and she was not without the milk of human kindness.

'There!' said Miss Fielding, banging herself down on the camp stool, 'I don't expect we shall be here for long. The stove will soon burn up. How foolish it all seems, doesn't it? So senseless.'

Miss Burton, whose lugubrious small face looked out of her fur coat like a mouse in a muff, made a vague and dismal sound.

'I wonder where Betty and Vartouhi are,' pursued Miss Fielding, handing her cousin a packet of Maltesers and taking two herself. 'I hope Vartouhi will have the sense to take cover.'

'And Ken—poor Ken—*out* in it!' put in Miss Burton, who felt so much better when large, kind Kenneth was there to pat her on the shoulder and make little jokes.

'Oh, he enjoys it,' said Kenneth's sister at once. 'I never waste any sympathy on *Ken* in a raid. When he was three he loved bangs, the bigger the better, and he's just the same now.' She glanced discontentedly round the shelter and started whistling through her teeth, which she always did during raids. In a moment, Miss Burton knew from experience, she would begin to accuse people of things. Miss Burton had never fathomed why air-raids affected Miss Fielding in this way; she only knew that they did. Perhaps it was the confined atmosphere of the shelter, which made her feel like a conspirator fulminating against his Government in a cellar or perhaps she thus worked off her irritation at having her normal activities interrupted. Whatever it was, she began at once by announcing that Vartouhi smoked too much; it was very bad for her; she smoked seven or eight of those strong cigarettes a day and she, Miss Fielding, was going to speak to her about it for her own good. Vartouhi disposed of, Miss Fielding passed on to Betty and demanded if Miss Burton had not noticed that Betty's manner with Kenneth was increasingly flirtatious and silly? Miss Burton truthfully replied that she had not. (She had, in fact, observed a change in the manner of one member of the household towards another, but she was not going to mention the matter to Miss Fielding.)

'And besides,' she went on, more frankly than usual as she knitted very fast and badly and the guns banged, 'what does it matter if she is flirtatious? They're old friends and there's no harm in it.'

'I don't want Betty getting ideas into her head,' said Miss Fielding sharply. 'Kenneth is a very good match and Betty's getting on. If she wants to settle herself comfortably for her old age she hasn't much time left.'

Miss Burton, to whom the idea of marriage for any reason but love was actually horrible, knitted faster than ever and said that she was sure such an idea had never entered Betty's head.

'And besides,' she went on illogically, 'why shouldn't Kenneth marry if he wants to, Connie? Betty would make him a very good wife, I'm sure, and we know her, and *I* think it would be very—oh, my *goodness*, was that a bomb?'

'No, it's that new gun near Cowater. Kenneth is not the type to make a good husband, Frances. You know as well as I do how many times I've stopped him making a fool of himself in that way. He's so selfish and set in his habits, too. And besides . . . remember!'

'If you mean Uncle Eustace——'

Miss Fielding nodded meaningly and took three more Maltesers. 'Kenneth has inherited all that. I look on it as a sacred trust, left to me by Our Mother, to see that Kenneth never marries.'

He would if he really wanted to, thought Miss Burton, dropping stitches madly. It isn't *you* that's kept him from marrying, it's having been jilted by Betty when he was only a boy, and always being so henpecked by you and Joan and Aunt Eleanor, and being so comfortable here, and not being very attractive to girls, poor old Ken, they laugh at him. There are about six different reasons that have kept Ken from marrying, so far, but if he *really* wanted to, he would, and you couldn't stop him. Oh dear, this knitting is in more of a muddle than ever.

Miss Fielding had now passed on to Richard and was wondering how much longer he intended to stay at Sunglades; the thirty shillings a week that he paid her did not cover his food, let alone his lighting and heating and laundry and baths and besides she disliked him personally. He was rude and had no ideals. The guns continued to bang at intervals, and Miss Burton continued to drop stitches, and the evening wore on.

Kenneth was coming back from a Home Guard meeting through the raid, whistling *Roll out the Barrel* as he walked along the moonlit road with his martial shadow trailing behind him. Occasionally he heard the noise of engines high up in the cloudless sky as night-fighters went over after the raiders in the direction of St Alberics, and stopped to stare up into the purple air among the tiny remote stars, trying to make out the machines in the moonlight; then he walked on again. Just as he came to the old stone bridge that was half a mile from home he saw something moving between the black and silver hedges on the road ahead of him. It was a cyclist, pedalling slowly along and apparently admiring the view. He gave a closer look, then called out:

'Vartouhi! Is that you?'

She stopped the bicycle and jumped off and turned to meet him as he came up with her. She was smiling, and as she curtsied her hair glittered in the moonlight.

'Good night, Mr Fielding,' she said.

'What on earth are you doing out here? Why aren't you at home? Does Miss Fielding know you're out?' he demanded (a comic echo sounded in his mind but he would not let himself smile).

'Is my evening away, Mr Fielding. I say to Miss Burton that

I go to the pictures but I have no money so I go to the station to see if my hat is find.' She sounded quite undisturbed.

'You ought to have waited in a shelter. You might get hit by shrapnel or machine-gunned—cycling along as if to-morrow would do!'

'I am in Portsbourne when they come all night, every night in a week. I am in a house when a house near is hit with a bomb. Is only a small raid, Mr Fielding,' and she glanced up at the sky with a nose wrinkled in criticism.

'That's not the point. You oughtn't to be out in it at all. I'll take that thing. Come along now, and let's get home, they'll be worrying about you.'

He wheeled the bicycle for her and they went on together, through the still cold air. It was about nine o'clock. Presently Vartouhi stated:

'You have angry at me, Mr Fielding.'

'No, I'm not, but what would your father and mother say, a little girl like you out all alone in a raid?'

'They would be please because I am enjoy the raid. And I am not knowing there is to be a raid when I am go to find my hat, too also.'

'Well, no, of course not. But you oughtn't to be out alone at night *at all*,' he said firmly.

'Because of wicked soldiers.'

'Er—yes. Lots of rough customers about in the country since the war, you know.'

'I can bite and kick. And in my stocking I have my little knife too also.'

'Good Go—have you? By Jove, that's the spirit,' and he glanced admiringly at the small creature, with the little cap that looked so foreign perched on top of her braids. 'Not that you'd ever have to use it over here, of course. We've got the police to tackle that sort of thing in England.'

But she went on, in a pensive tone and gazing at the

ground—'In Portsbourne I am sticking it into a sailor's lag. I am telling Mrs Mason who keeps the café but she is taking nothing notice and laughing. So I tell the police at the corner but he is laughing too also. The next time that sailor comes and touches me here'—she spread her hand for an instant upon her breast—'I am sticking it into his lag.'

Kenneth glanced at her quickly, but this time he was silent, for the story had shocked his kind heart.

'He is not an English sailor,' she went on.

'I'm glad of that, anyway,' he muttered.

'I am glad too also, because in Bairamia we all are liking English sailors, my father and my mother and my sisters and me too also.'

'Did you? Good.'

'It is the nuns who halp my sister Yania to go to America,' she said, after a pause.

'Oh, you've got a sister in America, have you?'

'Yas. She is work in a flower shop with an American lady who halp her. She is vary pratty, my sister Yania.'

'Too also?' said Kenneth, turning to smile down at her.

She laughed delightedly.

'Thank you, thank you, Mr Fielding! You mean I am pratty!'

Kenneth nodded, relieved at the turn the conversation had taken. Flower shops and compliments seemed to him more suitable subjects for discussion with a girl of twenty than knives in sailors' legs.

'Are all your people safe?' he went on.

'Oh, yas. They are all live in our fruit farm until the English come and kill the Italians,' she said cheerfully. 'My nice Medora is in Turkey with many old nuns, and my father and mother and my other sisters stay in the Khar-el-Nadoon.'

'Oh—er—what's that? I'm afraid I'm very ignorant about your part of the world.'

'Is the Valley of Apricots, the Khar-el-Nadoon,' she answered.

It was the first time that he had ever heard the name. Soft as a breath of air scented with fruit blossom, it echoed strangely under the English winter sky, and yet he liked the sound, in the same way that he liked the old greenhouse in his kitchen garden and the peach trellis along the south wall.

'Khar-el-Nadoon,' he murmured to himself, trying to imitate the way she said the words; just then the Raiders Passed began to sound far away, and an exhausted voice called:

'Is that you, Kenneth?' and they both turned to see Betty coming slowly towards them down the road.

'Hallo, my dear—are you all right?' he called anxiously, going towards her. She was carrying the small suit-case in which she always brought home her work from the Ministry and looked very tired.

'Perfectly, thanks,' she said, giving him the case and taking his arm and beginning to laugh. 'Except that like a certain famous gentleman I missed the bus—only he didn't have to walk all the way home from St Alberics. I haven't *got* any feet *left*—and I'm *frozen*. Hallo, Vartouhi, my child, whatever are you doing here? For heaven's sake, Ken, you don't think we shall have to go a-Little-Frimdling to-night, do you? I don't believe I *could*.'

'We'll get you both indoors and then you must both have a hot drink,' he said, shepherding them across the frosty lawn and Betty suddenly realized how good he had always been at looking after women. Dick was wonderful at it too, she thought. It's part of his generation's charm. Now Richard is no use at all at taking off your shoes and mixing you a drink, though he'll let you *talk*, if you want to, until further orders. But then, his young women all seem able to take off their own shoes.

Vartouhi was reluctant to leave the exciting night, where the noise of battle still seemed to be thundering through the frosty silence. She lingered at the front door, and had to be shouted at, albeit kindly, by Kenneth. He had gone straight into the drawing-room with his arm round Betty, who pulled off her hat and dropped it on her son's face.

'——purely nervous reaction,' he said earnestly, removing it and finishing the sentence he was uttering to Alicia. 'Hallo, Betty, are you all right?'

'All the same, I still think it's better than a double whisky,' Alicia said, meaning the Raiders Passed. 'Hallo, Mrs Marten—*are* you all right?'

'No feet left. Missed the bus,' smiled Betty, and sank down on the hearthrug in front of the fire. 'But I'm quite all right, thanks.'

Without a glance at anyone Kenneth knelt beside her and pulled off her shoes and began to rub her feet in their beautiful but darned silk stockings.

'Oh that *is* nice, you *are* an angel,' purred the woman of 1914, while Alicia looked on with an impassive face, and at that moment Miss Fielding stalked into the room, carrying rugs and pulling Miss Burton in her wake.

'Oh, I am so glad you've all got back safely!' cried the latter. 'Constance,' piteously, 'do you think we could have some tea? I know you don't approve of it at night, but——'

'Vartouhi!' cried Kenneth, looking up from his task.

'Here!' cried a voice from the kitchen.

'Make some tea, will you? and get the whisky out, and then come and get warm. Here——' he got up from his kneeling position—'better now?' to Betty, who nodded with a grateful smile—'I'll come and help you,' and he strode off to the kitchen, whence laughter and the Bacchic clashing of cups could shortly be heard.

Miss Fielding slowly seated herself in her favourite chair and put out her feet to the fire. She was much disturbed and annoyed by what she had just seen. A man, mused Miss Fielding, did not rub a woman's feet unless he was very much attracted to her. And Betty's feet were small; too small, Miss Fielding had always considered, for her height, and they had looked even smaller than they were when nursed—yes, he had been *nursing* them—in Kenneth's big hand. It was the sort of contrast, reflected Miss Fielding as she absent-mindedly fumbled for a Malteser where no Maltesers were, that appealed to men, silly middle-aged men like Kenneth. Something would have to be done, thought Miss Fielding.

'Tea for the troops!' said Kenneth, wheeling in the dumbwaiter.

'What a really admirable idea,' said Richard, raising himself on his elbow, and then, as he saw Vartouhi, he realized that for two hours she had been out in an air raid and he had not once thought of her danger. But that is only to be expected, he thought, considering that I don't love her as a person at all, only as an enchanting face—'*to love is a bad fate like that in the fairy stories, against which nothing avails until the enchantment has ceased,*' as Proust says. All the same, I'm glad she's all right.

'Hallo,' he said, smiling at her, but to his dismay she put her tongue out at him with a malicious smile and carried a cup of tea right past his nose and bestowed it upon Miss Burton.

'Oh, how delicious—you kind girl,' said Miss Burton gratefully.

'It will keep you awake, Frances,' warned Miss Fielding.

'Anybody fire-watching to-night?' suddenly demanded Kenneth.

'I am,' said Betty. 'I should have been home just in time to go on duty if I hadn't missed the bus.'

'Father was asleep when I left, he'll carry on from midnight,' put in Alicia. 'He's crazy about it, Mrs Marten. He looks forward to it all the week.'

Betty laughed and said it was comforting to hear of somebody liking it.

'Great nonsense women having to do it at all,' said Kenneth, gulping hot tea. 'Plenty of able-bodied men in the neighbourhood. You need never bother about it when I'm at home, Betty.'

'That's very nice of you, Ken; I'll remember.'

126

Miss Fielding, having refused tea from principle rather than from disinclination, was jealous of everybody else sitting weakly sipping with oohs and ahs of satisfaction, and heard this exchange between Kenneth and Betty with deepening alarm. Fire-watching provided excuses for wandering about the house in the small hours wearing scanty clothing; fire-watching took place when everyone else was asleep, and morale and resistance were at their lowest ebb. What might not happen if Kenneth and Betty got together at four in the morning? To do her justice, Miss Fielding's mind did not usually run upon this track, for it was what is curiously known as 'healthy,' but she was ever on the watch for nonsense where Kenneth was concerned, and she could feel it in the air at this moment. He's going to make a fool of himself again, she thought.

'Did you enjoy the pictures. Vartouhi?' inquired Miss Burton; when Vartouhi had sat down next to her with a cup of tea.

'I am not going, Miss Burton. I have no money.'

'Oh, my dear, what a shame.' Miss Burton was slightly embarrassed.

'So I am go to find my hat, instead.'

'Oh, really—to the station? And had they found it?'

'That old man has stolen it,' pronounced Vartouhi.

Everybody laughed, but Miss Fielding said reprovingly, 'Now, Vartouhi, that is not kind or true.'

'He hide it in the porter's room. I am seeing it—I think,' said Vartouhi.

'Now, now!' Miss Fielding wagged a finger.

'What's the time?' Kenneth looked at the clock. 'Just on ten. Too late for any rehearsal to-night, Con.'

'Nonsense, Kenneth. Everybody must be wide awake after all that tea and ready for work.'

But everybody was so stimulated by the raid and their various adventures that there were stout cries of 'No!' and 'Have a heart!' and 'Pack it up!'—this last uttered in an experimental tone by

Richard. 'That's right,' said Alicia, nodding at him kindly, and was pleased to see him look conscious.

'Well, you *must* all come in for a reading to-morrow night, or we shall never have it ready by the 26th,' warned Miss Fielding.

'So what?' muttered Alicia, heard only by Richard. No one else said anything.

'I think I shall go to bed,' said Miss Burton, getting up. 'I'm tired.' She paused by Vartouhi's chair, and instantly Vartouhi's eyes were lifted in respectful inquiry above the rim of her cup. 'Vartouhi, if you will come up to my room to-morrow morning, I think I can find you a hat, if you would like one?'

'What colour will be, Miss Burton, please?'

'Well, there are several. A beige one and blue one and a white one.'

'Thank you, Miss Burton. I will come. That hat the porter steal is a rad.'

'Good!' said Kenneth. 'I like a girl in a red hat. More tea, anybody?'

Richard and Betty passed their cups, while Miss Fielding shut her eyes. What a foolish and undignified thing to say! Yes, Kenneth was certainly ripe for trouble. However, she dismissed the subject from her mind while forcing out of her victims a solemn promise to attend another rehearsal on the following evening. Miss Burton and Vartouhi then went upstairs to bed.

Alicia watched Vartouhi with a new interest, for she had surprised an unguarded expression on Richard's face when Vartouhi first came into the room. The discovery was rather the last straw, and she almost decided to throw in the towel; she did not fancy competing for Richard's favours with a refugee in a ropey little cap. After all, there were plenty of men in England just now, more men than there had been for years, and some of them were more or less hers and seemed to like it. Why should she bother about Richard Marten? But she liked him. She admitted the fact, and she wanted more of his interest and attention. I'll hang on for a bit and see what happens, she decided. It will be something to do in the long winter evenings, anyway. He can't have fallen seriously for that little number; she looks like an early Myrna Loy produced by Capra.

She was used to competing with tall, perfectly groomed, sophisticated young women like herself, and could not realize that a man could be attracted by a girl with none of the conventional attractions. To her, Vartouhi was a joke, and not a very good joke at that; and she did not see that Richard was attracted to Vartouhi by exactly the same quality that she, Alicia, found attractive in Richard himself: *differentness*. The thoughts and feelings that lit up Vartouhi's face were not those of an ordinary girl, any more than the thoughts and feelings that lit up Richard's face were those of an ordinary young man. But in both cases the result was very attractive to some people.

After Alicia had said good night and declined Kenneth's offer of an escort, and gone home, the others lingered on over a last cigarette. Miss Fielding, who did not smoke, did her best to spoil the peace of the evening's end by starting vigorously on Alicia; how hard and bitter she was, how old for her age, in spite of being a very young soul.

'I thought she seemed more cheerful this evening,' said Betty, as neither of the men would be drawn.

'What precisely is the matter with her?' demanded Richard. 'Obviously something is, but I supposed it was the usual unconscious guilt felt by a rich and useless young woman.'

'She does work in a factory all day, dear,' said his mother mildly.

'From choice—from choice,' he said impatiently. 'I don't regard that as a virtue, when freedom of choice exists. If she didn't like working there she could leave.'

'She *is* doing her bit,' said Betty.

'The contemporary version is "doing a grand job of work,"' said Richard. 'Well, what is the matter with her?'

'She was mixed up in a divorce case with someone who let her down,' said Betty.

'Oh. Quite an ordinary story.'

'Did you expect something more original?'

'Something less conventional, certainly. She isn't quite an ordinary person.'

'It was bad luck.'

'Or bad management,' said Richard, but nevertheless silently registered it as a point in Alicia's favour that she had not told him her sad story.

Young men, on hearing that a young woman has been betrayed, do not clench their fists and call the betrayer a villain. If they are good young men they make a note to avoid the young woman as a possible bore and if they are bad young men they make a note of her telephone number. While we are on this painful subject it may be added that a recitative on her sufferings from the young woman's own lips to a new young man is about as favourable to her hopes as if she had proffered him arsenic.

Kenneth had been staring into the fire and had not heard a word of all this. He now roused himself, and said abruptly:

'Con, did you know Vartouhi was a waitress in a low-class café in Portsbourne before she came to us?'

'No!' exclaimed Miss Fielding. 'Well! Frances suggested as much but I didn't agree with her. Did she tell you?'

'Not directly. I gathered it from something she said this evening.'

'Poor little thing,' said Betty. Richard said nothing.

'Yes, she must have hated it,' said Kenneth, turning eagerly to Betty. 'She had a pretty beastly time.'

'She could always have left,' said Miss Fielding. 'There is no need for anyone to put up with that sort of thing an instant longer than they want to. There are the Labour Exchanges and the Young Women's Christian Association and the Girls' Friendly Society and, since the war, countless refugee aid societies.'

'But of what use are those, dear lady, if they exist in one stratum and Vartouhi in another?' asked Richard in his silkiest voice. He was so much moved and so resented his pain that he lashed out like a wounded snake. 'The societies exist; Vartouhi exists; but at no point do their activities intersect.' His mother glanced at him, surprised.

'That's what I meant; she ought to have gone to one of them and they would have helped her, silly little thing. She isn't quite as bad as she was when she first came, but she's still very secretive and peculiar,' said Miss Fielding. 'I suppose she made quite a mouthful about it to *you*.'

'Oh, no, she didn't say much,' Kenneth answered, getting up. 'Well, I don't know about everybody else but I'm going to bed.' He was glad that he had not told them about the sailor and the knife. None of them understood, not even Betty, sympathetic as she was. And I'm damned if I give Con that to chew over, he thought.

'A good idea; the evening has been wasted so we may as well "call it a day," as they say,' said Miss Fielding, also getting up. 'Well, Vartouhi seems to be quite happy here, that's one good thing, and I will write to Charles Omopoulos to-morrow and ask him for the latest news from Bairamia and the Khar-el-Nadoon. That ought to cheer her up.'

Not necessarily, thought Richard, struggling up and supporting himself upon the stick which he now used. Maddening woman! She will write to Charles Omopoulos to-morrow; she always does what she says she will; and so strong is the blend of coarse kindness with detestability in her character that one is denied the comfort of whole-heartedly disliking her. I give her up; I renounce and abandon her; shade of Marcel Proust, she is yours.

Kenneth went round locking up the house, having told Betty to run off to bed and not fuss when she murmured something about her fire-watch. The cat Pony yawned and stretched enormously at him from its blanket in the hot tidy kitchen where the clock ticked loud and fast. He peered into the quiet glowing interior of the boiler and slammed its doors to. Everything was in order. Someone (Betty, no doubt) was running in bath water upstairs. Kenneth felt restless and gloomy. The sound of his sister's clear voice briskly uttering the name 'Khar-el-Nadoon' sounded on in his mind, drowning the echo of another voice that had made the words sound very different.

'Have you heard of the European Reconstruction Council, dear?' inquired Richard, as Betty came into his room half an hour later to say good night. He was in bed, with the reading-lamp shining on his gaunt face and Montaigne's *Essays* and the *Economist* on the pillow.

Betty sat on the bed, and thought for a minute and then shook her head.

'I had this from them this morning.' He held up a letter. 'They are opening a training school at Blentley shortly and want me to give some lectures during the coming term, on the financial systems of the invaded countries.'

His mother nodded. 'I see. Getting ready for after the war.'

'Exactly. Fully trained students will be sent to Europe immediately it is possible to deal with the social problems. (Well, you knew that, of course.) The Council is sponsored and financed by the Government.'

'It should be quite interesting.'

'I think so. And I have only three pounds left, so the money is very necessary too. The lectures won't take up all my time, so I shall get some part-time work in a small factory as well. That ought to be possible.'

'If it doesn't knock you up, darling,' she said, looking at him fondly.

'I shan't undertake anything that I'm not capable of performing. That would be foolish, as well as a disguised form of vanity. It appears that my name was suggested to the Council by Sir William Beveridge.'

'Oh—ho! Nice little compliment, Rick.'

'Well,' he looked down with a demure smile, 'I am not insensible of the honour. The point is: does Miss Fielding object to my being here so strongly that she will seize upon this change in my habits as an excuse to get rid of me?'

'I should take no notice of Connie,' said Betty with decision, 'I think she really likes us all being here, only she must have someone to grumble at. Her bark is worse than her bite.'

'You will observe,' said Richard, lying back on the pillows, 'that we both assume that she is head of the household. Fielding really does dislike me but the fact fails to register with me.'

'Poor old Ken,' said Betty vaguely, and slid off the bed. She had on an amber dressing-gown over an amber silk nightgown that made the best of her dark hair and tea-rose skin. 'I don't think he really dislikes anyone. Well, he *isn't* the head of the household, of course. Good night, dear.'

'Good night. You are a pretty and delightful and good woman, Betty.'

'My dear boy! Aren't you always telling me I'm not your type? Thank you, all the same. You wait until you've got a household of your own!' she added teasingly.

'When I have, I shall be head of it,' said Richard, opening Montaigne's *Essays*.

15

The next morning after Kenneth and Betty had gone to work and Miss Fielding had settled herself with *The Times*, Vartouhi went upstairs to Miss Burton's apartments.

It was raining, and the cold light came through scudding clouds into Miss Burton's sitting-room with its summerlike furnishings of white paint and blue flowered chintz and basket chairs and many photographs, and made them look flimsy and uncosy. But the room was well warmed by a large electric fire and by it Miss Burton sat with Ouida's *The Massareenes*. She herself preferred the later and less romantic novels of this writer to the earlier ones; it was her mother who had been the fervent admirer of *Wanda* and *In Maremma* and the rest and who had passed her collection on to her daughter; but Miss Burton liked to pull out one of the novels while she was dressing or digesting her lunch and read a few pages. She now put the book down and smiled at Vartouhi.

'There you are, Vartouhi. I hadn't forgotten. Look,' she indicated a table where the hats had been put out, 'there they are. See which you like.'

'Thank you, Miss Burton.'

'That looks charming!' exclaimed Miss Burton in a minute; she had been interestedly watching the trying on of the beige hat and the white one and now admired Vartouhi in a large pale blue felt. 'But you can't see yourself properly in that glass; let's come into the bedroom.'

'Oh, yes, you must have that one!' she said as Vartouhi smiled at herself in the long mirror as a country girl of fifty years ago would have smiled at cherry ear-rings.

'Vary pratty,' announced Vartouhi.

'Very. Highly unsuitable and becoming,' drawled The Usurper, looking out of Miss Burton's amused eyes for a moment. Her visits were becoming rarer as Miss Burton grew older.

'You'd better have them all,' she went on with abrupt kindness, 'I shan't ever wear them again.'

'Three hat!' murmured Vartouhi, staring at them as they lay on the bed. 'This morning I have no hat, now I have three hat. Oh thank you thank you, Miss Burton!'

'You needn't thank me. I like you to have them.'

'I do something for you,' said Vartouhi eagerly.

'Oh no, my dear, there's no need for that, really.'

'Yas, yas, I do something for you. You tell me what you like, I do it.' Her gaze moved round the room, looking, at once, for something to do. Miss Burton's gaze went with hers, and lingered on a half-open drawer stuffed with coloured wool and knitting needles and embroidery frames.

'Well,' she said, laughing but slightly ashamed, 'if you really do want to be a kind girl you can tidy up that shocking drawer for me.'

Vartouhi went over to the drawer and looked down into the confusion of brilliant wools and silks. Suddenly she violently shook her head.

'No! Miss Burton, I will not tidy. I *make* you a thing, a pratty thing, all colours. You have old sheet, old rug, old something, I make you a pratty thing.'

'Oh, well, really——' said Miss Burton, attracted but foreseeing some objections to the plan, including protests from Miss Fielding at Vartouhi's wasting her time. 'That would be very nice, but——'

'Yas. I do it.' Vartouhi interrupted her vigorously, kneeling in front of the drawer and plunging her hands into the silk. 'All this red, all this yellow, all this green, I make a *beautiful* thing. You find out old sheet; I make.'

'Well, that's very kind of you, Vartouhi. Er, what would I use it for?'

'Put it on you bed,' answered Vartouhi with a flashing smile, 'Yas, Miss Fielding! I come!' and she ran downstairs in response to a distant bellow.

'So tiresome,' said Miss Fielding, standing in the hall with *The Times*, 'Mrs Archer hasn't turned up and I particularly wanted to see her to-day to ask her about her grandson doing Little Frimdl. Can you look in there on your way to the town, Vartouhi, and find out what is the matter? I hope to goodness she's not ill. I will do the beds to-day,' and Miss Fielding stalked back into the drawing-room to finish *The Times*, irritated by the prospect of doing the beds.

In the little study, Richard was stamping a letter to the European Reconstruction Council, which accepted the post they offered, and deciding that he would try to walk down the road to post it, for he must get the normal powers of his ankle restored as quickly as possible if he was to undertake daily journeys to work in the New Year. His satisfaction at the prospect was twofold, for he looked forward to doing some congenial work again and also to earning some money. He had saved fifty pounds during the time he had been working with the Dove Players but, as he had told his mother, that money was nearly all gone now.

The rain had stopped and an icy wind was ruffling the pools in the road as he limped out of the gates. Sky and fields and trees were steely with winter yet wet with cold rain, and only the delicious freshness of the air compensated for such an unpleasant day. Richard never took much notice of weather or made many concessions to its variations and on this occasion he had no hat and an enormously long scarf of faded blue wool twisted three times round his neck, an ancient trench coat, and a pair of beautiful boots, hand-made by Hill's, that he had bought for thirty shillings from an aristocratic Leftist friend. He had practised walking in the garden during the past week and it was with some confidence that he set off slowly down the road.

'Hey! You get cold in you head!' called Vartouhi mockingly, as she came up behind him. He turned and smiled at her.

'No I shan't, I never wear a hat. Where's the bicycle this morning?'

'It has burst in its wheel.'

'Oh. Are you going in to shop?' he said, a little confused by being alone with her. He noticed vaguely that she looked different this morning, and, when he brought his mind to bear on the matter, observed that she was wearing a large pale blue hat.

'Your hat is new, isn't it?' he went on.

'Miss Burton give me. Vary pratty,' she said proudly.

Richard said nothing to this, but looked down at her with so much meaning that she was compelled to do something about his look, but all she did was to give him a smile which, not for the first time, disconcerted him by its malice. He suddenly remembered the smile of a five-year-old child belonging to some friends of his when scoring off a younger brother. She *really* doesn't like me, he thought. But her eyes and the full curve of her sallow cheeks were so enchanting against the pale blue of the hat that his thoughts were suddenly scattered by a rush of feeling.

'Vartouhi——' he said, quickly, 'you are so lovely!'—and then stopped, unable to continue because of a conviction that he was addressing something that could not possibly understand, like a flower or a kitten.

'Oh yas!' said Vartouhi, looking pleased but scornfully half-shutting her eyes. 'I know you think so I am lovely. You look at me all the time.'

'Well, yes, I do, I'm afraid. Er—I can't help it. Don't you like me to look?'

'Make me laugh,' said Vartouhi, and did so, putting her little hand over her mouth and giggling at him through it.

The gesture was astonishingly foreign and he was instantly reminded of those silly charming Asiatic faces seen so many times in travel films, flying from the camera or peeping rapturously round doorways and veils. He did not like it. A feeling very like repulsion touched his mind for an instant.

'I'm glad I amuse you,' he said stiffly.

'Now you are cross to me. I don't care. Make me laugh again,' and she repeated the gesture but now her eyes were sparkling angrily.

'Well, no one likes to be laughed at,' he said more mildly.

'I like it. But I do not like to be angry at. Make me angry too also.'

'I can't laugh at you,' he said slowly, stopping to rest on his stick for a moment while he looked down at her. 'You make me feel too much.'

'I am varry pratty,' she said complacently, 'that is why you feel. There were some many man in Bairamia ask my father to marry me.'

'I'm sure they did, Vartouhi.'

'He say, no. They have no money enough.'

'Well, I haven't either.'

'I see, Rich-ard. You have bad clothes and no money at all.'

This time Richard did laugh, though the mixture of exasperation and fascination into which he was floundering was no laughing matter.

'Here's the pillar-box,' he said, stopping under a long wall where the rhododendrons dripped, 'I'm not coming any further.'

'Good-bye, Rich-ard,' said Vartouhi gaily with a nod, and continued on the road towards Mrs Archer's, while Richard limped homewards, thinking that the situation between himself and Vartouhi showed signs only of becoming less satisfactory: for it was by no means a case of simple desire and it was most certainly not a case for the remedy of marriage; you don't marry a kitten or a child of five. No; it is simply the '*bad fate like that in the fairy stories*,' he thought once more.

Mrs Archer lived in an old cottage at the end of a long narrow garden which in summer blazed with flowers and even now had a cold pink rose or two on the leafless bushes above beds of sturdy winter spinach. The cottage had an undulating roof of rotting dark silver thatch where starlings nested, and very outside sanitation, and Mrs Archer longed to get out of it and go and live in one of the Council houses on the St Alberics road. People (not Archers) had been living in her cottage for nearly two hundred years and, what with the pump and the sanitation and the starlings and their mess and the tiny coal fire which was all she had to cook on, she felt it was time the place had a rest. She had long since stopped noticing how pretty it was.

The front door was shut, and as Vartouhi went down the cinder path she heard excited voices. She looked with contempt at the cottage. This was the kind of house that her father's fruit workers lived in, small, old and cramped, a pitiful place compared with the spacious stone rooms of her own home and the gorgeously carpeted and curtained mansion, flowing with tinned music and hot water, where dwelt her employers. She marched up to the door and gave a loud knock.

In a minute Mrs Archer opened it. She was flushed and excited and behind her Vartouhi saw a tiny dark room crowded with people; an old woman and a small boy and a young woman and several middle-aged ones, all staring towards the door.

'Yes?—oh, it's you,' said Mrs Archer. She never addressed Vartouhi in any other way.

'Good morning, Mrs Archer,' retorted Vartouhi with a passable imitation of Miss Fielding's manner. 'Miss Fielding ask why you do not come this day morning.'

'Come to see why I didn't come to work, I expect, haven't you?' pursued Mrs Archer, who always kept up a running translation of Vartouhi's remarks. 'Well, we've had a bit of excitement here. Our George has won a medal!'

'I do not understand.'

'For fighting. My George, my son. He went for three of those Huns in some place in Norway on one of those Commando raids—you know—bang! bang! shoot Germans!' and Mrs Archer imitated somebody firing a rifle.

'That's not the way you handle a tommy-gun, Gran,' interrupted the small boy, pushing his way between the females to the door. 'Like this—pr-rr-rr-rr!' and he slowly moved his arms to and fro, machine-gunning

'Ah-ha! I know!' exclaimed Vartouhi, smiling. 'I see on the pictures. Your George do that?'

'Yes. In Norway. In the snow. Mopped up three of them and took a position all on his own. The Government's given him a medal and he's come home on leave this morning, unexpected. So that's why I'm having a holiday to-day.'

'Medal—like this, see?' interrupted the small boy, who had personally undertaken Vartouhi's enlightenment. 'These are my gran-dad's. For killing Germans in the old war. Medal—see?'

'Sidney Archer, you put those back at once!'

'I understand.' Vartouhi had been examining the case he held out to her, and now looked up smiling. 'I am so please. He is very brave and good, this man. I would like him to see.'

'He's upstairs now, having a bit of a wash,' said Mrs Archer repressively, and the young woman came slowly over to the door and put her pretty face over Mrs Archer's shoulder, without speaking.

'Is good for you, Mrs Archer. So brave a son,' said Vartouhi. 'I tell Miss Fielding.'

There was some murmuring from the interior of the room and the words 'do her good' could be detected.

'That's right. You tell her I shan't be in to-day because my son's got a medal———'

'Mum!' exclaimed a confident male voice from somewhere upstairs, 'come and find me a shirt, will you? and spare my blushes!'

'You get along, George Archer!' said his mother. 'That's Miss Burton's hat, isn't it?' she added, looking with interest at the pale blue felt.

'She give me it,' said Vartouhi haughtily. A woman who lived in a small dark house like this, though she did have a brave son who killed Germans, had no right to proclaim that people's hats were second-hand.

'Summer before last she had that. I remember thinking at the time it was too young for her. Well, you'd better be going now. I'll be in to-morrow, you tell Miss Fielding.'

'Good-bye, Mrs Archer.'

'Good morning.'

Vartouhi went away down the path with her dancing walk.

'Who on earth's she?' demanded the pretty young woman as Mrs Archer shut the door. Mrs Archer explained.

'Oh—a refugee. Poor thing. What a day to wear a hat like that! I s'pose it's the only one she's got.'

'It looked O.K. to me,' said the voice from upstairs. George had been reconnoitring above the window curtain.

Vartouhi was so excited and filled with admiration at George's medal that her mood lasted all the time she was filling her rucksack with provisions and household requirements in St Alberics, and when she got home she hurried to tell Miss Fielding about it. Miss Fielding was standing at the table dabbling absently in some pastry with her eyes fixed upon a book about monads.

'Did you get the fish?' she demanded.

'Yas. Four bit cod. Miss Fielding, Mrs Archer son get a medal!'

'I presume that was why she didn't turn up this morning,' said Miss Fielding coldly.

'Yas. Miss Fielding, George (that his name, George) kill three

Germans in the snow! There was many people there, a little boy and a pretty girl and some old ones too also.'

'A small boy? Mrs Archer's grandson, do you mean?' asked Miss Fielding. 'What was he like? Did he look intelligent? I want him to do Little Frimdl.'

'He show me how to fire a gun—pr-r-r-r-r——!' and Vartouhi, smiling broadly, machine-gunned the kitchen.

Miss Fielding shut her eyes. 'And I was Relying on him,' she muttered. 'He does not sound the right type at all. How tiresome. Vartouhi, finish this pastry, will you? it seems to be too wet, I think,' and she retired with her book to the drawing-room.

But Vartouhi put it in the boiler and made some fresh.

16

It was now three weeks before Christmas, the time of ever-darkening days, and breakfast by artificial light, and thick mists that dripped from the black trees, and colds in the head. The inhabitants of Sunglades were all fairly healthy, as health goes in the winter in England, for they had money with which to buy such extra nourishing food as was legally obtainable, the house was warm and comfortably furnished, and none of them—except Vartouhi who was very young, and Richard who was used to the weight of his secret cross—was suffering deep anxiety.

Richard's ankle improved rapidly and he was able to go for longer and longer walks, including one excursion into Blentley, famed for its beautiful Roman Catholic church, which gave him, despite his disapproval of Roman Catholicism, considerable pleasure. It had been a severe trial to him to be unable to walk, for he had what someone has called (the quotation is made from memory) 'the characteristic passion of the wise and good for walking,' and a walking tour had been part of his yearly programme ever since he had been old enough to take holidays by himself. He liked equally well to walk alone or in company, but if he took a companion, their conversation must be impersonal yet entertaining and their step must suit with his own, or else their next suggestion of a walk was met with the most courteous of refusals. Despite the dreariness of the weather there were occasionally days when walking was possible, and he continued to be out two or three times a week in that country which was so lacking in surprises and so full, to him, of charm.

The rehearsals for *Little Frimdl* continued with regularity, and the play even made some progress as a whole, for as it had no drama and the characters were abstractions, questions of licking it into shape and putting it across and building up a part and all the rest of it simply did not arise: you came on as Peace or Ignorance or Non-Co-operation and said your piece and that was all there was to it. Richard, who considered that one of his most useful gifts was a capacity for conserving his energies, made no attempt to produce anyone, but concentrated on showing them all how to wear their clothes, and on constructing some non-naturalistic scenery out of plywood, brown paper and black-board chalks, and fixing up a simple but effective lighting system. Miss Fielding's collection of theatrical accessories that were left over from other plays in the past came in usefully here. He was busy for the rest of his time working up his lectures for the European Reconstruction Council and received weekly parcels of books from the London Library, his subscription to which was one of his few self-indulgences.

One afternoon he took the early bus into St Alberics to consult the public library, and, on being informed that the particular book he wanted was not to be had there, asked if there was any other library in the town. He was told that there was; at Telegraph House he would find a small but up-to-date library where, the librarian was sure, he could obtain the work he wanted. On entering Telegraph House, a Victorian mansion of the 'sixties now converted into offices, he was surprised to see in its hall a portrait of the same lady who reigned above the mantelpiece in the drawing-room at Sunglades. It appeared from the inscription below the picture that the late Mrs Fielding had been the prime mover in the founding of the Telegraph House Library, which consisted of three rooms lined with technical volumes and works on economics and sociology, supported by private subscriptions and a small charge to the public and a tiny yearly income left by the lady herself. The books were renewed as the facts they contained became out of date. Richard obtained the one he wanted, and the little institution, with its voluntary assistant and its thrice-weekly opening, appeared to him to be admirably administered and performing a useful public work. He felt a respect for Our Mother which he certainly had not felt before.

As he came down the steps he seemed to hear someone blowing a car-hooter. The street was almost empty as it was tea-time, and after bringing his mind back from where it was wandering, he decided that the hooter was being blown at him. He looked down at the foot of the steps and saw a sports car.

'Hallo—can I give you a lift?' called Alicia.

'If your driving has improved—yes, thank you,' he answered, limping down towards her.

'Actually, I don't drive as badly as most women,' she retorted, opening the door for him. He got in beside her and put his books at the back. 'Do you want to go home?'

'Well, is there somewhere we can get some tea near here? I want to talk to you; I have been meaning to write to you but I've been very busy lately. Is that a place over there?' peering across the road.

'It looks ropey to me,' said Alicia, suddenly feeling happy.

'Never mind—never mind, it won't hurt us for fifteen minutes,' he said impatiently, collecting his books again, and she drove across to the Myrna Café, which had a dish of dark, damp sausages displayed beside a vase of red paper flowers in its steamy window.

'Cripes,' muttered Alicia as he opened the door.

'You must be used to this sort of thing if you're working in a factory,' he said, sitting down at a marble table.

'Our canteen is so clean you could eat off it if you had any appetite,' said Alicia waving and smiling to someone dimly seen through steam and cigarette smoke at the other end of the room.

'Who's that?' demanded Richard, turning round.

'Two girls from my factory. I don't know the boys.' The girls had rich yellow curls on their shoulders, men's jackets over sweaters, and trousers, and heavy, expensive shoes. Their grubby little hands had painted nails and the paint was thick on their eighteen-year-old faces. The boys were in battle-dress. All four looked soft and sleepy with happiness.

> *There'll be blue birds over*
> *The white cliffs of Dover*

hummed Alicia, in time with the roaring wireless. She liked being here so much! in the hot, greasy noisy room with the smell of tea and stale frying, under the red shaded lights, with the gathering winter dusk outside. Richard had piled his books on the table and unwound his blue scarf and presently she slipped off her fur coat.

'Two cups of tea, please,' said Richard, to the thin little girl who came to take their order.

'Sometimes the cake is quite good at these places,' suggested Alicia. 'What they call cut cake.'

'And a piece of cut cake,' added Richard austerely.

'Don't you want any?'

He shook his head. In fact he had come out with half a crown, as his supply of money was almost at an end and he would have no more until a cheque arrived for an article he had written for an American paper, and he did not intend to spend a farthing more than he must.

The tea was hot and weak in thick cups and they were each given one teaspoonful of sugar by the little waitress. Richard watched her all the time she was serving them, noticing her spotted dark dress and the white marks on her nails, her childish thin neck and the coloured slide on her lank hair. Alicia watched him curiously.

'When *everyone*,' he said suddenly, and drank some tea, 'when everyone (and when I say everyone I include the last and most besotted Indian in Mexico and also all the Japanese) has enough to eat and his share of what's good in the world, then, and only then, will I cease from mental fight. What I wanted to ask you was——'

She had been watching the colour that had come into his thin face, and now interrupted him——

'I don't believe you eat enough.'

'I eat *enough*. I don't pay much attention to what I do eat or eat as much as most people think necessary, possibly.'

'That isn't awfully sensible, if you're not strong, is it?'

'It may be subconsciously due to my health; I don't know. In any case, by this time it is a habit, and not an interesting habit either. And it's part of my political beliefs not to overeat. As I was going to say, is there any part-time work to be had in your factory?'

Alicia's common sense had warned her that he would not want to ask her anything romantic, and she was able to answer almost without disappointment.

'I'm afraid not. We did think of getting it started but the work doesn't lend itself to part-timing. Why? Do you want a job?'

He explained what he did want, and she was able to give him the address of a friend who worked in a converted shed with other part-timers in the town, sorting rivets. He thanked her and made a note of it, then glanced at her plate, where she had left half a slice of pale wettish cake.

'Don't you want that?' She shook her head.

'You shouldn't waste food,' he said calmly, and ate it himself. Alicia gazed at him, fascinated. He certainly has the most original line, she reflected. Any other man on this planet would have said, *I'm so sorry—it looks awful—I should never have brought you here.* But then no other man would have brought me here.

'Is that why you don't like to see food wasted—because so many people haven't enough to eat?' she asked, and he nodded.

'I've never thought about it,' confessed Alicia suddenly, longing to abase herself.

'Well, it would be surprising if you had,' answered Richard

judicially. 'Miss Fielding tells me that your father handles Government contracts for clothing which brought him in, before this war, an income of something like ten thousand pounds a year. Unless you were an outstandingly unusual woman, like Barbara Bodichon or Beatrice Webb, you could not possibly enter imaginatively into the lives of the poor.'

'It's not quite true that I've *never* thought about it,' she said, ashamed of her first impulse, 'since I've been in the factory I've thought about it quite a lot, as a matter of fact.'

'You seem to have the desirable quality of being honest with yourself,' said Richard approvingly. 'But of course, the workers in your factory are not poor.'

'No, that's true. Those girls down there,' jerking her head towards the back of the room, 'get plenty to eat and as good a time as I do, in their own way.'

She hoped he would ask her if she did have a good time, but there was more than one disappointment for Alicia that afternoon. He only nodded again and offered her a case with two cigarettes in it.

'You——' she said as he lit her cigarette with a match; he seemed to have no lighter, 'I suppose you care about the poor more than anything, don't you?'

It was a clumsy speech, but she was moved, and could only speak clumsily. In this hot, noisy café, so sordid and full of ordinary people, where there was nothing beautiful or serious, she felt closer than she had ever been in her most intimate moments with H. to what she vaguely thought of as 'real things.'

Richard did not answer at once. He leant forward and stared down at the table as if intently thinking. Then he began to say slowly:

'You used the right word when you said "care." *The poor you have always with you*, as Jesus said in another sense, and part of my mind always aches with the knowledge of them. They ask so little. At least 90 per cent. of the British want a small house and a garden; a vote recently taken among men in the armed forces showed that that was what 95 to 98 per cent. wanted, and an inquiry made in Birmingham proved that 96.7 of the city's population wanted it too. If you ask almost any of them casually what they want from life, the answer's invariably the same—"nice little house and a bit of garden." Some of them are greedy, of course, but they haven't the monopoly of *that* vice. Most greed is innocent and the frightened greed of the poor is the most innocent kind. "A nice little house and a bit of garden" and the wish is probably true for the poor all over the globe. That's all; and we have so mismanaged *the wasted garden of the world*, as some writer[1] called it, that they can't even have that. It isn't that they can't have art and riches and leisure (which most of them don't want anyway); they can't have enough food, or time to rest their overworked bodies, to make love, or delight in their children without fear for their future.'

He stopped, and coughed. Alicia did not say anything, and after a moment he went on:

'What I feel about the poor shapes the pattern of my whole life. I seldom talk about this, but since you asked me and because I like you, I have spoken of it. Now if you agree we will talk about other things.'

He stopped talking, and carefully tapped the ash from his cigarette, without looking at her. Alicia still said nothing. Colour came into her face, and she drank some tea without noticing that it was cold. The words *Because I like you* still sounded in her mind and she was ashamed because she remembered them, and only them, clearly out of all the words he had spoken. Presently she said:

'You didn't tell me all this the other night when I asked you what you liked doing best.'

[1] Ouida.

'You were talking about what gave me pleasure. I can't say my feelings about the poor do that.'

'You said that this feeling—sort of—influences your whole life. How do you mean?'

'I believe that I can help to alleviate, though of course in a microscopically small way, the lot of the poor all over the world by teaching Economics and supporting the Communist movement. I do both those things. And I live entirely on what I can earn. An aunt left me three pounds a week when I was twenty-one, but I pay that into the Communist Party funds for four months out of the year, and the rest of it goes to help the prisoners from the Spanish Civil War who are still interned in France and other countries. When I am destitute, which does not often happen, I borrow from my mother—no one else. And I even pay her back!' He gave the smile that Alicia was beginning to watch for, and she smiled too.

'Are you a Communist?' she asked.

'I am not a member of the Party, but what political views I have approach nearest to Communism, I suppose.'

After thinking this over, Alicia said candidly:

'You know, I think you must have a ropey time. Worrying about the poor, and giving all your money away and not eating much. And you say you're happy!'

'I am,' he said instantly. 'Don't I look it?'

She studied his face, with its high forehead and beautiful mouth, and had to admit to herself that happiness, though of a kind most unlike what she was used to calling happiness, did shine there.

'Well, yes, you do. But I'm damned,' said Alicia, forgetting to be charming as she thought bitterly of her own unhappiness, 'if I know why.'

'I like the human race, and I'm doing what I think is my duty. And, fortunately, I like that too,' said Richard, beginning to cocoon himself up in the muffler.

'Pi!' she jeered.

He took no notice beyond smiling indulgently at her, and beckoned to the waitress.

'Are you going to drive me home?' he asked.

'If you like. Why?'

'This is all the money I've got,' holding up the half-crown, 'and I want to leave the change for the child.'

After he had paid the bill, Alicia watched him put the coppers and silver under a plate. She did not offer to pay for her own tea. Why should she? It had not been a very nice party; she felt as if her shins had been barked. But she went on liking him, and a vague comparison between himself and H. continued in her mind. H., with his money and his cigars! she suddenly thought. It used to be enough to choke you.

'I thought Communists didn't approve of tipping; isn't it an insult?' she said maliciously, as he helped her on with her coat.

He did not answer, but gently shooed her out of the café with outstretched palms. She turned at the door to wave good-bye to the munition girls, who waved dreamily back, and then they went into the black-out.

'Damn, it's snowing,' she said, feeling a tiny icy touch on her face. 'And I haven't got the hood up. Shall we bother?'

'Splendid,' he answered absently. 'No; it isn't wet snow.'

'Won't you get a cold or something?' She was adjusting the windscreen wiper as he settled himself in his seat.

'I think not. My clothes are old but very thick and warm.'

'You never bother about them, do you?'

'I have them cleaned,' he answered mildly. 'I buy his old suits from the Earl of Swanage, actually.'

'It's a pity he doesn't go to a better tailor, Richard,' said Alicia, who had heard of the eccentric young peer.

'He economizes on cut rather than on cloth, Alicia.'

She drove on through the darkness. The windscreen wiper ticked steadily and their shoulders became covered with fine snow; the dim roads were white.

'I'm sure you'll get a cold,' she said presently.

'I may, of course. But I am very fond of walking in the snow, and if this lasts I shall walk to Blentley on Sunday. Will you come too?'

The simplicity and sweetness of this request completely bowled Alicia over and she just prevented herself from exclaiming 'Will I not!' by answering pleasantly, 'I'd love to—if I don't have to work. I like walking in snow, too, and I badly need some air.'

Arrangements for the excursion were made and they parted amiably at the gates of Sunglades without having touched again upon serious subjects. Richard limped away into the blackness with his books protected under his coat, and Alicia drove home thinking—My beaver boots and the green suit and my beaver coat and cap. Oh, boy! Communism my foot. But much of this was bravado.

Bravado for which there was no need, for on Saturday Mrs Marten telephoned to say that Richard would be unable to walk on Sunday as arranged because he had influenza and a temperature of a hundred and four. Her voice sounded worried, and it took a definite effort of will on Alicia's part to confess that she was responsible for his illness because she had not put up the car's hood against the snow. 'I always seem to be doing things to him,' she concluded ruefully. Betty assured her that she was not to blame: Richard never took normal precautions against the weather and he always had influenza just before Christmas anyway. And she promised (without being asked and rather to Alicia's embarrassment) to ring up again in a day or two and let her know how he was.

Well, she certainly isn't like most young men's mothers, thought Alicia, sighing as she replaced the receiver. But I'm thoroughly browned off.

However, London was full of men eager to be amused and to spend money on an attractive young woman, and there were even unattached men in St Alberics, Canadians and Free Frenchmen and boys in the R.A.F., and for the weeks before Christmas she managed to have her customary good time with dances and parties and pub-crawls and did not consciously think much about Richard. But underneath her usual half-bitter, half-good-natured acceptance of anything that turned up, the thought of him was always there, and she was pleased when his mother rang up in a few days to say that his temperature was down and that he was feeling better.

Alicia expressed a polite relief and did not suggest that she should go round to see him with something to read. For she had, in addition to a natural talent for getting on with men, strict rules governing her relations with them which she had drawn up for herself ever since her earliest affairs. She never made scenes or asked awkward questions or suggested that she should meet a man; she did not write long explanatory or demanding letters, or discuss her admirers with her few women friends. And she contrived that her orderly feminine life, with its war-work and appointments for shopping or hairdressing, should go on in apparent tranquillity whether she was having a love affair or not; and this was another attraction to her men friends. The little dears are always intrigued by someone who isn't in a mess, she thought, and they aren't satisfied until they've made you into one. And then they aren't satisfied.

Because she liked men and had always behaved beautifully towards her own, like an expert fencer or dancing partner, Alicia still felt bitterly towards H., who had broken down her rules with his passion and drawn from her emotion and suffering and then decided that he did not want to spend the rest of his life with her. She felt that she had not deserved such treatment from luck or Fate or whatever it was. She, who had taken such care to behave within her code! who had 'used her loaf' as the Army says, and never clamoured or whined! It was not fair; and she was still sore with H., though not so sore as she had been before she met Richard.

In the dark icy days before Christmas, Richard lay in bed recovering from influenza and feeling so weak that he could only concentrate upon the necessary reading for his lectures for a short time in the morning and evening. He was much alone, for Miss Fielding said that the atmosphere of a sick room depressed her and darkened her constructive powers, Miss Burton was merely afraid of catching the influenza, and his mother was of course out all day, while Vartouhi hurried in and out with his meals, calling him 'Poor Richard!' in a tone that gave him no pleasure, and could never be persuaded to linger for a moment.

One afternoon, when he had been lying for an hour or more watching the dark trees moving ceaselessly against the lowering sky, and thinking of Occupied Europe and his friends who had been killed in Spain, she came in with the tea, turning on lights and drawing the curtains and awakening the dull room to warmth and comfort. As she put the tray by his bed and gave him a fleeting smile, he suddenly caught at her hand, muttering:

'Vartouhi—be kind to me. I love you.'

She snatched her hand away and put it behind her back.

'Oh, you love me! You are ill, you are always ill!' she said scornfully. 'You get well varry quick and then I have no more carry these trays to you!'

'Is that what you really feel? Aren't you sorry for me at all?' he asked, pain and anger forgotten in sheer scientific curiosity to find out if she were really as monstrously unkind as she seemed.

'Not at all, not at all,' said Vartouhi, vigorously shaking her head. 'Rich-ard, I hate the rain in England, I like the sun all day, I like to ride on horses up in the mountains, I like to go asleep all in little red flowers, and I hate ill people.'

'Go on about the red flowers,' he said in a low voice, watching her face.

'Little red flowers and white flowers in the mountains in my country.' She lingered for a moment by the bed, and although she was looking down at him he knew that she was seeing a picture, far away. 'I go with my sisters on horses. We climb all day, and go asleep there in the afternoon. We see the sea, a long way off. So blue.'

'Go on.'

'First manny white flowers, then manny red flowers, then the sea, a long way off. And the varry hot sun. That is what I like. Not ill people, Rich-ard.'

'I know, Vartouhi. I shouldn't have bothered you. I'm sorry.'

'Oh yas, you are sorry, I know! Soon you try to touch my hand again.'

'No, I won't. I promise. What do you wear—what dress?— when you ride up in the mountains with your sisters?'

'White, white, all white, with boots,' she said impatiently, hurrying away, 'and yellow on the top, varry pratty, *here*,' and she touched the collar of her overall. 'And there is bells on the horses that ring all the time in the hot sun,' she ended, and shut the door.

I suppose (he thought, as he lay there with his eyes shut) if an Englishwoman told a Bairamian that she lived in a country where there were green meadows with rivers where blue and yellow flowers grew, and stone churches a thousand years old whose bells rang above black trees, that would seem as romantic to him as Bairamia does to me. I can't stand much more of this; I must get a room in Blentley as soon as I'm up again; and meanwhile a counter-irritant is strongly indicated. He drank some tea and wrote a note to Alicia Arkwright suggesting that she should come to see him on the following Saturday afternoon, if she were not working, and bring him something to read—'*the newest whodunit complete with maps and quotations from Plotinus, and the 'New Yorker' and 'Esquire' and 'Vogue.' Not the 'Tatler,' please, although I know that you read it.*'

She is an attractive girl, and I like her, he thought as he stamped the letter, and what I need right now is some civilized feminine society.

It was the hour of the afternoon post. Vartouhi saw the letters come through the box as she ran downstairs; and took them into the drawing-room where Miss Fielding was sitting bolt upright in front of the fire and severely reading.

'Ah, letters!' exclaimed Miss Fielding, slamming down her book. 'Nearly time for black-out, too,' and she glanced out at the darkening garden where dead leaves were blowing along the stone paths. 'We'll have tea, Vartouhi,' and she began to open her correspondence.

Some time later Miss Burton, who was just about to put out the stove in her room and descend to the drawing-room for tea, was surprised to see her door open and Miss Fielding come in. She looked mysterious and disturbed, and in one hand she held a letter.

'Constance! What is the matter?' said Miss Burton, anxiously, going towards her. 'Is it bad news?'

'The worst,' answered Miss Fielding sepulchrally, and handed her the letter. Miss Burton read it hastily, exclaiming: 'Good gracious!' and 'T't, T't!' at intervals, then gave it back to her cousin, saying:

'Oh dear, Constance, whatever *shall* we do?'

'We can do nothing. We are Helpless,' said Miss Fielding, sitting down upon the bed. 'I cannot refuse him house-room. It is my duty to let him come and I must.'

'Oh, dear, it *will* be so uncomfortable!'

'And stay as long as he likes.'

'Oh, *Constance*! And he has no money, he says.'

'Yes, that is something new. It is very ominous, I feel.'

'Let me see—how long is it since he was here?'

'It must be twenty years—at least. I saw him last in London three years ago, and he said then that he had not been here for twenty years.'

'Oh, dear, there will be such a lot to do . . . where will he sleep?'

Miss Fielding shut her eyes. 'He must have Richard's room; it used to be his.'

'But poor Richard—what will he do? He's ill.'

'He must get well at once and find a room somewhere else,' said Miss Fielding decisively, getting up, 'and I may have to ask Betty to go too.'

'Oh dear, why? I'm so fond of Betty. Doesn't he get on with her?'

'Too well,' said Miss Fielding. 'That is what I am afraid of. And taking *other circumstances* into consideration, it is just as well that she should go. Oh dear, oh dear,' she went on in a sort of hushed lament as she tramped downstairs followed by the dejected Miss Burton, 'what crime have I committed in another life that I should have this burden thrust upon me? When I opened that letter this afternoon, Frances, I could not help wondering *why*, when so many *better* and *older* souls have Passed Over, *he* should still be with us, a cause of disappointment and grief to us all. Promoting night clubs! At his age!'

'Night clubs——' murmured Miss Burton.

'Yes. Didn't you read the letter?' sharply.

'Oh yes, of course, but I was so confused and upset, I hardly took it in properly. Night clubs!'

'Go along, Pony, now you know you are not allowed in the drawing-room,' said Miss Fielding crossly to the enormous cat who was stalking across the hall. He stopped short at the drawing-room door and gave her one look, then slowly retreated to the kitchen.

'We can't have you in here to-day, Vartouhi,' Miss Fielding went on as she sat down in front of the tea tray, 'Miss Burton and I want to talk private business.'

'Yas, Miss Fielding,' said Vartouhi cheerfully, and went into the kitchen with Pony, where they sat on the table and ate margarine and toast together while staring out at the wintry garden.

17

After her talk with Miss Burton, Miss Fielding wrote a letter to London and posted it without telling Kenneth or any other member of the household except Miss Burton what she had done. Kenneth is such a fool, she thought, as she tramped through the cold windy night to the posting-box down the road, flashing her torch to light her way. He would have wanted to send a wire saying, 'Come at once, delighted.' Now we'll see what will happen; I hope this will keep him off for a while, at any rate.

Despite this disturbance of the usual pleasant calm of her existence, and her increasing worry about Kenneth and Betty, Miss Fielding did her Christmas shopping as usual. She refused to abandon her custom of giving handsome presents to her friends and acquaintances because of the war, and she went up to London in a day or two with her handbag full of notes and returned in a discontented mood laden with leather blotters, book-ends made like elephants, and gilt fir cone posies. She said that the choice in the shops was very poor and everything was shockingly expensive and it all seemed so senseless, while the difficulty of obtaining the customary attractive wrappings and tyings kept her on the grumble until the very eve of the holyday. Kenneth's presents were all bottles, filled with scent or whisky.

Miss Burton was having an austerity Christmas and making bedroom slippers, traycloths and needle-cases of scraps of silk and brocade from her piece bag. She did not concentrate on one gift at a time but darted feverishly from one to another and became progressively more exhausted as time went on and none were finished. Betty bought book tokens for everybody, for she was so overworked at the Ministry that she could not spare the time to hunt for other presents in the denuded shops and she was glad to take this easy way out. She had been dowered with that best of Heaven's gifts, a happy nature, and did not usually worry, but just now she was worried both by the slowness of Richard's recovery from influenza and by his passion for Vartouhi, which he had been too ill to hide from his mother. It was the first time that she had ever been troubled about one of his love affairs. She had always taken them as gaily as he took them masterfully and felt that he could look after himself and, as for the girls, he was too kind and good to hurt a girl badly. But this affair was different. She had seen the passion and pain in his face when he heard Vartouhi's voice in the distance and had felt helpless and grieved for him. That was why she had telephoned to Alicia, as the nearest civilized attractive girl to hand, and one (Betty thought), who was herself attracted to Richard. Anything to take his mind off that little goblin, thought Betty as she replaced the receiver, being less than just to Vartouhi because she was annoyed with her.

Meanwhile, unmoved by everybody else's worries, Vartouhi climbed the stairs to Miss Burton's rooms whenever she had a spare moment and placidly worked at the beautiful bedspread. Miss Fielding had of course lost no time in asking her what she did up there every evening but had indulgently consented to ask no more questions on being told that something beautiful was being made, for she assumed it to be a present for herself.

One silent night when the countryside was hidden beneath an icy mist, Vartouhi was up there working. She sat on the floor in front of the stove with one cheek flushed by its heat and Miss Burton sat in her low chair cobbling away at a slipper. The room was warm and quiet and scented by some white and purple hyacinths blooming in a bowl on the table; and, although she was bothered by the lopsidedness of her slipper, Miss Burton had been thinking what good company Vartouhi was; how cheerful and kind, and brave (for after all she may never see her family

159

again, thought Miss Burton) and how pleasant it was to sit thus and work together. She stole an affectionate glance at the head crowned with the fair braids, and wished that Miss Fielding would not presently break up the party by roaring for Ovaltine. Really, thought Miss Burton, this war *has* brought home to one the pleasure in quiet pastimes. Oh dear, this slipper.

'Miss Burton.'

'Yes, Vartouhi?'

'I want ask you something.'

'Well?'

'In Mr Fielding bedroom I see a picture of soldiers.'

'Oh yes? That would be some of Mr Fielding's regiment in the last war, the 47th London Territorials, I expect. What about them?'

'I count them. Eleven soldiers. And at the end of soldiers on a chair is a young man.'

'Yes?' The Usurper, always ready for mischief, suddenly glanced with a gleam out of Miss Burton's eyes.

'Is Mr Fielding, Miss Burton?' demanded Vartouhi, looking up from the bedspread with her needle poised. 'Is Mr Fielding, that young man?'

The Usurper nodded, smiling.

'Yes, Vartouhi. That is Mr Fielding as a young man of twenty-five.'

'But so han'some!' breathed Vartouhi, still with the needle poised. 'And so big too also! I look at that picture because I am liking look at soldiers always and there are none pictures of soldiers in this house, and I say, No, no, it is not Mr Fielding. But now you say, Yas, yas.'

'Certainly I do. That is Mr Fielding, as he looked when he was a soldier fighting in the Great War.'

'He is fight?' cried Vartouhi, jabbing the needle into her work and edging herself along the floor closer to Miss Burton while she gazed excitedly up into her face. 'He is killing wicked Germans?'

'Oh, yes. He was in France for four years, and saw a great deal of action—he fought a lot, I mean.'

The Usurper was beginning to enjoy herself. The conviction that his sister had interfered with Kenneth's affairs of the heart was always strong in Miss Burton's mind, and whereas she herself, alone, might have had scruples about encouraging Vartouhi's interest in his war record, The Usurper had none. She went on mysteriously, leaning closer to Vartouhi——

'And he has two medals!'

'*Two* medals? Mrs Archer's George have only one!'

'Yes; the Distinguished Service Order and the Military Cross.'

'What for does he have them, Miss Burton? You tell me all about it!'

The Usurper's sparkling mischievous eyes were looking teasingly down into Vartouhi's ardent questioning ones, and to Miss Burton the quiet hyacinth-scented room seemed to echo with the ghostly music of *There's a Long, Long Trail a-winding*. Her lips were parted to begin on a story of twenty-five-year-old battles and the half-forgotten bravery of the men of 1914 when a distant shout, winging its way up from the hall below, broke the spell.

'Vartouhi! Ovaltine!'

'There's Miss Fielding calling you; we shan't have time this evening,' said Miss Burton hurriedly, The Usurper having retreated and left her to it. 'Run along now; I'll put this away.'

But on the following evening when they were again seated by the stove and the 'beautiful thing' was growing under Vartouhi's hands, the tale of Kenneth's medals was taken up again and related, this time without the mischievous touch of The Usurper, from the depths of Miss Burton's affectionate heart.

She sat with the lamplight falling on her faded face and ageing hands as she carelessly feather-stitched a needlecase in red silk, and Vartouhi sat at her feet, with the moorland colours of green and brown and purple wools and the sheen of brilliant silk skeins scattered all about her.

'It was at a place called La Bassée, in France,' began Miss Burton. 'It happened in 1915 (before you were born, my child). The war had been going on for a year and the Germans had taken all Belgium and a lot of France. It was all so terrible——' she went on dreamily, letting the work fall from her hands, 'this war is not half so terrible, I think. You see, we weren't *used* to the idea of war, as you young people were for years before war came. One year we were all safe, playing and working and living our lives, and the next——'

'Tell about Mr Fielding's medal.'

'Oh—yes—of course. Well, the English were attacking. It was a very big important battle and every soldier felt he must fight as hard as he could. (Oh dear, I am telling this so badly! I wish I could make you *see* it all.) Well, the Germans had their guns on a little hill above one of the villages and they were shelling the village all the time and killing our men as they tried again and again to get into the village. Mr Fielding—Captain Fielding, as he was then—ran with his company—that's about sixty men, but there weren't as many as that under Mr Fielding because some had been wounded—and got right past the German guns and into the village. And they held it against the Germans until reinforcements came up. The Germans came down the hill and fought in the streets but Mr Fielding and his men held on, and in the end they drove the Germans right out onto the guns of our reinforcements.'

'Was very brave,' said Vartouhi, who had been listening with closer attention than Miss Burton had ever seen her show.

'Yes, splendidly brave. He had always been a soldier you know, even before the other war came, and his mother and sisters used to jeer at him about it and try to get him to give it up. But when the war came, of course, he was properly trained and got made an officer very quickly.

'What is "jeer," Miss Burton, please?'

'Oh—laugh in an unkind way. Like you do at Richard,' said

Miss Burton, whose sympathies had been moved on behalf of the invalid. (Richard would have been annoyed had he known how many women suspected his feelings for Vartouhi, but fortunately he did not think about this aspect of his case; he only did his best, instinctively, to conceal his feelings. But—as his Spanish friends would say—*Love and a cough cannot be hidden*.)

Vartouhi moved her shoulders indifferently, and went on——

'His mother and sister jeer at Mr Fielding, you say, Miss Burton?'

'Er—well, yes, they did.' Miss Burton was wondering if she had not gone a little too far in her championship of Kenneth. After all, Miss Fielding was the girl's employer.

'They are fools,' said Vartouhi, gathering up the silks and beginning to work again.

'Really, Vartouhi, you mustn't say that.'

'Is true. They are fools. Is good to have a soldier in your house. Then if fighting happens, you have a soldier all ready.'

'Quite a number of people would agree with you,' said The Usurper, sparkling. 'But, you see, Mrs Fielding and her daughters believed that if you have a lot of soldiers, you make a war come.'

'That does not matter if you have planty soldiers, because then you win. These women are fools, I say so again. Tell about the other medal, please, Miss Burton.'

'The Military Cross? He got that for having been in France for the whole length of the war, from 1914 to 1918, and having seen a great deal of fighting.'

Vartouhi nodded but said no more. However, Miss Burton was sure that she was thinking about Kenneth and his medals, and once or twice during the remaining evenings before Christmas she returned to the subject and asked Miss Burton to describe the medals and to tell again the story of how Kenneth and his company held the village. Miss Burton did so, and was pleased to find that she could express more and more of the tale's colour and drama with each repetition.

Christmas was now only a week away and Miss Fielding, one Saturday morning at breakfast, said that green boughs and holly must be brought in from the woods to decorate the house; and at once an argument arose as to the propriety of using the car for this purpose. Miss Fielding (who had exchanged a relieved glance with Miss Burton after glancing through the morning's post and seeing that it consisted of two letters for Betty and the *Spanish News Letter* for Richard), saw no reason, except the war, why the car should not be taken out, and said that if they filled it sufficiently full with evergreens everybody would think they were doing it for the hospitals and there would be no unfavourable comment. 'We might pinch one of those "Doctor" notices to stick on the front,' murmured Betty to Kenneth, who gave a loud laugh. But Kenneth thought that a walk to the nearest wood three miles away would be jollier, and more patriotic. He and Betty would go.

'And Vartouhi and I will come too and help you carry your treasure-trove, won't we, Vartouhi?' said Miss Fielding brightly. 'It's a lovely day; if we start immediately after lunch we shall have plenty of time to get all we want before it gets dark. I don't suppose you'll come, will you, Frances?'

'Oh yes, why not?' said Miss Burton, glancing out of the window at the cold green garden lit up by the low, bright winter sun. 'I will wrap up warmly. I shall enjoy it.'

'On the birthday of Kemal Ataturk,' announced Vartouhi, getting up and beginning to clear away the breakfast, 'we put a roll of flowers over the fron-door—red and white and yellow flowers like the colours on our flag in my country.'

'Do you, Vartouhi? How interesting!' said Miss Fielding gaily. She was growing more cheerful with every day that came and did not bring a certain letter from London. 'I am *sure* you will enjoy taking part in our ancient English custom this afternoon. It used to be called Bringing in the Yule Log, but of course——' and Miss Fielding followed Vartouhi into the kitchen and gave her an exposition upon Christmas customs in England. Miss Burton wandered upstairs, and Kenneth and Betty were left sitting at the breakfast table with their cigarettes.

'Damn,' he said, looking across at her. She had on her silvery suit and her little ear-rings of green jade and the morning sun deepened the tea-rose tint of her skin. She giggled. It would of course have been pleasanter to walk through the winter woods alone with Kenneth, without Miss Fielding observing his every glance and Miss Burton falling into rabbit holes and tearing her stockings, but what she was really thinking about was Richard, who would have a lonely afternoon and a late tea. However, when she spoke to him about it later in the morning he seemed indifferent and said that he had plenty to read and would not want any tea at all.

In fact he was envious of the others, who would go laughing through the silent leafless woods, pulling down the bitter-smelling laurel and the holly and come home through the frosty dusk with their arms full of stiff, dark-green branches and ivy trails; and particularly did he envy Kenneth, who would only see Vartouhi as a pretty little girl in a woollen cap. Vartouhi in the woods would be wasted on Kenneth, thought Richard, and resigned himself to an afternoon of controlled suffering. He had forgotten that he had invited Alicia to tea.

After lunch the party set out, very talkative and gay with Miss Fielding walking between Kenneth and Betty; and the house was left to solitude and the invalid. He read for a while, then became sleepy and fell into a doze.

He was aroused by something small and hard falling on the bed. He sat up and examined it. It was a pebble, and at the same instant a voice called from the garden below:

'Yoo-hoo! Richard?'

'Hallo,' he called. 'Is that you, Alicia?'

'Yes. I've brought you something to read as per instructions but I can't get in; everybody seems to be out.'

'The kitchen door is unlocked.'

'All right, I'll go round.'

In a few minutes she came into the room, wearing a beaver coat and cap and carrying a bundle of books and papers which she put on the bed.

'I've been staying in town for the last few nights and didn't get your letter until I got back this morning,' she said, pulling up a chair for herself and sitting down. She took off her high cap and put it on the floor and passed one white, faintly stained hand over her dark hair. 'Are you better?' leaning back and looking at him.

'Not quite, thank you. I've still got this temperature. It was rather reckless of you to throw that pebble; it might have blinded me.'

'Rubbish.'

'And how did you know this was my room?'

'I guessed,' smiled Alicia. She was ridiculously happy to see him again. He looks like a beautiful thin wise young owl in pyjamas, she thought. 'Where is everybody?' she went on.

'Gone a-maying,' said Richard rather sourly. 'That is, picking evergreens for Christmas decorations, up in the woods.'

'Oh, bad luck. I should think you like that sort of thing, don't you?'

'I do. And I am very annoyed at having to stay here—browned off, I should say—and quite glad to see you.'

'That's big of you. Well——' glancing at the books—'I've brought you the latest Agatha Christie—my father happened to bring it home last night—and *Vogue* (though what you want *that* for I can't think, and it gets sillier every month anyway) and *Men Only*.' Richard shut his eyes in imitation of Miss Fielding but Alicia only thought how long his lashes were; the beautiful eyelashes of the consumptive. Neither of them thought of Mr Arkwright, who happened to be reading the latest Agatha Christie.

'——and the *Sunday Express*. I adore Nat Gubbins, don't you?'

'Sally the Cat,' said Richard instantly.

'*Love* her,' said Alicia. 'Do you know, Father got so browned off with Garvin in the *Observer*—you know, Now Is The Issue Joined and all the rest of it—he gave up the *Observer* and took to the *Sunday Express* because we love Believe It or Not and Gubbins, and the very week we started to take it, Garvin joined the staff. Father was fit to be tied.'

They both laughed, and Richard said, 'It was a pity we didn't get our walk.'

'Yes. The snow lasted, didn't it? It was a lovely day that Sunday. Are you very keen on walking?'

'Very, but I usually prefer to walk alone.'

'Like Kipling's Cat,' she murmured.

He nodded. 'People will talk about themselves or their love affairs. Have you ever marvelled at the way people use the countryside and the patience of their friends as safety valves for their own passions and misfortunes? When one considers what enduring pleasure may be derived from the mere contemplation of natural objects, it seems to me so strange that people do not exert themselves to the utmost to rid themselves of personal preoccupations, in order to enjoy this delicate yet lasting pleasure to the full. Doesn't it to you?'

'One can't always rid oneself of them,' she said.

'One should be able to. And there should be a special punishment for people who tramp through an exquisite countryside bawling about love. Will you make us some tea?'

'Yes, of course.' She went downstairs whistling and explored the kitchen and in a little while came back with tea on a tray and some little buns.

'I thought we'd toast them,' she said.

'Excellent,' said Richard, who was staring out of the window. He's thinking about the little number, thought Alicia, but she felt confident and calm, because she was used to getting what, and whom, she wanted and the little number seemed to her, in connection with Richard, to be what an aunt of hers used to call Most Unsuitable. She's not his type at all, thought Alicia, gazing peacefully into the electric stove and toasting buns. She would make him wretched if they were to get married—not that I suppose he's thinking of that for a moment. He would be wasted on her, and I like him and I don't want to see him hurt and anyway I don't see why she should have him.

She arranged hot buns and tea conveniently on the tray for him and then sat down by the stove with her own tea. There was a long silence. The sun was setting behind the black trees and the garden was full of cold violet shadows and brilliant yellow light. The earth of the flower-beds was purple and the grass a rich unearthly green under the frigid blue sky. Presently Richard said:

'It's so pleasant, the way you don't talk much.'

'Oh—is it?' She stifled a yawn, and went on, 'I'm sorry, I'm sleepy. I wasn't in bed until three this morning.' Her eyes were still shadowed and her voice slightly hoarse from a three-day party in London, which had ended in the small hours so that people could get some sleep to enable them to get through their day's work, and then continued on the next night. At this party she had met a man who worked in the building that was also adorned by the authoritative presence of H., and had learned that the latter was known to his subordinates as Sexy William. This information, and the already fading memory of many kisses, was all that was left of the party.

'Do you like parties?' she went on.

'Some parties,' said Richard cautiously. 'But the thing to bear in mind about parties is to have all you want of them, and at them, when you're young and then you will not want them when you're old.'

'You might get to like them so much you couldn't do without them.'

'You might, certainly. But that is a risk that must be taken.'

'I go to a lot of parties.'

'Indeed? Is there another bun?'

She took one across to him, pleased to see him eating, and said as she put it on his plate:

'You said you were happy, the other day. I'm not.'

She felt the desire for personal conversation with him, and thought that the liking between them was now strong enough to bear it, but Richard was tormented by pictures of Vartouhi's bright hair and dark eyes against the glossy evergreen leaves as she laughed and thrust her arms among the branches, and he never welcomed personal conversations and the last thing he wanted was one now. He answered:

'That is probably because you are not free. To be a slave to anything—an idea or a person—is repulsive. You won't be happy until you are free.'

'No, I suppose not,' she answered indifferently, knowing she had made a blunder and feeling very annoyed with herself, 'More tea?'

'No thank you. Will you smoke?'

'Are you allowed to?'

'Oh, good heavens, yes,' he said impatiently, and held out his case. As she put out her hand, he took it in his and held it for a moment.

'Beautiful,' he said, turning it palm upwards and gently pushing it back to her with a cigarette in it.

'I can't get the stains out,' said Alicia, whose heart was beating fast.

'They only make it more beautiful, to me,' he said, and she thought: he means that, it's because the stains make it more like a poor woman's hand and he loves the poor. He *does* like me! he really does. She sat down by the fire again and suddenly began to talk very entertainingly and soon they were laughing.

In the woods, all was apparently mirth and jollity. There was

169

plenty of holly; that is, there were plenty of berries on the holly trees, which is all that ever matters about holly, and they enjoyed themselves hooking down the branches with a walking-stick brought for that purpose. The beech leaves lay in deep copper drifts in the hollows and the dark silver trunks towered solemnly upwards to the cold, fading fairy light in the sky. Kenneth sliced off branches of hawthorn laden with soft dark crimson berries, and Betty cut rhododendron sprays with their pale green buds, while Miss Burton rustled through the leaves in a dream, quoting Tennyson to herself and not listening to Miss Fielding, who was explaining about Druids.

Vartouhi was excited by the stillness and the scent of dead leaves and moss, the blue gleam of the sky on a black pool, the sudden rustle of grey pigeons' wings among the highest grey branches, and she took off her cap and ran among the trees, singing in a strong little voice. Miss Fielding, who was concentrating upon procuring the holly for which the party had come out, watched her with an indulgent eye and frequently sent her to assist Kenneth and Betty, particularly when they lingered over some bush behind the rest of the party. She enjoyed the freshness of the air and the wintry hues of the leaves and bushes, but her enjoyment was tempered by her sisterly anxieties. It was hard, she reflected, that she could not fling herself unreservedly into the pleasures of the afternoon, but this had been her cross ever since Kenneth had been of an age to make a fool of himself. They had never been on a picnic, or a water-party, or a tennis party, that she had not breathed a sigh of relief to have the pretty girls left behind and Kenneth safely seated, alone once more, opposite to her on the homeward journey.

Gradually their arms grew full of branches and sprays; trails of ivy with dark jade green leaves, the bright black berries of the honeysuckle, dim red rose-hips and the fans of the fir tree, and at last Miss Fielding said that they had enough and announced that they would go home. Darkness came down very quickly; the last light faded from the woods and they became spectral and chill with shade. As the party came out onto their homeward road the icy moon was rising and threw their shadows at their feet. The thought of tea was of course now uppermost in everybody's mind and they walked smartly homewards, with their beautiful spoils nodding fantastic shadows on the moonlit road as the bunches moved in time to the walking. Everyone was in high spirits and Miss Burton did her best to forget that she was undoubtedly starting a cold. Miss Fielding spoke at length of *Little Frimdl*; how it grew upon one with each rehearsal, and how sad it was that the work of a man like Dr Stocke should be held up by the war, and how tiresome it was that Richard's illness should be holding up the rehearsals. Aeroplanes were active overhead while she was talking, and presently the distant sound of the Alert went faintly up into the dusky, cold rose sky. But the Raiders Passed sounded as they reached Sunglades, and Betty at once went upstairs to see how Richard was.

The sound of laughter greeted her as she opened the door, and she was pleased to see Alicia lying back in a chair by the fire, while Richard turned to smile at his mother with a more cheerful face than he had had for days.

'Hullo, darling; hullo, Alicia, how nice to see you; have you had some tea?'

'Yes, thank you,' and Alicia indicated the tray.

'Good walk, Betty?'

'Delightful. Look——' she put a little posy of a dark fir spray, a rose hip and a pale rhododendron bud on his pillow—'aren't they delicious? It's ages since I've had a walk in the woods in winter and I'd forgotten how lovely they can be.'

'It always seems so strange to me when I come home from a walk with wild flowers and see them in an ordinary room, to think that I've been all day in a place where everything is like that,' he said as if to himself, inhaling the posy's sharp cold scent.

Alicia thought: now that's *definitely* over my head. But H. did like orchids and carnations.

At this moment a distant clamour was heard downstairs in which the word 'buns' was wailingly reiterated.

'Oh God, have we eaten their buns?' inquired Alicia guiltily.

'It is without importance,' said Richard, and went on to tell his mother how he had invited Alicia to tea, when Vartouhi bounced into the room demanding:

'Rich-ard, you have taken some buns to eat them? Oh, Miss Ark-wright is here. Good afternoon.'

'Hullo,' said Alicia pleasantly.

'You did cook and eat the buns?'

'Yes, I'm so sorry. I didn't think,' said Alicia.

'Now there are none for Miss Fielding tea!' said Vartouhi tragically with a beaming smile. 'Oh dear, oh dear, Rich-ard!' Everyone laughed.

Vartouhi stood at the door with her cap in one hand and a spray of scarlet berries in her coat, laughing and looking into the room, at Alicia's peaceful pose by the fire and Richard's face, happier and less tired than it had been some hours ago. He was looking at her, but more detachedly than usually, and there was no pleading in his eyes.

Vartouhi suddenly said crossly:

'Was very annoying thing to do. Now there is *nothing* for *anyone* tea,' and she went out and shut the door sharply after her.

Doesn't like him getting matey with me, thought Alicia, standing up and putting on her coat with a cheerful face. 'I must go; I'm working to-night.'

'Thank you for the books and a very pleasant afternoon. Come again soon,' said Richard tranquilly.

'I will. I'll tell Miss Fielding about that 'phone call on my way down. Good-bye.'

Meeting Miss Fielding, who greeted her rather gravely, in the hall, she said:

'Oh, London tried to get you on the 'phone this afternoon, Miss Fielding, but whoever it was wouldn't leave any message and rang off when I said you were out.'

'Was it a man or a woman?' demanded Miss Fielding agitatedly; then went on more calmly as Alicia glanced at her in surprise, 'I expect it was my sister; she is coming to us for Christmas if she can be spared.'

'It was a man, I think, but the line was so bad, I couldn't hear a thing.'

'Oh—my brother-in-law, I expect. I will ring them up this evening. Thank you, Alicia. Don't forget the rehearsal on Wednesday. Good night.'

But after Miss Fielding had got through to her sister after supper and talked with her, she put a very disturbed face round Miss Burton's door on her way to bed; and whispered to her that there was no doubt who it was who had telephoned that afternoon, and that now she was afraid they must be prepared for the worst at any minute. Miss Burton said, 'Oh dear, and just at Christmas, too, how tiresome and worrying it all was.' With which verdict Miss Fielding sombrely agreed.

18

Joan Fielding, who was also Mrs Henry Miles, arrived after lunch on Christmas Eve. She was a large woman of fifty-six, more fashionable than her sister, and her favourite expressions were Nonsense! and Rubbish! which she served up with a loud short laugh like Kenneth's. She had a war job of some importance in London with an office to herself and four people whose luck was out working under her. Her husband, who belonged to the higher ranks of the Civil Service, had seen to it that her talents—which were genuine—had received this recognition early in the War. Mrs Miles did not share the international interests and outlook of her sister, but concentrated with vigour upon the work in hand; she enjoyed making people do what she wanted them to, never wearied of detail or routine, and did not take the long view. Her three grown-up children all had war jobs outside the Services which she had found for them and were, so she said, doing well. She fascinated Richard, who found the spectacle of a person without imagination curiously restful. Mr Miles was to arrive late that evening, when he should be released from his duties, and then the Christmas party would be complete.

Miss Fielding took her sister away for a long private talk after tea. They were going out to dinner that evening with some old friends in the town, and must start early to catch the bus. In spite of the festive green branches that decorated the house and the mysterious parcels arranged about a tiny tree in the dining-room, and the atmosphere of suspense and happiness that filled even this childless household on Christmas Eve, Miss Fielding's manner was so preoccupied and worried that the party seated about the drawing-room fire noticed it.

'Is something the matter with Constance?' inquired Betty of Miss Burton. 'She seems worried.'

'Well, yes, she is, a little,' replied Miss Burton mysteriously, 'but I hope it will be all right.'

'It isn't anything serious, I hope?' pursued Betty.

'What is it?' demanded Richard (who was now downstairs again) looking up from his book. 'We should both like to know, and I dislike mysteries.'

'Really, Rick,' said his mother feebly.

'Well——' Miss Burton leant forward and lowered her voice, 'as a matter of fact, it is Uncle Eustace.'

'What is Uncle Eustace?' asked Vartouhi loudly, putting half a bun into her mouth.

'S-sh! Miss Fielding's father.'

'She have a father! And so old!'

'Not so very old—only seventy-eight,' retorted Miss Burton stoutly, but with an inner conviction that seventy-eight *was* rather old for the facts which she was about to relate. 'I ought not to be telling you this really only you may as well be prepared in case he comes here——'

'Comes here!' said Richard, putting down his book. 'Is there a chance of his coming here?'

'Oh, more than a chance, I'm afra—I think. He wrote and said he was coming for Christmas. Constance wrote at once and told him that the house was full, but we have heard nothing since—except that telephone call on Sunday which we think *must* have been from him—and Constance thinks it very likely that he will just—blow in,' ended The Usurper, giggling.

'If he does I shall certainly try to get a room in Blentley,' said Richard. 'Miss Fielding won't want the house overcrowded, and I was thinking of going anyway.'

'You go away, Rich-ard?' murmured Vartouhi, who was sitting next to him in a fireside chair. For the last few days she had been a little more friendly towards him, but he derived no

175

happiness from this change, because he thought that she was only amusing herself by changing her tactics.

'Yes,' he said. 'It will be easier for me to work.'

'Will be lonely without you, Rich-ard,' said Vartouhi, so sweetly that he paled, and glanced away from her. You little wretch, I would like to beat you, thought Betty.

'She does not like him, her father?' inquired Vartouhi, turning to Miss Burton. 'Why is she not glad to have him come?'

'Well, he has always been rather *difficult*,' said Miss Burton carefully. 'He likes his own way——'

'You remember, darling; he's always floating night clubs,' said Betty to Richard. 'He left old Mrs Fielding nearly twenty years ago and he's never lived at home since.'

'Of course, his children have seen him in London,' Miss Burton hastily assured Richard, anxious to make the situation seem as wholesome as possible.

'Are you exaggerating when you say that he is *always* floating night clubs?' asked Richard.

Betty shook her head.

'No; he has a real talent for it. He gets the club going and then puts in a manager and takes a percentage of the profits.'

'It sounds extraordinary, I know,' put in Miss Burton.

'It *is* extraordinary,' retorted Richard. After a moment's reflection, he asked:

'Is he talkative?'

'He used to be, rather, I'm afraid,' said Miss Burton reluctantly. After reflecting again Richard announced:

'He sounds like an exhausting personality; a "character"; I dislike them, I shall certainly go to Blentley,' and he returned to his book.

'Darling, you will be a character yourself long before you are seventy-eight,' murmured his mother. 'Why is he coming?' she went on to Miss Burton.

'Well—he says he is temporarily out of funds.'

'Oh, my goodness,' muttered Richard, without looking up.

'I remember him as a charming man,' said Betty.

'I expect he is greatly changed and aged,' said Miss Burton. 'The war, and everything, you know.'

'What is a night club?' asked Vartouhi. 'I take away these cups with old tea in because Miss Arkwright is coming presently soon to do the play.'

'I will help you,' said Richard, getting up.

'Now you all know what you have to do!' cried Miss Fielding, sailing in with spirits apparently restored by a course of Nonsense! and Rubbish! and wearing a fur coat down to her ankles. She was followed by Mrs Miles, wearing a smarter coat.

'*You* ought to be coming with us, not frowsting by the fire! It would put you right in no time,' said Mrs Miles playfully, pointing a large kid finger at Richard. 'It's a topping night and the stars are galopshous.'

'No, I want him to take the rehearsal, Joan,' said Miss Fielding, as if there had existed a possibility of Richard's following Mrs Miles's advice. 'Vartouhi—where is she?—oh, in the kitchen, never mind—she can read my part. Frances——' Miss Fielding drew her cousin aside and confided to her in a low rapid tone that Joan thought it most unlikely that Father would come; he had always been so opposed to family parties and with all his faults he could take a hint; besides he had so many congenial friends all over England, and so on. Wishful thinking, thought Miss Burton, but she knew better than to disagree with her cousin aloud.

After the sisters had gone, a peaceful silence fell. Vartouhi stared into the fire with the pungent smoke from her cigarette wreathing up into the air and Richard read steadily and occasionally made a note; Betty was making an undergarment for herself and Miss Burton was pleasantly doing nothing.

Miss Fielding said that the heart and eye needed more than ever in war-time the refreshment that flowers alone could bestow, and therefore she saw to it that the porcelain vases held proud snowy chrysanthemums, each like a Chinese prince, and wonderful pink giants with silvery underleaves. The lampshades floated in the warm, dusky firelit air like moons and a delicious smell came from the burning logs. In Europe, Richard suddenly thought, they keep children in bed because there is no fuel to heat the schools. I'm getting soft here. I will go to Blentley.

The front door bell rang.

'Is the old Fielding!' cried Vartouhi enthusiastically and ran out of the room pursued by Miss Burton's decisive—'Vartouhi, you must *not* call him that!'

But it was Alicia, with a silly little Christmas present for everybody, including a tiny Hammer and Sickle made of marzipan for Richard.

'Don't let's rehearse; I'm much too comfortable and anyway Kenneth isn't here yet,' said Betty, when they had all laughed over their presents and thanked Alicia and everyone had thought how much pleasanter she had been lately. 'He's seeing a client at Cowater and won't be back until supper-time.'

'What are you going to do about supper, Alicia?' inquired Miss Burton. 'We were just going to have Something on a Tray.'

Alicia held up a packet and said, 'Spam, but I'm not hungry, anyway.' Her eyes were shining, for she had passed the afternoon with a man she had met at the three-night party, and she was in her mood of not caring if she died to-morrow because life was such fun and went so fast that there was no time to get browned off.

'I think we ought to rehearse, Connie will be annoyed if we don't,' said Miss Burton.

'Right. We will do half of the play now, then eat, and the other half when Mr Fielding comes in,' said Richard, and stepped into the middle of the room, and began straight away upon his opening speech as the Spirit of Pity:

'*I look north to the icelands and what do I see? I look east to the ricelands and what do I see? I look west to the cornlands and what do I see? I look south to the grapelands and what do I see?'* He paused, and said very quietly and seriously: *'Dark, Dark, Dark, Dark.'*

'You know,' interrupted Alicia, 'I do think this is awfully bad. I mean, I'm not highbrow, but even I can see that. Don't you agree?' to Richard.

'It is so bad that it is below an intelligent person's notice' he answered. 'I take care that performing in it does not exhaust energies which I require for other purposes; otherwise, I never think about it. Go on, please, Italy.'

Alicia came forward and made a speech intended to express misguided patriotism; and they rehearsed conscientiously until seven o'clock, when Kenneth came in, cheerful and scented with whisky, and insisted on holding a sprig of mistletoe over the four ladies and kissing them. Richard detected a little contempt in Alicia's eyes but she was the only one; the other three simply giggled and enjoyed the fun. They all got supper together, to the sound of the big radio-gramophone which Kenneth and Richard wheeled into the hall, where they also rolled up the rugs.

'After supper we'll dance,' said Kenneth with satisfaction. 'Now, this is my idea of fun.'

It was Vartouhi's, too. She darted about helping to get the supper, wearing two squares of brilliant Bairamian embroidery pinned on her head and round her waist as a cap and apron, while her eyes danced and her two little sallow cushions of cheeks were constantly pushed upwards in laughter.

'Enjoying yourself, little girl?' asked Kenneth kindly, going across the hall with a tray of beer, and smiling down at her.

'Oh *so* I enjoy myself, Mr Fielding!' looking up at him glowingly, 'This is the firs' time in this house I am enjoying so much, laughing all the time!'

'Good. That's the spirit. Must be a bit dull for you here usually, I'm afraid, with no one young about the place.'

He spoke without an afterthought or a pang for his own youth, lost long ago in his broken engagement and the Other War, for something of that youth lived on in his heart, and made him amused at the simplest jokes and ready to enjoy a sunny morning, the discomforts of Home Guard duty, an unexpected adventure, as if he were still twenty-five.

Vartouhi nodded. 'Is rather dull a bit sometimes, Mr Fielding, but I am like be here. Is a grand rich large house, Mr Fielding, and *you* are so kind, too also.'

'I am? Oh—well—I don't know about that, Vartouhi. I'm—we're all fond of you, you know, and want you to be happy here. Some day when all this beastly business is over you'll be going back to your own country and we want you to have good memories of England.'

'You are so kind, Mr Fielding,' repeated Vartouhi earnestly, not seeming to hear what he said. 'You let me walk by the peach trees in the summer when I am so unhappy liking for my home, and you take so a care of me when I am out in the raid. I *never* seen you unkind, Mr Fielding, even to Pony the cat.'

Kenneth threw back his head and laughed; then patted her hand. She smiled in sympathy, watching his face.

'I say a funny joke again?'

'No, no, it's all right. You're a dear little girl, Vartouhi. And to-morrow—ha! ha! We shall see! Present for a good little girl!'

'Is a prasent, Mr Fielding? Is a prasent for me?'

'Ah—ha! That's tellings! If we don't take this beer in the chill will be off it—come along!'

She followed him into the drawing-room. Richard had inadvertently overheard this conversation from the kitchen and was reflecting upon it as he sliced bread. She likes him, he thought, just as she dislikes me. She looks up to him because he's older and richer and more sensible and reliable than I am—and than she is, too. How naturally he said *No one* young about the place—and I am only twenty-six. That is young, though it never

THE BACHELOR

occurs to me to think of myself as young. It never does occur
to the young, of course, except when they think of their youth
as an intellectual concept which explains their difficulties. Neither
he nor she is intelligent, but what does that matter? She enchants
people, and he is the type of man, simple and tough and kind
and brave, that wins wars and founds empires. It is surprising
how irritating those fundamental virtues can be at close quarters.
Now there is Geoffry, who is neither simple nor tough nor even
particularly kind, though he is certainly brave, yet because he
tries to tell the truth to himself and is scrupulously careful not
to grab or be a bore, he and I get on admirably together and I
respect and like him as I could never respect or like Fielding. It
is a question of temperament, I think, not of age. I don't find
Uncle Howard and Uncle Prosper bores. And all this analysis of
the situation does not prevent my being jealous of Fielding.

He carried the sandwiches into the drawing-room and found
Alicia arranging plates on the hearthrug.

'We shall make crumbs,' said Miss Burton resignedly.

'So what?' said Alicia. 'What's this I hear about your going to
Blentley, Richard?' She spoke lightly but she was annoyed; at
Blentley, four miles farther off, he would be unseeable unless
she walked there on purpose.

He explained about old Mr Fielding, for he was not going
to tell her that a hopeless passion was torturing him and that
he felt the Spartan framework of his life was being undermined
by the comfort at Sunglades; and Alicia listened without feeling
or expressing much interest in the returning wanderer and
aged impresario. She had come—rather earlier than most of her
contemporaries—to a time when her life was a search for satisfaction. It was no longer a prolonged joke or party or love
affair, and her interest in 'characters' and 'marvellous stories' and
ludicrously embarrassing situations had simply faded. All that
sort of thing, which had seemed so funny five years ago, was
rather dim nowadays. She did not foresee the day when the

interest would revive, concentrated upon the funny sayings and doings of her own and her friends' children.

'Oh—rather a bore,' she said at the end of Richard's explanation. 'Still, it is his home, I mean.'

'That is what I feel, though I appear to be in a minority of one,' said Richard. 'His return is viewed with apprehension, not to say dismay, by those who should be most relieved and delighted, namely, his children.'

'Ssh——! Mr Fielding doesn't know yet!' said Miss Burton, with a nervous glance towards the kitchen.

Richard and Alicia both raised their eyebrows. It was a simultaneous expression of surprised disapproval from their generation, and as they did it, they both realized that they were experiencing the same feelings. Miss Burton glanced scaredly at their faces, which suddenly looked young and severe, like two prefects come to judgment.

'Isn't that a little odd?' said Richard pleasantly.

'Won't he get rather a nasty jar?' asked Alicia.

'Yes, well, I'm afraid he will; I did say to Constance that it wasn't fair,' said Miss Burton nervously, still glancing towards the kitchen, 'but Mr Fielding—Kenneth, you know—can be very *difficult*, and if he took it into his head to *encourage* his father to come here——'

At this point, any other human being would have demanded stoutly, 'Why shouldn't he?' But Richard and Alicia simply withdrew from the conversation. Richard made it a habit never to discuss other people's problems because it wasted energy, and Alicia, as we know, was no longer interested in 'priceless situations.' It was Miss Burton's bad luck that she should have been drawn into a discussion with two such unnatural people.

'Oh, well, it's Miss Fielding's affair, of course,' said Richard indifferently, and Alicia said, 'Will that be enough watercress? There is some more outside.'

'You and I have rather the same way of thinking about some

things,' he said to her, when Miss Burton had gone out of the room to wash her hands for supper.

'Do you think so?'

'Yes. Don't you?'

'I really hadn't thought about it,' she replied dishonestly. 'I think skeletons in the dirty linen cupboard are a bore, if that's what you mean.'

'It is what I mean. Do you know of a room to let in Blentley?'

'How much do you want to pay?'

'As little as possible. I shall want meals included.'

'I should think some of the new houses on the Luton road let rooms. I suppose you'd get something for about thirty shillings a week.'

'Twenty-five would be better. Thanks. I'll walk over when the holiday's over and make inquiries.'

She looked at him as he stood leaning against the mantelpiece, a very tall, fair young man with cheeks thinner than usual from illness. The thought of the man she had been with that afternoon was still warm in her memory, and she could look at Richard more detachedly than usual. But her decision was still, yes, he's attractive.

'This preoccupation with personalities——' he went on thoughtfully, staring into the fire, 'is a *bourgeois* disease that will disappear with capitalism. People like this old man, whose personalities are swollen beyond normal size, exhaust ordinary people and waste their time by provoking endless discussion and argument and marvellings at their behaviour, and the principle even extends to nations; we have the swollen state which draws unnatural attention to itself by roaring about its misfortunes and rights. The beauty of a team of actors such as the Russians and the French produce, or a field of buttercups or a swarm of fish, the beauty and fitness of the norm, is lost on these personality drunkards. Do you know what I like, Alicia?' turning towards her, 'I like to lose myself in a crowd. Then I'm most myself.'

183

STELLA GIBBONS

'You couldn't lose yourself; you're too tall,' she said, laughing. 'Don't people always look at you?'

'I might be much more conspicuous than I am,' he said, displeased. 'Being looked at is largely the result of wanting to be looked at. *You*, a woman, should know that.'

'And you're a "character" yourself,' she went on maliciously, 'I never met anyone the least like you, anyway.'

'Possibly your world is a narrow one,' he retorted, and then the rest of the party came in and grouped itself about the fire. Vartouhi knelt between Alicia and Richard and offered him sandwiches with a grave, innocent face, most unsuitable to one who had just been viciously poking a tiny green doll's umbrella, her Christmas present from Alicia, down the kitchen sink. She had noticed his growing friendliness with Alicia and resented it. He had admired *her* first; he must go on admiring her, and she would not put up with a rival, especially one like Miss Arkwright, whom she hated because Alicia had two fur coats. She did not think Alicia pretty or fascinating or mind her being a rich man's daughter, but she did envy her those two fur coats, and why should she get attentions from her, Vartouhi's, admirer? Is a beastly girl, thought Vartouhi, forgetting to hand Alicia the sandwiches.

If she's going to be as rude as this, he can't go on caring about her, surely, thought Alicia as she tranquilly ate a sandwich to which she had helped herself. He dislikes 'characters' and personality-bores; suffering cats! What else is she, with her plaits and her ropey little apron? Hold on, Arkwright; patience and tidy hair will yet win the day—if we want it to be won, that is. This afternoon has made everything seem a bit different.

Conversation at supper was very cheerful, as conversation always is when carried on in the absence of some severe and worthy soul who would disapprove of its being so; in this case there were two souls of this type, so the conversation was doubly cheerful. It was the guilty conviction that a dozen times throughout supper Miss Fielding's finger would have been held

184

up in smiling reproof and Mrs Miles's shout of Nonsense! and Rubbish! have resounded on the air that made Richard's speeches so silky and Kenneth's jokes so hearty, Alicia's wisecracks come out with so inimitable a drawl and The Usurper's wit flash so brilliantly. Betty and Vartouhi were the audience, the one contributing her pretty laugh and the other her delighted little face, to the general gaiety. The firelight danced over their laughing faces as they sat in the circle of empty plates and crumbs scattered on the carpet, while above them the curled, massive heads of the Chinese prince-flowers in their white and silvery-pink stared raptly out into the dusk.

After supper the rehearsal was resumed with hilarity. They did make some attempt to do it seriously but unfortunately everybody was in the mood when even ordinary remarks seem exquisitely funny, and *Little Frimdl* had just no chance at all. Every one of Dr Stocke's sentences either had a double meaning or was funny enough as it stood, and when Richard came to his big speech, he could get no further than——

'Misled and unfed are the ricelands——'

which he gaspingly repeated three or four times and then collapsed into a chair, crowing into his handkerchief while the rest of the Spirits of Co-operation and Non-Co-operation stood round him whooping weakly and offering him beer.

It was while all this noise was going on in the drawing-room that the scullery door, which led out into the garden, might have been observed slowly opening into the brilliantly lit, deserted kitchen. A face, crowned by a fashionable soft hat with a decidedly American cast, came cautiously round the door out of the black-out, and was followed by a small man in a long overcoat whose superfine cloth was finished by a rich, soft, luxurious collar of sable. The rest of the visitor's dress was to match in opulence; his gloves were fine pale hogskin only faintly marked by the stains of a journey and his American shoes were finished off with white spats. In his buttonhole he had an orchid, protected from the cold of the winter night by a little hat of cellophane. He had a pointed silver beard and a fresh healthy face with blue eyes.

As soon as he saw the kitchen was empty he straightened his shoulders and smiled. Then he took a biscuit off the table and ate it, listening with his head on one side to the noises that came from the drawing-room.

'A party,' muttered Mr Eustace Fielding. 'Can Constance be dead, and the house let to strangers? But certainly on Sunday I was told that she was *out*. Not dead. Ah! I hear Kenneth's laugh, poor boy.'

Putting another biscuit into his mouth, he set out in the direction of the cheerful sounds, smiling to himself as he listened. Across the hall he went, glancing from side to side at its familiar furnishings, and finally pushed open the drawing-room door. Giant flowers, and firelight, and the laughing faces of pretty women made a charming picture among the soft blue-green and rust colours of the room, but everybody was making such a noise that he had been there for quite half a minute before anyone noticed him. Then Betty glanced down the long room and saw the open door with the old man standing beside it, and gave an exclamation. Everyone turned to look, and the next instant Kenneth and Miss Burton were hurrying forward with exclamations of welcome.

'Father! Of all people! How are you?' and Kenneth seized one of his parent's hands and heartily shook it. 'How ever did you get here? and why didn't you let us know you were coming? Have you had any dinner?'

'No, and I should like some, please,' replied Mr Fielding senior in a light, pleasant voice while his eye roamed keenly among the ladies in the background as if selecting types for a floor-show. He speaks with simplicity and directness, at least, thought Richard, who was watching the scene with some dismay. But what an old bounder. And the stuff on his back would keep a nursery school for a fortnight.

'Uncle Eustace! It must be five years since we met,' said Miss Burton, taking her uncle's hand and shaking it, 'how are you after all this long time?'

'I am very well, thank you, Frances, my dear. And you?'

'Very well too thank you, Uncle. We'll get you something to eat at once—Vartouhi—I'm afraid there isn't mu——'

'I have thought of that,' interrupted Mr Fielding, and dived into one capacious pocket and produced a flat black case. He dived into another on the other side and produced a flat black flask.

'Whisky——' said Mr Fielding, 'and'—he flipped open the other case and disclosed to the fascinated eyes of his audience a large expanse of bloody meat—'steak.'

'Your ration! How thoughtful of you, Uncle!' cried Miss Burton.

'Oh, I ate my ration for lunch yesterday. I got this from a man I know in London,' and Mr Fielding made his way to the most comfortable chair and began removing his outer garments and handing them one by one to Kenneth, while he keenly yet amiably studied the group by the fire.

'Betty! Betty Marten!' he suddenly cried in a satisfied tone while unwinding a silk scarf. 'I was sure I knew that pretty face. What a delightful surprise! What are you doing here?'

He stood up, beaming with pleasure, and Betty came forward and greeted him and introduced Richard, whom he remembered seeing once twenty-five years ago in his pram. (Or says he does, thought Richard, uncharmed.) Mr Fielding did not remember Alicia but did remember her mother, after whom he inquired, nodding smilingly on hearing that she was now married to someone else. After he had eaten the steak Vartouhi cooked for him, and congratulated her upon its excellence, he brought out and lit an excellent cigar. Slowly that ultra-masculine, undemocratic, old-fashioned fragrance diffused itself throughout the chaste apartments of Sunglades, winding over the copies of *The Aryan Path* and past the paintings of blue spirits with no legs and making the place smell like the foyer of the Empire Music Hall.

19

It was this unfamiliar yet nevertheless unmistakable smell that greeted the old gentleman's two daughters as they walked home across the garden about half-past ten that night. The air was brilliant with moonlight and Mr Fielding, who took a childlike pleasure in air raids, had been standing on his doorstep hopefully surveying the heavens and smoking a few moments since. The smoke lingered on the motionless air.

Miss Fielding and her sister stopped dead, sniffing, and exchanged a glance of horror.

'Cigar-smoke!' breathed Miss Fielding. And Mrs Miles said deeply:

'*Father!*'

As one woman, they began to hurry towards the house. As they drew near to it the sound of music could be heard; heard very loudly. They exchanged another glance and Miss Fielding shook her head. Mrs Miles said nothing. Each knew what the other was thinking and feeling.

Behind the front door, the brilliant lights shone on the gleaming expanse of the parquet hall, where Kenneth was waltzing with Vartouhi to the music of *Live, Laugh and Love*, gayest of tunes from a fairy-tale Vienna. Down the long shining floor they waltzed, with Vartouhi's little feet in their shabby black slippers twinkling obediently after Kenneth's big ones, her gaudy cap fluttering in the wind of their dancing and her laughing face lifted to his. On the stairs were grouped Miss Burton and Richard and Betty and Alicia, watching and laughing as they hummed the catchy tune. They had all been dancing, even Richard, who had ignored his weak ankle as he led out Alicia, and now they were resting and watching the two who were agreed by all to be the experts. Half-way up the stairs, like a little Father Christmas in the shadows, sat Mr Fielding, with shady boughs of fir and red, glittering holly framing an old gilt mirror above his head, smiling sympathetically upon the scene and wondering if it couldn't be worked up into a cabaret number. It was upon this orgy that Miss Fielding and her sister opened the door with their latchkey.

'Well! *What* fun!' exclaimed Miss Fielding playfully, advancing into the hall and stopping the waltzers in full flight like shot swallows. 'And how long has *this* been going on, I should like to know? How much *rehearsing* has been done, you bad people?' All the time she was speaking, her eyes were searching into the darker corners of the hall for her father, and she suddenly detected him, skulking (the word came immediately into her mind) half-way up the stairs. Typical.

'Father!' exclaimed Mrs Miles, detecting him at the same moment. 'What a——' she checked herself. One of her unpleasant virtues was a chronic truthfulness, and never mind *anyone's* toes; and as she could not on this occasion say that her father's visit was a surprise, she just repeated 'Father! Well!' which did not sound cordial.

'Yes,' said Mr Fielding simply, coming down the stairs and coming across the hall, looking small yet prosperous, to pat his two large daughters on the arm.

'*Have* you dined?' inquired Mrs Miles with enormous earnestness, peering down at him. He just nodded.

'I get Ovaltine,' said Vartouhi suddenly, darting away.

'Oh *good*,' said Mrs Miles, still addressing her father and hurling her fur coat onto a chair. 'Did you have a good journey down? And by the way, is Henry here?' glancing round as she suddenly remembered her husband.

'He telephoned about nine o'clock to say that he can't get away after all,' said Miss Burton, coming forward with a guilty look, as of one caught furtively sipping gin.

'Oh, too *bad*,' beamed Mrs Miles tragically and absently, sinking into a chair and fixing her father with a severe stare that seemed to go into his future, as well as over his past. 'Oh, I *do* call that *bad luck*.'

'What is bad luck?' demanded Miss Fielding sharply, from her place at a side table with the drinks; she feared that her parent might already be unbosoming himself of his troubles.

'Henry! Henry cannot get away after all,' said Mrs Miles.

'How tiresome. But perhaps it is just as well: we shall be rather a tight fit as it is and one more would make it impossible,' muttered Miss Fielding, her mind busy with plans as to who should sleep where.

In the kitchen Vartouhi was preparing the Ovaltine and thinking how much more cheerful the house had been lately. Is because of Mr Fielding the young one, thought Vartouhi. At last he sees how foolish he has been for many years to let his sister rule him and make his manhood a mockery. Now he begins to remember his bravery as a soldier and his medals. He thinks: I am a Man! and so he rejoices and buys me a present—how I wonder what!—and kisses the women of the house with laughter and asks his honoured ancient father to spend the feast of Christmas beneath his roof. Is a very good thing, concluded Vartouhi, carrying the tray of Ovaltine into the drawing-room.

Betty and Miss Burton were conferring in the now deserted hall—where the rugs had been replaced and the gramophone removed.

'He will have to go on the Kumfi-Slepe in Richard's room,' Miss Burton was saying. 'Just for to-night——'

'Richard hates sharing a room,' said Richard's mother.

'Well, I am dreadfully sorry, Betty,' said Miss Burton fussily, 'but it isn't my fault—you know what Uncle Eustace is—one never knows what he is going to do next—we never have—and Constance seems so upset at his coming—Joan too—anybody would think they had had no warning, and I know for a fact he wrote to Connie at least a week ago——'

'I know, Frankie—I didn't mean to be tiresome,' Betty soothed her, 'I'll break it to Richard,' and she hurried away.

'Good heavens,' said Richard, on being stopped halfway upstairs to his bedroom by his mother and informed that he was to have a stablemate. 'But—good *heavens*, Betty.' He looked excessively tired, and had escaped from the now rather subdued revelries in the drawing-room on the plea of his recent illness. He gazed wanly at her.

'I know, darling. It's tough——'

'Tough!'

'I'll tell him you've been ill, darling.'

'Please don't tell him anything. I am going straight to bed and when he comes in I shall be asleep. And tomorrow I shall go and look for a room in Blentley.'

'To-morrow's Christmas Day, darling.'

'Well, on Boxing Day, then.' He resumed his ascent of the stairs. 'I will not endure two nights of it.'

'Oh, Connie will have got the spare room ready for him by to-morrow night,' Betty promised, but even as she did so she remembered that Mrs Miles was occupying the spare room.

The Kumfi–Slepe in all its nakedness was exposed in Richard's room with sheets flung all over it. It was at the foot of his bed; he had naturally, whenever he looked at it, supposed it to be a chair. He now silently pushed it over to a far corner, where it looked very obviously isolated, and went unhappily to the bathroom.

Downstairs, a final drink was being had. The party was now definitely subdued, for Alicia had gone home, after wishing them all a Merry Christmas, Vartouhi and Miss Burton were collecting bedding, and Betty was getting out some pyjamas of Kenneth's. Why (she thought, as she went into Richard's room with them) has he got three out of the five women in the house waiting on him? We don't wait on Ken or my poor Richard. I believe it's because he takes it for granted that we shall. Wicked old man. I like him, though.

Mr Fielding was alone with his three children.

He sat in the most comfortable chair and sipped his own whisky, and gazed rather glassily into the fire. Kenneth stood by the mantelpiece, also sipping, and Mrs Miles and Miss Fielding sucked up their Ovaltine with grave faces.

Kenneth was embarrassed. He had always been fond of his father but even in his boyhood the expression of his affection had been influenced by the attitude of his mother and sisters, who disapproved of Mr Fielding senior's frivolous attitude to life, his lack of desire to improve the characters and habits of his acquaintances, and his lack of interest in his wife's public work. The three strong-minded women kept up this steady attitude of disapproval without ever relaxing, and as a result Kenneth, a warm-hearted but not strong-minded boy, found his love for his father opposed to the admiration and fear he felt for his mother and sisters, and the affection was defeated, and forced to take refuge in his secret heart. He had kept in fairly close touch with his father since the old man had scandalized St Alberics twenty years ago by leaving home for no apparent reason. He usually knew where old Mr Fielding was, and what his latest plans were, and whether his health was good or bad, and sometimes he ran up to town for a week-end and visited, in company with his father, one or two of the night clubs the old man had promoted.

It may here be pointed out that there are night clubs and night clubs; there are the orchids of the night world and its deadly nightshades, and there are its gay pink camellias, sophisticated yet cheerful, scentless and shallowhearted yet immediately pleasing to the man in the street. It was in the pink camellia class that the night clubs promoted by Mr Fielding belonged; if you had to have night clubs, his were the best kind to have. Innocence we do not claim for them, nor spirituality, nor depth (whatever that may mean), but only an ass would look for those qualities in a night club, and they had gaiety and elegance, chic rather than chi-chi, and no one shot themselves or took drugs in their precincts. Mr Fielding wanted people to enjoy the world they lived in. He, like God, found it good; he still found it good at seventy-eight, although its deeper joys had evaded him (his family would have said that he had evaded them) and as he had no taste or talent for improving minds or organizing bodies, he concentrated his gaiety, his sociability, his taste in wines and his love of women and pink lights, on the twenty-four square feet of parquet and the fifty little tables of the night club, and there, miniature and attractive, he let them sparkle.

Kenneth was embarrassed because he sympathized with his father, who had not been inside his old home for twenty years and must be feeling pretty bad. But affection does not necessarily bestow insight upon the person who feels it, and therefore Kenneth was distinctly shocked when his father roused himself, turned with a genuinely cheerful smile to Miss Fielding and said:

'Well, Connie! I congratulate you. A delightful evening—I never remember the house being so cheerful.'

'Yes, the atmosphere of Sunglades is very changed,' replied Miss Fielding sombrely, and Miss Burton, who now glided in to make her good nights, chimed in with something about 'the old gracious ways being gone for ever.' No one could make out whether this applied to Sunglades or the world in general, and she said good night to them all rather effusively, anxious to show that she was on everybody's side and understood everybody's point of view. When she had glided away, Mr Fielding resumed his congratulations.

'It's delightful to see so many pretty faces. That Arkwright girl is very well turned out. And your little companion with the unpronounceable name is charming. As for Betty—well, Betty always was a favourite of mine and she gets prettier every time I see her. I do think,' he went on in a plaintive humorous tone, 'that some of you girls might have looked a little older. But none of you have changed at all. You all look as young as you did the last time I saw you. You're looking very well too, Kenneth.'

'Thank you, Father. That's the Home Guard. Soldiering always did suit me.'

'Ah, yes, of course.' Mr Fielding looked vague, as he always did when anything to do with the war was mentioned. 'How do you come to have the house so full, Constance? and where are all your foreign friends? I made sure the place would be full of them. A splendid opportunity for you!'

Miss Fielding replied shortly that most of them were lecturing in America.

'But England is still full of foreigners,' said Mr Fielding. 'When you told me in your letter that the house was full, I made sure that you meant full of refugees.'

His goaded daughter replied still more shortly that she had had evacuees billeted on her for eighteen months and this had given her more than enough to do.

'No doubt you intend to extend hospitality to refugees at a later date,' suggested Mr Fielding.

'I don't think so, Father. The difficulties of catering and shopping nowadays are almost insuperable; I assure you I have my hands full from the moment I get up until the moment I go to bed.'

'Ah well, I wouldn't know,' laughed Mr Fielding. 'One isn't bothered with that sort of thing in hotels.'

'One is fortunate,' put in Mrs Miles loudly.

'If you stay at an hotel where they've known you for years, it is possible to live quite comfortably,' pursued Mr Fielding. 'There is occasionally a limited choice of fish, but only occasionally. Even the question of alcohol; I hear people complaining of a shortage, but I must say that personally I have always been able to obtain what I wanted. When it is a question of obtaining supplies for licensed premises, of course, there *are* difficulties,' admitted Mr Fielding handsomely. 'However, like most difficulties, they can be overcome by money and tact.'

They were listening to him in silence, and while Joan and Constance were looking down their noses, Kenneth was looking sulky. His father had spoken of Constance's letter. Then the girls *had* known the old boy was coming! Why the blazes hadn't they told him? It was absurd. They all treated him as if he were still a schoolboy; even his father had written to Constance instead of to him. He was glad to have the old boy here, and would have liked to have gone to the station to meet him. Never heard of anything so extraordinary, Father creeping into the scullery like a parachutist, he thought. But then of course that's just what he would enjoy. I wonder just how hard up he is? He must be cleaned out or he'd never have come here.

The clock on the mantelpiece softly chimed twelve, and Mr Fielding yawned and stood up.

'Merry Christmas!' he said cheerfully, smiling round on the glum faces of his three children. 'I will go to bed, I think, Constance, if you will excuse me.'

'Of course, Father. You must be tired.' Miss Fielding spoke more kindly than she usually did to her father: the most upright and sensible of persons is softened by the chime of midnight on Christmas Eve. 'You're in Richard's room—your old room—on the Kumfi-Slepe.'

'Excellent; Kenneth can help me move it into his room,' said Mr Fielding briskly. 'I sleep very little as I get older and am usually awake by five o'clock. I want a word with you, Kenneth, and if we are sharing a room we can talk more easily; I don't expect there will be much chance to-morrow, Christmas Day is always a busy time. Are you having anyone in?' to Miss Fielding.

'Father, you can't begin moving furniture at this time of night,' said Miss Fielding firmly. 'No, I am *not* having anyone in. Mrs Archer, my help from the village, very tiresomely refused to work on Christmas Day, and——'

'I meant friends; people; a party,' interrupted her father. They were all moving towards the door. 'Oh, nonsense, Kenneth and I will do the whole thing in ten minutes.'

'You will awaken Betty,' warned Mrs Miles, not wishing to refer to Betty in her bed, but feeling painfully certain that Mr Fielding would be deterred from making a noise by the picture thus painted.

'Ah! Little Betty!' said Mr Fielding, with his head on one side and only too plainly visualizing Betty nestling into her pillow. 'No, we'll be as quiet as mice. Come, Ken, let's get it over.'

And he ran up the stairs.

Richard was just falling asleep. The door opened, a broad ray of light came across the room onto his face, and a voice said, not in a whisper:

'Ah, just as well we are going to move it. Surely you all remember I can't sleep with my head to the east? and it gets worse as I get older. I'll take the bedding, Kenneth, and you take the bed. I'd better put on the light.'

Richard slowly opened his eyes and expressionlessly surveyed the fatigue party. Kenneth grinned at him as his father went out of the room with an armful of bedding. Do that young prig good to be shaken up a bit—though he has been ill, poor blighter, he thought. Mr Fielding nodded pleasantly at Richard as he went.

It must be wonderfully restful never to think about other people's comfort or feelings, reflected Richard.

'Sorry to disturb you, my boy,' said Mr Fielding, coming back for pillows. 'We shan't be a minute.'

'That's all right,' Richard answered mildly: as so often happened, his scientific interest in people's behaviour had conquered his indignation at its peculiarity. I should have been a biologist, not an economist, he thought.

Bump, bump, scrape, bump, scrape, went the Kumfi-Slepe across the landing.

'Oh dear, is it a raid?' called Miss Burton's voice dismally from upstairs on her landing. 'Whatever is the matter?'

On being told that it was only Kenneth and Father moving the Kumfi-Slepe into Kenneth's room, she returned to her bed, and the household gradually settled down for the night. If Kenneth had seemed surprisingly calm over his father's announced intention of having an important talk with him in the small hours, it was because he knew his father's habits: Mr Fielding's belief that he was a light sleeper needing less sleep as he grew older was not supported by facts. He fell asleep at once like a baby and did not awaken until half-past eight on Christmas morning.

20

Vartouhi awoke at seven o'clock as usual, for it was to be a very busy day for her. She cheerfully said her prayers, as she always did now, ever since she had first felt so grateful to God for her pretty bedroom. They were an inaccurate version of the formal sentences of praise that she had heard her older relatives use, and this morning she repeated them with even less fervour than usual because she was wondering, and had been from the moment she opened her eyes, what her present from Mr Fielding was going to be.

Then she went downstairs into the warm dark house and made tea for everybody and took it into their bedrooms. The moon and stars were still shining and the ground was covered with glittering grey frost. She found Richard awake and reading, and he declined his tea and said he would come down and help her get the breakfast, which he did, while she examined the pastry and other things that she had prepared yesterday, and made an exotic stuffing for the two chickens which were to be eaten for the Christmas dinner.

'Avrybody is old in this house except you and me, Rich-ard,' she suddenly remarked while they were setting the breakfast.

'My mother is only forty-five,' he answered, wondering what was coming next and thinking how delightful it was to be alone with her like this, engaged in the ancient and simple tasks of boiling water and toasting bread, before anyone else was up.

'Is vary pratty, your mother. Is kind also, too. She gave me a drass with flowers on, all silk. Is too long for me but I sew it up. In my country the women with old sons like you, Rich-ard, would be old too also, and all wrinkle.'

'Yes, I think my mother is pretty, too.'

'You love her?'

'Very much,' he said, smiling down at her.

'How old Mr Fielding is?' she suddenly asked, arranging cups on the table.

'Old Mr Fielding? Seventy-eight, so I am told.'

'*Young* Mr Fielding.'

'Oh—forty-seven or forty-eight, I should think.'

'Is old, forty-seven,' she murmured. 'Rich-ard, will you make toast? I make porridge.'

'Right you are.'

Just before nine o'clock the older members of the party began to come downstairs and express mild surprise at Richard's being out of his bed and domestically employed. I hope he hasn't been *proposing* to her, thought Betty uneasily, gazing out of the window with a tranquil face at the pale Christmas roses in the still dusky garden.

At breakfast Vartouhi was busy helping to pass porridge bowls and make more toast, and hand milk and people's sugar ration, but all the time she was wondering what her present would be, and whether she would have any time in the evening to work at her bedspread. She glanced round the breakfast table and hoped that to-day would be as cheerful as yesterday evening had been. Mrs Miles and Miss Fielding were talking loudly about war savings. and the old Fielding and Mrs Marten, who were sitting next to each other, were laughing over a funny joke. Only the young Mr Fielding and Rich-ard were not talking. Both of them were looking at her, and as she slowly moved her gaze from Rich-ard's face to the young Mr Fielding's, they both smiled. Is a good thing to have two men smiling at you, thought Vartouhi, and jumped up and began to collect the plates.

She was very busy all the morning, basting chickens and boiling potatoes and anxiously filling up the bubbling water in the pot where that pudding was boiling away; that pudding which must be holy, since the young Mr Fielding had been cross about it with his sister, and said that they must have one, no matter what the difficulties were, since Christmas would not be Christmas without it. So many many things had gone into it! and it had a dark, rich, holy look like the inside of the great church at Ser which was now an anti-God museum. Miss Fielding and her sister walked all over the house shouting at each other about their families and the war all the morning, and the young Mr Fielding went out to march with his soldiers, and Mrs Marten made the old Fielding go to church, still laughing, and Rich-ard helped her to do the brussels sprouts.

Just before the chickens were put on their dish, while everybody else was listening to the one o'clock news, Richard came over to her where she stood at the sink, dishing up potatoes, and said nervously:

'Vartouhi.'

'You speak as if you would touch my hand, Rich-ard,' said Vartouhi instantly, not taking her eyes off the potatoes. 'I am busy with these potatoes. Go away from me.'

'No, I don't mean that, really, it's only that I've got a little present for you—not much, only I hope you'll like it——'

Down went the potato saucepan, and Vartouhi turned round with a smiling, delighted face.

'A present for me! Oh, Rich-ard, thank you! What is?'

'Well, it's—open it, and see,' and he held out a pretty little box covered with gilt sprigs of mistletoe and tied with green ribbon.

'So pratty!' murmured Vartouhi, and wiped her little damp hands on her overall before she began to untie the ribbon.

'Vartouhi! Vartouhi! It's ten past one and we're all starving!' came a distant roar from the hall, and footsteps were heard approaching.

Richard darted to the door and went out to face Miss Fielding.

'The pudding boiled dry but it's all right. It'll be ready in ten minutes,' he assured her, and managed to get rid of her.

When he turned back into the kitchen, Vartouhi, with a dreamy smile of delight, was holding his present up to the light. It was a bracelet of airy elegant links of chased silver, set with pale green stones that deepened to blue as the light changed, and fastened by a tiny safety catch.

'Is lovely!' Vartouhi was murmuring. 'Is *so* pratty. Never have I seen such a pratty thing, Rich-ard. How good and kind you are!' And she lifted a glowing face to smile at him.

Richard, who had never touched her, lost his head, and the next instant had her in his arms. But he kissed her only once on the mouth before he instantly let his arms fall at his sides and said unsteadily:

'I'm awfully sorry, but you looked so lovely.'

Vartouhi did not seem very cross. She had struggled a little in his arms, but she was smiling, though surprised, as he stepped back, and she lifted the bracelet to the light once more so that the colour of the stones changed. She gave him a sidelong look out of her long eyes.

'Is the first time anny man has kiss me,' murmured Vartouhi, smiling still.

Richard put his hand to his forehead and said a little wildly:
'Vartouhi, will you marry me?'

His mother, whose suspicions about his state of mind had been steadily deepening all the morning, opened the kitchen door in time to hear the end of Vartouhi's answer, which was partly muffled by giggles:

'No, no, Rich-ard, because you have no money and I do not like it when you kiss me!'

'But——' he was beginning desperately, then turned and saw his mother standing there.

'Darling, do you want any help?' she asked gaily. And because it was so plain that he did, and because she was unable, as all mothers are at the long last, to give the help he needed, she could not bear the look on his face and went on in the lightest possible tone, 'we're all starving and I've had rather a wearing morning of it with the Night Club King; if I *could* strain the sprouts for a change——'

'Of course; we'll be glad of any help, shan't we, Vartouhi?' he said at once, turning to the stove and beginning to move saucepans about while he recovered himself.

'Look what he give me!' said Vartouhi gaily, holding up the bracelet.

'How charming, do let me look,' said Betty, who knew how little money Richard had and guessed that this—though it was not expensive—had taken most of his latest cheque from America. As she murmured graciously over the bracelet, she felt really angry with this shallow, cruel little girl, and full of pain for Richard. It was as if he were a little boy again, suffering the miseries that even happy children must endure, and she suffering for him and with him but powerless to help. She handed the bracelet back to Vartouhi with a smile, but for the moment she *could not* say anything pleasant.

'Ah! May I come in? All hands to the pumps!' exclaimed a cheerful voice, and Mr Fielding advanced upon the trio. Betty and Richard, who would have been equally pleased to see a rattlesnake at that moment, summoned every civilized quality they possessed to deal with the situation, and soon the kitchen resounded with jokes about puddings and the voices of Miss Fielding and Mrs Miles, who could no longer be kept from their food. Amid general gaiety, the Christmas dinner was dished up and carried into the dining-room. The bracelet sparkled upon Vartouhi's slim sallow wrist, and every eye in the room was immediately riveted upon it, and everybody wondered what had been happening. Such are the pleasures of conducting a courtship in a house full of people.

So far, Christmas Day has been most happy, thought Vartouhi, rolling up her sleeves the better to display her jewel. All is gay and cheerful, and after all this dark holy pudding tastes good to eat.

The old Fielding, whose place I sat next to his son, has moved himself to sit by Mrs Marten. Miss Fielding and Mrs Miles have noticed this. Ah! here is young Mr Fielding. This evening when we have presents from that strange little tree with the toys on it I shall have my other present. And a English man has asked me to be his wife! I will write a letter to Yania in the United States of America to tell her this. But I like better to have presents than to be asked to be a man's wife. You can be only one wife but you can have many presents.

After dinner, Richard excused himself on the plea of needing exercise after all that food, and hurried out on a long walk over the freezing countryside; past cottages with lights already burning in their windows as the dim December light began to fail, and along lonely lanes where the only colour was an occasional dark green holly or russet mass of lingering beech leaves. The sky was lowering and almost motionless and the peculiar hush that belongs to Christmas Day was in the air. The pure scent of cold leaves and moss and the subdued colours and the silence, broken only by the occasional solitary whistle of a robin, calmed him after he had been walking for some time and he was able to think, rather than only to feel.

He realized that he had put the happiness of both their lives in danger, simply by asking her to marry him, because he had been momentarily overcome by his longing to have her beauty and gaiety and charm always with him, and he soberly thanked Heaven that she had refused him. But below the congratulations which his reason uttered, there was an increasing pain, which became almost unendurable as he repeated over and over again to himself her devilishly cruel words. The fact that she had refused him began to dominate his thoughts. It was all over. He had asked, and he was not to have his heart's desire. For weeks he had, without knowing it, clung to hope because he had never put his hope to the test: he had kept on telling himself that it would be idiotic to propose to her, in case she said 'yes'; that they would never hit it off together; that he might find himself bound for life in one of those horrible yet fascinating bondages of the spirit which only the death of the sufferers can destroy; and then again he thought it might be all right because he loved her so wildly and he could not, he knew from experience, love what was wholly bad. And all these questionings and doubts had been a waste of energy, that energy which meant so much to him because he was not strong, because she had refused him instantly, without a thought, as mercilessly as a child.

He gave a kind of groan, and stopped in his frantic stride, gazing about him. He was in a lane enclosed by tall leafless hedges and occasional groups of large old elms. The quiet grey sky was beginning to get dark and the distant woods across the fields looked clear, as they do when rain is coming. I'd better get back, he thought, recognizing that he was some four miles from home, and he turned round and began to retrace his steps, more slowly now, for he was very tired.

Vartouhi found time in the afternoon to work on her bedspread in Miss Burton's sitting-room while the latter enjoyed a refreshing sleep. Half of the older members of the party did the same; and Mr Fielding both had his cake and ate it, for he not only got Kenneth alone for ten minutes in the morning-room after dinner and borrowed five hundred pounds from him but also fell sweetly asleep in front of the drawing-room fire for an hour and a half, and awoke at half-past four demanding tea and the whereabouts of Betty just as the trolley was wheeled into the room by Vartouhi, with Betty (whose thoughts were away with Richard) following it. When they had been at tea for about ten minutes Richard came in, looking unusually pale but otherwise as usual, and Vartouhi, with a smile and a coquettish little movement of her head, offered him the hot toast.

Is not so gay as everything was at dinner, thought Vartouhi, eating her own toast and letting her long brown eyes wander lazily from one face to another. The old Fielding is even more gay but Mr Fielding is silent (how I hope he has not broken it, my present) and Miss Fielding and Mrs Miles are cross at something. The old Fielding sits with Mrs Marten and looks at her and laughs but her heart is full of fear because Rich-ard has been out walking on this cold day because he is sad because I say I am not to be his wife, and she is afraid he will have another illness. How I wish it was time to put all the lights on and play the music and have the presents from that little tree!

She encourages him, thought Miss Fielding, carefully not looking at her father and Betty. Giggling at everything he says in that silly way, thought Mrs Miles. It would be perfectly easy for her to choke him off, goodness knows she's had enough experience, thought Miss Fielding. I wonder she isn't ashamed, in front of Richard, thought Mrs Miles. Surely he can't mean to——? thought Miss Fielding. At his age——? thought Mrs Miles. No dignity, thought both sisters together.

After tea there was a diversion caused by Henry, Mrs Miles's husband, who telephoned to say that he feared there was now no hope of his getting away over the holiday at all. Everybody had forgotten about him, and such was the intensity of their personal preoccupations that most of them even experienced a momentary difficulty in remembering who he was, but they all expressed hearty regrets which Mrs Miles boomed at him down the telephone. Miss Fielding was so relieved that he could not come that she insisted on telling him herself how sorry she was. Mrs Miles was glad too, for he wasn't very happy and that made him rather a nuisance to people who thought that they were.

Everybody was cheered by the putting up of the black-out and the lighting of all the lamps once more. The pink and silver and white chrysanthemums gleamed, the pearly moons of the lamps floated in the golden air. Mr Fielding switched on the radio, as he would call it, and the house became full of loud gay music and there was much making of cold chicken sandwiches and preparing of coffee. Will this day never end? thought Richard, shutting his eyes for a moment as he lingered in the kitchen.

'Headache?' inquired a voice heartily at his elbow; he opened them and looked down into the friendly face of old Mr Fielding, peering up at him like one of the dwarfs in *Snow White*. 'I've got some things upstairs that'll get rid of that for you in ten seconds; wonderful things; man I know in New York sends them over for me.'

'That's extremely good of you; thank you very much,' said Richard with real gratitude, but hoping that he was not going to have to deal with the additional burden of Mr Fielding's sympathy. And he hadn't a headache anyway.

The wonderful things were pale green and as large as a thumbnail and he failed to swallow them adequately and the resultant taste was vile beyond belief; nevertheless, in ten seconds he certainly felt 'better,' if a sparkling inner indifference to everybody, as if he were looking down on them from the star Arcturus, could be described as 'better.'

This passage between the old gentleman and the young one had been observed with dismay by Miss Fielding and Mrs Miles as they stalked between the kitchen and the drawing-room with trays. Trying to get round Richard now, thought Mrs Miles. Making up to her son, thought Miss Fielding. Everything has gone wrong ever since he came into the house, thought Mrs Miles. Nothing seems to have gone right since he came, thought Miss Fielding. Richard is upset about something and what is the matter with Kenneth, and Betty is worried too, and why did Richard want to give Vartouhi a bracelet? Surely there can't be any nonsense going on *there*? they thought together.

I shall hear all about it after everyone has gone to bed, thought

Miss Burton, who had spent an interesting ten minutes earlier in the day questioning Vartouhi, with apparent idleness, about her bracelet. She had *not* been rewarded by a complete confession, for Vartouhi could still assume the polite reserve of her nation whenever she wanted to, but she had put two and two together, and made them into a romance. She looked in smiling silence at the girl for a moment, then patted her hand and turned away. No, she doesn't suspect anything yet, I'm sure, was Miss Burton's curious reflection. Dear old boy, I do hope it comes off.

After the coffee and chicken sandwiches had been partaken of, with many amusing anecdotes from old Mr Fielding and with laughter from everybody except his two daughters, Kenneth announced that it was time to 'have the tree.'

Everybody stood up, and Kenneth and Richard carried the table on which the tree stood over to the fireplace. It was a well-shaped little tree, decorated with pink and green balls and little houses and fantastic birds made from fairy-glass, as the children call it. These toys had been carefully preserved by Miss Burton from the days when Mrs Miles's children had been young enough to enjoy a Christmas tree, and every year she brought them out and decorated the tree with them. Usually this custom was looked upon by her cousins with mild amusement, but this year, as the strangely heart-stirring little tree was set down in front of the fire, and its blue and silver and gold decorations tinkled themselves into glittering stillness once more, Kenneth looked across at her and said with a smile:

'A good thing you've always saved the decorations, Frankie, there aren't any to be had this year.'

'I always knew a time like this would come,' answered Miss Burton, and then Kenneth began to give out the presents and cries of 'Just what I wanted!' began to sound in all their falseness upon the festal air.

Richard was watching Vartouhi. The icy sparkle, as from Arcturus, that had temporarily relieved his pain was beginning to subside, leaving him just reckless enough not to care if people noticed or not that he was watching her. Her hands were clasped like a waiting child's, and her bright eyes were fixed upon the heap of presents round the tree. All the household had remembered her; Miss Fielding had presented her with a small picture of some green spirits with no legs in a passe-partout frame; Miss Burton had sewn her a scarf from three broad brilliant ribbons with fringe at the ends, and even Mrs Miles had produced, evidently from some emergency store, a little bag full of rather stuffy lavender.

She received all these gifts with her usual polite curtsy and smile, but it was painfully clear to Richard that all her interest was concentrated upon the large parcel addressed to her in Kenneth's writing, which he had left until last.

Oh, my darling, don't look at her like that, thought his mother, glancing at him above the heap of presents that was slowly collecting in her own arms; she isn't worth it. As if that ever made any difference!

At last Kenneth took up the parcel and held it out. 'Vartouhi,' he said, smiling at her across the circle.

Everyone was watching, for this was the last present to be delivered.

'Oh thank you, thank you, Mr Fielding,' said Vartouhi, dropping a very low curtsy, and then, while Miss Fielding and Mrs Miles were still apprehensively regarding the size and obvious opulence of the parcel, she began with flushed face and sparkling eyes to undo it.

Everyone was quiet. What a pity he didn't give it her while we were all busy with our presents, thought Miss Burton, but of course he's so inexperienced.

Vartouhi exclaimed with delight as the wrappings fell away from a long golden box. She opened it, loosened some gold ribbons, and slowly took out a bottle of cut glass decorated with gilt scrolls and flowers and containing a pint of White Rose scent. The extravagance of it dumbfounded everybody for a minute; even such spiritual beings as Miss Fielding knew what a pint of White Rose scent, in a bottle and a box like that, must cost in war time.

'Is scent!' cried Vartouhi, holding it up for everybody to see, as though their eyes were not fixed upon it already. 'Never before I have had scent! Oh thank you, thank you——'

'What a lucky girl,' interrupted Mrs Miles, 'just as if there were no war.'

'Glad you like it,' muttered Kenneth. He glanced at the clock. 'Want to hear the news, Connie? It's just on nine.'

'Yes, Kenneth, I think we will to-night,' said his sister in a repressive tone, as if they all needed pulling back from an orgy of scent bottles and fun to the grim present; and he turned on the wireless.

The rest of the evening passed quietly. Richard sat exhaustedly behind a book and dozed off and awoke at intervals, and Betty and Kenneth joined the two more frivolous members of the elderly quartet at Bridge. Vartouhi had retreated with her loot upstairs. Miss Fielding and Mrs Miles sat in front of the fire, the one with some tapestry and the other with some horrible civilian knitting, and worked in silence. Occasionally, at some frivolous remark from Mr Fielding and a giggle from Betty, they glanced at one another or compressed their lips, but their minds were now seething over the bottle of scent and they could think of nothing else. What could Kenneth have been thinking of? Wasting all that money on a little refugee! Whatever would everybody think? It was only too plain what everybody would think. And Vartouhi too, sly little thing. She must have been making up to him all this time while I thought he was being silly over Betty, thought Miss Fielding. Poor Constance has been taken in *on all sides*, thought Mrs Miles.

The house is full of women with designs on Father and Kenneth; it's too dreadful. How could she have let things come to such a pass? It is a pity I can't spare the time to stay here for a week or two; I'd soon have them out of it.

Her sister was quite silent until bedtime. She was trying to think of a convincing pretext for dismissing Vartouhi.

211

21

Miss Fielding was so used to confiding her difficulties to Miss Burton that she did so on this occasion, sweeping into her bedroom with a torch at half-past six in the blacked-out morning and frightening her very much and asking her if she thought there was any nonsense going on between Kenneth and Vartouhi?

Miss Burton, half-asleep, yet had sufficient command of herself to say stoutly that she was sure there was not. It was Richard who was sweet on Vartouhi, not Kenneth. Constance knew how silly Kenneth had always been over a pretty face and how easily he was upset if anyone was in trouble. He had only meant to be kind to Vartouhi because her country was occupied, and she was a refugee and all that.

'But seven guineas! Joan says that scent couldn't have cost a penny under seven guineas, Frances!'

The Usurper said airily that Ken probably knew a man in the scent business who let him have it cheap.

'Just like Father, he always knows men who let him have things cheap,' put in Miss Fielding gloomily. 'In *every way*, Ken is even more like Father than I feared. And then there's Betty and Father! He hardly left her side all day yesterday! And Father has borrowed an enormous sum of money from Kenneth; five hundred pounds! Imagine! Joan and I suspected something was up and we got it out of Ken last night after you'd all gone up to bed.'

Poor Ken, thought Miss Burton.

'What does Uncle Eustace want it for?' she asked, lying back on her pillows and gazing up at Miss Fielding's large troubled face by the light of the bedside lamp.

'Need you ask? He has an idea for another night club. Apparently they aren't so easy to run nowadays with all these restrictions (and a very good thing too) and he has lost a great deal of money lately.'

'How long is he going to stay?' asked Miss Burton.

Miss Fielding's face became less troubled.

'Well, he said something about leaving us after the holiday. That's one good thing; apparently he won't be here for long. But the harm is done! He has got five hundred pounds out of Kenneth, and goodness only knows what will happen with Betty—I dare not think!'

Why not? thought The Usurper, but Miss Burton thought that it was better not to say it aloud.

'And Betty does *nothing* to discourage him!' burst out her cousin, 'it's positively indecent, at their age! And Richard giving presents to Vartouhi, and all the time she must have been sucking up to Kenneth behind our backs—really, I don't know what the house is coming to—it's like—a—like a *farmyard*!'

'Oh really, Connie, I think you're making too much fuss about it,' said Miss Burton very daringly. 'Everybody naturally feels friendlier at Christmas and you know Kenneth and Uncle Eustace always have been—er—attracted to the opposite sex' (*women*, thought The Usurper scathingly). 'They don't mean anything by it. After all, Vartouhi doesn't encourage Richard, and he really behaved very well yesterday, poor boy: I'm sure he proposed to her and was turned down; he looked so odd at dinner.'

'Then it was very silly of him, and even sillier of her to lose a good chance,' said Miss Fielding crushingly. '*I* thought Kenneth was so glum because Father was carrying on with Betty, but I suppose, if what you say is true, he was glum because he was jealous of Richard carrying on with Vartouhi. Jealous of *Richard*! At his age! Disgusting!'

'I don't think anybody is jealous of anybody,' said Miss Burton, determined not to let her go from the room with all these suspicions still in her mind. 'It's all much—much lighter than you think, Constance. I'm afraid it's Joan who has made you take such an exaggerated view.'

'Joan is worried, naturally, Frances.'

'Joan is overworked and needs a good rest,' retorted Miss Burton and The Usurper thought, So does Big Ben. 'Couldn't you and she agree not to talk any more about it to-day?'

'Impossible,' said Miss Fielding, getting up. But she looked less worried, and at the door she paused and said, looking back at her cousin curled like a mouse in the large bed, 'Of course, it would be very awkward to have to get rid of Vartouhi. She really suits us very well and before this affair I quite liked her, quaint little thing. I don't *want* to have to sack her.'

'I hope you won't, Connie,' said Miss Burton earnestly, raising herself on her elbow, 'you know we were both getting quite worn out with the work before she came and you don't want us to be landed with any more evacuees, do you?'

'Well, I will see; you may be right,' and Miss Fielding tramped downstairs again to her own room.

Love—thought Miss Burton, lying on her side and staring at the Christmas roses on her bedside table. And she tried to have some beautiful thoughts about Love, but really, all she could think of was how much she wished they had three good maids again and the war was over and it was possible to buy a chicken for lunch if you wanted one, and then she was shocked to find herself thinking that Love was only one more nuisance to deal with. So she got out of bed and began to get up.

I will keep them all busy rehearsing *Little Frimdl* to-day, thought Miss Fielding, as she coiled and pinned her hair, and that will keep them under my eye. I will *not* have a repetition of yesterday, with Father and Betty in each other's pockets all day and Richard getting up before it was light to hang round Vartouhi in the kitchen, and then going off in that peculiar way after lunch without saying a word to anybody. Betty *can't* want him to marry a little foreigner who isn't much better than a servant. I shall speak to her about it to-day—if I can get her to attend to anything else but *her own affairs*—and if she hasn't noticed anything, I shall tell her straight out what's going on. It's most peculiar; *I* never noticed that Richard was mooning after Vartouhi. Perhaps Frances is imagining the whole thing. But I must say she's always been right about that sort of thing before. Only I don't take any notice of what she says about Betty and Father. Of course there's something in it. I suppose I can believe my own eyes. It's simply that Frances is fond of Betty and so she makes excuses for her. And as soon as the holiday is over I will see about getting rid of Father, and Betty and Richard too. And Vartouhi as well, if Kenneth doesn't pull himself together. Oh dear, oh dear, why must people make such fools of themselves and upset everything? Thank goodness I was never that way myself, and Joan was always most sensible, even when she was engaged.

The fact is, Sex is a Destructive Force, more often than not used by the Evil Principle for its own ends, and I will not have it rampant and unchecked in my beautiful home where Our Mother spent her last years.

Such were the plans of Miss Fielding for Boxing Day. But (as in a 'whodunit' in which the house party is cut off from the rest of the world by a snowstorm and everybody is plotting against everybody else) the other members of the party also had their plans; and when she announced playfully yet firmly at breakfast that to-day presented the perfect opportunity for getting in two good long rehearsals of *Little Frimdl*, she was annoyed to be greeted by a series of rebellious murmurs; Richard was going to spend the day in town with friends; Kenneth proposed, as it was not raining, to do some digging and tidy the greenhouse; Betty murmured something about writing letters and mending; and even Vartouhi said that she was going to sew on the beautiful thing. Miss Burton said nothing, but Miss Fielding knew from experience how *she* could slip away to nowhere just when you wanted her. The only support for her plan came from Mrs Miles, who announced in a solitary bellow, of course, what a grand idea, and from Mr Fielding, who was always ready to talk and bustle about. *His* support was rather disconcerting, for he was very out of favour with Miss Fielding and her manner towards him throughout breakfast had been markedly grave.

The fact was that the more sensitive members of the party had not yet recovered from the shocks of yesterday, and felt the need of solitude and reflection to restore their composure. Kenneth had been made to feel his imprudence in lending his father such a large sum of money; both his sisters had pointed out that doubtless this was the Beginning of It and the Thin End of the Wedge, and so on, and these prophecies had strengthened his own sense of recklessness and guilt. In these times! when unearned incomes were dwindling steadily beneath the pressure of unforeseen circumstances and Income Tax! Lending money to promote a night club! He must be mad!

He had not dared to tell them that it was to be called The Last Banana.

He had slept badly because he was worried, and this morning he wanted to get away from everybody and work in the garden; with the dark wet winter earth and the bundles of bast and the flower pots and seedling boxes, moving them about and re-arranging them in the quiet of the December day until he had soothed himself into his usual state of mind.

Richard had decided that another day like yesterday would— would give an importance to their little group that would be false when compared with what was happening in Europe, and so he was simply going to run away; to know when to do this, and not to feel ashamed of doing it, was a famous conserver of energy, he had always found.

As for Betty, she was wishing it was time to go back to work, because the holiday was being both dull and full of anxiety for her; and old Mr Fielding, beside her at the breakfast table, was planning to sit over the drawing-room fire with her for most of the day, smoking and laughing and gossiping.

In the face of so much quiet but steady opposition, Miss Fielding found it impossible to press her plan and she got up from the breakfast table in a bad temper. Vartouhi, who was more fortunate than she realized in having a fixed programme of work to occupy her day, immediately began to clear the table, and the others dispersed upon their own affairs.

'Betty——' said Miss Fielding ten minutes later, opening Betty's door—'are you there? I want to speak to you—oh, now *why* are you making your bed? Vartouhi can easily do it.'

'I thought I might as well. I don't mind, really.'

Miss Fielding shut the door and sat down upon the dressing-stool. Betty went on making the bed. Surely she can't be going to tackle me about the Night Club King? she thought incredulously—though I wouldn't put it past her. Anybody would think I enjoyed having the poor old sweet dancing round me, instead of praying for nightfall.

'Do you realize that Richard is—er—is very attracted to Vartouhi?' began Miss Fielding abruptly.

Betty looked at her across the bed, as she sat firmly on the dressing-stool, fresh and neat in her good dark woollen dress, with her lips pressed purposefully together, and thought what an interfering bosser she was. Betty was also (as at most of the 'scenes' and 'good long talks' at which she had unwillingly assisted) conscious of a strong desire to giggle. But she was also determined to protect her son.

'Oh—is he?' she said mildly. 'I know he likes flirting with her, of course; anybody can see that, but I don't think it's serious.'

'He proposed to her yesterday,' said Miss Fielding solemnly.

'*Did* he? How *thrilling*! How do you know?'

'I don't know for a fact, but Frances had her eye on the two of them all day and she is sure he did,' said Miss Fielding, taken aback by this girlish flutter of interest.

'Frances is a romantic old goose,' said Betty, straightening the eiderdown. 'She loves that sort of thing.'

'All the same, she is usually right, Betty. And I do feel that you ought——' Miss Fielding paused, anxious to choose words which should have a strong effect—'you ought to take a very serious view of the matter,' ended Miss Fielding.

Betty, also choosing her words, rejected the 'Why?' that rose to her lips and replied soothingly:

'I will, Connie. Thanks awfully for telling me.'

'But you don't!' exclaimed Miss Fielding, suspecting not without reason that she was being soothed and resenting the fact. 'You don't seem at all upset. I cannot make you out, Betty. Now if *I* had an only son, who was delicate and clever (at least, some people seem to think he's clever), I should be very deeply distressed at the idea of his marrying a refugee, a foreigner, a girl who may be pretty, but who isn't much better than a servant. Besides,' Miss Fielding went on dropping her voice a couple of notes and looking meaningly at Betty across the bed, 'that sort of thing . . . you never know where it may lead, and we don't know what Vartouhi's morals are.'

'Possibly not, but I know what Richard's are,' said Betty, beginning to feel angry.

Miss Fielding sniffed, but said nothing.

'Yes; I know that he wouldn't lead anyone astray unless they were willing,' said Betty.

'My dear!' Miss Fielding was deeply shocked. 'I should hope he wouldn't behave like that to *anyone*, whether they were willing or not! If I thought that he would, I should be very sorry to think that he had ever stayed under my roof.'

'Especially not a girl much younger than himself, an exile from her own country, with no money and hardly any friends,' Betty went on. Colour had come into her face.

'Well, I am very relieved to hear it,' said Miss Fielding, not sounding in the least relieved. 'In that case, if what you say about him is true, don't you think it is very likely that he has asked her to marry him?'

'I'm sure he hasn't,' said Betty decidedly, 'because he has no money. He can't afford to marry for years yet, until he has an academic job with a good salary. We have often discussed it,' she ended, with her prettiest smile.

'Oh, then he *does* discuss his affairs with you?' asked Miss Fielding, looking at her keenly.

'Oh yes. *Everything*. Ever since he was tiny,' lied his mother.

'And has he talked to you about Vartouhi?'

'Oh yes, quite openly. He thinks she's a charming little thing (which she is, of course) but nothing more. I'm sure there's nothing to worry about, Connie. It's very kind of you to bother about Richard, but he can take care of himself.'

'Oh well, so long as you're satisfied,' said Miss Fielding, getting up from the dressing-stool and marching towards the door. 'I still think you're taking it too lightly but of course you never *did* worry about anything, did you? even as a girl.'

'I'm afraid not. Awful of me.'

'Our Mother always used to say—I'm sure you won't mind my telling you this, you know her funny joky way and how she always spoke out so splendidly, just what she felt about people— "Betty is a *lightweight* in the boatrace of life."'

She got muddled with boxing, thought Betty but she only nodded and continued to look pleasantly attentive.

'And *I* always say that you care about nothing but *Richard* and *hats*!' cried Miss Fielding; laughing jovially.

'And handbags!' said Betty, laughing too.

'Well, you are very lucky *not* to worry,' said Miss Fielding, going solemn again as she felt the conversation taking a lighter tone. 'I suppose it hasn't——' she hesitated, then went on, 'I know you won't mind my saying this to you, as that old affair between you and Kenneth was so many years ago—but you haven't noticed *Kenneth* looking at Vartouhi, have you?'

'Ken? Good heavens no, Connie! What an idea!'

'But the scent—the scent, Betty! Joan says it can't have cost a penny less than seven guineas.'

'Ken's so kind; he wouldn't think about the price of a thing if he wanted to give someone pleasure,' Betty said warmly, glad to be able to say something truthful at last. 'He's sorry for her, that's all.'

'Yes—well, I *hope* so,' said Miss Fielding doubtfully, shaking her head as she went out of the door, 'but you know what a fool he's always been about a pretty face.'

And, nodding and smiling, she shut the door behind her and tramped downstairs.

Betty sat down on the bed and swore; then put some powder on her nose and went downstairs (we are sorry to say with malice in her heart) to find old Mr Fielding.

She found him in the hall, telling Richard where he could get a pre-war meal in London if he didn't mind paying for it. He did not add 'or ask where it comes from,' but Richard, looking huntedly at him, filled in this gap and was more anxious than ever to be off.

'. . . a thick juicy steak and those little button French mushrooms and plenty of onions. *And* something to wash it down with!' said Mr Fielding, all twinkling and rosy, looking up at Richard, who had four slices of Spam and half a loaf in his pockets, as iron rations to take to his friends in London.

'You surprise me,' said Richard, 'but not very much.'

'Ah ha! Well, they say you can buy anything in London and Pekin if you've got the money, and it's still true, in spite of the war. Now don't forget, my boy; the second turning on the left down Windmill Street. I shall be interested to hear how you get on—and give my love to Bebbini, he and I are old friends. Enjoy yourself! Good-bye.'

Richard blew a kiss to his mother and shut the front door.

'I've just told him where he can get a first-class feed,' said Mr Fielding to Betty. 'Hope he does; it will do him good; he's too thin for his height.'

Betty only smiled. This was usually enough; but Mr Fielding went on:

'Nice boy. I didn't like him at first, you know.'

'No?' said Betty.

'I thought that he was highbrow. But there's good stuff in him. Well—there would be—he's your son,' and he suddenly gave her an adoring smile, and patted her arm.

Oh goodness, if only it were time to go back to the Ministry, thought Betty.

Miss Fielding, happening to cross the hall at this identical moment, observed both the arm-patting and the smile.

'Let's take a turn round the garden,' suggested Mr Fielding, and Betty, still feeling revengeful but not so revengeful as she had been, went to get a coat.

In the kitchen garden, Kenneth had carefully closed the door that shut away the outside world and pulled an old hat over his eyes and turned up his coat collar and was pottering about. The day was cold and still with a veiled sun gleaming fitfully in a cloudy sky. Frost lingered on the ground under the big cabbage leaves. He went into the greenhouse and began to tidy it; untangling bast and rolling it into neat balls and arranging the flower pots in rows and sweeping down the racks and shelves with an old broom. It was very quite in there, and everything was still except the clouds moving slowly across the sun and casting their faint shadows on the ground. The warmth of two hundred summers seemed distilled in this ancient glass house, for the air was never really cold there even in the depths of winter. He had been worried enough when he came into the garden; about his father, and the loan to his father, and the anger of his sisters, and about some feelings of his own which he had not clearly thought out (for he belonged to the generation that has not the habit of telling the truth to itself about its feelings), but gradually he began to feel peaceful and soon he ceased to think about anything, and worked on in a trance of contentment, aware only of the rough surfaces of the pots and shelves as he handled them and the smell of dry earth and warm wood. He began to whistle softly.

When he had been working there for some time he saw out of the corner of his eye something moving across the garden. It was Vartouhi, carrying a white basin in which she was evidently going to gather winter spinach. He felt irritated. She'll come in here bothering, was his first uncontrollable thought, for the habits of half a century of bachelorhood are not easily broken down and, although he had been a model son and was now almost a model brother, as well as a devoted admirer of women, his life-experience of them was that they usually did bother. They were not fond of solitude and silence, and the prettier they were the more they shrank from those two pleasures, and the more (it seemed to him) did they bother. Well, it's only natural, he thought vaguely. But he pulled his hat over his eyes, as if in the hope that she might think he was somebody else.

In a moment or two she had worked her way across to the greenhouse—although it was true that the best spinach grew in a bed immediately outside it—and was busily filling her bowl, without a glance in his direction. She had on gumboots and her brilliant Bairamian scarf tied round her head like a peasant. He kept on glancing at her through the dusty panes, and presently began to wish that she would look at him. At last he opened the greenhouse door and called to her:

'Want any help?'

'No thank you, Mr Fielding,' answered Vartouhi, all smiles and sunny surprise. 'Is planty of spinach here.'

'Yes, it's done well this year; better than last year.'

She continued to fill the bowl, and he stood at the door filling his pipe (which Miss Fielding, like someone running a mansion in the 1870's, did not encourage him to smoke in the house) and watching her. He wanted her to come into the green house; he suddenly thought it would be delightful to have Vartouhi beside him in the old place that he was so fond of, and he called to her:

'Come and see how tidy I've made it.'

'Is warm in here,' said Vartouhi, stepping over the threshold with her basin balanced against her hip.

'It always is, even in cold weather. It catches all the sun; it's a regular sun trap.'

'You should have tomato in here, and grape too also,' she said, glancing round rather critically.

Now, if either of his sisters, or even Betty, had made this suggestion Kenneth would have thought, there you are, what did I tell you? Bothering, as usual. Bless them, but they do bother. But when Vartouhi uttered the words, his mind obediently did a somersault in order to retain its opinion of her, and he said heartily, 'Splendid idea! I might try it this summer. I've never tried grapes. Do you know anything about growing them?' He turned a box upside down for her and she seated herself upon it with the basin of spinach on her knees.

'Oh yas, Mr Fielding, we all have them in my country. We eat manny. You put them in the sun where it is varry hot and you give them blood to eat.'

'Oh yes, so you do. Dried blood. I remember now. By George, it sounds rather sinister, doesn't it? feeding them on blood. Where do you get it from?'

'We kill a goat or a sheep,' she said indifferently, glancing round, 'and cook him up with spice and use his blood. We eat him up for ourselves. Mr Fielding, I think grape would look pratty, *there*,' and she pointed to the whitewashed wall opposite to the door.

'Do you? Well, so do I. If I get a vine and start it off in here, will you help me look after it, Vartouhi?'

'Will be *varry* pleased, Mr Fielding! Always at home I am help with the fruits and here in England I am sad without doing it. All the girl help with the fruits in the Khar-el-Nadoon.'

'Ah, that's the place you told me about before, isn't it? The Valley of Apricots.'

'Yas. Is so pratty, Mr Fielding. All the pink flower on the tree in the spring.'

'Pink? I thought apricot blossom was white—but I suppose you might call it very pale pink.'

'Is pink in the Khar-el-Nadoon.'

'Oh. What's the soil?—I mean, when there's a spring of water, is the ground all round it a sort of red?'

'Yas. And the water taste——' Vartouhi made the gestures of one who dislikes the taste of the water and he laughed.

'That's the iron in it. I expect that's what makes the apricot blossom a deeper pink, too; it's supposed to have that effect.'

'Is pratty,' said Vartouhi, and stood up. 'Mr Fielding,' she began, and stopped.

'Yes?' His kind eyes looked at her, so betrayingly from under the brim of his old hat, but she was gazing down into the bowl of winter spinach and did not see.

'Is a beautiful, beautiful bottle of scent you give me.'

'I'm very glad you like it, Vartouhi.'

'Never have I had scent before. Nor a bracelet, too also. And now you give me scent and Rich-ard a bracelet! Is varry nice. Never have any men give me prasents except in Bairamia a man give my father a goat for me. Was rather old, too also.'

Kenneth did not laugh. He said glumly:

'Do you like the bracelet better than the scent?'

Vartouhi considered, gazing at the spinach. Then she said, lifting her eyes to his with a wicked smile:

'Soon the scent will be use up. The bracelet will not use up.'

He roared, though he was not pleased, and then he said eagerly, leaning towards her:

'Vartouhi, let me give you another bracelet, will you?'

'A necklace?' she breathed, catching his eagerness and leaning in her turn towards him with shining eyes. 'Better to have a necklace because I have a bracelet, too also.'

'Right you are, then. A necklace—the prettiest one I can find. What kind would you like?'

'All gold and bead,' said Vartouhi promptly.

'All gold and beads. Right you are.' He foresaw that a visit to any shop in one of the flashier London arcades would provide him with something to delight her heart for about two guineas, and he was relieved. If she had asked for diamonds, he would have had to get them for her, and would have done it with that exasperation and pride that is the mark of infatuation in men, but he would also have felt utterly different about her. With her childish demand for 'gold and bead' she had wrung his heart into a new tenderness and the greed on her little round face enchanted him with its innocence.

But a sobering thought now struck him.

'Er——' he began, and hesitated. How could he warn her not to let Miss Fielding see the necklace? If he did warn her it would spoil his pleasure in giving and her pleasure in receiving and make a shady secret out of a harmless little transaction. Dammit, why *should* he warn her? Why should Connie always mess everything up for him? He would defy Connie.

'Nothing,' he said, smiling and standing up. 'Well, I'm afraid I must be getting on with my work.'

'I must go, too also.' Vartouhi paused at the door and absently raised the spinach bowl onto her head, where it balanced, under Kenneth's fascinated gaze, as if it were growing there. 'Is how we carry the apricot in basket,' she explained, then went on earnestly, looking up at him, 'Mr Fielding, I shall not tell Rich-ard you will give me a necklace because he want marry me. I say, No! but he is still want, and he will see the necklace and be angry at me. Is a nuisance, Rich-ard. So I will say, my sister Yania give me this necklace from the United States of America. Is a wicked lie, you think? So the old nuns would say that teach me speak English.'

'Er—no. Not wicked,' said Kenneth, very taken aback by the news that Richard had actually proposed, and at once feeling twice as jealous and apprehensive. 'But why should you have to tell a lie at all? It isn't any of his business if I give you a necklace. You aren't engaged to him,' ended Kenneth, working himself into a righteous indignation over Richard's impudence.

'Yas, is none of his business!' echoed Vartouhi heartily, evidently relieved to have moral support. 'I will say, Mr Fielding give me this because he is kind and good and is none of your business, Rich-ard!'

'Er—yes, something of that sort. Right you are, then; I'll look out for your necklace and we'll—keep it just a secret between ourselves, shall we?'

Vartouhi nodded and went off, but outside the door she turned back. Beneath the basin still balanced on her head her little face was excited.

'Mr Fielding! I have a secret too also. Is something varry nice—but I will not tell you yet!' she said mysteriously, and hurried away.

What a dear little girl she is, he thought. Not like most women. Now, she *doesn't* bother; and he sighed as he went on with his work. To his thoughts about his father and the anger of his sisters over his loan to his father, there were now added thoughts about Richard and his proposal to Vartouhi and thoughts about his private feelings, and he no longer felt peaceful. He had decided that Vartouhi had not come bothering, and he was too loyal to admit that the result was precisely the same as if she had.

22

Richard found a room outside Blentley for twenty-five shillings a week, which sum covered his meals and baths. It was in a little new bungalow, jerry-built and decorated in shades of beige and biscuit and brown, and furnished with mass-produced furniture and crockery in mean designs. None of the inanimate objects in the house were older than three years and the combined ages of its inhabitants, Richard and his landlady and her two little boys, added up to only sixty-four years, but this did not make for gaiety and a careless youthful atmosphere, as the little boys were *very* little and unnaturally good and given to catching colds and adding unbearably to the burden already carried by their mother, who was also little, and very meek and timid and good, and only lived for the postman's daily visit which might bring a letter from Daddy away in the Middle East.

Richard had begun with the intention of having no social intercourse with his landlady, but the kind heart he had inherited from his mother and his own detached yet passionate interest in human beings as social units soon did away with that plan, and he found himself inquiring after the boys' colds and bringing home friars balsam and camphorated oil in his pockets when their mother could not leave the house, and making comforting remarks when there had been a long gap without letters from the Middle East and she went about looking like a miserable little ghost. Neither she nor her boys ever made demands on Mr Marten's time and patience: they were so polite, so patient and good and quiet, they wanted so little to make their dim, peaky faces light up, that they completely won Richard's head and heart, and slowly he began to return, with feelings of mingled

227

shame and relief, to the first love that had filled his life before he met Vartouhi—the love of ordinary, helpless people all over the world.

Romantic love had seemed to him, before he fell a victim to it himself, a sort of beautiful bane——

> *Even bees, the little almsmen of spring-bowers;*
> *Know there is richest juice in poison-flowers,*

and he had disliked the thought of it, just as he disliked a romantic attitude towards politics, and leaders, and religion. When he fell romantically in love he had therefore been surprised at himself, and this surprise helped him to keep a part of his mind detached from his own sufferings. Knowing that Vartouhi could never play an orderly part in that 'blue-print' which he had drawn up for his life, he had known that he must either try to marry her and thereafter submit to a lifelong enchantment and an unending domination of his higher impulses, or else he must run away. He had seen more than one man bound body and mind to sorceresses; women without scruples or reason, possessing the immeasurably ancient power which may be called Eve. It was a rare type nowadays, and so rare among Englishwomen as to be practically non-existent, and it was his bad luck that he should have encountered a foreigner who was dowered with Eve in excess. He knew that he had been right to run away.

If I had had more physical strength, and had been vital and ambitious, so that I was capable of dragging her along and doing my work too, I might have married her and subdued her, he sometimes thought, but I have only one lung and a vast amount of work to get through in the next fifty years and it's a bore, subduing people. And his reflections always ended with the bitter thought: *she wouldn't have me, anyway.*

But gradually, as the quiet winter days went on with their routine of work and meals and long walks, he began to feel healed. The drabness and etiolation of the little house did not get on his nerves because, in spite of his physical delicacy, his nerves were healthy and his tastes were not those of an ivory-tower dweller. His landlady liked (loved was too strong a word to use of such a dim little person) her triangular teacups and her fumed oak furniture, and to the little boys and the absent soldier-father it meant Home, and Richard was not one to shudder aesthetically over what contented ordinary people. He could escape, if he wanted to, by looking at one of the many hundreds of pictures in his memory: a garden in Spain with azure tiles set in its brown walls and its colonnade, wreathed in budding vines, opening on a pool fringed with white and yellow iris; a swelling brown field in Sussex with a mass of golden young oak trees springing out of it. He could whistle 'Tell me, fair ladies,' or murmur the verse about 'The shepherds on the lawn' from the 'Ode on the Nativity.' Kingdoms of the mind; they could not provide all that the heart desired but they could provide one kind of freedom.

He neither grieved because his landlady had not had his opportunities nor deplored the fact that she liked her anaemic bungalow. Let us get everybody properly fed first, he thought always, impatiently, and then, when the vitality of the peoples rises, so will their taste for rich strong beauty in all the arts, including those of everyday living.

He lived like a peaceful hermit for nearly a month. January had come, with snow and violets, and nearly gone, and he delivered his first lecture at the European Reconstruction Council's training school. It dealt with the degree of industrialization reached by the States of the Danube Basin up to 1939, and was a success; that is, his fellow lecturers and teachers praised it and the people who were there to learn from it, did learn. He had the supremely satisfying experience of working hard and seeing his finished labours perform the task they were meant to do. He was also well paid for his work and that was very pleasant too.

He sent half of his first cheque to the Spanish Republican Internees Comforts Fund and paid his mother back three pounds that he owed her. And he meditated—for he was no anchorite by temperament and disliked a life without feminine society—writing to Alicia Arkwright to suggest that they should lunch in London and go to a film together—'and I shall warn her that it must be inexpensively,' thought Richard.

Alicia was having a dreary New Year. The man she had met at the party had been sent out of England on a Government job and she was temporarily without anyone regular to kiss, while even her excellent health had broken down under the daily journey to the factory in a freezing bus full of coughing women, and she had had a heavy cold. She stayed away from the factory for a day or two, sitting up in bed in a snow-white fluffy jacket tied at the throat with red velvet ribbons, her dark hair caught up with a childish bow of the same ribbon on top of her head, and every morning her father, who was fond of her, came in and inquired, while folding his newspaper, did she want anything from Town—though Heaven knew that there wasn't much to be had even if she did. She usually gave him some small commission, for he was a man who enjoyed spending money on women and his daughter thought this a trait to be encouraged. Then he would go off in the car that he was still allowed to run because he was head of a firm fulfilling very large Government contracts, and Alicia would be left alone, to read and blow her nose and stare out of the window at the garden under melting snow. In a lowered state, with time on her hands, she not unnaturally indulged in gloomy reflections about being twenty-eight next July and having no plans and not much hope for the future, and so on and so forth, and even wrote a depressed letter to her best friend, Crys, another tall cool girl like herself, with a commission in the W.R.N.S. Crys's consolatory letter arrived by the same post as Richard's invitation to go to London and see a film, and she was ridiculously pleased to hear from him, and at once wrote to explain why she could not come, ending with an inquiry as to why he always wrote letters, the telephone had been invented about 1890, or thereabouts, she believed.

'I dislike the telephone,' he wrote back on a post card of Milan Cathedral, 'and never use it unless I cannot avoid doing so. I am sorry you have a cold and I will write to you again in a fortnight to see if you can come then.' The post card was signed 'Yours affectionately, Richard.'

'"Affectionately"!' exclaimed Alicia, throwing the post card down on the bed, 'what a way to sign oneself! Just like Mash.' (Mash was the old governess of her childhood.) She picked the post card up again and after studying it severely, tore it in pieces. 'But that's rather how I feel about him—"affectionately." He's the sort of odd old thing you do feel affectionate about.'

With which serene piece of self-deception, she picked up *Vogue* and became absorbed in it.

Meanwhile, what was happening in that forcing-house of the passions, Sunglades?

Everybody was relieved when the holiday ended and they could return to their normal avocations, and the spirits of Miss Fielding were further lightened by the departure of her father for London, with hints that he would probably not return for at least a fortnight, if at all; he would let them know. But her rejoicing was of short duration, for he returned in three days, more depressed than she had ever seen him, and it became alarmingly clear after he had been back a few hours that the cause of his depression was that he missed Betty. He cheered up wonderfully when she came in from the Ministry about seven o'clock, and Miss Fielding's heart sank to zero when he announced, sparkling and joking his way through dinner, that they must make up their minds to seeing a great deal of him in future—a very great deal.

'Thinking of settling down here again, Father?' said Kenneth, who was also in excellent spirits, and had been so ever since *he* had visited London earlier in the week. Everybody, indeed, was cheerful except Miss Fielding. Betty was always cheerful, and Vartouhi was all smiles because she had had such a pretty necklace made of gold filigree beads and red jewels from her sister in America. She had met the postman in the lane that morning on her way into St Alberics, and he had given her the parcel. It was quite a handsome present and must have cost at least ten dollars, perhaps more, in Miss Fielding's estimation. Vartouhi *was* a lucky girl! three hats, and a bracelet, and scent! and now this charming necklace whose deep red and gold glowed against her smooth throat. No wonder her long eyes gleamed with delight.

'Ah—yes—well, perhaps, perhaps,' said Mr Fielding, smiling and twinkling mysteriously and nodding at Betty, whose private reaction was Mercy on us! 'It depends; it depends.'

Miss Fielding heard this with feelings close to despair. What! settle down again near St Alberics, and spend the remainder of his days—and he was sure to live to ninety-odd; not that, of course, she wanted anything to happen to him—popping in and out of Sunglades borrowing money from Kenneth and upsetting him by his bad example? Reviving scandalous memories in the minds of all the old friends and neighbours; perhaps marrying some highly unsuitable person years and years younger than himself— good heavens! perhaps marrying Betty! He looked at her as if he was going to propose that very evening; and all Miss Fielding's possessive instincts rose in fury at the thought. Why should he, who had caused Our Mother so much worry and distress (even Miss Fielding could not pretend that Our Mother had been broken-hearted over his departure), why should he, at the very end of his misspent life, settle down with a shallow frivolous woman like Betty who took no interest in world problems and had led an almost useless existence? Our Mother's memory would be profaned by such a marriage, and Kenneth encouraged thereby to make a fool of himself in every direction. And what would they live on? Father had been practically penniless when he arrived at Christmas, Kenneth said. It would mean continual loans; perhaps even a settled quarterly allowance; endless complications. And above all there was the indecency, the sheer inappropriateness, of remarriage at seventy-eight. There might even be a paragraph in the *Evening Standard* about it. Miss Fielding's face was red with rage as she cut up her corned-beef pudding.

There was no more talk of his going away again. In the middle of January he spent a day in London and came back very pleased with himself and assured Kenneth that his loan was in a fair way to be repaid very shortly with interest, and he brought chocolates for Vartouhi and an enormous bunch of sweet pale violets for Betty and a large cake for Miss Fielding and Miss Burton. The latter was touched, and her heart was won. He's a dear old man, she thought, as she sat at the piano playing *My Love had a Silver Ring* in the firelight, and I like having him here. How disagreeable Connie is, always trying to stop people from enjoying life and having an easy time if they want to. Heaven knows there's enough misery in the world—and what does it matter if he does propose to Betty? I'm sure she won't have him.

And she went into the next room to take a refreshing peep at Vartouhi's beautiful bedspread, which was half-finished and by now very beautiful indeed; gorgeously, dazzlingly so. Vartouhi still came up for two or three evenings in the week to work at it. She had been slightly subdued ever since Christmas, and Miss Burton was amused, but rather disturbed, to learn that she found the house duller now that Richard had gone away.

'You're like "Barbara Allan,"' said Miss Burton disapprovingly.

'Who is that, Miss Burton, please?'

'Oh, a girl in an old song. First she let the young man die for love of her and then when he was dead she made a dreadful fuss and ended by dying herself from remorse.'

'What is re-morse, please?'

'Being sorry you've been naughty.'

'I am not sorry, Miss Burton, because I have not been naughty to Rich-ard.'

'Well, I think you were, very unkind and naughty, but never mind that now. I thought you'd miss him when once he had gone.'

'Is no one to look at me with love now, Miss Burton.'

The Usurper laughed.

'Is a nice feeling to have a man want marry you, Miss Burton. Though you say "no, no," is a nice feeling.'

'I quite agree, Vartouhi.'

'I think I will go and see Rich-ard in his new house?' She glanced up innocently at Miss Burton, who looked as severe as she could.

'Now you don't want to do that, Vartouhi!—digging him up just when he's probably getting over it.'

'Is a kind thing to do,' said Vartouhi, embroidering busily. 'He is lonely, perhaps.'

'Not at all,' said Miss Burton vigorously. 'His mother saw him yesterday and she says he seems perfectly comfortable in his lodgings and likes the work very much.'

'He has forget me, all,' said Vartouhi, and giggled.

'A very good thing too.'

'All the same, Miss Burton, perhaps I shall go,' said Vartouhi, and smilingly fingered her necklace.

Miss Burton, who had definite plans of her own for Vartouhi's future, hoped sincerely that she would not go, but was powerless to stop her if she meant to, except by giving advice. She was most anxious that Vartouhi should not see Richard alone in doubtless comfortless lodgings; the girl's charm would glow with more than its usual power in such surroundings and was almost certain to revive his passion for her, while she would see him, pale and moved and an exile for her sake, and perhaps her heart would be touched at last. And then what becomes of all my fine schemes? thought Miss Burton. What a wicked little thing she can be!—but only where men are concerned. She is a good, loyal, kind little girl to me and Betty and even to Connie.

Oh dear, I do hope she won't go.

But on a Saturday morning towards the end of January, a mild wet day when the country seemed as colourless as it could be, Vartouhi walked to Blentley and knocked at the door of the bungalow where Richard lived. One of her three hats, a brown one with a feather, was arranged right on the back of her head like the hat of a lady she had seen in a woman's paper brought into the house by Betty, and she wore her necklace outside her old tweed coat and had bare legs and heavy shoes. Richard's landlady opened the door and looked at her with mild inter-rogation on her small face.

'Is Mr Marten live here?' asked Vartouhi with her most spark-ling smile. (What a small house! and so brown!)

'Yes,' said the woman, staring. She was fascinated by this visitor, who would have looked striking even in conventional clothes and was doubly so in the blend of shabby garments with surprising hats and jewellery that her circumstances and taste compelled her to adopt.

'He is in the house?'

'Oh yes. But he's just going out. Did you want to see him?'

'Yas, please.'

'I'll just go and tell him, if you'll step inside.'

Vartouhi did so, looking with lively scorn at the furniture and walls. Brown, all brown! Is like the inside of a parcel.

She heard voices, and Richard's tones sounding surprised, and a moment later his tall form came out into the hall, stooping towards her. He was in his overcoat and was evidently just going out.

'Oh——' he said, stopping short, 'it's you—Vartouhi, I mean. This is—this is a surprise,' he ended, very coldly. 'I thought it might be Miss Arkwright. I'm meeting her in town. Er—won't you come in?'

He stood aside, and she sauntered past him into the room. To her it seemed all brown, like the rest of this stuffy little house, and quiet and chilly, with not much light in it from the small windows. Papers and books were scattered on a table.

Vartouhi turned to smile at him as he followed her into the room. There was silence for a moment.

'Er—have you a message from my mother or Miss Fielding?' he asked courteously, looking down on the odd enchanting little figure from his great height. All his pain revived at the sight of her. He recognized with resignation that he was not so healed as he had hoped.

'Oh no, Rich-ard. I come to see you. I am thinking you are lonely perhaps so I am coming to see you and cheer you up, too also.'

'That's very kind of you,' he answered with perfect gentleness and no trace of irony; all the same, Vartouhi knew that she was most deeply unwelcome. She smiled impudently and moved her shoulders but just for a moment she could not think of anything to say. She had hoped that he would look at her with that pleading which had so often pleased her vanity at Sunglades, but his eyes were only friendly and calm.

'You do not want marry me any more?' suddenly demanded Vartouhi, sitting down on a chair and gazing up at him while clutching at her hat, which nearly fell off the back of her head with the abruptness of the movement.

He shook his head. He simply could not think of words in which to answer her. Had she come to say that she would have him after all? God forbid! and yet——

'You *sure*, Rich-ard, you do not want marry me any more?' she repeated, looking at him with narrowed eyes.

He found his voice.

'I've decided it wouldn't do, Vartouhi, even if you would have me.'

'I thought you do not want any more, Rich-ard. When I see

how you look at me, I thought it.' He could not tell from her tone what she was feeling, but he hoped that she was wounded by his apparent indifference. He said still more calmly:

'Why do you ask? You didn't—come to tell me you've changed your mind, did you?'

'No, *no*, Rich-ard!' cried Vartouhi, bursting into giggles. 'But I like to have a man want marry me, though I say I will not marry him, no. So I come to see if you still want.'

'Typical,' murmured Richard, gazing at her pensively and thinking how a less intelligent young man than himself might have sneered something about 'making sure the moth was still on the pin.'

'Please?'

'It's all right—nothing. Well, I'm still in love with you, even if I don't want to marry you. Does that make up at all for the disappointment?'

'You still are loving me, Rich-ard?'

He nodded, looking down at her.

'Is a good thing,' said Vartouhi cheerfully, getting up from her chair and rearranging the hat. 'You are going to London now?'

'Yes—and I must go or I shall miss the bus.'

'To see Miss Arkwright?'

'Yes.'

'You like her?'

'Yes, very much.'

'Is a horrid girl,' said Vartouhi vehemently. 'She has two fur coat. Is bad in war-time.'

He burst out laughing and made his shepherding movement of driving her out of the room. 'Go on with you—you're hopeless. The Barbarian in Our Midst. Miss Arkwright is charming and you're jealous.'

'I am not—I am not! I do not care you see her at all!'

'Oh, not jealous of *me*, jealous of the two fur coats.'

'Is a bad wicked thing in war-time,' she said obstinately, going in front of him down the hall.

He shut the front door behind them.

'Is my day off,' explained Vartouhi sunnily, walking beside him down the road, 'so I come in the bus with you—so far as St Alberics.'

'That will be delightful; thank you,' he said with irony.

He had expected to be a little embarrassed in the bus by the attention which Vartouhi's unusual appearance and queer English would inevitably attract, but he was surprised—and his passion for her was increased—by the sober air she at once assumed, which eclipsed her personality and presented only a faintly smiling courteous mask to her fellow passengers. It was the first time he had ever been with her in a public place and he found the experience interesting as well as painfully delightful. Of course, he thought, watching her as she sat opposite to him gazing politely out of the window, she comes of a race famous for concealing their feelings under their good manners. It's only because she has got to feel familiar with me by living under the same roof with me for six months that she tells me the truth— how polite she was to me that first day, when she carried my rucksack! If only she had been really like that! courteous, gay, with a heart growing steadily sweeter as it unfolded. But it makes no difference, blast it. Have I only been in love with her for six months? It feels like six years.

'Good-bye, Rich-ard,' said Vartouhi, as they parted at the bus stop in St Alberics. 'I go to eat lunch in the Fedora Café and then I go to the Fedora Pictures to see some Germans and some Italians and some Japanese all blown up. Is a varry good thing. Good-bye.'

'Good-bye,' said Richard.

23

Round about twelve o'clock on the same Saturday morning Betty was sitting in her room at the Ministry of Applications, working.

The Ministry, it may be recalled, was housed in the large buildings of a girls' school that had been evacuated to Cornwall, and though at first there had been room for it, it had grown considerably in three years and had recently overflowed into a network of small rooms made from patent boarding erected in the school grounds. Although the rooms were painted in pleasant white and green and attempts had been made by hardy individualists to brighten them up with vases of flowers and calendars and even on some of the more important desks with photographs, they continued to give to sensitive minds an unpleasant suggestion of cells, and although any ordinarily robust person could have kicked her way out through them in ten minutes, some of the clerks had a faint but permanent claustrophobia when the doors were shut.

But Betty's cheerful temperament made the best of her little cell, appreciating the bright cold light of the northern Home Counties that poured in through the well-designed windows, and the tiny electric stove provided by a benevolent Government, with the warning that it must not be used between certain dates when, it was assumed, the weather would be warm. Of course it never was, but you cannot run a country at all unless you ignore some of its peculiarities.

This morning the little stove was at half-pressure and the room was too hot and the windows could not be opened because when they were the fine rain drove in all over Betty's chief's desk. He had been out all the morning at a conference and had left her in charge. She had Mr Fielding's violets in a white vase on her desk and was sorting letters from applicants.

Precisely at twelve o'clock, an old gentleman in a beautiful grey tweed overcoat and grey felt hat presented himself at the little hut which guarded the entrance to the school grounds, and inquired of the porter if he might see Mrs Marten? Having filled up a form with his name, his address, and the nature of his business (Personal), he waited while the porter communicated with Betty by telephone. On hearing that she would see him at once, he looked gratified, and waited while his pass was stamped with a little circle representing a clock set at twelve-five, the hour he entered the building; he watching this ritual with his head on one side and the indulgent smile of one who murmurs Bless their little hearts! Finally, holding his pass airily between finger and thumb, with his hat in the other hand and his bright blue eyes glancing amusedly from side to side as he went, he traversed the corridors between the numbered doors until he came to Room 87.

'Come in!' called Betty, sitting back in her chair and gazing at the door with an expectant smile, though she felt apprehensive.

'Well!' she said, as Mr Fielding came in all smiles, 'this *is* a surprise! Have you come to take me out to lunch? because——'

'Delighted; nothing would give me greater pleasure,' he said promptly, 'but first of all——'

'Because I'm terribly sorry but I can't manage to-day; my chief is out at a conference and I'm going to have something sent in from the canteen,' she interrupted dexterously, 'I'm in charge, you see.'

'Charming!' cried Mr Fielding, gazing at her in delight. 'It's delightful to see you with your typewriters and your files and your telephones, pretending to be a business woman! And so you're "in charge"! Well, no office could have a prettier guardian,' and he put his hat down on the table and glanced about him for somewhere to sit down.

You maddening old man, you ceased to think somewhere round about 1908, thought Betty, but you're rather a pet too. Is that how you talk to the cabaret girls?—*charming, charming, how delightful to see you pretending to wear nothing but a scarf, with your lipstick and mascara, you playful puss.* 'Oh, do sit down on our Applicant's Chair,' she said, and opened a cupboard and out fell its solitary occupant; a folding chair of intimidatingly utilitarian design which nevertheless wobbled.

'Thank you,' said Mr Fielding, and sat down so carefully that they both laughed.

'You see your violets,' said Betty quickly; she was so nervous that she made this dangerous remark without thinking where it might lead. 'Don't they smell delicious?' and she put her dark head down to the fading flowers.

'They remind me of you,' said Mr Fielding, folding his hands on the crook of his umbrella and looking at her with his head on one side.

Oh dear, thought Betty.

She smiled at him and sat down at her desk again. There was a little embarrassing pause. She moved some letters about.

'Won't you——' she was beginning.

'You must know what I came here to say to you, my dear,' interrupted Mr Fielding suddenly, bending towards her with, as the old saying has it, his heart in his eyes. 'I'm never sure of getting you alone in *that place*' (he meant Sunglades) 'so that's why I came here, in the hope——'

'I wish—oh dear—I'd really rather——' began Betty, looking down at the typewriter in distress. And then she added that last request of the soft-hearted when driven into a corner and very afraid of giving pain to the person who has driven them there—'Please don't.'

But he did.

★

Alicia arrived at their rendezvous at the same moment as Richard did, and he gave her a good mark, for he himself, though absent-minded, was by no means chronically unpunctual. She was dressed in elegant rain-clothes and had an oiled silk umbrella.

'Hullo, Richard. Nice to see you.'

'Nice to see you too, Alicia. Shall we go and lunch at once? I thought we'd see *Casablanca*. Do you approve?'

'Grand. I adore Humphry Bogart.'

'And I admire Ingrid Bergman, so we shall both be happy.'

They walked away past the ruins of the Café de Paris, livid under the lowering grey sky. Rain danced lightly on the dark stagnant water of the reservoir and drifted in their faces as they moved along the crowded streets. Men were selling bunches of snowdrops outside the big cinemas.

Alicia would have liked a drink. Her usual meetings with her friends always began with a drink or two. But she decided not to suggest going in for one because she knew that Richard had not much money and drinks were very expensive nowadays, and she did not want to suggest paying for herself.

'Look here,' she said lightly, as they stepped in at the almost hidden entrance of an obscure little restaurant near the National Gallery, 'we're going Dutch to-day, aren't we?'

He shook his head.

'Not to-day. I've just had my first cheque from the European Reconstruction Council and I have enough money to take you out and I'd like to. I did warn you, though,' smiling down at her, 'that it would be very inexpensively, didn't I? The next time we go out together, if I'm very hard up, we'll go halves.'

The next time we go out together, thought Alicia, as they sat down at a table by a large spotted mirror wreathed with tinsel leaves and grapes. She arranged her wet raincoat over the back of her chair while Richard (having consulted her, but not much) ordered the lunch. What is it he does that makes quite ordinary remarks sound charming? He doesn't try to be charming like poor H. used to. It's because he never shoots a line or puts on an act, I think. Anyway, I'm happy.

She continued to be happy throughout the afternoon, sitting beside Richard in the escapist dusk of the pictures while he held her hand. Sometimes he turned to smile at her, or she at him, when they were both amused, and both were pleased to find that they were amused at the same things. He neither stroked her hand nor pressed it but held her long fingers gently and safely in his own. I'm perfectly happy, she thought dreamily, with her shapely turbaned head lifted a little towards the screen and her eyes watching the convincing sufferings of the hero and heroine. Crys would laugh, and say Simple Pleasures. So what?

Richard gradually began to feel calmer, too. The morning's encounter with Vartouhi had disturbed him deeply, more because it had proved to him that he was not yet healed than because of her unkindness, for he was used to that. But he took care that Alicia should not suspect that he was suffering, for he strongly disliked talking about his troubles to anyone and was inclined to despise people who could not keep their woes to themselves but unloaded them on their friends.

As they came out into the rainy dusk he said, with his hand under her elbow to steer her through the hurrying crowds:

'The only unconvincing note in that, as hokum, was the part where he got drunk and cried.'

'Yes, I thought that too. In my experience,' said Alicia dryly, 'women sit and drink and cry over men oftener than men sit and drink and cry over women.'

He laughed.

'It's a question of temperament, not of sex. Do you mind the same little place for tea?'

By this time she would definitely have preferred a bar, but she thought that if he had wanted a drink he would have said so and as she did not want to disturb their harmony by suggesting plans of her own, she said that she did not mind at all.

When they were sitting again under the mirror with the tinsel grapes and drinking tea and smoking, he said:

'You have a calming effect on me, Alicia.'

'Men don't like being calmed as a rule,' she said impersonally.

'It isn't anything you do or say, it's what you are—or appear to be.'

'Oh, I am fairly calm, I think. I never have flapped much about anything.'

'I like it, anyway.'

'Thanks.'

But nevertheless a little shadow came over her contentment. She did not want to be a walking bottle of soothing syrup for Richard Marten. She had known more than one girl who had been calm and friendly and always there when men wanted comfort, and then the men suddenly married exciting women with red hair and fiendish tempers and the calm friendly ones never saw them again. And he's just the sort that would marry that little number over a week-end, she thought, and found the idea depressing.

At the entrance to the tube station he said good-bye to her, for she was spending the night in London.

'Thanks awfully, Richard, I've had a lovely time,' she said. Her eyes were very blue beneath the black turban as she looked up at him.

'So have I. It displeases you,' said Richard, looking down into her eyes, 'if I say that you have a calming effect on me, so I will not say it again. But have you ever spent a long day on the river in still weather, drifting along between the trees with only the lovely musical sound of the water going past the boat?'

She nodded, still looking up at him.

'Well, that's how I feel. Thank you, dear. Good night.'

He stooped his head and lightly kissed her cheek, then turned away and went down the steps into the Underground.

Alicia hailed a taxi and told it to go to Knightsbridge, which—after some oaths, and some promises from Alicia—it did.

I really can't sort out my feelings at all, she thought, as the taxi went on through the deepening black-out. Perhaps I'd better not try.

About nine o'clock that evening Richard was sitting in his room making notes on the value of the export trade from Holland to Sumatra in the years from 1935 to 1939, when his landlady opened the door and announced that there was a lady to see him. *This is gettin' monotonous*, as Billy Bennet would say, thought Richard, standing up and peering over her shoulder out into the dim hall, but when his mother, looking pale and tired and amused, followed the woman into the room, he knew at once that something had happened and that she was upset.

'Rick, darling,' said Betty, pulling off her hat and dropping it on the table and going up to give him a kiss, 'I'm so glad you're in.'

'This is my mother, Mrs Arnold,' said Richard.

'Oh yes, Mr Marten,' said Mrs Arnold, dimly returning Betty's friendly smile, and went out of the room murmuring 'Good evening, Mrs Marten.'

'What a dreary little room, sweetie,' said Betty softly, looking about her.

'It is not festive, but it is adequate. I'm afraid,' looking at her searchingly, 'that all the same you're glad to be here, Betty.'

'Well, I am, dear, "as a matter of a fack," as you used to say when you were small. That little stove gives out quite a good heat but what a smell! It can't be good for you.'

'Does it smell? I hadn't noticed it. This is the only comfortable chair,' pulling it up to the stove for her, 'and here's a cigarette. I know what's the matter; someone's been proposing to you.'

'Yes—the Night Club King—and it *is* all so uncomfortable——'

'You didn't walk here, surely?' he interrupted.

'Oh no, Ken brought me, he had to go to a Home Guard

meeting and he dropped me here on the way; he's going to pick me up on his way back in about an hour. It's so nice to be with you, Ricky. I really couldn't bear the atmosphere of that house another minute, with the Night Club King being dreadfully cheerful and gallant and obviously feeling utterly miserable, and Connie looking at me as if I'd stolen her sugar ration and Frances being all knowing and sympathetic and trying to get me into corners for a nice long cosy chat, and Ken being bluff and embarrassed——'

'But it has nothing to do with any of them. I don't see——'

'Of course it hasn't; he's free, white and seventy-eight; but you know what people are. And Connie really is very queer with her dislike of the idea of any of them getting married: it makes her angrier than anything. She's a sort of Old Miss Barrett about it. She needs psyching.'

'Or telling not to be selfish.'

'Oh, it's more than just selfishness. It's a sort of bossy elder sister attitude; Ken mustn't make a fool of himself, he wouldn't make a good husband, he's too like Father, and so weak, and all the rest of it. She always has been like it. I remember when we were all young——'

'Was she responsible for breaking off your engagement to Kenneth?'

'No, I fell in love with your father, darling, and just forgot all about poor Ken; we were married two days after we met— I've told you so often. Besides, that affair with Ken wasn't a pukka engagement, you know, it was only an understanding, and a boy-and-girl sort of affair.'

'On the rare occasions when I have given any thought to the matter I have wondered if he never married in later life because of that shock to his sexual vanity in youth.'

'What a way to put it, dear! I don't think it upset him all that. He wrote me a very sweet letter saying he hoped I'd be happy. He's a pet, really. Rather an old stick, of course, but a great dear.'

Without any warning, tears came up into her eyes. She blinked them away, for she was sitting outside the light of the table lamp, and continued in the same amused tone while a sudden unbearably vivid picture of her husband's face slowly faded into the darkness of memory, 'It isn't really my fault, you know.'

"'*Why, oh, why will gentlemen desert their chosen intendeds for my sake?*'" quoted Richard, grinning at her.

'It's all very well, you little brute! but it *isn't* my fault! The Night Club King pursued me into the Ministry and proposed in my office—thank god Fowler happened to be out at a conference or he would have thought it most unsuitable, he doesn't encourage followers—and it took me nearly half an hour to let him down gently, poor old sweet.'

'Poor Betty.'

'You may well say so.'

'What did he say?'

'Now, Richard: None of your Mass Observation please!'

'I'm interested.'

'It isn't done. *You* ought to know that.'

'On the contrary it's done all the time—not by persons whom you and I would consider of any value, of course, but it's undoubtedly done. You'd better come clean and then you'll feel better.'

'Oh—well, he said a lot of very nice things which he obviously meant, poor old man, and then he said he felt it was time he settled down——'

'Good heavens.'

'I know. But he quite saw the fun of it, he was laughing. I liked that, you know. And he told me quite frankly what a good time he could give me for the next few years. He's on his feet again with regard to money, he says.'

'Poor old boy.'

'Rick, I'm so glad you think so too. He *is* nice, you know. He said he longed to take care of me.'

'That's understandable. I often feel you oughtn't to be knocking about as you do, even though you are in your prime of beauty and health.'

'I enjoy it, darling. I could always go to Salters if I wanted to settle down, but it's more fun to live the way I do.'

'That's a little weight off my mind. I sometimes get a conscience about you.'

'You needn't, Rick.'

'Not in any way?'

'Not in any way, dear. Later on I should like some grandchildren but there's heaps of time for that.'

He studied her for a moment. She was reclining in the deep chair, with the shadows beyond the circle of lamp-light softening her face and hair to a tender beauty that they sometimes lacked in broad daylight because she was always so gay and so on her guard against heaviness and sorrow. Yes, she's even happy, he thought. That one deadly blow in her youth immunized her for ever afterwards and she has instinctively avoided any entanglements that might let her in for suffering again. There are people who would call that selfish. How I *hate* suffering! tears, and agony, and all the long-drawn-out, dismal appurtenances of misery! My dearest mother, you are doing what Alicia would call a grand job of work simply by being pretty and gay.

'Will I do, dear?' inquired his parent meekly, as the pause in the conversation grew prolonged.

He laughed.

'Very well indeed, Betty. So you let him down gently?'

'As gently as I could. You see, Rick, the trouble is that he keeps on *saying* he's old, but he doesn't *feel* old.'

He nodded.

'*He* feels as if I'd rejected some gay lad in his prime. I had to tell him at last that I just couldn't ever marry anyone again,' she ended in her airiest tone.

'Did he see that?'

'I think so—at last. It was rather wearing, though—explaining it.'

'I can imagine.'

'People are a nuisance,' said Betty, lighting another cigarette, 'the way they will fall in love.'

'Indubitably, Miss Squeers.'

'But they *are*, Rick. Look how this has upset things at Sunglades.'

'Well, it's an upsetting agent, in its raw stages. It only begins to be constructive after marriage. Shall you go away?'

'I really don't know. I don't want to. I'm very comfortable there and I'm fond of Frances and Ken and I like Connie too, though goodness knows why. I hope that he'll be the one to go away.'

'I expect he will. I had to,' said Richard, suddenly lowering his defences under the influences of the dusk and his mother's soft voice.

'Is it working, dear?'

'Not now. It was until this morning, and then I had a visitor.'

He did not know everything about his mother, in spite of being sure that he did, and he would have been very surprised to know how much dismay Betty was concealing when she asked in a casually interested tone:

'Oh? What was the reason for that?'

'To see if the moth was still on the pin, I presume.' Richard's youth and his bitterness sounded in his voice for a moment; then he was ashamed of his own melodrama and went on self-consciously, 'I mean, to see if I was still in the same state of mind, I presume. I can't think of any other reason.'

His mother said nothing. With a dreamy, absent expression on her face she was wondering if she could manage to get Vartouhi sacked from Sunglades. She did not seriously consider this last idea, for she avoided intriguing as she avoided emotional entanglements, but her mind did just touch on the possibility.

'Oh. Well, allowances must be made,' she said at last, implying that Vartouhi's youth and foreignness and hapless situation in a strange land must all plead for her. 'But I don't think it shows a kind heart,' she ended mildly, unable to keep the remark back.

'No, it doesn't. But I knew that, and unfortunately it makes absolutely no difference,' he said, getting up. 'Would you like some coffee? I've got the things here to make it with.'

'Love it.' She was watching him sorrowfully from her seat in the shadows.

While he was walking about the room assembling the cups and milk and saucepan, his tall form throwing a shadow on the ceiling, he went on talking.

'It won't be allowed to make any difference to my life-pattern, you know, so don't let it worry you, dear. I shall ignore it.' He looked across at his mother and they both smiled, for that was what he used to say when he was a child and one of his frequent minor ailments threatened to prevent his taking part in some promised excursion. 'This kind of thing happens to people sometimes, just as malaria does. One gets over it.' He lit the flame under the glass carafe and turned the wick down.

'I don't like your being worried, Rick.' Her casual and airy voice was almost pure sound, so light was the weight of meaning she made it carry.

'I'm not worried all the time. Only sometimes.'

He was thinking how restful were these two women with whom he had spent the day and evening; and how, after listening to their cool voices and the nuances and reticences of their conversation, any more dramatic method of dealing with emotions became unbearable by contrast. And yet, he thought, it's just that force and merciless honesty that attracts me in the other one.

'It will depend on how they all go on whether I go away or not,' said Betty, stirring her coffee. 'If they continue to go round looking as if I'd murdered somebody I shall get out pretty quick.'

'Where will you go?'

'I shall have to try to find somewhere in the town,' she said, shrugging her shoulders.

'I wish you could come here but there isn't another bedroom.'

'I wish I could, Rick dear, but don't give it another thought; I'll manage somehow.'

There was the sound of a car stopping outside and a moment later the front door bell rang.

'That's Fielding; I'll go. Mrs Arnold's in bed, I expect,' said Richard, getting up and going out into the hall. Betty heard voices and Kenneth's laugh and the next minute he followed Richard into the room, looking even burlier than usual in his Home Guard greatcoat, whose shoulders were dark with raindrops. He had his forage cap in his hand and the dim light shone on the bald crown of his head.

'Coffee?' inquired Richard. 'It's not good, I'm afraid. I have no talent for cookery.'

'No thanks. I've just had a couple with Arkwright and the lads at the local.' He sat down on the table, which creaked ominously, and he got up again and sat down by Betty.

'Don't hurry,' he said to her. 'It's a beastly night, pouring again.' Now that he was away from Sunglades and his sister, his manner to her was as affectionate and unembarrassed as usual. By Jove, if Dad did pop the question I don't blame him, he thought, looking down admiringly at her as she held the cup in her slender pale fingers with their glittering rings. Her eyelashes cast a little feathery shadow against the side of her nose. All very awkward, of course, thought Kenneth, and the old boy's taking it very hard. I expect he'll go away now.

'The "Black Bull" was full of Yanks,' he said suddenly.

'Oh?' said Betty. 'Was that nice—or wasn't it?'

'We got on all right. I like them,' said Kenneth.

'I don't,' said Richard. 'An expansive and emotional race.'

'We'd look rather funny without them, anyway,' said Kenneth, who had had more than a couple.

'That only increases my dislike,' said Richard. 'Can you tell me where Abbot's Lane is, in St Alberics?'

'Yes; it's an alley opening off Abbot's Hill just before you get to the High Street,' said Kenneth, half glad to have the subject changed and half spoiling for a fight.

'Thank you,' said Richard, and went on smoothly to talk of other things. In a little while Betty finished her coffee and kissed her son good night and ran out into the rainy black-out to Kenneth's car. Richard shut the front door on them, hoping that his mother would not have too dreary a drive home.

24

But it was rather dreary, for Betty was worried about Richard and Vartouhi now, in addition to her worry about Mr Fielding's proposal and its unfortunate results; and although she would have liked to talk to Kenneth about the trouble Vartouhi was causing Richard, she felt unable to do so because she suspected (in spite of her incredulous words to Miss Fielding) that her old friend was himself attracted to the trouble-maker. And as the car approached Sunglades Kenneth's own manner became silent and restrained, as does that of the prisoner who returns to the prison house after one day out on parole, and Betty felt quite cross with him.

It's utter nonsense, she thought vigorously, as she let herself into the hushed, dimly lit, warm house, while Kenneth was putting the car away. The presences of the three elderly inmates (though they had presumably retired to rest) could be felt therein as disapproving entities.

What has it got to *do* with Connie and Frances if Mr Fielding proposes to me? thought Betty. It isn't even as if he lived at home and his remarrying would upset their lives. No; it's because they live in such a backwater that they have an exaggerated sense of the importance of their own affairs; and Connie has this absurd notion about no one in the family marrying. Heaven alone knows why, for she isn't in the least morbid or neurotic. She's just selfish to the bone, and she would fight to the last ditch to keep her life running along in the smooth easy comfortable way it always has. I suppose (she smiled guiltily to herself as she went upstairs) in a way she and I agree; we both think strong feelings are a nuisance. But I don't go so far as to want other people not to marry! I wish Rick *would* marry somebody civilized and sensible who'd know the right way to look after him. He looked desolate to-night, poor pet, though he is so sensible about it all; and she gave a little sigh.

She opened her bedroom door, and then stopped short, for there was a light in the room and the stove was burning. By it, clad in a silk dressing-gown inappropriately embroidered with the calm and lovely water-lily, sat Miss Fielding.

'Ah, there you are,' said Miss Fielding, quite unabashed and in a severe voice. 'No doubt you are surprised to see me here.'

'No, not very,' answered Betty and went over to the dressing-table and dropped her hat on it and glanced at herself in the glass.

Miss Fielding nodded.

'I felt sure that you must have suspected from my manner earlier in the evening that I intended to have a talk with you,' she went on.

Betty sat down on the bed and opened her cigarette case. She was more tired and depressed than angry, and she glanced surreptitiously at the clock. It was half-past ten. She held out her case to Miss Fielding with an inquiring look.

Miss Fielding surprised her by accepting one; she seldom smoked. She lit it from a spill at the stove, and then went on, between the ungraceful puffs of the rare smoker:

'Have you anything to tell me, Betty?' in a sepulchral voice which Betty found so absurd that she was unable to repress a giggle. Miss Fielding raised her eyebrows. I know what it is, thought Betty, staring at her fascinatedly, she's never grown out of being the Straightest Girl at St Agatha's. Right now, she's tackling the Senior Prefect who's been caught using scent, and she's smoking herself to put the Senior Pre. at her ease. Poor old Con. But really, it's too much; I can't play.

'Only that your father asked me to marry him to-day and I said "no,"' she answered, with disarming mildness.

'So I suspected,' said Miss Fielding, compressing her lips and nodding.

'Suspected I'd said no?'

'Yes. Father has been so strange in his manner all the afternoon that I Guessed.'

'Oh. Well. That's all right, then, isn't it,' said Betty, hiding a small yawn. 'I'm very sorry if he's upset, of course, Connie. I felt bad about it. But it really isn't my fault——'

'Yes, Betty, it *is* your fault,' interrupted Miss Fielding, in a deliberate tone. 'Both Frances and I consider that this undignified and painfully embarrassing situation would never have arisen if you had not encouraged Father.'

'Oh, don't be so *silly!*' cried Betty, losing her temper and standing up. 'I never did a thing! If you and Frances think I enjoyed having him stringing along wherever I went, you couldn't be more wrong.'

'A woman should be humbled by a man's devotion,' said Miss Fielding, in a reproving tone and with maddening illogicality, '*and* grateful. After all, it is the greatest honour a man can pay a woman.'

Though she deplored the situation which had arisen, she was not going to let Betty deprecate the value of Mr Fielding's devotion, for Mr Fielding was her father, and as such, however deprecatable his own qualities might be, he was to be highly valued.

'I *am* grateful! Of course I am. But it was *not* my fault.'

'Your manner was thoughtless, Betty. You laughed and joked with him more than was necessary. Frances and Kenneth and I all remarked on it.'

'Oh, *nonsense*,' said Betty, violently, for her, 'I don't want to be catty, Connie, but if you put a susceptible man down in a houseful of women and three of them sit on him and the other one doesn't, what do you *expect* to happen?'

'I was not aware that I 'sat on' my father, Betty. Nor, I am sure, did Frances intend to do so. And as for Vartouhi——'

'She took her tone from you and was off-hand with him.'

'Better off-hand, Betty, than flirtatious. As a matter of fact, bearing Father's and Kenneth's unfortunate weakness in mind, I dropped a word of warning to Vartouhi.'

'I thought you must have. She isn't usually rude to anyone,' said Betty with a little bitterness, 'except Richard.'

'I told her to avoid lingering in conversation with Father as in England it was not considered respectful for the young to monopolize the attention of the old. But that is beside the point. As you are such an old friend—and I speak from my heart, Betty, when I say that I hope you will *remain* one—I can say things to you that I could not say to a stranger. I am sure you will agree with me that in the circumstances it would be far better if you left us, at least for a little while.'

'Of course,' said Betty, sitting down on the bed again. 'I'd been thinking that, too.'

'It will save embarrassment for everybody,' said Miss Fielding, looking relieved and relaxing the severity of her facial muscles.

'It will be an awful bore, though, Connie,' sighed Betty, delicately ruffling her hair. 'I wish I needn't.' Her anger, always as short-lived as a starry firework, had gone out.

'It will be better in the long run. We must take the Long View,' said Miss Fielding.

'I've been so marvellously comfortable here.'

'Sunglades *is* comfortable.' Miss Fielding's tone was a little softer with housewifely pride as she glanced about the pretty bedroom. 'And the old simple virtue of hospitality is very dear to me. As you know, I would never refuse anyone bread and salt.'

'Oh, I know,' murmured Betty.

'It grieves me very much to have to make this suggestion to you. I know that it would have grieved Our Mother too. Although things are sadly changed here since the war, we still know how to make life pleasant at Sunglades.'

'Yes, indeed.' Another murmur.

'And now for the time being your sojourn with us is over,' said Miss Fielding, rising from her seat and swaddling herself in the water lilies, while a look of playful affection replaced her former disapproval. She could afford to be playful. To-morrow she would tackle Father, and if she did not persuade *him* that it was best that he also should leave them, her name was not Constance Fielding. 'But we shall see you often, I hope, and of course I will leave no stone unturned to find you some "digs" in the town.'

'I don't want to live under a stone,' muttered Betty frivolously, beginning to unbutton her dress as a gentle hint.

'It will be so much better for us all,' Miss Fielding promised her, moving towards the door. 'Father will become his old self again, and I shall get over this little feeling of resentment I have against you, you naughty girl! and you will have an easier journey to work.'

'And there will be less for Vartouhi to do,' murmured Betty, from under the cloud of dark hair she was brushing over her eyes. 'Such a comfort.'

'Yes, indeed! Oh, it will be a better plan all round!' cried Miss Fielding blithely. 'We will talk it over properly in the morning. Good night, old girl!'

'Good night,' said Betty pleasantly; and as the door closed upon the victor she added, 'old beast.'

Miss Fielding went along the landing as if tramping upon air. How easy it was to deal with people if only you knew your own mind and stuck to your guns! She had always done that; and hence she had what some military correspondent has called the habit of victory.

As she approached her father's bedroom door a thought struck her. Why not begin to work upon Father this very night? She would not say anything very definite or tell him that Betty was going to leave them, but she would sound him as to his future plans and drop a hint or two about the amount of work that his presence there made for Vartouhi, and make a casual reference or so to her own failing health and that of Frances. It could do no harm; it would prepare the ground for future attacks; and she believed in acting while her vibrations were in harmony and she was charged with energy, as she was to-night.

Without pausing to think further, she knocked briskly upon his bedroom door.

There was no answer.

After waiting for a moment Miss Fielding opened the door a few inches. The room was in darkness, but she could just make out the smooth empty bed. Curious! She had certainly seen him go upstairs an hour ago, looking dejected and pleading tiredness (which deceived nobody) as an excuse for his early retirement. Tiresome old man, he must have gone downstairs again to speak to Kenneth, or perhaps he was still monopolizing the best bathroom.

Miss Fielding swept downstairs.

The house was quiet. It was a quarter to eleven; the chimes struck musically from the clock as she crossed the hall.

Kenneth was sitting by the drawing-room fire with the evening paper and glanced up as she opened the drawingroom door.

'Hallo, Con. Thought you were asleep long ago.'

'Have you seen Father, Kenneth?'

'Not since before I went out. Isn't he in bed?'

'No, he isn't!' Miss Fielding, tying the water-lilies tightly round herself as if taking action stations, gazed at her brother with dawning surprise.

'Oh well, he's probably in the bathroom or the——' Miss Fielding frowned loftily, so he ended, 'I shouldn't worry, anyway,' and returned to his paper.

Miss Fielding retorted, 'I am not worrying, Kenneth,' and moved about for a minute or two, fiddling with various objects, in an aimless way; then she went out of the room.

The kitchen was dark, and she supposed Vartouhi must be

in bed. But as she crossed the hall, glancing keenly about her ('for no reason that I could name, Frances, it was pure instinct— and how thankful I am that I *did*'), her gaze happened to linger on the kitchen door, and suddenly her heart gave an uncomfortable jump, for slowly it began to open.

Miss Fielding stood quite still for a second. Then (for she was no coward) she strode silently forward, laid her fingers upon the handle, and gave the door a good push.

There was a gasp and a cry of pain and Vartouhi stood revealed by the light from the hall, with her hand up to her nose.

25

'Vartouhi!' trumpeted Miss Fielding. 'What on *earth* are you doing?'

'You hurt my nose, Miss Fielding!'

'Serves you right, you silly child. What do you mean by creeping about like that? I thought you were a burglar.'

'It bleed—it bleed!' Vartouhi held up a crimson finger, but Miss Fielding ignored the blood and concentrated upon something else. As her eyes became accustomed to the dusk she saw that Vartouhi wore her coat and cap and that both were sparkling with raindrops.

'You have been out,' proclaimed Miss Fielding, in a voice solemn with anticipation of the revelations that she felt must be to come. 'Vartouhi, where have you been?'

At that moment, Kenneth came out into the hall clutching his newspaper:

'What on earth's the matter?' he demanded. 'You'll wake up everybody in the house.'

'Miss Fielding make my nose bleed!'

'Vartouhi came creeping out of the kitchen in the dark and I naturally thought it was a burglar and pushed the door onto her.'

'It bleed—it bleed!' repeated Vartouhi, very angrily.

'Vartouhi has been Out, at This Time of Night, in The Rain,' continued Miss Fielding, switching on the lights and sweeping into the kitchen, 'and I think I have a right to know Where She Has Been. Vartouhi! Take your fingers away so that I can see— there, that's better.'

She stooped slightly and peered at the swollen little nose and so did Kenneth, and the two middle-aged faces, tired at the end of the day and showing all their wrinkles, were thrust forward into the angry young one as they earnestly surveyed the damage. Vartouhi's eyes sparkled furiously. No pain is so maddening as that from a bumped nose.

'It's very swollen. I'll get some boracic——' muttered Kenneth and hurried away to the little cloakroom opening off the hall where the First Aid box was kept.

'My handkerchief is all blood,' hissed Vartouhi, flinging it on the floor.

'I will give you mine, though you don't deserve it, you naughty deceitful little girl,' snapped Miss Fielding, pulling out a large snowy one from the depths of the waterlilies. 'We'll get you tidied up first, and then I intend to know exactly what has been going on.'

She was convinced that it was Canadians.

Kenneth came back with a basin and some cottonwool and made Vartouhi sit down at the kitchen table and bathe her nose over the boracic and water. Miss Fielding stood impatiently by while this was going on, wishing to heaven Kenneth had been in bed when it had happened. To see the fuss he made anybody would think there was nothing queer about the incident and all that mattered was the tiresome little thing's nose.

'Is better,' announced Vartouhi at last, coldly. She had not shed a tear. 'It stop bleeding.'

'Ah-ha! Just the job!'

'To-morrow I wash your handkerchief, Miss Fielding,' said Vartouhi. 'Oh, how kind and good you are to lend me!' and she held it out to Miss Fielding with a look of the purest spite.

'Keep it, and return it to me when it is clean,' said Miss Fielding, icily.

There was an awkward pause.

'I go to bed,' said Vartouhi sunnily, switching on her national smile. 'Good night, Miss Fielding; good night, Mr Fielding,' and she curtsied first to one and then to the other, which she had not done for some time.

'No, Vartouhi,' Miss Fielding stayed her with an authoritative hand. 'You are not going to bed until you have told us where you have been this evening. It is not your free evening, and you did not ask me for permission to go out, and while you are in my employ I stand in relation to you as your father and mother would do. And I am sure that *they* would not like you to be out late at night in the rain without permission. Now, come along, please. Where had you been?'

'Down to the corner of the road, yas, Miss Fielding,' replied Vartouhi with a promptitude that took her employer considerably aback.

'Oh. Well, that's truthful, at any rate. Er—what were you doing there?' pursued Miss Fielding, approaching the hypothetical Canadians with a faint hesitation.

'I shine a torch,' said Vartouhi at once.

'Shine a torch! Don't you know you might be arrested for doing that? How very silly and thoughtless of you, Vartouhi! Whatever for?'

'So there could be light.'

'Well, of course.' Miss Fielding's voice was the more impatient because she detected out of the corner of her eye a faint smile on Kenneth's mouth. 'But why *else* did you do it? What was your *reason* for doing it?'

'So that someone could see with their bags.'

'With their——?' Miss Fielding glanced reprovingly at her brother, who instantly straightened his face. 'What on earth do you mean, Vartouhi? Now, you will just tell me everything at once, please, as plainly as possible. Your English is quite good enough now to make yourself perfectly clear. Who—er—who was down there with you, and—er—what were you doing?' A mutter from Kenneth which sounded like 'I say, Con, steady on, you know' was ignored by Miss Fielding.

'Mr Fielding is down with me, Miss Fielding,' answered Vartouhi, putting her hands behind her back and speaking with polite patience. 'He carry his bags down there to meet the car and I carry the torch so he can see not to fall in the mud. Would be a pity.'

'Mr Fielding? My father?' exclaimed Miss Fielding, turning in bewilderment to Kenneth, who now looked as surprised as she did. 'What car? How did he come to be there?'

'After dinner,' began Vartouhi in a cosy voice, evidently warming to the possibilities of her subject and glancing dramatically about the kitchen, 'I am in Mr Fielding bedroom with his hot-water bottle, and he is there too and he is very sad. So I said to him, "Mr Fielding, you are so sad," and he said, "Yas." So I said, "I am sorry," and he said, "You are kind little girl. More kind than some." And I think that he has been ask Mrs Mar-ten to marry him and she said "No, no," like I said to her son. Then I remember that you say it is not the custom here in England for young people to talk much to old ones, so I am going away, but he said to me, "I wish I could go away, away on this very night here now this minute." So I said, "Yas, Mr Fielding, would be a good thing." So he said, "When is there a train?" and I said to him, "I do not know." (You are in the bath and Mr Kenneth is out with Mrs Mar-ten, Miss Fielding.) So he go and make a telephone and then he said to me, "Vartouhi, Vartouhi, if I could get a car I could just make the nine-forty-five." Yas, the nine-forty-five. Is a train, I think. So he makes another telephone but no car will come, no taxi, no bus. Is nothing. He is varry sad because he has packed all his two bags with me to help. So he then said, "Ah! the Arkwright girl!" and he make another telephone and Miss Arkwright is away in London but her father said he will come because he is just home with his car, and it is not in its bed yet, too also. (Mr Fielding tell me all this.) So Mr Fielding was varry please and he told me to come with him and carry the torch and he carried the bags and we found Mr Arkwright dressed like a soldier in his car and he said, "Ah Fielding, in you get." So Mr Fielding got in Mr Arkwright car and he was driven away to the station and I came home but he told me not to tell anyone until to-morrow; so that is why I come in quietly, Miss Fielding,' ended Vartouhi reproachfully, but smiling still.

As this narrative proceeded, Miss Fielding's anger found itself slowly shifting its focus from Vartouhi, who had been deceitful but no more, and concentrating upon that only too familiar target, old Mr Fielding. What an extraordinary thing to do! Sneaking off in the middle of the night without telling anybody and treating Mr Arkwright as if he were the station car! And now that he had gone, Betty would of course think that there was no need for *her* to go, and, with the deplorable object-lesson of his silly old father removed from his sight, Kenneth would become more besotted with Betty than ever. There was No End to It. It is fortunate that my vibrations are naturally harmonious, thought Miss Fielding, while gazing severely down at Vartouhi's cheerful face, or I do not know how I should bear it. A weaker woman would have sunk beneath it all long ago.

'Did Mr Fielding say when he was coming back or leave any address?' asked Kenneth, in a quiet sensible tone that seemed to remove much of the oddness from the situation.

'He is not ever coming back. Regent Palace Hotel,' said Vartouhi, promptly.

'Oh well, he'll be all right; they know him well there, and I'll run up in a day or two and see him,' said Kenneth to his sister, and as she was anxious to preserve as much as possible of the 'not before the servants' attitude that she had always supported, she answered in a matter-of-fact voice:

'Yes, that would be best. Now, Vartouhi, you go off to bed. You are a silly little girl to come creeping in like that; there was no need to make such a secret of it. Mr Fielding did not want to—er—disturb Miss Burton and me, that was all.'

'Yas. He told me, "Do not let them hear, Vartouhi. S'sh!"'

'Yes, well—er—that was very considerate and kind of him. Does your nose still hurt?'

Vartouhi cautiously felt it, and nodded.

'I will give you some ointment, if you will come to my room. Will you get Pony in, please? he had better not be out in this rain, we don't want him to get another cold.'

'Is in.' Vartouhi pointed under the table, where the enormous cat sat sulkily blinking at them all.

'Yes, very well, then. Good night, Vartouhi.'

'Good night, Miss Fielding. Good night, Mr Kenneth.'

'Good night, Vartouhi.' They went out of the kitchen together.

Alone, Vartouhi brought out from her pocket and smoothed with an admiring look, a pound-note.

'She must think it so odd,' fumed Miss Fielding as they went across the hall.

'I don't think she does, Con. Foreigners are all slightly crazy and they don't expect people to behave normally.'

'I'm sure she knows everything that goes on in the house, she's as sharp as a needle underneath all those smiles and curtsies.'

He said nothing. He thought that what his sister said was true but the fact only amused him. Vartouhi had enjoyed the whole thing, like a schoolgirl. It was bad luck that Con had caught her.

'I shan't ever feel quite the same about her,' announced Miss Fielding, pausing at the foot of the stairs. 'I *know* now that she is sly.'

Kenneth wanted to say irritably, 'Oh rot, Connie,' but he controlled the impulse and was silent. The one thing he must avoid was the arousing of his sister's suspicions. They had been stirred by the gift of the scent at Christmas but fortunately seemed to have fallen asleep again while she had been making such a fuss about his father and Betty. He was not going to make a fool of himself like that again. Any fun he and Vartouhi was going to be carried on under the rose, his favourite flower. There was no harm in their little secrets but he knew what Con was. To his relief, his sister showed no disposition to discuss the evening's events any further, and he was able to go back to the drawing-room fire and his newspaper and such comfort as could be had from his thoughts.

After Miss Fielding had gone upstairs, with the obvious intention of arousing Miss Burton and telling her all about it, he sat in solitude until past midnight, dozing and reading items of news over and over again and every now and then thinking uneasily how unsettled life at home had recently become. He was not more given than the average man to dreams of tender domestic happiness; if such a state had come to him in the natural course he would have welcomed it warmly and been completely content with it, but he did not consciously sigh over his unmarried state. His straightforward, affectionate and strongly repressed nature had been steeped from his early manhood in the thought, instigated by his mother and sisters, that he was the type of good-natured old ass that girls liked but did not fall in love with, and when his first youthful passion had been killed by Betty, he *had* (Richard's guess was a true one) suffered as deeply as he could suffer, and his bachelorhood was largely due to that one wound received in youth.

But his was too healthy a nature to brood over an old sorrow, and if he had been asked whether his years from twenty-five to forty-five had been happy ones he would have unhesitatingly answered 'yes.' He had the never-failing interest and pleasure of his garden, his affection for his mother and sisters and his pride in their talents (Mrs Miles, we forgot to say, painted in her spare time in a downright, between-bouts-of-active-service fashion, rather as a bustling Prime Minister might), a profession which interested him without exhausting his energies and upon which he need not rely for his ample income, and a large comfortable house in which there was always enough social activity to make the time pass pleasantly and even to keep him abreast with affairs in the great world, for Miss Fielding's protégés had included some harmless *déracinés* with political contacts in their native lands.

And, besides, he had never quite known what he wanted. Few people do, and he was an average person. His desires had always been vague; if he ever thought about what he would have liked his life to be, he pictured himself as a soldier, with a foreground of active service in far-off lands and the dim figures of a pretty wife and some children in the background. But his ambitions had always been so vague, and never supported by Ambition itself, which drives the dreams of love or fame remorselessly forward until they crystallize and come true; and his home was so comfortable, the pattern of his life so uniformly pleasant, that the roots of desire for the life of a normal human being had steadily withered.

They were almost dead when Vartouhi and Betty came to live at Sunglades six months ago. Another ten years, even another five, and Habit and Comfort and Humorous Self-deprecation, the great stones that lie on such roots and bleach and dry them, would have done their work. But the two women had arrived just in time; the roots were stirring with fresh life; and Kenneth sat dejectedly before the fire on this February evening, with the snowdrops and violets and daffodils in the green Chinese bowls and vases, and thought how uncomfortable life had been lately and wondered why.

Perhaps there are too many women in the house, he thought, standing up with a sigh that ended in a yawn and folding his paper neatly for salvage; and yet it was no better when Richard and Father were here, because they were both so hard hit they were no use as ballast.

The fact is, he thought, going gloomily round tweaking the black-out close and switching off lights, this isn't an ordinary household. (The enormity of this thought, coming from himself, never struck him, although six months ago he would have been simply incapable of thinking it. So far had the roots grown in strength.) None of us here are married or have any children (can't count Father, he isn't like a father anyhow and never has been), or are even engaged. A normal household, thought Kenneth as he went slowly up the stairs, a normal household has children in it or young people just growing up and falling in love and perhaps a grandmother or an aunt or something like that. Old people and young people and little boys and girls, with a man in his prime at the head of it. There's something wrong with all of us, he thought even more gloomily, as he stalked into the bathroom. Father's too gay by half for his time of life, and Con's so down on everybody, and Frankie's an old maid, and Betty's never got over Dick's death, and Richard's a highbrow, and I'm an old stick, and Vartouhi—she's a dear little girl but I sometimes think she's got an eye to the main chance, like the rest of them nowadays.

He went to sleep thoroughly dissatisfied with his housemates and himself.

The following morning at breakfast Miss Fielding lightly revealed that her father had gone to London overnight and it was uncertain when he would return. The proper comments were made, in which polite regret mingled with a little surprise at the suddenness of his departure, and then the establishment almost audibly set itself in train to resume the uneventful routine that had preceded his arrival. Betty was too cautious to assume immediately that she would not now be expected to leave the house, but she did go so far as to postpone making inquiries for a room in St Alberics, which she had proposed to do that morning, and her optimism, as the week went on, was justified, for Miss Fielding said no more about her departure and even made references to plans for the summer in which she was included.

The fact was, Miss Fielding had suddenly decided that it would be best if Betty stayed on. After all, she was an old friend, and however sensibly she had received the suggestion that she should leave, her departure was bound to leave a little unpleasant-ness, and that was never desirable. Now that Father was gone, the chief reason for her leaving had been removed, and although Kenneth, no doubt, would continue to make sheep's eyes at her, that was irritating, but it meant nothing more than it ever had. And, most persuasive factor of all, on the very morning after Father had left, one of those women called with a paper wanting to know how many bedrooms there were in the house. That settled it; Miss Fielding patiently replied that there were seven, five of them permanently occupied and two likely to be reoccupied at any moment; and decided that she would say no more to Betty about the incident.

Now that Christmas was hardly a memory, and the evenings were beginning to draw out and fill with blue light, and the snowdrops to lift their delicate heads from the garden earth, Miss Fielding's thoughts turned once more to *Little Frimdl*, whose presentation had been so long delayed, first by the deplorable slackness of the cast and secondly by the arrival of old Mr Fielding and the subsequent falling in love of all the inmates (or so it seemed to her) of the house. Miss Fielding thought that it would be an excellent idea if everyone purged themselves of their recent preoccupation with the Destructive Force by starting rehearsals again.

It was with indescribable dismay that the former cast of *Little Frimdl* witnessed his resurrection. What! were they not harassed enough by convalescence, love and their war work and the spring weather, were not their inward sufferings from their emotions and their outward ones from colds, enough that they must once again struggle with the Spirits of Mutual Mistrust and the Very Old Man and all the rest of it? They could hardly believe what they heard. But they were weakened by months of emotional strain and the long winter nights, and also they were taken by surprise. They all found themselves enrolled again, and Betty's feeble attempt to get Richard exempted by explaining that he had recently taken on part-time work in a rivet-sorting factory in St Alberics was defeated by Miss Fielding's brisk demand for his address in Blentley, so that she might write to him and get everything arranged.

When he received her letter Richard was really annoyed. He had got his emotions into order again after Vartouhi's visit to him in January, having found satisfactory work for his mind with the European Reconstruction Council and for his hands in the rivet-sorting factory; and he was emphatically not going to risk having himself disturbed again. He wrote to Miss Fielding by return of post, saying courteously but very firmly that he was too busy to undertake a part, and wishing the play all the success it deserved. He then dismissed the matter from his mind.

There was a strong contrast between the two places where he worked, and he appreciated it. The European Reconstruction Council was housed in a mansion designed by one of the many English disciples of Palladio, standing in a small secluded park among the low hills some miles beyond St Alberics. The long windows looked out across the stars and ovals of flower-beds which had been laid out by a Victorian owner of the house (overruling the assurances of experts that a house of that period should have a wild meadow sweeping up to its very loggia), and thence down a gentle slope to the waters of a lake surrounded by groups of stately beeches and—an exotic touch—deodars planted by another experimenting owner. The flower-beds were now planted with potatoes, and in the loggia was a long rack containing bicycles belonging to the Council, but the severe, noble lines of the house and the placid beauty of the lake with its dark sweeping trees could not be marred by such contemporary details. Richard looked forward to his first sight of the great mansion, in colour neither grey nor cream but a blending of the two, as he turned the curve of the drive in the morning and the lake and the trees and the low hill crowned by the house were first revealed. He had managed to buy a bicycle, which was extremely useful to him, as Cobbett Hall was some five miles from Blentley and it was only the senior members of the Council who had the tacit right to use the Council bus; but the man he envied was the one who rode up to the mansion twice a week on a beautiful dark grey mare and who made a picture of himself and his mount, despite his own unpicturesque person, because Cobbett Hall had been designed in the age when horses were a natural part of any picture.

Within, the delicate touches of gilding on the cornices and the sea-green or terra-cotta walls served to emphasize the strict beauty of the house's lines, as did the shadowless light that illuminated every corner and filled the rooms. Wood, stone and plaster were so happily married here, and in the more domestic parts of the house their lines were so gently softened by two hundred years of service, that the prevailing atmosphere was one of harmony; before a chair or a picture or a flower had been put into the house, its proportions, and light, had furnished it perfectly for as long as it should stand.

The rivet-sorting factory was housed in two tall dilapidated sheds in a back street near the cathedral, named Abbot's Lane. The wall of an old cemetery ran along one side, and on the other there were some squalid dark cottages, and others of the same kind stood opposite. Glimpses of machines and moving figures could be detected behind the dusty windows of the sheds, and occasionally when the doors, painted grey, were opened to let one of the two-hour shifts come out, there was a smell of hot oil. Most of these voluntary and part-time workers were women, and sometimes their children stopped on the way home from school to wait for Mother to come out from the factory, and the narrow silent little street, where the hum of the machines could faintly be heard, was disturbed by the brisk cries of marble-players and the arguing of little girls.

There was a yard at the back of the sheds with some old boxes and half a motor-car in it, and on sunny days Richard and others of the sixty workers would sit out there for half an hour and listen to Works Wonders on somebody's portable wireless while eating their lunch. A wall kept off the wind that blew across the old cemetery with its tangled grass and neglected graves, and over the place there was the shabby peace, the comfortable obscurity, that is the favourite atmosphere of seven human beings out of ten whether they know it or not.

So Richard began to find life orderly and manageable once more.

26

Sunglades was a sadder and a wiser house as the spring advanced. There was the feeling that a number of very bad rows had just been avoided; rows in which old grievances would have exploded and people would have had large jagged pieces of other people's minds thrown at them, and this had a sobering effect upon the older members of the household who had learned to value peace. *My Love had a Silver Ring* echoed from Miss Burton's rooms at the top of the house more frequently than it had for months; on the lengthening evenings of March the romantic notes floated down to the daffodils and narcissus swaying in the windy garden or sounded through long afternoons of cold spring rain. Mr Fielding had now been in London for some five weeks, and Kenneth had had a gallant little letter from him saying that he was leaving the Regent Palace and going to spend a week or so with some friends in town. Apparently he was still taking it hard. Kenneth was very sorry for the old boy; he knew what it was; but meanwhile he undoubtedly found the house a pleasanter place than it had been for months. It was Betty and Vartouhi who brightened it for him, now that both his rivals had departed; but Vartouhi especially. She was like sunlight in the house, he thought, with her ready smile and her topsy-turvy English and her frank delight in the secret little presents of flowers and trinkets and scent which he gave her from time to time.

She was made even more cheerful than usual towards the middle of March by a letter from her sister in New York, enclosing one from the Mother Superior at the Convent where all the five Annamatta sisters had learned to read and write. It told Yania that her father and mother and Djura and Yilg and K'ussa were alive; and that Medora was still safe with the nuns in Turkey, and that the farm had been forced to produce fruit for the enemy but was not producing very hard. The Mother had seen them all at the farm on the very day that she wrote, having obtained permission from the Italian authorities to visit an old dying lay-sister, who lived in the village nearest to the Annamattas' home. The crop was not good this year and they had been forced to hold the Feast of the Fruit in secret; but they had held it, and they were all alive, and they trusted in God the All-Merciful who would one day set them free.

'Soon, perhaps, Vartouhi,' said Kenneth, wishing that he were twenty-five again to sail with that new crusaders' fleet.

'Is a good thing!' was all Vartouhi would answer, reading the letter over and over again. He thought, as he looked down at her little face which was unwontedly soft with love for her family, and with happiness that they were safe, that Con and Betty and Frankie were all wrong when they said she was a hard-hearted child. She was only unawakened. Her heart was tender and true; and she'll make a wonderful wife one day, for some oily Bairamian, thought Kenneth with an unconscious sigh.

Alicia had not seen Richard for a month, and that seemed to her too long. She liked her friendships with men to progress, or to finish. But she followed her usual procedure and neither telephoned to him at Cobbett Hall nor wrote to him at his lodgings. More than once (even while in the arms of the man from the three-day party, who had come back to London) she thought, 'I believe he and I had something there, if only things had gone on.' But she did nothing about it. She had had a most bitter lesson, and never again was she going to lower her defences to a man nor advance one step towards him until he advanced, and probably not then.

So when she got Miss Fielding's post card announcing that

the next rehearsal of *Little Frimdl* would take place on March the 12th, she was actually pleased and her first thought was, 'I shall see Richard again.'

She wanted to talk to him. There were so many problems she wanted his opinion on; problems that had vaguely bothered her ever since she was a child, which everyone in her family and social circle had always been too busy to answer, on the rare occasions when she had broken through her reserve and asked. She thought she would like to sit up all night talking to Richard and hearing what he thought about this and that. And then she thought, well, perhaps not all night, and smiled to herself, as she tilted the gun-barrel into a new position and watched the blue figures below settle busily onto it with their tools. She wrote to Miss Fielding promising to be there.

Richard's letter announcing that under no circumstances could he take a part in *Little Frimdl* rather had its thunder stolen by another letter, in a typed envelope with an American stamp, which arrived for Miss Fielding by the same post. The household was at breakfast

'From Dr Stocke,' said Miss Fielding in a tone of satisfaction, opening the letter with the American stamp. Betty saw the one in Richard's handwriting with a sinking heart: she could almost guess the words in which his refusal would be phrased.

'He always finds time to write to you, Connie, in spite of being such a busy man,' she said, partly from the wish to put Miss Fielding into a good humour but partly from her instinct to give pleasure.

'We are old friends,' replied Miss Fielding, absently, for she was reading, but with complacency. Suddenly she gave a faint exclamation.

'Bad news?' inquired Miss Burton, rather hoping that it was, and the tiresomely peripatetic and efficient Stocke for once up a gum-tree.

'Oh no—no—quite the reverse. He is coming to England!'

There was a pause, which Miss Fielding was too busy reading to notice.

'Oh—er—good!' said Kenneth loudly and heartily at last. Betty and Miss Burton could not for the life of them refrain from exchanging a glance. Everyone hung on Miss Fielding's next words.

'In about three weeks!' she exclaimed, hastily turning the pages of the letter. 'He will fly of course, by way of Lisbon—hopes to see something of our plans for *reconstruction*—(how like him! ever forward-looking, even in the midst of Armageddon!) and will give some talks on the social services in his own country to the European Reconstruction Council—why, aren't those the people Richard is working with, Betty?—and would be gla——'

Miss Fielding ceased abruptly. Everyone gazed at her in surprise. She rustled the pages of the letter about, coughed, and then resumed in a voice strangely different from her usual confident tones:

'Would be glad if we could offer him hospitality for a while. But of course! How splendid!'

There was another pause. Miss Fielding continued to read the letter to its end. It is not too much to say that into the hearts of the remainder of the breakfast party there came a feeling very like despair. Each had always pictured Dr Stocke as an Arch-bore, a Grand Master and Adept in that ancient Lodge and Hierarchy, who would never stop talking in an exhausting foreign accent about social evils and their remedies, and insist on everybody else talking as well, so that they could neither go secretly to sleep nor crawl away under cover of an inconspicuous silence. More; he was the author of *Little Frimdl*; the creator of the Very Old Man and all those Spirits and Entities and those interminable speeches about the Ricelands and the Cornlands. And the first thought of everybody (except Vartouhi, who was eating porridge and staring out of the window) was: *He will take the rehearsals himself*.

'Well!' said Miss Fielding briskly at last, laying down the letter and glancing round at the faces of her housemates; 'isn't that splendid news? He has not visited England for nearly ten years. He will find great changes.'

'Nothing to eat, for a start,' said Kenneth, who now seemed in a bad temper, 'or drink.'

'Oh, that won't trouble Gustav Stocke!' cried his sister joyously. 'He is a total abstainer and while there is a glass of cold water left in England, he will fare royally!'

'The water usually tastes filthy, nowadays,' said Kenneth, determined that Dr Stocke should not enjoy himself. He was thinking angrily how different the reception of his father had been; what long faces, how grudging the hospitality. Why should this foreigner be taken in with open arms?

'I will write this morning and say we shall be delighted to give him bread and salt for as long as he wishes,' said Miss Fielding very firmly, observing signs of rebellion in Kenneth's manner. She began to roll up her napkin. Kenneth said nothing. His silence and his sullen look were embarrassing.

'Is it really ten years since you have seen him?' asked Betty, breaking what threatened to grow into an awkward silence.

'Oh quite that. It must be nearer eleven years.'

'I wonder if you will find him much changed?'

'I think not. I feel, somehow, that I shall not.'

Miss Fielding's manner had become even brisker and more confident than usual since reading Dr Stocke's letter. Miss Burton looked at her idly, and The Usurper wondered if she were quite as brisk and confident as she appeared. Both Miss Burton and The Usurper could remember days when the non-arrival of a letter from Dr Stocke had made Miss Fielding very low indeed; really cast down, as she used to be in her teens when she had suffered for a time from religious doubts. When a man was the sole masculine interest in a woman's life, and when the woman had not seen the man for ten years, surely the natural attitude on hearing that she was going to see him again was one of slight apprehension? And even Connie had her weaknesses. There was that Christmas party—in 1905, was it?—when the Bargle boy kissed her under the mistletoe and she cried for an hour, mused Miss Burton, eating toast with her head on one side. Well, it will be a great bore having him here, but if he succeeds in humanizing Connie it will be almost worth it.

'Con——' said Kenneth, opening the door of his sister's little morning-room half an hour later, as she sat writing letters, 'can you spare ten minutes?'

Miss Fielding looked up in a patient way and removed her glasses and sat expectant.

'It's about this chap coming here,' he went on, advancing into the room, 'look here, have you thought what a deuce of a lot of extra work it's going to make?'

Miss Fielding shut her eyes. Then she opened them again and fixed them severely upon her brother's ill-tempered face.

'I have taken all the difficulties into consideration, Kenneth. You may be sure of that.'

'Oh—er—good. I thought you mightn't have realized, that's all.'

'I fully realize.'

'He's over here in an official position, or semi-official, you know, and that means he'll be out at all hours seeing people and going over places and——'

'Dr Stocke's investigations are those of a private individual interested in peaceful international relationships,' interrupted Miss Fielding. 'He has no official support from his Government.'

'I see. If he gets his face pushed in, that's his funeral,' muttered Kenneth. 'Very convenient for his Government.'

'He has greater freedom of action and speech as a private individual. Naturally, his Government approves of his activities.'

'Yes, well, that's all right, but all I meant was, he'll be wanting meals at all sorts of odd hours and that'll make a damned lot of extra work for Vartouhi,' burst out Kenneth very irritably indeed.

'Has Vartouhi been complaining?' Miss Fielding's voice was as sharp as his own.

'She's never said a word. But I can see what's it's going to mean.'

Miss Fielding replaced her spectacles and turned again to her correspondence.

'I have eight letters to write before luncheon, Kenneth. You may be quite sure that everything will be properly organized and that Vartouhi will not be given any more to do than she is capable of doing. Bairamians are a hardy race.'

'She'll need to be,' he muttered. Then, after a moment's hesitation, he broke out again with:

'And another thing, I'm not at all sure I want him here. Foreigners all over the place . . . There are too many of them in the country now, and I'm not the only one who thinks so. A neutral, too!'

'Most mercifully, *yes*,' said Miss Fielding, not looking up and scribbling away like mad.

'I don't like neutrals coming over here and poking their noses into our war and eating our carrots.'

Miss Fielding flung down her pen. She sat upright. Her eyes blazed. She glared at her brother.

'Kenneth!' she said very loudly. 'I will hear no more! You are the essence of selfishness! I seem to hear the voice of the Evil Principle itself! An old and valued friend, who knew Our Mother, an ardent worker for peace, asks bread and salt of us and you would have me refuse! I regard it as a sacred duty to offer hospitality to Gustav Stocke. It is a form of *peace-work*; the first I have been able to do for months. He is a messenger from a saner world than ours, a true emissary of civilization, and were I to refuse his request I should feel ashamed to my dying day both for myself and for you. Besides, I haven't seen him for ten years and I *want* him to come here and he *shall*!' suddenly concluded Miss Fielding with a stamp of her foot on the floor. 'Now let us regard the matter as settled: I feel the Evil Principle all about me and my vibrations are disturbed; please go away at once, *before worse things happen.*'

Kenneth, who detested and dreaded scenes, hastily went. He had not succeeded in getting in a word about Father and the way *he* had been received. Might as well have kept my mouth shut, he thought gloomily, Con always gets the best of it.

This was not the end of the matter, however. Vartouhi was unusually silent throughout lunch and clashed plates about while she helped Mrs Archer to wash up. When Miss Fielding was settled in the drawing-room with *The Times*, Miss Burton having gone upstairs to take her afternoon rest, there was a tap at the door. In response to Miss Fielding's 'Come in,' Vartouhi entered, looking extremely polite.

'What is it, Vartouhi?' demanded Miss Fielding, looking at her over her spectacles.

Vartouhi marched up to her employer's chair and stood looking down at her with hands behind her back.

'Miss Fielding, I want talk to you.'

'Very well then, Vartouhi, but don't be long about it, please.' In spite of her crisp tone Miss Fielding's heart sank. She had retired to the drawing-room for an hour or so in solitude, to think over the forthcoming visit of Dr Stocke, about which her usually concise thoughts were somewhat confused. Was that visit to be marred by domestic rebellion?

'A man friend of you is coming to stay here,' announced Vartouhi abruptly.

Miss Fielding inclined her head in dignified assent, overlooking the colloquial form of this statement.

'There will be much for me to work at. Much, much.'

'Who told you that Dr Stocke is coming to stay here?' demanded Miss Fielding, suspecting Kenneth and very annoyed.

'I hear you say so, Miss Fielding, at breakfast.'

'Indeed.' Miss Fielding gave what in vulgar circles would be described as a nasty laugh. 'I did not think you were listening. You were looking out of the window.'

'I look out of the window *and* listen too also.'

'I am afraid you often do, Vartouhi. You are a sly little girl, I am very sorry to say.'

'No I am not. In the pictures I sit with an American soldier and he said I am not. He said the British are all frozen up except me. So I am not, Miss Fielding.'

'I said *SLY*, Vartouhi, not SHY,' explained Miss Fielding with commendable patience. 'Sly means deceitful, hiding your real thoughts. Shy means——'

'Averybody hides their real thoughts.'

'Yes, well, never mind that now. We seem to have wandered from the point. By the way, Vartouhi, though of course you must be polite and pleasant to any foreign soldiers—poor misguided men!—who have come to England, you must be careful—er—not to be *too* friendly in your manner.'

'Why, Miss Fielding, please?'

'Because your *mother* would not like it!' Miss Fielding, who did seem unlike her efficient usual self to-day, lost her temper for the second time. 'Now that's enough; hurry up and tell me what you were going to say and run away.'

'There will be too much work for me when this man he comes.'

'Dr Stocke, Vartouhi; not "this man"; that is a rude way to talk.'

'Dr Stocke, Miss Fielding.'

'Now, Vartouhi, understand this for once and for all; there will *not* be a lot of extra work for you to do when Dr Stocke comes. There will be no more for you to do than when Mr Marten and my father, Mr Fielding, were here; not so much, in fact, because they were two and he is only one. And I know for a fact that Dr Stocke makes a habit of helping with the work when he stays in the houses of his friends. So——'

'Is varry good and kind.'

'Yes. Yes, he *is* good and kind.' Miss Fielding suddenly stifled a sigh. How long it seemed since she had enjoyed a really interesting, fruitful talk about her work with anyone! I live in a spiritual desert, she thought; Ruth in tears amid the alien corn. 'Now, is all that quite clear to you now, Vartouhi?' smiling mechanically at her and taking up *The Times*.

'Yas, thank you, Miss Fielding. Dr Stocke is varry good and kind and he will help me with the work.'

'Er—yes. Perhaps not quite that. We shall have to see when he comes. But he will certainly do his share of the household tasks, that I know. Now run away, Vartouhi; I am busy.'

Vartouhi curtsied and smiled and went.

Alone once more, Miss Fielding let *The Times* fall upon her lap, and gazed into the fire with an expression which gradually became thoughtful. Thought, that wears and hollows the face to which it is habitual as water erodes the bed of a stream, had left no marks on her face, with its habitual decisive expression. Now it lay across her stubborn rosy features like a shade. She began by thinking how long it was since she had seen Dr Stocke, and went on to an effort to recall the details of his appearance, and to wondering if they would be much changed by the passage of eleven years, and then to wondering whether *he* would find much change in *her*. My hair is greying now, of course, she thought, lifting one hand to it; and then her thoughts (softened perhaps by pleasant memories of many a splendid long talk with Dr Stocke about Peace and International Goodwill and the League of Nations, and by the firelight dancing dreamily over the bowls of delicate spring flowers), imperceptibly took a more personal and frivolous turn; and an hour or so later when she was presiding over the tea tray with Miss Burton she suddenly observed, after a longish silence, that she thought she would go up to town and buy a new dress.

'Something light,' said Miss Fielding, crunching her firm white teeth on a piece of toast, 'and springlike.'

27

So it happened that some three weeks later, as Richard was sitting at luncheon in the long dining-room of Cobbett Hall, he was disturbed to see Miss Fielding sweeping in through its double doors, plainly in search of provender and *supported*, rather than followed, by an enormously tall, broad handsome man in the middle fifties, with Nordic eyes and hair and a Presence.

The long windows revealed the uncertain blue sky of March and the wonderfully clear light shone down on the dark faces, the scholarly or worn or foreign faces, of the members of the Council and their trainees, who were patiently, and in most cases absently, moving past the service counter, carrying their own cutlery and plates. There were long trestle tables covered with white cloths washed and bleached in the great laundry and drying-ground of the mansion, and vases filled with wild daffodils and early purple orchids from the woods on the estate. The long room was piercingly cold and most of the people in it wore their overcoats.

Richard was hoping fervently that Miss Fielding and her friend would not see him, when they did. Miss Fielding, who had a pink dress under her fur coat and had done something to her hair, made a remark to her companion and waved. The big man at once turned his full attention upon Richard with courteous concentration. It was like being focused by a search-light. Richard gazed vaguely at the two through his glasses and pulled his book closer to his plate; but Miss Fielding, with plates and cutlery in one hand, waved again, so Richard stood up and bowed: such is not the casual manner of the day, but the Council and the trainees were used to handshakes at odd times and clickings of heels and kissings of hands and no one took any notice.

I am not going to be branded as an unwashed Leftist with bad manners, thought Richard, as he sat down again.

A moment later they were upon him.

'Well, Richard, here is the author of *Little Frimdl* in person!' cried Miss Fielding merrily, 'Gustav, this is Richard Marten.'

The gentlemen exchanged smiles and how do-you-do's, and then Dr Stocke observed in grammatically perfect English with a slight accent:

'May we sit here with you, Mr Marten? I have looked forward to meeting you, and I am glad to do so now; I do not know much about the European Reconstruction Council, although I have been invited to lecture for it, and should be grateful if you can enlighten me a little. Constance, you have no spoon for your pudding. I will go and get you one, if you will both excuse me.'

'It's rice. I don't think I will have any; I don't like it,' said Miss Fielding, with a schoolgirlish giggle.

'You had better have some, Constance. It is a mistake not to eat whenever, and whatever, you can, and take advantage of the admirable, the truly admirable,' turning to Richard, 'organization and distribution of food in this country. To me it is a never-failing source of amazement, for I have recently been staying in countries where there is very little food and what there is is badly distributed. I will go and fetch you a spoon for your pudding, Constance. Excuse me.' He smiled at them both from his clear blue eyes and marched away.

'Well, Richard! It was very naughty of you to say that you couldn't be in *Little Frimdl*,' said Miss Fielding, settling herself opposite to him and loosening her coat. 'What have you to say for yourself?'

'What I said in my letter, Miss Fielding.'

'But it's nonsense! You must have *some* spare time!'

'Oh yes, I have. I use it for my personal recreation.'

'Very selfish of you.'

'Yes. Will you forgive me if I go on eating; I have a lecture to give at two o'clock and my cabinet pudding is getting cold.'

'Is there cabinet pudding? I thought there was only rice.'

'I had the last portion, I think.'

Miss Fielding had nothing to say to this, and Richard went on with his luncheon, reflecting that her manner was more animated and youthful than heretofore. He did not think the change an improvement.

'Here is your pudding spoon, Constance.' Dr Stocke loomed above them once more.

'Thank you, Gustav. Now do sit down and eat your lunch; it will be cold.'

'I do not mind. In the last three years, during my itinerary, I have learned to eat and enjoy anything that is not actually putrid.'

Miss Fielding glanced at Richard as if to say, *Isn't my friend magnificent?* and went on, 'I have just been telling Richard, Gustav, that he has no excuse for not acting in *Little Frimdl.*'

'Indeed? Why has he no excuse?' inquired Dr Stocke, eating steadily away and indulgently turning the searchlights full upon Richard. Richard was not embarrassed. His cause, he considered, was just; and he intended to make a stand.

'I am too busy, Dr Stocke. I give four lectures a week here, which need considerable preparation, and I am also doing part-time work in a rivet-sorting factory.'

'Making instruments to destroy his fellow-men,' put in Miss Fielding, with a little shudder.

'I should hardly describe a rivet as an instrument of destruction, Miss Fielding,' said Richard. 'Rivets hold things together—or so I hope. They do not blow them apart.'

'They hold things together which are used for blowing things apart,' said Miss Fielding gravely.

'And what do you do in your leisure time?' asked Dr Stocke. His tone was politely interested rather than inquisitorial.

'I play the gramophone and read astronomy and walk.'

'Excellent,' nodded Dr Stocke, demolishing the last of his savoury vegetable pie. 'Your time is fully occupied. Even your recreations require application and intelligence. I agree that you have no time to act in my play.'

'But Gustav!' protested Miss Fielding, 'it's almost impossible to get another man for the part! And he has rehearsed so often.'

'You are not eating your rice pudding, Constance. You should do so. It is excellent.'

'I don't fink I *like* wice-puddie!' said Miss Fielding, naughtily pushing her plate away.

'Ha! ha! It is very amusing to hear a grown-up woman talking like a little girl!' laughed Dr Stocke (but Richard could see that he was going to have his way). 'Do you know what I do to naughty little girls who will not eat their pudding? I smack them!' said Dr Stocke, nodding his head meaningly at Miss Fielding, 'I smack them on their naughty little hands!'

'Oh—well—in that case I *must* be good,' said Miss Fielding hastily, colouring and beginning upon the despised pudding. 'But,' she went on, straightening her face and assuming a plaintive air, 'it is a great disappointment to us, Richard, that you will not change your mind.'

'Is it?' smiled Richard, taking out his cigarette case.

'It is not a disappointment to me, Constance,' interrupted Dr Stocke authoritatively and rapidly, finishing the last mouthfuls of his rice pudding. 'I am sorry if you are disappointed. I had not realized that the performance of the play meant so much to you. In fact, I had almost forgotten it. Although I was deeply moved at the time that I wrote it, for I never create a work of art without experiencing the true creative urge, for the last two years I have been engaged upon work that is so much more important and satisfying that I recalled the play almost with surprise when you mentioned it to me.'

'Oh, it has meant so *much* to us——' murmured Miss Fielding.

'Yes, indeed,' said Richard, offering Dr Stocke a cigarette.

'Thank you. You said that with irony,' observed Dr Stocke, accepting a cigarette.

'Well, yes,' Richard adjusted himself quickly to the impact of what he now realized was a most unusual personality. 'I did. The truth is, we were rehearsing your play at a time when I was overworked and very run down and I didn't enjoy the rehearsals at all.'

'It is understandable.'

'Thank God you see it like that,' said Richard cheerfully, getting up to go. 'Are you going to be here this afternoon?'

Dr Stocke nodded. 'I have an appointment with Sir Lawrence Barwood at half-past three, to discuss the form and subject of my talks. I shall probably be free at a quarter-past four.'

'Then would you care to have tea with me? We haven't had a chance to talk about the Council, and I can probably tell you anything you want to know.'

'Thank you. That would be very pleasant.'

'Till four-fifteen, then. Good-bye, Miss Fielding,' and Richard, with another slight bow and smile, walked away.

'A clever and attractive young man,' pronounced Dr Stocke.

'Oh, do you think so, Gustav? I've always found him so *difficile* and rude.'

'That is natural, Constance, for he dislikes you,' said Dr Stocke calmly. 'May I smoke now, if you have eaten all of your pudding that you intend to eat?'

'Oh, please do. *Does* he dislike me, do you think? I always get on so well with young people—I thought——'

'Yes, he dislikes you very much. It is because you wish to arrange his activities for him. He resents that. Men,' said Dr Stocke, turning the searchlights full upon Miss Fielding, 'men of mature age who are experienced in the conduct of life are not angered by such attempts on the part of women, as a young man is. Mature men find such attempts amusing, even attractive.

For they know well how to deal with them,' concluded Dr Stocke. 'Will you smoke a cigarette, Constance?'

'Thank you,' said Miss Fielding meekly. 'I don't often smoke———'

'I have observed that. It is as well. In one respect, and in one only, concerning the activities of your sex, I am old-fashioned. I do not much like to see women smoking, especially in the street. Let them organize, govern, teach, do what they will———'

'Oh, I *do* so agree!'

'———towards the making of the new world which shall emerge from the senseless ruins of the old, but do not let them blow tobacco smoke all over me, because I do not like it.'

'I must be careful!' laughed Miss Fielding, waving her cigarette smoke away from him.

Dr Stocke looked at her indulgently. 'Have no fears, Constance. You do not smoke often enough for me to find the habit offensive in you.'

They spoke no more for a little while, but sat watching the hall gradually emptying of people. At length Dr Stocke said, glancing at the old gilt and painted clock high up on one of the walls, 'Now, if you have finished your cigarette, you had better go home, Constance. The bus passes the end of the beech avenue in twenty minutes and I do not want you to miss it. Adjust your scarf closely about your neck, for the wind is very cold to-day.'

She did so, and he stood up and waited courteously with his cigarette between his fingers.

'Good-bye, Gustav. Shall you be in to dinner?'

'Indeed I shall, with much news for you, no doubt, and I shall not be late. Good-bye.'

He bowed, smiling down upon her from his impressive height, and stood until she had gone out through the tall doors.

Richard's verdict upon Dr Stocke after passing an hour or so alone with him was that he was an ass but a well-informed ass, and he was even disposed to like him, in a mild and amused way; besides, it was such a satisfaction to see the Fielding woman put down, really in chains, ordered about like any Fascist Frau, for all her fine talk! But he must be exhausting at close quarters, thought Richard. Dr Stocke for his part found that Richard had all the marks of the ancient European culture, and had even begun dimly to see the light about international relationships, although he was grievously pig-headed—misled and mistaken, that is to say—about the Nazi War, not scrupling to say that it was a filthy job that had to be done. Still, on the whole Dr Stocke approved of him, and what with pleasant acquaintances and the excellent hospitality at Sunglades, he was thoroughly enjoying his visit to war-time England.

This was more than could be said for the weaker spirits at Sunglades, who crept about their affairs oppressed by Dr Stocke's omnipotence and size and habit of sitting up until half-past one every night having splendid long talks with Miss Fielding about international goodwill. His voice was loud, and it carried all over the house, Miss Burton going so far as to say that it boomed in the chimney and made her think it was the guns. But no one could hint a protest, for Dr Stocke was most considerate when he did at last come up to bed, shutting doors noiselessly and tiptoeing about and generally demonstrating that he was qualified to live in a civilized community.

It was not what he *did*, it was what he *was*; so large, so clever, so humourless and merry, so sharp at pouncing on any little sly dig in conversation and dragging it out into the light of day; above all, so dreadfully, dreadfully interested in the way everything worked, from the points rationing to the Sunglades refrigerator on its special low war-time allowance of gas instituted by Kenneth.

He also helped in the house. Miss Fielding seeing to it that it was she, and not Vartouhi, whom he assisted to lay the cloth. Vartouhi, not being a weak spirit, was not oppressed by Dr Stocke. She did not take any more notice of him than was necessary for daily normal politeness. He seemed very old to her, and she had also gathered that he, like Miss Fielding, did not approve of the Nazi War and wished to make peace immediately. This was quite enough to give her a deep scorn for him, which, being a Bairamian, she had not the smallest scruple or difficulty in concealing; and, besides, Mr Kenneth did not like him, and Mr Kenneth was unhappy because he was in the house. Is a wicked thing, thought Vartouhi, placidly wiping up plates or sorting laundry. Mr Kenneth sees his ancient and honoured father driven away because Mrs Mar-ten does not love him and because Miss Fielding will not give him shelter in his old age. Now this one comes along, full of health and strength and a fool, and he is made welcome, while the poor old Mr Fielding who said I was a kind girl and gave me the one pound note money is in London far away. Is a wicked bad thing. If only Mr Kenneth would drive this one angrily away!

Dr Stocke made his own bed, and would have helped Betty and the rest of the household make theirs, if Betty (keeping a straight face with difficulty) had not assured him that this task was Vartouhi's and that an elaborate and efficient timetable would be disrupted if he intervened. Dr Stocke, a methodical man, could appreciate this (besides, he enjoyed making beds no more than any clever man—or clever woman—does), and so he made no more offers that would take him up to the bedrooms. But he carried coals, he washed up, he made—so far as the milk supply would permit—superb coffee, he lit fires, and he would even have dug, wearing an old national costume that he carried about with him for this very purpose, had not Kenneth made it very plain that Dr Stocke was not wanted in the kitchen garden.

Miss Fielding had not felt so harmonious for years. How delightful it was to have a kindred spirit under her roof! to let her fancy soar and her eloquence too! to plan the Brotherhood of Man with a man; a clever, solid, courteous, masterful man! He *is* a little masterful, thought Miss Fielding, not unpleasantly moved by this discovery, but I must confess that I find it rather a relief. For so many, many years I have had to be the man of this household, poor Kenneth being so weak-willed and unreliable; and it is a positive relief to me to let the oars rest, and drift downstream while Gustav steers.

These novel sensations were not confided to Miss Burton, who shared Betty's amusement at seeing Connie brought to heel. There was a little malicious pleasure in watching Connie having her hair waved, and buying new hats, and even abandoning the chalk-white powder which she had used for years and purchasing a pink one to dull the apple-shine on her rosy skin.

Although Miss Burton was not made a confidante, she missed no move in the situation, and she and Betty found their sole relief from the oppressiveness of Dr Stocke's presence in marvelling and smiling over Miss Fielding's subjugation. Each knew that Connie had for over ten years taken great pleasure in Dr Stocke's friendship and letters, but neither had been prepared for the rapidity with which she succumbed to the charm of his actual presence. And he himself never failed in courtesy and protective kindness towards her. Betty and Miss Burton murmured together over the fire in the latter's sitting-room in the evenings when Miss Fielding and Dr Stocke were booming away downstairs, and wondered indeed how it would all end.

Kenneth sat alone in the little study on the nights when he was not out with the Home Guard and sulkily read detective stories. He was thoroughly out of temper nowadays and made but little effort to conceal his feelings. The beginning of his anger had been his sisters' unkindness to his father at Christmas, but his tranquillity had been vaguely disturbed for months before that. No sooner did one domestic storm die down than another arose; and these storms were not the endurable ones inevitably arising out of a full and expanding family life; no, they were imposed by extraneous and unnecessary circumstances such as the visits of dam' bores of foreigners. And he was worried about his father, from whom he had not heard for a month. The weather was wretched, with icy winds and sweeping rains, and he had an uneasy feeling that the old man might be ill. Presumably he had gone to stay with his friends in London but so far Kenneth had received no address.

Well, Con would go on making a fool of herself until this fellow left, he supposed, and he prayed that it might be soon. After that, they could settle down to await the next disturbance of their peace.

On a very wet evening towards the middle of March he was sitting as usual, reading the latest Agatha Christie with less than his usual attention. By the afternoon post there had come a letter from Mrs Miles taking him to task for various happenings; his father's behaviour in going off and leaving no fixed address ('so *peculiar*, now that he *has* got in touch with us again *after twenty years*'); Constance's preoccupation with this man who was living in the house ('*so unlike her*, I have had no answer to my last *two* letters; *what does it mean*?'); and finally a strong hint that Betty was setting her cap at him ('I suppose Mrs Marten is still with you. She must feel quite like *one of the family* by now.').

This epistle had rendered poor sweet-tempered Kenneth even crosser than was usual nowadays; and as he sat alone in the little room, with the deepening blue of the March twilight making him annoyedly aware that it was within a few minutes of black-out, he looked a thoroughly disgruntled middle-aged man. Sheets of rain swept against the windows every now and then, and the trees tossed wildly in the gusts, while the budding tulips and the fading daffodils alike were being beaten down by the storm. In spite of the closed windows something of the evening's wild rainy spring freshness entered the room and increased his restlessness.

The telephone bell rang in the hall.

There was an extension line in the little study, and he reached across and took off the receiver.

After some preliminary noises and inquiries from the exchange, a man's voice, nasal and over-refined, inquired:

'Is that Treme 15? Mr Kenneth Fielding's house?'

'Yes. This is Mr Fielding speaking. Who is that please?'

'Judson, sir; the Mr Fothergills' man. Mr Fielding is staying with the Mr Fothergills, and 'as asked me to 'phone up, sir. Mr Fielding——'

The line crackled and the next words were lost.

'What? I can't hear you?' said Kenneth loudly.

'——very poorly indeed,' were the next words he heard. 'A kind of a chill, it seems to be, sir.'

'Mr Fielding—my father—he's ill, did you say? Do speak up; the line is appalling.'

'I'm sorry, sir.' The voice rose to an outraged yet controlled shout. 'Yes, sir. Mr Fielding 'as been poorly for about a week. The Mr Fothergills are away for a few days in Wiltshire and Mr Fielding is alone 'ere. He asked me to 'phone you up, sir.'

'Yes—quite right—where are you speaking from? I'll come up at once.'

'Very good, sir. It's Number 11 St Charles's Street, round at the back of Fortnum and Mason's.'

'All right. I'll be up there this evening. Is——'

'I shall 'ave to go out, sir, later on. A person promised to let me have a bit of fish for the Mr Fothergills when they return to-morrow to luncheon. I don't know quite how long I shall be. Wha——'

'Well, all right, I suppose there'll be someone to let me in?'

'I'm afraid not, sir, me being alone in the flat with Mr Fielding, and him in bed. What time will you be here, sir?'

The warning three pips sounded.

'As soon as I can get there. Surely you can wait——' began Kenneth irritably, and then was cut off in the middle of a sentence from the other end about the Mr Fothergills having ordered a bit of fish and this person having——

Kenneth swore, and went upstairs to find Betty, who put a few things into a suitcase for him and telephoned the station about trains while he was breaking the news to his sister and Dr Stocke. Miss Fielding did not seem seriously disturbed out of her pipe-dream, and made no more than conventional expressions of regret; it was Dr Stocke whose manner conveyed interest and concern. This did not decrease Kenneth's irritability, and as he drove the car away down the lane under the trees streaming with rain, a man more torn between bad temper and anxiety could not have been found that evening in the whole of Hertfordshire.

High up in her attic bedroom, Vartouhi was sitting at the window watching the rain, and every now and then putting a stitch into the bedspread, which flowed in brilliant waves of colour across her knees. Violet clouds hurried across the darkening grey-blue heavens, and the trees, their trunks and branches already lightly veiled in brown buds, swayed sighing in the wind. Vartouhi was singing to herself the *Song of the Lilac-picker*:

> *I pick the heart-leaves,*
> *I pick the purple flowers,*
> *Honey is in the flowers*
> *And love is in my heart,*
> *I give you the leaves and flowers*
> *And I give you my heart.*

Is Mr Kenneth driving away quickly, she thought, leaning forward the better to see the car go down the drive, and dimming the rainy window pane with her breath. She rubbed the mist away with one hand that held a needleful of brilliant yellow silk. Is gone, she thought. Is something the matter. And she resumed her little song.

I pick the heart-leaves——

In the clear twilight the colours on the bedspread glowed like a mosaic of dazzling summer flowers.

28

After a disagreeable journey, Kenneth arrived at 11 St Charles's Street at ten o'clock that night and found that the Mr Fothergills lived in a block of old-fashioned service flats standing between a shop that dealt in old masters and a shop that dealt in hand-made shoes. The impenetrability of the black-out on this moonless night and the comparative inaccessibility of St Charles's Street, together with the extreme and aristocratic smallness of the ancient shops, which caused them to resemble two cupboards that had strayed into the world of trade and barter by mistake, almost made him miss the entrance to No. 11.

A dim light burned in the hall, and he was able to discern that Mr Fothergill and Mr A. Fothergill inhabited Flat No. 3. He went up a softly carpeted stair; all was rather luxurious in a slightly Edwardian fashion, with palms in majolica pots and velvet curtains over the black-out. He wondered what the Mr Fothergills were like, and also reflected how little he knew of his father's life. How did he come to be lying ill in the flat of these two, who were apparently friends of his?

Judson turned out to be a thin reproachful little elderly man, rather sour, and plainly concerned only with the comfort of Mr Clifford and Mr Aubrey and—also plainly—regarding Mr Fielding, senior, as a nuisance likely to interfere with his lustrations. He showed Kenneth into an unexpectedly large bedroom whose size, however, was almost halved by the luxuriance of the velvet curtains and the thickness of the Aubusson carpet and the profusion of paintings of pretty dancers and naked girls by *petits maîtres* on the amber-brocaded walls. Each piece of furniture was antique and a treasure; the bed in which the old man lay uneasily sleeping was a little French four-poster with draperies scattered over with forget-me-nots and carnations. A fire was burning cheerfully. Kenneth glanced round him distastefully, reflecting that the old boys—he hoped, at least, that they were old—did themselves dam' well, and wished heartily that he were in the greenhouse on a fine day at home.

The doctor, it appeared, had not been summoned. Judson had been engaged for most of the day in polishing the silver and making a layer-trifle of which Mr Clifford and Mr Aubrey were particularly fond and which they had ordered for luncheon to-morrow. They would be put out, said Judson immovably, to find Mr Fielding so poorly. He had been a bit poorly when they left on Monday but they had been sure he would be better by the time they came home. It was very awkward, ended Judson, standing by the door and gazing reproachfully at the figure in the bed.

It ended with Kenneth arranging with his father, who awoke from his restless doze about midnight, that he would find a doctor to-morrow morning. Mr Fielding was rational in manner and speech and pathetically glad to see his son, and Kenneth was relieved to hear him say that a pain in his side was better than it had been earlier in the evening. After swallowing some hot drink reluctantly prepared by Judson, he fell asleep again; and Kenneth further shattered Judson's world by announcing that he must spend the night there. Where could he sleep?

It appeared that there was only Mr Clifford's room or Mr Aubrey's room. Judson seemed to think that this settled the matter, and Kenneth would now be prepared to curl up like Fido on the mat. However, on being impatiently told that his guest would sleep in whichever room was nearest to that of the invalid, he led the way to a smaller bedroom, every muscle of his person breathing forth indignation and dismay, and finally established Kenneth between fresh sheets of wonderfully fine linen, lavendered and monogrammed, and in the midst of more brocade-covered walls, tulipwood chairs, Dutch marquetry chests-of-drawers, and luscious little Renoir and Corot landscapes.

Thank heaven, thought Kenneth drowsily as he dozed off, at least it doesn't smell of scent.

With the morning, the problems of the previous night reappeared, but augmented. Mr Fielding was certainly worse; he complained of the pain in his side and of headache, and could not even drink the tea prepared in silence by Judson. Kenneth went out before the meal and with some difficulty found a doctor, who promised to come in an hour, which he did, and pronounced Mr Fielding to be suffering from pneumonia.

There is no need to recount in detail the events of that most trying day: the mounting agitation and final despair of Judson on hearing that the patient could on no account be moved and that a night and day nurse must immediately be installed; the bustling return of Mr Clifford and Mr Aubrey at luncheon-time, pleasantly ready for their bit of fish and layer-trifle; their dismay at finding Fielding a sick man and his son here; their complete lack of any attempt to hide that dismay, and the string of suggestions they made, all tending towards getting their friend out of their flat as speedily as possible.

Kenneth gathered that these two personable, very wealthy and gay brothers in their middle sixties had become acquainted with his father some four years ago when all three were interested in the same theatrical venture into which they were putting capital. He had been in the habit of spending a night at their flat from time to time, and his perfect health and lively powers as a raconteur made him a welcome visitor when he had recently come to stay with them for a longer period. But they had never intended him to have pneumonia there; *they* were never ill; they knew nothing about illness; it bored and frightened them; and here they were, at the beginning of the fine weather, with a thousand things to do and see, and an old man with pneumonia and his large dull, obstinate son on their hands. The Mr Fothergills could have wept.

They made themselves so unhelpful during the first half-hour of Kenneth's meeting them that he was dismayed at the prospect of seeing a good deal of them during the next week or so. However, he need not have worried, for when he returned from the post office where he had been telephoning the news to his sisters (he had not liked to ask more favours of the Mr Fothergills), he found Judson packing a great number of elegant clothes and a few cherished *objets d'art* and was informed that Mr Clifford and Mr Aubrey were moving temporarily into rooms at a nearby hotel. He was to be left alone with his father and the two nurses.

He apologized profusely for turning them out of their home; indeed, he did feel very distressed at the trouble he and his father were causing them, but his distress was considerably mitigated by their grudging acceptance of his apologies. Dammit, thought Kenneth, if this is the worst they ever have to put up with, they'll be lucky.

To his immense relief Judson went with them.

He now settled down to a strange dreamlike life. He felt cut off from the outside world by his anxiety for his father and by the muffling luxury of the flat and the bright nunlike cheerfulness of the two nurses, although both were pleasant girls, and he grew to rely on them for help and company. All his boyhood love for his father was revived by this time of anxiety for his life; and he promised himself that if the old man lived he should be offered a home at Sunglades for the rest of his days, and hang Connie. He did not suppose that his father would ever be so sprightly again, for the illness had taken a serious form and at his age people do not recover completely from such experiences, and if the old boy had suddenly grown old and feeble there was all the more reason to see that he was properly looked after. It would be company for himself; and there'll be two of us to stand out against Connie, he thought.

The prospect stretching before him did not seem cheerful, as he reflected on it in the evenings while sitting in the exquisitely furnished little drawing-room with an unread book across his knees. There would be three ageing people and a very old man living in that large house, which would seem to get larger and quieter as houses always did as the occupants shrank in size and grew more fixed and subdued in their habits. There was youth still alive in Kenneth and it stirred protestingly at this dismal picture.

He got up and stood at the window, which had a pleasant view across the trees of St James's Square to the sober façade of the London Library. A little girl was crossing the road with her hand in her mother's, and he could distinctly hear, above the distant sounds of the traffic in Piccadilly, her clear little voice. It's a sad thing when a man gets old without any children, thought Kenneth, turning away from the window.

His depression was increased by his dislike of the Brothers Fothergill, in whom bachelorhood had, so to speak, run to seed and provided a warning to those not yet completely enmeshed in it. A couple of selfish old tabbies, he thought them, with their pictures and their bits of silver and their special teacups which they could not do without and their slavish Judson. They made him think of those lines of Burns's, a poet whose warm and vigorous rhymes he had loved in his youth:

> O wad some Pow'r the giftie gie us
> To see oursels as others see us!

It must be years since they thought about anyone but themselves, he reflected, and probably they've no idea how they strike other people. Probably I haven't, either, and I'm as bad.

He began to long for the time to return to Sunglades, which was temporarily at least enlivened by the presence of a gay pretty woman and a charming child. It'll seem all the duller, though, after they've gone, he thought.

Mr Fielding's illness approached its crisis. There came a day when Mrs Miles arrived in a taxi and conferred in low tones with her brother as to the advisability of sending for Constance. But that day passed, and the old man lived; and from then on he began to get better. He was very weak, and seemed to cling to Kenneth, who saw that it was impossible yet to think of leaving him.

As soon as he was out of danger a new feature presented itself; the popping in and out of Judson, who of course had his own key and perfect right to come in and out whenever he chose, to fetch some bit of Spode or Georgian jam-spoon that Mr Clifford could not bear to be without for another minute. He nipped in and out without speaking to any of the invaders, but he invariably shut any windows that might be open (and both the nurses liked open windows) for fear the gales of St James's Square might damage the Tissots. These visits did not add to Kenneth's comfort and by the end of a fortnight he was wishing heartily that he and his father were at home again. He had kept in touch by telephone with his partner, Mr Gaunt, and had obtained compassionate leave from the Home Guard (not without robust inquiries made in private by Mr Arkwright as to why the blazes one of those Fielding women couldn't have gone instead), and when he spoke to Connie on the telephone she assured him that 'everything was all right.' Nevertheless, he was anxious to be at home again.

We must now return to Sunglades and find out if everything really was all right.

The first few days of Kenneth's absence passed pleasantly for Miss Fielding. She was not fond enough of her father to feel painful anxiety about him, although of course her sense of family duty prevented her from being completely indifferent to his fate, and the absence of Kenneth, with his unconcealed dislike of Dr Stocke, was decidedly a relief. Miss Burton and Betty remarked

301

occasionally how queer the house seemed without Ken and how glad they would be to have him home again, and Vartouhi surprised everyone (and even caused a little suspicion to arise in the Stocke-bemused mind of Miss Fielding) by inquiring determinedly every morning at breakfast, 'How is the father of Mr Kenneth to-day, Miss Fielding, please? Is a varry poor old gentleman,' and by showing in various ways that she pitied the invalid and wished heartily that he might recover. She also missed Kenneth; his kind ways, his smile, and his ready attention to, and interest in, her small problems and doings. But this feeling she kept to herself.

So all went well at Sunglades, until a certain morning when Kenneth had been away for nearly a week.

29

It was an extremely cold day. An east wind was blowing round the house, turning the petal-tips of the white and pink tulips an ugly brown and giving to the sky that peculiar light, with shreds of grey cloud floating low, that is only seen when the wind is in this quarter. All the household were peacefully eating their cornflakes and reading their correspondence when suddenly an exclamation from Dr Stocke caused everyone to start.

'Ass!' cried Dr Stocke (but in his native tongue) and he dashed a letter down upon the table, 'Stupid and unfeeling boy! It is too late!'

'Is something wrong, Gustav?' inquired Miss Fielding with more anxiety than had ever been heard in her voice for the misfortunes of her own family, while Betty and Miss Burton murmured something about hoping that it was not bad news. Vartouhi, behind her tea-cup, looked pleased.

'Yes, it is bad,' replied Dr Stocke, immediately recovering himself but speaking with an angry sparkle in his eye, 'Thank you for your kind inquiries. Constance, I must go to London at once. I should be most grateful if you would telephone to the Council for me and say that I shall be unable to address a gathering of students there this afternoon, but that I hope to do so to-morrow at the same time. Will you do this for me?'

'Of course,' said Miss Fielding, brightening slightly at the indication that he would not be long away, 'Er—shall you be in to dinner?'

'I must ask, Constance, if you will be kind enough to let me leave that question in doubt,' said Dr Stocke, his accent growing more noticeable as he paused to address her on his way to the door, 'but I shall certainly return by luncheon time to-morrow, and I must apologize most sincerely at having thus upset the domestic arrangements. If I might speak to you alone in the small study in fifteen minutes I will tell you briefly what has happened.'

Dr Stocke then hurried upstairs to pack a bag of needments while Miss Fielding retired, presumably to await the appointed hour; and Betty and Miss Burton looked at one another and simultaneously exploded into giggles.

'I must ask, Constance, if you will be kind enough——' said Vartouhi, also giggling and prancing towards the door with a recognizable imitation of Dr Stocke's voice and walk, '. . . if I might speak to you *alone* . . .' and up came her hand to her mouth and behind it her dark eyes danced in malicious delight. 'Is a fool, that man,' ended Vartouhi with a long sigh, wheeling forward the dumbwaiter. 'Praise be to God the All-Merciful that he will not be here to lunch!'

As the words left her lips, Miss Fielding's head came round the door, which had been left ajar. Betty and Miss Burton sat frozen: she had heard every word. She was looking extremely cross, and said very coldly:

'Get the table cleared at once and then wash up as quickly as you can. I want some things fetched from St Alberics. Don't waste your time, please, and don't giggle in that ill-bred silly way.' And she slammed the door.

'She's worried,' said Miss Burton, in excuse for her cousin.

'I do not care,' and Vartouhi gaily put out her tongue as she wheeled the dumbwaiter away.

Miss Fielding's face was no more cheerful half an hour later when she encountered Miss Burton on the landing and confided to her that Dr Stocke's eldest son, a youth of eighteen, had been misguided enough to join one of the Air Forces of the United Nations, flying to England especially for that purpose with a party of young men from one of the occupied countries whose frontier ran parallel with his own. They had stolen a bomber that was under repair from a Nazi airfield, and taken off in a snowstorm on one engine (Miss Burton could not keep back the 'How splendid!' that burst from her lips at this point), and after a hair-raising trip had pancaked down on an airfield in Scotland, very pleased with themselves. No wonder Dr Stocke was annoyed.

Miss Fielding recounted this saga in a low shocked voice as if it were something shameful out of one of the more popular Sunday journals, and her temper was not improved when, at the end of it, Miss Burton said stoutly, 'Well, I still think it's splendid, Constance. Dear boys! And fancy them knowing *how* to fly a bomber at all, that's what's so wonderful. You or I couldn't fly one if it was to save the British Empire.'

'*I* would let it perish,' said Miss Fielding grandly, 'and I am surprised at you, Frances, and disappointed too, I must say. What do you suppose Gustav can say to his Government—all so very awkward—and the German Embassy in the capital is bound to make inquiries—his son is well known there—and the boy's father on a visit to England—it all looks so suspicious—the German Embassy will think——'

'Oh *let* it!' cried Miss Burton. '*Really*, Connie! Who cares what they think, the—the—the dirty dogs? *I* think it's glorious!'

And Miss Burton swept away to her own quarters, leaving Miss Fielding—between sympathy with Dr Stocke and disappointment at his absence and fear lest he should after all not return on the morrow—in a bad temper.

Nothing happened as the day wore on to improve that temper. Vartouhi was unusually late in getting back from St Alberics and when she was reproved she only laughed and cheerfully displayed some of Kenneth's favourite biscuits for which she had stood in a queue. 'Will put them in a tin for his tea when he comes home,' said Vartouhi with satisfaction, and went into the kitchen swinging her cap and whistling, leaving Miss Fielding in the hall quite breathless with annoyance. The wind continued to moan drearily round the house, occasionally rising in force to an angry shriek, and Miss Burton complained of neuralgia.

After lunch a hush settled down on Sunglades. Miss Burton retired to her bedroom with a hot-water bottle and a book, and Vartouhi vanished on her own affairs. Miss Fielding sat alone in the drawing-room, which was even darker than usual to-day because of the lowering sky, and glanced disconsolately over *The Times*. Then she took up some embroidery and worked for a little while; but then she laid it down again, and glanced out at the desolate garden—the more desolate because the spring flowers with their promise of warmth and loveliness were shrivelling under the freezing wind—and sighed. It was impossible to settle to anything. The house seemed so dreary without Gustav. Usually if he were away for a few hours she had the pleasant anticipation of his shortly returning to a meal, but to-night there would be no firm knock at the front door, no manly tread across the hall, no cheerful tones greeting her as she turned to smile at him from her favourite fireside chair; and in her present gloomy mood she thought it unlikely that he would return to-morrow either. It is all the fault of that wretched boy, she reflected, angrily pulling her silk through the material. How selfish young people are. No thought for his father. I don't see what good Gustav can do by going to London, though I suppose—*bother* this silk! And she stuck the needle viciously in and folded the work up and shoved it away. I will write some letters, she thought, and remembered that one concerning some repairs to the house which had to be answered was upstairs in the old desk which Kenneth kept in his bedroom.

She went upstairs to get it.

The house was very silent. As she mounted the stairs she could see the red glow of the stove through the half-open kitchen door, with the great cat Pony lying asleep before it. Half-way up, there was a long window in which stood a bowl of spring flowers beautifully grouped by Miss Burton, and she paused to rearrange one or two that had been disturbed by the violence of the gale flinging itself against the window panes. She glanced out across the garden, brown and green with its freshly cut lawns and dark beds of earth under the low grey sky. Gustav will have had a cold journey, she thought, and went on.

She crossed the landing and opened the door of Kenneth's room and then stopped on the threshold, with her mouth open in amazement at the sight that confronted her.

Kenneth's room was furnished with a soldierly plainness that contrasted with the prettiness of the rest of Sunglades. There were faded photographs of rowing groups and his regimental mess on the brown walls and the furniture consisted of some slightly shabby pieces brought from their old home in St Alberics where the family had lived before the three younger members had come into their inheritance. A worn green carpet completed the sober effect.

All was as usual—but the bed! The bed, which was habitually covered by a green quilt and eiderdown! The bed was transformed!

Eiderdown and quilt were lying anyhow on the floor, as if the perpetrator of this outrage—who stood in the middle of the room admiring her work—had flung them there in her eagerness to replace them with the object that now concealed the whole of the large bed and hung in stiff folds down to the very floor.

It was a bedspread, truly, but what a bedspread! It blazed with brilliant yellow, blue, crimson, green, black, and white; it was stiff with massy open flowers and pink silky buds coiling away among their brown leaves in a deep border round its edge. Queer little stiff soldiers in purple turbans marched across its middle towards a rose-like blossom that made the centre; a white-and-yellow flower with elongated thorns of scarlet silk. On the other side of the great blossom was another army of fair-haired warriors in white tunics who carried black spears.

And all about the rose were green trees heavy with glowing pink and yellow peaches and apricots, swelling and fruiting upon the white background where every available space was filled by a tiny red or blue flower.

At the foot of the bed Vartouhi stood, with her head on one side, smiling with pleasure at the pretty thing she had made. All the grey light of the March afternoon could not dim the marvellous glow of colours on the coverlet or make less the life that danced in her eyes. In spite of her plain dress, she and her bedspread looked like two sudden visitors from the gorgeous East; she might have sailed into this sober English bedroom on the magic carpet that now covered the bed, and so exotic was the picture that all Miss Fielding's ill-temper and anxiety and apprehension burst at once into a blaze of rage. Vartouhi— in her brother's bedroom—and disarranging his bed!

'*Vartouhi!*' she exclaimed, so loudly that it was almost a shout. 'What are you doing here? How dare you come into Mr Fielding's bedroom and put your rubbish on his bed? Take it off at once!'

Vartouhi stood quite still. But her eyes, sparkling and suddenly angry, slid sideways to look at Miss Fielding like those of a little wild animal. She began to smile politely.

'You are angry, Miss Fielding,' she said softly.

'Yes, I am angry, and I should think so, indeed. Throwing bedclothes on the floor! When you know how everything has to be taken care of nowadays! and wasting time and wool and silk on that gaudy fancywork when you know perfectly well the Red Cross are crying out for materials! You ought to be ashamed of yourself!'

She paused, literally for breath. Her face was red and her heart was beating fast. Outrageous, outrageous, was the word that repeated itself again and again in her head, mingled with angry memories of Vartouhi's insolent words about Dr Stocke that morning. And there was something in the opulent colours and strange, bold, easy design of Vartouhi's work that struck at her deepest convictions. Propriety, common sense, prettiness—all were nullified by the gorgeous barbarity before her. She felt actually frightened. What idea was in the girl's head— flinging a thing like that across a man's bed? It was really disgusting! The foundations on which Sunglades stood were being attacked.

'Take it away, this minute!' commanded Miss Fielding.

But Vartouhi did not move.

'Is a prasent for Mr Kenneth,' she said, still softly and politely. 'I gave him no prasent at Christmas, so now I make him one.'

'Mr Kenneth doesn't want presents from a silly little girl and it's very impertinent of you to offer it. Take it away, now at once! or I will!' said Miss Fielding, growing angrier every minute.

'Will not!' Vartouhi suddenly said in a low tone that trembled with rage. 'Is a beautiful thing I made for Mr Kenneth to cheer him up when he comes home sad to this miserable house. *Will not!*'

Miss Fielding wasted no more words. Before Vartouhi could guess what she was about to do, she had twitched the coverlet from the bed and held its considerable weight, stiff with silk and padded flowers, in her arms.

'There!' she said with a nod, her eyes blazing triumphantly, 'now it's going on the kitchen fire!'

The absurdity of this threat struck neither of them. Vartouhi sprang forward and, taking her by surprise, managed to snatch the quilt from her arms and, turning, darted towards the open door. She was half-way across the landing, with Miss Fielding in pursuit, when she bumped into Miss Burton, who was coming down the stairs with an alarmed look on her small face.

'*Oh!* Vartouhi! Whatever is the matter?' cried Miss Burton, just managing to recover her balance. 'Connie—have you both gone mad?'

Vartouhi and Miss Fielding paused in their flight and Miss

Burton stood between them, a bewildered figure in a housecoat, glancing from one to the other.

'Why, it's your bedspread, Vartouhi! What's the matter, Constance—don't you like it?' demanded Miss Burton.

'*Like* it? a vulgar hideous thing like that? I think it's—it's disgusting. And she was putting it on Kenneth's bed!—with the eiderdown all over the floor!'

'*Kenneth's* bed? Why were you doing that, Vartouhi?'

'Is a prasent for him,' said Vartouhi sullenly, standing at the head of the stairs with the gorgeous massive folds gathered up in her slight hands and sweeping opulently to her feet.

'A present for Kenneth? Why, I thought it was for you, Constance!' cried Miss Burton, hastily saying the thing she thought safest.

Her remark did not have the soothing effect she expected. Vartouhi, drawing the breath in through her dilated nostrils, spat on the floor at Miss Fielding's feet.

'For *her*?' she shouted, 'I make a prasent for *her*—the wicked woman who rules her brother's house and sends her ancient honoured father to be ill away in London? In my country we would cut the hair off such a woman! Mr Kenneth is varry sad in his heart and he has no joy in his house because of her. And she say he does not want my prasent! Is a wicked lie. I put it on his bed to make him happy when he come home— oh yas, oh yas, is a varry *nice* house, varry *comfortful*, but is nothing *pratty* in this house!' shouted Vartouhi, stamping her foot and glaring at the silent English ladies and speaking in a tone of savage sarcasm. 'Is so *nice* here—is no laughing, no dancing, no children, no singing! Is all talk talk talk and read read read all day, sometimes I think I will *burst* like the thing on my bicycle!'

She paused for breath, and drew the back of her hand across her moist mouth. Both ladies were still silent, staring at her.

'So now?' taunted Vartouhi, advancing upon them with the

bedspread defiantly clasped to her bosom, 'so now you will be *varry* angry with me, Miss Fielding, and Miss Burton too also, who I like, because she is look like a varry old nun I know in my own country? You will punish me, Miss Fielding, yas, I think so.'

'Vartouhi, you're a very naughty——' began the counterpart of the very old nun, feebly. Her voice died away.

'I shall certainly punish you,' said Miss Fielding icily, after a long pause. 'You are a wicked, uncontrolled little savage, not fit to associate with civilized people. You must go away from here this afternoon, at once, and never come back.'

'All-right,' said Vartouhi contemptuously, shrugging her shoulders. Miss Fielding quelled a protesting murmur from Miss Burton with one look.

'And I shall not give you a reference.'

'I do not care at all.'

'You will find it hard to obtain another post without one.' ('Oh, Connie——' murmured Miss Burton.)

'Still I do not care, too also.'

'And I shall *not* give you a month's salary,' snapped Miss Fielding, still angrier at being unable to awe the culprit.

'*Still* I do not care, too also! I have some pound. Mr Fielding the old honoured one give me three of those pound money notes at Christmas and I save five shilling a week and I sell a little hat I make for some shilling to a girl I talk to in a tea place in St Alberic. So I shall be all-right, Miss Fielding, you wicked woman.'

'I am sure I hope so,' said Miss Fielding, recovering some of her grave reproving dignity. 'Now go at once and pack up your things. I do not wish to see you again before you go.'

'I wish not see *you*, Miss Fielding. At the café at Portsbourne there was a wicked sailor call Mrs Marshall a bish but I shall not call you a bish because is a bad wicked name, Mrs Marshall say, and the nuns say I must naver call names. So good-bye, Miss Fielding,' and Vartouhi made an elaborate sarcastic curtsy which

Miss Fielding did not see because she was already half-way down the stairs.

Vartouhi gathered up the bedspread once more and turned to Miss Burton, who had seated herself despondently upon the lowest stair.

'Oh Vartouhi, *dear*,' said Miss Burton sadly, looking up at her.

'I go to pack away my clothe,' announced Vartouhi, ignoring the remark and pushing past her. The bedspread trailed its exotic pattern behind her as she went.

Miss Burton got up, and followed her into the pretty room where she had said a prayer of gratitude to God eight months ago. The rainy light poured in between the dark leaves of the jasmine creeper as it shook in the wind. All Vartouhi's possessions were already strewn on the bed; her one thin dress, the trousers she had bought secondhand in St Alberics, her little woollen cap and some exceedingly worn and sketchy undergarments. Kenneth's bottle of scent was there, and Richard's bracelet, and one or two other trinkets and pretty things that Miss Burton had not seen before. She now guessed that they were presents from Kenneth. He loved this crazy child. Even if he did not know it, he loved her; and what would he feel, poor Ken, when he came back and found her gone?

'Vartouhi,' Miss Burton said urgently, leaning across the bed, 'you will write to us—to me or Mr Kenneth—the moment you get settled somewhere, won't you?'

Vartouhi set her lips as she buckled a strap on her rucksack, and shook her head. 'Oh no, Miss Burton.'

'But why not? Vartouhi, don't be so silly! We shall all want to know how you are getting on, and I'm sure Mr Kenneth will make Miss Fielding have you back again.'

'Is no use, Miss Burton. I hate you all now. I would not come.'

'Oh, Vartouhi! How can you be so silly!'

'Is not silly. You like me, I like you. You hate me, I hate you.'

'I don't hate you, I'm very fond of you, and so is Mr Kenneth, I'm sure; very, very fond, Vartouhi.'

'Well, so perhaps I am fond of you and him too also, Miss Burton,' said Vartouhi, buckling another strap. Miss Burton's anxious eyes could detect no trace of grief on her face. She looked absorbed in her task, determined and even gay. 'But is all ended now. Is a pity.'

'Yes, it is a pity, Vartouhi. If only you hadn't—er——'

'*This*,' said Vartouhi, and mimicked her spitting with a spiteful smile.

'Yes—that was really dreadful, you know; I don't wonder Miss Fielding was angry.'

'Is a bad wicked thing, that,' said Vartouhi indifferently, glancing about the room to see if she had overlooked anything. The rucksack was nearly full.

'Vartouhi, do write to us, *please*.'

'I will see, I will see,' said Vartouhi cheerfully, tying on another of her extraordinary little caps; a mackintosh one this time, that had belonged to Mrs Archer's little grandson.

'Is raining now,' she added, looking out of the window as she put on a shabby old trench coat that was too big for her. She had no stockings. She swung the heavy rucksack onto her back and adjusted it.

'Vartouhi, you can't go like this, my dear—just walking out into the rain. You've had no tea——'

'Miss Burton,' said Vartouhi, pausing at the door and looking into the older woman's eyes with her own long, sparkling, un-Western ones, 'I am young, you are old. All the English are old, I think. So manny, manny things in their house, so manny clothe, so much to eat. I come from a place where all is stone or made of wood, and not much clothe. We do not mind to get wet in the rain or not eat much. We do not have manny things; no, not manny things. We have our stone house and our family and we like to dance and sing and grow the fruit. I can be all-right, Miss Burton. I am not a English girl, I am a Bairamian girl. Perhaps I go to New York to see Yania, my sister; yas, perhaps. Good-bye, Miss Burton. Give to Mr Fielding the pratty thing I made for him and say to him I like him, he is very good and kind, too also. Good-bye!'

And she ran downstairs with the heavy rucksack bumping against her shoulders. Presently Miss Burton heard a distant shout of 'Good-bye, you wicked woman!' and then the front door slammed. She had gone.

Miss Burton, bewildered by the suddenness of events, hurried across to the window and, opening it, leant out into the rain. The wet leaves of the jasmine brushed her hair. In a moment she saw Vartouhi come out into the drive and hurry away, with head bent against the driving rain. She went out through the gates and turned into the lane and Miss Burton lost sight of her. She had not once looked back.

30

'Whatever has been happening?' asked Betty, hurrying into Miss Burton's room soon after she got home that evening. 'All I can get out of Connie is that Vartouhi did something dreadful and she sacked her. She's in an awful temper and snapped my head off. Has Vartouhi really gone?'

'Oh yes, unfortunately.' Miss Burton was sitting by her fire and looked depressed. 'I'm afraid Constance is very annoyed with me too, but I can't help that; I really had to say what I thought for once. And getting rid of a splendid little worker like that— however does she think we shall get anyone else? And what Ken will say I really don't know.'

'Whatever happened? It all seems so sudden; I can't believe it.' Betty sat down and offered her cigarette case to Miss Burton who accepted with a heavy sigh and proceeded to relate what had occurred, Betty listening with the deepest interest. When the bedspread came into the story, and Miss Burton fetched it from the cupboard where she had hidden it, Betty exclaimed aloud with astonishment and admiration.

'Yes, isn't it a wonderful thing? She's a real artist. I told her she could sell it in London for pounds and pounds but she only laughed.'

'I thought Mohammedans weren't allowed to reproduce flowers and fruit and human beings on any work of art; they aren't allowed to on their mosques, I know,' said Betty, curiously examining the little warriors.

'Well, officially Vartouhi is an atheist, like the rest of her country, only she happens to live in a remote part of Bairamia where some of the old customs linger on. (And they aren't exactly Mohammedans, either.) They still have the prayer at sunset and sunrise there, she told me. So I suppose she didn't feel that the ban on representing living things mattered.'

'I can't imagine her taking much notice of a ban, anyway,' said Betty, whose feelings were a mingling of dismay because the house would now be domestically uncomfortable and relief because the source of Richard's unhappiness had been removed.

'I *do* hope that she will write to us!' Miss Burton was saying unhappily while she put the bedspread back into the cupboard. 'She was in such a rage! and she went off without once looking back, although she must have known I was looking out of the window. But it's Ken I'm really worried about.'

'Oh yes, of course, he's fond of—her.' Betty just stopped herself from saying *the tiresome little thing.* A very attractive woman herself, and on the whole a soother of life rather than a disturber of it, she had small liking for temperamental, if alluring, young women.

'He loves her,' said Miss Burton dramatically.

'My dear Frances! Isn't that putting it rather strongly?'

'I tell you he *loves* her!' Miss Burton had been much upset by the events of the day, and she now actually thumped her fist upon her knee. 'Things were going beautifully, and in another month he would have proposed to her.'

'Then I'm very glad she's gone,' said Betty, more decisively than was common with her. 'I'd no idea he felt as strongly as that and I must say I think it would be disastrous if they did marry. Ken—and Vartouhi—oh, it's absurd, Frances! You're romancing!'

Miss Burton said angrily that she was not, and in support of her theory produced so much impressive evidence about secret presents, chats in the old greenhouse, and other details that Betty was all but convinced.

'Yes—well, you may be right,' she said at last, getting up, 'but I still think it would be a disaster. Ken's nearly fifty and thoroughly set in his habits and she can't be much over twenty and she's barely a European at all, and with that temper of hers—no, Frances, it wouldn't work.'

'Well, I'm sure it would,' said Miss Burton stubbornly. 'He would be just the steadying influence she needs and she would liven him up. You know, Betty, the fact is——' she hesitated, then came out with—'you've had Ken hanging round you for so many years that it's natural you should resent his turning to someone else. But he hasn't had what I should call a happy life, you know, and if the last twenty or thirty years of it *could* be happy—*really* happy—I should be so glad. He *is* such a dear old boy, and we none of us appreciate him.'

'Yes, he is,' said Betty, thoughtfully, looking down at her, with a very kind light in her eyes, 'and I don't resent anything, truly, Frankie. I quite see what you mean about their being good for each other. It *sounds* all right—but I still wonder whether it would work out in practice.'

'It won't get the chance,' said Miss Burton with a sigh. 'I've got a feeling we shall never hear from her again. Of course, I don't blame you for not liking her, and not minding very much that she's gone. She was so unkind to Richard.'

'Yes, she was,' said Betty quietly.

'I used to talk to her about it but I'm afraid I didn't make much impression.'

'Nothing makes much impression on that young woman, because she isn't civilized,' pronounced Betty. 'And, Frankie, what I think I *do* resent a little is her having collected Kenneth's scalp as well as my poor Richard's. It's just a bit too much. Why should she?'

'Well, she *has* that attraction,' said Miss Burton feebly.

'Apparently. Oh well, I suppose I just don't see it because I'm a woman.'

'But I see it, and I'm a woman.'

'You're a goose,' said Betty affectionately, and added 'Bo!' which feeble joke made them both laugh and sent them downstairs to prepare supper and face Miss Fielding in a more cheerful mood.

It was a pity that Dr Stocke was not at Sunglades that evening. If he had been, Betty and Miss Burton would have been treated to the interesting spectacle of Miss Fielding's righteous indignation and ill-temper wrestling with her desire to appear harmonious, womanly and calm in front of the object of her veneration. As it was, there was no restriction placed upon her sulks; and it was a very silent party of three that gathered at the table to eat reconstituted egg in the blue light of the long March evening. It's like a garrison that's being gradually reduced by the enemy, thought Betty. First Richard went, and then the old boy, and then Ken, and then Stocke, and now Vartouhi. How very glad I am I don't live here alone with Frankie and Connie, I don't think I could bear it. I never thought I should live to be sorry that Stocke wasn't here. Thank goodness Ken will be back soon, although when he is I suppose there will only be more trouble.

As the evening drew to a close, Miss Fielding's silence became more due to a dawning dismay than to the anger that had at first overwhelmed all more rational feelings. Miss Burton had made her realize how foolish she had been to dismiss Vartouhi without first obtaining other help, drawing a dismal but unexaggerated picture of the difficulty of running a large house inhabited by five people in war-time with only casual village help—as if Miss Fielding had not already experienced those difficulties, complicated by the Rigbys, before Vartouhi came—and pointing out that it would be impossible, if Dr Stocke were to be housed as comfortably as heretofore, for his hostess to spend so much of her time in his company. Then who was to do the shopping?—growing daily more difficult— and even supposing they were fortunate enough to obtain someone to live in, there would be all the tedium of getting her used to the household's ways.

Miss Fielding had cut her short by angrily exclaiming that the thing was done now and it was no use crying over spilt milk, and Miss Burton, perceiving that common sense had begun to reassert its command over passion, had said no more. Indeed, there was no more to say. Nothing could be done.

It was not wholly dismay at the prospect of domestic discomfort that kept Miss Fielding silent. She began to realize with what extraordinary violence she had acted. Reflecting upon her fury, she was amazed at herself. It was a direct invasion of my personality by the Evil Principle, she handsomely admitted to herself about ten o'clock that night, when the hour of Ovaltine drew nigh and she had to go out into the kitchen and make it for herself. Of course Vartouhi behaved badly—very strangely and impudently and I still cannot think what possessed her to put that gaudy rubbish on Kenneth's bed, but I admit that I was hasty, reflected Miss Fielding. I should have remembered that she is a very young soul and made allowances. Still, no doubt I shall hear from her in a day or two, and even if I don't, I can always get in touch with her through Tekla House. If she is really sorry and apologizes for that shocking display of temper I might even consider having her back again; she was certainly a splendid little worker.

With which generous tribute, Miss Fielding carried the tray of Ovaltine into the drawing-room and thrust her real apprehension—the return of Kenneth and the breaking to him of the news—into the background of her mind.

The house was duller without Vartouhi; even Betty admitted it. They missed her small strong voice singing the prettiest of her native songs, *The Lilac-picker*, over her bed-making and her cheerful rush when door bell or telephone sounded. They missed, a hundred times a day, her steady hard work in the house and her participation in all those small rituals that make up the pattern of a well-run establishment. Miss Burton was frankly doleful and said that she did not know *what* Kenneth was going to say when he came home; and Dr Stocke, returning on the following day to find no Vartouhi, said at length how valuable her work in the house had been and how much he missed one whom he regarded (in spite of a regrettable lack of interest in reconstruction) as the Archetype of Post-War European Youth. His surprise and disapproval put the final touch to Miss Fielding's depression, and she was unusually subdued, and only comforted herself by saying that of course they would hear from Vartouhi soon.

But the days passed, and there was silence.

Fortunately Miss Fielding assumed that Vartouhi had taken the bedspread away with her, and Miss Burton was able to look forward to the moment when she should give it, as Vartouhi had told her to, to Kenneth. What would happen after that she did not clearly imagine. Sometimes she fancied that Kenneth would declare his love and rush off to London to look for Vartouhi, but of course, he was getting on, and had a dread of changing his habits, like all bachelors, and perhaps Vartouhi's absence might wither the love that Miss Burton was sure had been budding in his heart. It was all too sad.

A week after Vartouhi had gone, Miss Fielding received a letter from Kenneth, in which he informed her that he would be home on the following Friday, bringing his father by car 'to make his permanent home with us, as he should have done years ago. He is still pretty weak and I don't want any fuss. Isn't it about time Stocke cleared out? Can't you drop him a hint?'

It was Wednesday when this letter arrived, bringing fresh agitation to Sunglades and causing Miss Fielding to cast herself, for the first time, upon Dr Stocke for comfort. The iniquities of old Mr Fielding were enlarged upon and the deplorable prospect of having him to live at Sunglades was drawn in the blackest shades, with frequent references to lack of harmony and the Evil Principle and the difficulty of resuming her Work after the war with a frivolous old man in the house to be looked after.

But Dr Stocke, to the surprise and pleasure of Betty and Miss Burton (who guessed at the course of the conversation without being actually informed of it), gave Miss Fielding a lecture in which he told her roundly that a woman's first duty was to her family and home. He mollified her by agreeing that her father's presence would be a severe trial, but said that she must support it, and added that he knew she could and would. After all, Dr Stocke pointed out, the voice of scandal would be busier over occasional visits from her eccentric father than it would be over a chastened (Dr Stocke was sure that he would be chastened) old man of nearly eighty living conventionally with his son and daughter. So great was Dr Stocke's influence over her and so admirable his power of managing females (one sort of female) that she emerged after an hour of it feeling brave and good and much tried, which is how we all like to feel; and ready to face the many trials of next Friday.

Betty had grown so tired of it all by Thursday evening that she telephoned Richard at Cobbett Hall and inquired if he would take his Mum to the pictures, which he said that he would be very glad to do. She had not seen him since Vartouhi's departure and was apprehensive about the effect it would have upon him. She felt almost sure that he would take it calmly; but there was just a doubt in her mind; did he care so much for that horrid little girl that he would go chasing off to try to find her? Betty thought not: it was only in books that people did such senseless things. Nevertheless, she wanted to break the news to him herself.

There was much to tell him while they were having a hasty drink and sandwich in the 'George' in St Alberics. She began with Mr Fielding's expected return with Kenneth on Friday.

'Oh dear,' said Richard, raising his eyebrows.

'Well, he's been very ill, Rick. I expect he's got over me by now. (*What is* that stuff you've got in your sandwich?)'

'(Liver sausage.) Don't you be too sure.'

'(How disgusting it looks.) Oh Rick, he must have.'

'(It tastes quite good.) We must hope for the best and expect the worst.'

'You are comforting, aren't you? Poor old boy. I'm glad Ken's bringing him home. It's quite clear what's happened; Ken's had one of those queer obstinate fits he gets sometimes when he does just what he wants to do and no one can stop him. And he always was fond of his father. But I'm afraid——' Betty opened one of her own sandwiches and peered interestedly into it as she spoke so that she need not look at her son's face— 'he'll get a shock when he does come home; Connie's sacked Vartouhi. (This seems to be corned beef; it's all right.)'

After a pause Richard said, 'Do you mean she's gone—left there?'

'Oh yes. She left nearly a week ago and we haven't heard a word from her since and I don't believe we shall, though Connie does (or says she does). There was an awful row. (Are you going to have some more beer?)'

'(Yes, if you will. I'll get it.) Oh . . . was there?' A pause. 'I don't want to hear about it, if you don't mind. I don't expect it's interesting, is it?'

'Not very, darling. I just thought I'd tell you.'

'Thank you, Betty. I'm nearly cured of that particular disease; but it's just as well to have the germ out of the way.'

'Rick!' said Betty illogically, 'aren't you rather hard? She's only a child and she's gone off in a towering temper and anything may have happened to her.'

'You don't expect me to *like* her, do you? The knight in *La Belle Dame Sans Merci* can't have been exactly full of lovingkindness towards his lady. She'll be all right. Barbarians and sorceresses always fall on their feet.'

He got up and glanced towards the bar; their table was in a far corner. The black-out over the door had just been moved aside, revealing for an instant the deep blue of the spring twilight veiling the ancient houses of the High Street, and Alicia came in. She was alone and looked tired. 'Now there,' said Richard, nodding towards her, 'is someone who won't always fall on her feet and whom I do like. *She* needs taking care of.' He picked up his own and his mother's glasses and went over to the bar.

The place was rather full and noisy and Alicia, pushing her way towards the bar, through the crowd of R.A.F. groundsmen and soldiers, had not noticed him. He came up behind her as she was ordering a double whisky and said, 'Hullo, Alicia.'

She turned quickly, and a smile of pleasure brightened her pale face. 'Richard! I *am* glad to see you!' she said, forgetting to be guarded and casual, and showing the happiness that always came over her in his company. 'I haven't seen you for ages.'

'I have been thinking about you a great deal for the last three weeks,' he said deliberately, smiling down at her. 'I'm having a drink with my mother and we're going to the pictures. Are you meeting anyone here?'

'No. I only felt I couldn't exist another minute without a drink on my way back from work so I hopped out of our factory bus and came in here.'

'What's yours, sir?' inquired the barmaid.

'Same again, please,' said Richard, pushing the glasses towards her. 'Come and sit with us, will you?'

'Grand.' She picked up her whisky, and Richard having obtained his beers, they carried their drinks across to Betty, who had been repairing her make-up. She looked up at Alicia with a friendly smile. She now understood and liked Alicia; a girl who was cool, well-groomed, apparently selfish and hard, and actually sensitive and a good friend; a brave reserved girl, with no creed and no standards except the contemporary one of not moaning or being a bore; the product of an expensive girls' school, from which every romantic trimming had apparently been pruned away. Yet her dark hair was rolled about her small head as gracefully as the locks of any girl for the last hundred years, and the long fingers clasped about the whisky glass were white and cool. Her full mouth was painted the colour of a dark red rose and her eyes, slightly bloodshot after the long exhausting hours in the factory, were blue as flax flowers. Alicia smiled and said she did hope she wasn't butting in, and sat down with her drink. *People are always saying civilization is decadent, thought Betty, but I think there's still a lot to be said for it. Good gracious, this beer is even weaker than the last. I shouldn't have believed it possible.*

'Has anything more been done about that dreary *Little Frimdl*?' inquired Alicia.

They explained to her what a lot had happened at Sunglades in the past month; she had heard of the arrival of Dr Stocke through her father, who constantly met Kenneth in their mutual Home Guard duties, but did not know that the doctor himself had discouraged the performance of his play. Nor had she heard of the departure of Vartouhi. She made no comment beyond observing that Miss Fielding would find it very difficult to get anyone else; but, tired as she was after nine hours' hard physical work and already slightly under the influence of whisky, she did let one swift unguarded glance at Richard escape her, and Betty caught the blue gleam. Richard happened to be looking at her as his mother spoke, and Alicia's glance encountered his grey eyes. He did not look in the least conscious, and Alicia instantly looked down at her drink again. But under her pale skin a blush slowly came, to the entertainment of the woman of 1914.

Certainly, after the news about Vartouhi, Alicia's spirits grew markedly more cheerful, and when Richard suggested that she should accompany them to the pictures, she first (more prettily than Betty would have believed possible) asked if she were truly not butting in, and, on being reassured, accepted with obvious pleasure. Betty was too tactful to plead a sudden headache and let them go alone; with such a moody creature as Alicia that might be fatal and startle her into her shell again. So they all went to the pictures and Richard calmly held Alicia's hand, and once dropped one of his light kisses on her cheek, as if Betty had not been there. She heard them, as they said good night, making an arrangement to meet on the following day.

On her way home to Sunglades, as the bus rushed through the black-out lit only by the splendid spring stars, Betty's thoughts were very pleasant. I really believe he means it, she mused. She certainly does. Oh, I do hope it comes off! Why didn't I notice all this before? I suppose because I've so seldom seen them together. Dear Rick! I'm sure she's just the girl for him. I never felt that about any of the others. (A saying of an old school-friend who was now the mother of four sons, *Mother's candidate never wins*, drifted through her mind and she smiled.) Such a contrast to that other little savage! That must be what attracts him, poor darling.

The weather continued cold and uncertain, and what with hurried preparations to receive a semi-invalid and the disturbance of the household routine caused by Vartouhi's departure, life at Sunglades grew steadily more disagreeable. Miss Fielding had been bolstering up her courage by *facing* her fear of having to meet Kenneth with the news; asking herself why she so disliked the prospect; and discovering that there was no solid reason except Kenneth's known dislike of change. And of course he had liked Vartouhi; he always liked pretty young girls, and he had made it plain that he enjoyed her being in the house; he had remarked to his sister more than once that she livened things up. In fact, when Miss Fielding came to recall certain small incidents that she had overlooked at the time they occurred, and added them to the incident of the bottle of scent at Christmas, she became convinced that something not unlike a flirtation had been going on between her brother and Vartouhi, and that the bedspread incident had been—or would have been—if the bedspread had ever reached Kenneth—the beginning of a serious 'affair.' The more she thought the matter over the more she congratulated herself (taking the long view) on having got rid of the girl.

She decided not to tell Kenneth about the bedspread and she warned Miss Burton not to tell him either, taking it so much for granted that her cousin would do as she was told that she did not even exact a promise. It will be quite enough, decided Miss Fielding, if I tell him she was poking about in his bedroom and spat at me when I caught her at it. He would not expect me to forgive that.

So there was really no need to be nervous about facing Kenneth and Miss Fielding was beginning to feel more cheerful when her spirits were again cast down to the earth by Dr Stocke's announcement that he feared he must leave his kind friends on the following Friday week. The last of his talks would be delivered to the Reconstruction Council on Thursday, and the following day he would leave for the north of England on the first stage of a journey to Argentina, in which somewhat stony ground he next proposed to scatter the seeds of international goodwill. He would have been at Sunglades exactly a month.

Miss Fielding was much disappointed. She had hoped for a stay of three months at the least, and reminded him that he said himself he had not had time to investigate half the reconstruction schemes that he wanted to. But Dr Stocke was adamant, and gave many irrefutable reasons why he should go, among them the honest one (for complete, even overscrupulous, honesty was a curious charm in his otherwise charmless character) that he thought it best for his Work to leave England sooner than he had intended as the German Embassy in his native capital was being most disagreeable and suspicious about his son's exploit and had even hinted that he, Gustav Stocke, was a pro-Allied sympathizer engaged in secret Anti-Axis propaganda—'I, who think they are *all* fools,' concluded Dr Stocke, swelling with indignation and looking more Nordic than ever.

Miss Fielding found some comfort for herself in comforting her friend, but his decision remained unchanged, and she was very sad. It might be years before she saw him again, she said; without false shame, for he made no secret of his liking for her, proclaiming it loudly several times a day. No, no, Dr Stocke brightly assured her, they would meet again before the year was out; and with this promise she was obliged to be content.

Alicia was not surprised that her friendship with Richard had suddenly taken a leap forward in intimacy, for her friendships with men often did that, but she was surprised at the gaiety and serenity with which it progressed. Never a cross word or a bad mood marred the happiness of the next few days. They met after work and sat in cheap cafés over bad coffee, and talked; or they walked out in the lengthening evening light to Blentley or Cowater, with bags full of the sketchy food to which Richard was inured, and sat on tree-trunks in the woods, listening to the song of the thrush and looking at the celandines glistening in the fresh green grass as darkness slowly came down over the countryside, and were silent.

Heretofore, Alicia had drawn a line between happiness and love. She was happy, for a little while, when she was steering a boat on a breezy, sunny day or dancing to a good band or laughing over a wisecrack with Crys or watching a good film. Love, represented by the feeling she had for H., and the man at the three-day party, had nothing to do with happiness. It was a troubling and imperious feeling, one whose appeasement was associated for her with secrecy, and transiency, and haste. She had always looked ahead, even in hours of passion, and thought: One day this will be over; and the prospect had had to be faced, as, when the time came, the break had had to be organized.

But when she was with Richard she was happy, and in his arms (in which she very soon found herself) there were only laughter and peace. The delight that she had experienced as the boat flew over the sunlit water with the rushing breeze, the dreamy pleasure of dancing across a shining floor—all these

sensations were now blent with what she felt when she was
with Richard. For the first time, happiness had become one
with love.

She supposed that sooner or later he would suggest that they
should become lovers, and in her new happiness she was content
to wait for him to speak, although she, with her bitter experience
of 'affairs', would almost have been content to go on as they
were. As soon as an 'affair' had reached its natural climax, it began
to move towards its end. And they were so happy! They were
such friends! She did not even want to think about their friendship ending.

However, as a modern young woman should, she was prepared
to acquiesce meekly in his dishonourable proposal and to delight
in the short midsummer of the sweetest and tenderest 'affair' she
had ever known. It was therefore with feelings so confused and
thrown out of their orbit as to take her breath away that she
found herself, some days after their meeting in the 'George,'
sitting on the top bar of a stile and gazing down at Richard's fair
head as he sat on the step, and listening to a proposal of marriage.

The evening was very still. It had been raining all day and now
the clouds had broken up into a strange sunset that flooded all
the heavens with fiery pink light although no rays or beams were
actually visible. The glow was diffused, seeming to come from no
particular quarter, while such few gulfs of clear sky as could be
seen were of a vivid turquoise blue. The clouds still moved restlessly, changing from moment to moment in rolling masses of
dark vapour penetrated now with amber light, now with rose red.
In this strange pink luminance every shade of green in grass, tree
and hedgerow was intensified with a distinctness and variety
inconceivable in ordinary sunlight; the brilliance of the young
hawthorn leaves contrasting with the glittering darkness of the
holly, and the mighty elms, which were not yet in full leaf, showing
shade on shade of rich green. The meadow that stretched before
Richard and Alicia was green as an alpine lake, and seemed to

shimmer with the intensity of its colour. To add the final fairy touch of beauty to the scene, every leaf and grass-blade trembled with its load of glittering raindrops and a delicious scent of soaked earth and young grass floated in the hushed air.

'*What?*' said Alicia, and nearly fell off the stile.

'I was suggesting that we should get married,' said Richard, a little more concisely. He glanced up at her and smiled. 'Are you surprised? I thought you might be.'

'I'm absolutely knocked flat, darling,' said Alicia in a dazed voice.

'I don't see any cause for quite so much amazement. I love you. I thought I had made that sufficiently clear.'

'Yes. Oh, yes. I—I love you, too. At least, I don't feel—but I'm perfectly happy with you,' she ended confusedly. So many thoughts and emotions were crowding in upon her that she found it difficult to speak. 'But loving people isn't the same thing as getting married.'

'It is with me,' said Richard austerely.

'Do you mean to say that every time you have an affair with a girl you ask her to marry you?' she exclaimed.

'Of course not. You are the second girl I have proposed to, and the first one I have proposed to deliberately, with my eyes open, knowing that if you say "yes" we shall have a favourable prospect of many years of happiness before us.'

'Gosh!' said Alicia weakly and started to laugh, but was stopped by a sudden thought. 'Who was the other one?' she asked in a quieter tone. 'Vartouhi?'

He nodded. 'In a moment of temporary insanity. I have never stopped thanking God that she only laughed.'

Alicia muttered something severely uncomplimentary to Vartouhi that he did not hear, and he went on:

'That's quite over. Yes,' nodding, and standing up so that he could look down at her, 'You are not being asked to accept someone on the rebound.'

He put his arm round her and drew her close. 'Will you, Alicia? I think we could be very happy. That's a rash thing to say nowadays, with the world in the state it is, but I believe we could. You see, I love you with all my heart, and all my reason too.'

She turned her cheek against his and shut her eyes.

'Being married is so serious——' she began quietly.

'Nonsense. Tremendous fun,' said the scholar vigorously.

'Suppose we didn't make a go of it?'

'We shall.'

'Of course, we could always get a divorce——'

He shook his head. 'Not with young children. That's one of the things I disapprove of very strongly.'

'There mightn't be any young children.'

'Nonsense,' he said again. 'I'm not very healthy, I know, but I come from a big family on both sides and you come of good working-class stock. You told me your grandfather worked in a Bradford mill.'

'That's why I've taken so easily to the factory. Don't they say it takes three generations to get back to the soil or something? But seriously, Rick darling——'

'If you are worrying about money, I can earn enough to keep us both in all the essentials, and later on when the children come I can work harder and earn more.'

'I've got about three hundred a year of my own.'

He shook his head. 'I don't mind you keeping a hundred, but three hundred is too much—not for you, but for us, with what I shall earn. Most people live on less than that. We mustn't be greedy.'

'Oh,' she said, and was silent. The pink light was deepening over the sky and the holly tree above their heads reflected the glow faintly upon its pale bark while its leaves glowed in lustrous green darkness. A few drops of rain fell.

'Rick,' she said at last, 'I wouldn't mind being hard up. I'd like making my own clothes and the children's and doing the housework—I adore messy jobs and feeling one's got to put up a good show on very little—that's why I went into the factory after Dunkirk——'

'You wouldn't have to do the housework. I don't want a Frau; I want a wife and a friend. Besides, your hands are so lovely,' and he kissed her fingers.

'They're like my mother's,' she said, spreading them out, 'she's a *real* lady. She married poor Dad for his money, I'm afraid. Oh well, if I did have to do the chores, I wouldn't mind. And I'd adore your children. But I'm frightened.'

'What of?'

'Oh—lots of things. I took such a nasty knock once before. And marriage is so—permanent.'

'That's exactly why you needn't be frightened. We shall have time to learn about each other.'

She hesitated for a moment, then said in a cooler tone:

'You don't mind about my not being——?'

He shook his head. 'We're talking about marriage, not an affair, and we're taking the very long view. You say you love me and I believe you. And I love you. The other thing doesn't bother me at all. If it comes to that, I'm not, either.'

'Oh—well. But some people would.'

'Then let us be glad that I belong in the category that doesn't,' said Richard. 'But, mark you, I do *not* belong in the category that lets its wives have affairs. A wife's best friend is her husband.'

'You mean you'd be jealous?'

'The problem will not arise,' said Richard amiably, and she had to laugh.

There was another short silence. The rain increased, then died away to a few scattered drops that shivered the brimming pools in the road reflecting the roseate sky.

'Listen, Alicia,' said Richard, giving her a little shake. 'It's time you grew up. You're tired of running around thinking you're enjoying life when you're not. And you know it. What I'm offering you—and myself—is a full human life, with children and adult responsibilities and satisfactions. In addition,' his clasp tightened, 'I love you with all my heart and I will not be unfaithful to you. (I shan't have the time.) Wherever we may be, we shall have a happy home and work and love. You know that's what you really want, and need, in your heart of hearts.'

She murmured something about being free.

'"Whosoever shall lose his life shall preserve it,"' answered Richard at once, 'You aren't free now. You're a prisoner to restlessness and discontent and the pursuit of happiness (which is a by-product, anyway).'

'The blue-print!' said Alicia, smiling up at him but with a troubled look. 'Do you remember?'

'Yes. I'm asking you to step into my blue-print. Come on!' He gave her another tender little shake. 'The water's lovely!'

But she held back from him for a moment.

'Oh Rick, it sounds such heaven, and it is what I need; you're quite right. But I'm still frightened. I suppose'—she hesitated for a moment—'couldn't we live together for a little while first? Suppose we don't hit it off physically——'

'The word "physically" is the idiot signature-tune of this generation,' exclaimed Richard. 'More nonsense is talked about that subject than any other except freedom. No, dear heart, I see no reason for behaving in any other way than the conventional one. And all my old uncles would have fits.'

'I offer to live with you and you talk about your old uncles!'

'I do appreciate the compliment, dearest.' He kissed her fingers again. 'And I do stipulate for an immediate marriage. Would the 30th of April suit you? That gives us five weeks.'

She still hesitated. Rain was beginning to fall again, showering down from the rosy sky with an appearance of indolence, as if clouds and light and the strange green fields and trees were too entranced to cease their crystal dripping and splashing. The petals of the celandines were clinging together with water and they drooped in the emerald grass.

'I love you and I want you,' said Richard suddenly, holding her close and kissing her mouth.

'All right——' said Alicia. 'Yes, Rick, darling.' She suddenly began to laugh, between their kisses.

'What's the matter? We're going to be very happy,' he said authoritatively, arranging his coat over her shoulders to protect her from the increasing rain.

'Darling, I'm almost sure we are. Only when you kiss me it's so much better than the adult responsibilities!'

'Look—look, a superb rainbow!' he exclaimed, standing up on the second rail of the stile the better to see. His tall gaunt figure was outlined against the magnificent fantastic sky, and she sat looking first at him and then at the bow in heaven. The delicate yellow and aerial pink and the pure turquoise blue curved solemnly across half the sky, every unnameable tint of colour shining against the smoky orange clouds. It had grown there while they were in one another's arms, and now vanished, the one end in a brilliant green hazel hedge at the opposite side of the field, and the other in a distant wood where the mists hovered low.

'Oh—a double one!' she cried.

Above the first rainbow appeared a second, like the delicate reflection of the first. Purer and more brilliant grew the colours, until even the green of tree and hedge and field and the fiery rose of the sky were subdued in wonder by the perfect loveliness of the double bow. They watched in silence until the last faint divine hues had faded into the dimness of evening.

31

Kenneth obtained a certificate from the doctor to take his father down to Hertfordshire by car, as old Mr Fielding was still weak and his son feared the fatigues of the journey for him. It was a cold rainy day when they set out with the east wind blowing again, and both were subdued. To Kenneth it was melancholy to see his father, whom he recollected for forty-seven years as an invariably cheerful person, changed into a quiet, patient old man. No doubt Constance would think the change was for the better, and Mrs Miles was already telling anyone she could get to listen how much improved poor Father was since his illness, but Kenneth felt sad.

The Mr Fothergills were so pleased to be getting back into their flat that they so far conquered their dislike of illness as to call on their aged friend the afternoon before he left, bringing with them a small bunch of rather unripe grapes from the hothouse of their connections in Wiltshire, and gleefully calling Kenneth's attention to the beauty of the bloom. Judson had spent the previous three days in silently airing and purifying the bedrooms. The Spode dishes had reappeared and so had the thin elegant Georgian silver. Soon Mr Fielding and Kenneth and the two nurses would be only a disagreeable memory at 11 St Charles's Street.

Farewells were said in an atmosphere of false cordiality, and the car drove away. Kenneth thought it unlikely that his father would ever see the Mr Fothergills again: if he were going to be old and live a dull life in the country they would have no use for him. Poor old boy.

'Kenneth,' said Mr Fielding in his faint hoarse voice as the car passed Victoria Station, 'can he stop a minute?'

'Yes, of course, Father.' Kenneth picked up the speaking-tube. 'Do you———?'

'Want a copy of *Men Only*,' said the invalid. 'Haven't seen it since I was ill. Damned dull stuff Aubrey and Cliff have got up there; nothing but *de luxe* editions of French books, all old writers and very dirty. Ask him to get *Post* and the *Daily Mirror* too, will you?'

Delighted, Kenneth gave the chauffeur half a crown to fulfil the commission, and presently the car was on its way again. Mr Fielding contentedly studied his papers and Kenneth looked over some documents sent to him that morning by Mr Gaunt. He felt happier. It was unlikely that his father would ever again have the energy to promote night clubs or shuttle between England and America financing leg shows, but it also seemed unlikely that he would be a delicate, discontented, depressing old man. By Jove, I'll turn him into a gardener yet, thought Kenneth, smiling at the thought as he put up his papers and glanced out of the window, to see that the car was within a few moments of reaching its destination.

Miss Fielding had put on a cheerful rose-coloured dress, one of her new purchases, in which to greet her chastened father. Rose-pink was a good colour, with peaceful and harmonious properties appropriate for the welcoming of a young soul which was beginning at last to grow old. She did not feel as cheerful as the colour of her gown, for the day which was to take Dr Stocke from her drew steadily nearer, and, despite her rationalizings, she still very much disliked the prospect of informing Kenneth that Vartouhi had gone; while the prospect of having her father living under the same roof with her until the day he died filled her with apprehensions. However, Dr Stocke's lectures had had a bracing effect, and she hurried across the hall as the car turned in at the drive prepared to do her duty.

The car stopped, and the chauffeur hastened to unload the luggage while Kenneth unwrapped his father from the enveloping rugs. Mr Fielding was still clutching *Men Only*, and it was the magazine's bright cover against his grey coat that first caught his daughter's eye. It gave her a distinct shock. What! that worldly paper again! Had she not burnt all the copies she had found in his room after he had left? What reading for a convalescent! Was Gustav wrong, after all, and her father unchastened?

'Hallo, Constance, my dear,' said Mr Fielding in his new hoarse and faint but cheerful voice, 'what a charming dress; years and years since I've seen you in pink.'

'Father!' said Miss Fielding, taking his arm and with Kenneth's help assisting him towards the house, 'I am so very grieved that you have been so ill. Now you must have a good long rest and get really well again.'

It was the kindest speech she had made to him for twenty years. Something moved her to make it as she felt his thin old arm within his coat sleeve, and remembered the far-off days when she had looked up at him from the height of his knee, and thought of him as her kind father from whom the sweets on Sundays and the weekly penny came. The copy of *Men Only* fell to the ground and she stooped to pick it up.

'Thank you, my dear,' said Mr Fielding, and glanced about him with a look of pleasure at the rosy hyacinths growing between the pavements of the stone garden, and inhaled the spring air, sweet despite the cold wind blowing gustily over the lawns. 'It's good to be here again. Ah, hullo, Frances! haven't got rid of me yet, you see!'

'So glad to see you, dear Uncle Eustace.' Miss Burton could not help one quick glance at Kenneth: but it was instantly obvious to her that he had not yet been told. 'Ken, dear, it is so nice to have you home again! We have missed you.'

'I'm very glad to be back,' said Kenneth, who was taking a first eager survey of the garden as he helped the chauffeur with the cases. 'Vartouhi out shopping?' he went on, 'and Stocke—is he still here?'

'Gustav leaves on Friday, unfortunately,' said his sister, with a tremor of her stomach nerves. 'He is out at present but will be in to tea.' She shepherded them all into the house, and went into the kitchen (it was almost twelve o'clock) to heat some soup for the convalescent, while Kenneth paid the chauffeur, and Miss Burton established Mr Fielding before the drawing-room fire. Mrs Archer was dusting in there, and withdrew after a respectful 'good morning.' It struck Mr Fielding, as he sat alone waiting for his soup, that the drawing-room was not quite so well kept as it used to be. The carpet looked dusty, and although there were the customary lovely seasonal flowers in the Chinese vases (white tulips and parrot tulips this morning) there were newspapers scattered about and the fire-irons needed polishing. Mr Fielding made a puzzled little face. It was most unlike Constance to permit slackness. What could have been happening?

He reclined against the cushions, gazing languidly at the flames. He was exceedingly tired; so tired that he felt no distress at the idea of meeting Betty again. His feelings for her seemed to belong to another life. Had he really asked her to marry him—a girl, a youngster in her middle forties? It did not seem possible. The tulips gave out a faint unfamiliar scent in the heat and the cushion behind his head was delightfully comfortable. He shut his eyes.

In the kitchen Miss Fielding stood face to face with her brother, but the news had not yet been broken. She had just told him of Richard and Alicia's engagement and he was expressing his pleasure.

'It's the best thing that could have happened to her!' he exclaimed. 'Of course, Con, I don't think he's good enough for her. He's a weak sort of chap with odd ideas. But she'll make a man of him; grand girl. Gad, I expect old Arkwright's pleased. He's been gloomy about her for years now: she's the apple of his eye and he's always wanted to see her settled down. How's Betty taking it? Pleased, eh?'

'She seems delighted.' Miss Fielding was pouring the soup into a basin with her heart sinking lower and lower. This news had put him into a thoroughly good humour, and when the other news came the shock would be all the greater. 'She has always liked Alicia.'

'*She* won't be the typical mother-in-law!' he chuckled.

'No, indeed,' said Miss Fielding, and could not help a repressive little smile.

'Vartouhi's late,' he said, glancing at the kitchen clock, and sat down on a kitchen chair and ate a biscuit. Miss Fielding went out of the room as quickly as the steaming bowl of soup would permit. The moment was almost at hand. In the hall she met Miss Burton, who gave her an agonized interrogative glance. Miss Fielding shook her head. 'I simply *cannot*,' she whispered. 'He's so pleased about Alicia's engagement—oh dear—Frankie, I suppose *you* couldn't tell him?'

'Not for *worlds*,' said Miss Burton with expressive gestures and followed her into the drawing-room and proceeded to administer the soup to old Mr Fielding with cheerful talk and little jokes. Constance has made her bed; now she can lie on it, she thought. I will give him the bedspread after lunch, before he has had time to feel really miserable. But I do wish it were over.

Miss Fielding gave herself a mental shake, invoked the Good Principle and her own indubitably righteous position, and returned to the kitchen.

Kenneth was still there.

'I must see about lunch,' said his sister, tying an apron over the pink dress without noticeable enthusiasm.

He stared at her.

'Won't Vartouhi do that when she comes in? Is this a new arrangement?' His tone was faintly disturbed: he disliked even the smallest variation in the daily routine.

His sister turned and faced him.

'Kenneth,' she began in a voice made louder than usual by

nervousness, 'I'm afraid this will come as an unpleasant piece of news to you, but Vartouhi has gone.'

'*Gone?*' he exclaimed, staring at her, while his face slowly began to turn a deeper red, 'How do you mean, gone? Left here?'

She nodded.

'A week ago to-day. I caught her prying about in—in one of the bedrooms and when I spoke to her she was very insolent. She spat at me. On the landing. So of course I had no choice but to get rid of her.'

'You mean you sacked her?'

She nodded. Their two red, agitated, handsome faces looked very alike at this moment.

'Sacked her for spitting at you? Good heavens, Connie,' he burst out, 'what a rotten thing to do—you know she's only a child and got the devil's own temper. What on earth possessed you to do that? Where's she gone?'

'I had no choice. She behaved insufferably. I don't know where she's gone; she left no address and she hasn't written,' said Miss Fielding, beginning to feel her righteous indignation mounting. He had no thought for the insult offered to his sister! All his concern was for that little savage of a girl!

'But——' Kenneth got up and walked about the kitchen, 'you mean to say you've no idea *at all* where she is?'

'Haven't I just said so? They may know at Tekla House. I must confess I'm still so angry with her that I haven't inquired.'

'I'll telephone them at once,' he said, starting towards the door, 'she must come back. Oh——' as his sister made a dignified gesture of remonstrance. 'She'll say she's sorry, of course. I'll make her. Little devil!' He gave a short laugh. 'It was very naughty of her. But you know what she is. And what a damfool thing to do, Con—sacking such a grand little worker! I suppose you and Frankie have been doing everything? I thought the place looked pretty grubby.'

'We cannot perform miracles,' said Miss Fielding, with dignity but also with furious annoyance.

'No need for you to try if you hadn't lost your temper as usual. Never mind, we'll have her back here tomorrow.' He opened the kitchen door.

'Kenneth!' Miss Fielding started forward. 'Remember Father! I don't really think he ought to be upset. If I were you I wouldn't tell him just now. And use the telephone in the little study.'

'Oh—all right. Perhaps you're right. But really, Connie, I can't get over—such a damfool thing to do! *What* do you say she was doing? Poking about in the bedrooms? Whose bedroom?'

'Yours,' she answered reluctantly.

'Mine?' He went even deeper red. 'Oh—er—what on earth for, I wonder?'

'I have no idea,' returned Miss Fielding stonily.

'Well, I'll get to the bottom of this somehow,' he muttered, and hurried out of the kitchen. Miss Fielding opened a patent chocolate pudding and began angrily to read the instructions for making it.

In the hall, Miss Burton was still hovering, and when she saw Kenneth come hastily out of the kitchen she gave a great start.

'Oh—Ken!' She beckoned to him mysteriously.

'Frankie my dear, I'm in a great hurry just now—Connie's just told me about Vartouhi and I want to telephone Tekla House—what is it? Can't it wait until later on?'

'I've got a message for you—from *her*!'

'Oh—well——' he hesitated, glancing irritably first at his cousin and then towards the door of the little study, 'in that case, perhaps I'd better——'

'Come upstairs to my room——' Miss Burton was already hurrying away, 'we can talk quietly there and I've got something to give you, too—from *her*!'

Kenneth hurried up after her, feeling more mystified and annoyed every minute. He even felt a momentary irritation with

Vartouhi; silly child, leaving secret messages and poking about in people's (he shied away from a more precise identification) bedrooms! What had got into her?

Miss Burton opened the door of her sitting-room and went in and he followed her.

'There!' she said, sitting down and preparing to enjoy herself. 'Do sit down, Ken. Oh, please shut the door. Will you smoke?' and she invitingly held out a box of cigarettes.

He waved them away and asked her impatiently if she would please give him the message; he wanted to get on to Tekla House without delay.

'How much has Constance told you?' demanded Miss Burton, puffing at her own cigarette and refusing to be hustled.

'Only that Vartouhi was very rude and spat at her and so she sacked her. Very naughty of her, I quite see Con's point, but——'

'Did she tell you what Vartouhi was doing in your room?' interrupted his cousin.

Kenneth went red again and shook his head.

'Ken,' said Miss Burton solemnly, rising (to his considerable apprehension) from her seat, 'she wasn't in there for any dishonourable purpose. I swear to that.'

'Oh—er—good.'

'She went into your bedroom to arrange a present that she had made for you and while she was arranging it Constance came in and caught her. She didn't mean any harm.'

'Poor little girl,' he muttered.

Miss Burton went over to the cupboard. 'Here is what she made for you,' she said, disdaining to spoil her effect by a longer speech, and shook out the bedspread at his feet.

He looked down at it. The dazzling closeness and richness of the pattern first struck on his senses, rather than on his sight, and then the feeling that it was savage. No civilized hands could have wrought such a thing. Every delicate piece of women's work he had ever seen paled into mere prettiness beside this square of cotton that was as orderly as a parade and as brilliant as a humming-bird. He was filled with admiration and so touched that he could only say simply:

'I say, what a glorious thing. She didn't really make that for me?'

Miss Burton nodded, fully satisfied with the effect she had produced.

'She started it before Christmas and finished it a week or so ago.' (She had forgotten that the bedspread had been originally intended as a present for herself.) 'And she left this message for you; it was the last thing she said to me. *Give to Mr Fielding the pretty thing I made for him and say to him I like him, he is very good and kind*; and then she just said "Good-bye" and went.'

'Poor little girl,' he said again. His feelings were very mixed. There was a little relief that the message was so innocent (although, indeed, all the words and actions that had passed between Vartouhi and himself seemed to him innocent), and a fresher grief at her loss because Miss Burton's careful repetition of her words brought her so clearly before him, and there was honest shy pleasure at her caring for him enough to make him such a beautiful present. Though it's more in the Fothergills' line than mine, he thought as he looked down at it. I can just see it on 'Mr Aubrey's' four-poster—only it would probably be the wrong period or something. Of course I can't put it on the bed; that would never do; but I'll keep it in my wardrobe. Bless her little heart.

'And now,' said Miss Burton sitting very upright, 'what are you going to do, Kenneth?'

'Oh, we must try to persuade her to come back, of course,' he said, clumsily folding the bedspread. 'Connie doesn't mean half she says and I can see she's sorry she lost her temper. Of course——' he hesitated, 'it *was* a rum thing to do, and I can understand Con being annoyed, all this worry about Father, too; that probably made her worse. But we can't have you and Con

342

doing everything; things were running so well before, and I don't think Vartouhi was overworked, do you? Did she ever complain?'

Miss Burton shook her head. 'Never to me. And I think she liked being here.'

'Did she seem sorry to go?'

'She was too cross to be sorry,' said Miss Burton.

'Didn't—er—cry or anything?'

'Oh goodness, no. If you could have seen her! She was *shaking* with rage—and then she suddenly didn't seem to care a bit: she just bundled her things together and went off into the rain without even waiting for tea.'

He said nothing, but stared at the floor.

'She didn't look back once, although she must have known I was looking out of the window,' enlarged Miss Burton.

'I'll go and telephone Tekla House, if you'll excuse me, Frankie,' he said, starting out of a reverie. 'Thank you for taking care of this,' holding up the bedspread. '*You*'d like her to come back, wouldn't you?' he added, pausing at the door.

'Oh very much, Ken,' said Miss Burton earnestly. 'I miss her terribly.'

'Good,' he exclaimed, and hurried down the stairs.

But Tekla House, though sympathetic, was not helpful. They were surprised and sorry to learn that Miss Annamatta had left her post owing to a misunderstanding in her employer's absence and were pleased to hear that she had been so satisfactory, and if they heard from her they would certainly get in touch with Miss Fielding at once. Meanwhile, she would of course have to report to the police in whatever district she might have settled and if all other methods failed that might be a way of tracing her. But they had no doubt that they would be hearing from her in a few days. And with mutual courtesies the conversation ended.

Kenneth hung up the receiver. The house seemed unusually dark. A shower was dashing against the windows and there was a pervasive odour of burnt chocolate pudding. It occurred to him that there might be other reasons for missing Vartouhi than her gaiety and prettiness.

He did miss her; more and more acutely as the day wore on. His sister was more amenable than he had anticipated, and only sighed when he announced his intention of doing everything he could, including doubling her salary, to get Vartouhi to come back. He did not mind her sighs; indeed, he did not hear them; he only thought that Con was taking it pretty well and that Stocke might have something to do with it. Or perhaps we're all getting older and the fight's going out of us, thought Kenneth despondently, as he tramped away in the rain to see what had been happening at the office in his absence.

'Well, Constance, I hear you have a young man staying here,' said Mr Fielding about half-past four as he sat snugly by the drawing-room fire watching Miss Burton toast the scones while his daughter made the tea on the spirit lamp. The firelight danced over the full-blown white tulips, which looked as if they were carved from mother-o'-pearl.

'Not a young man, Father; Gustav is older than I am,' said Miss Fielding without displeasure. She had changed her pink dress for a becoming blue one, a fact which her father's sharp eyes noticed at once. 'He should be in any moment now; he said he would be back to tea.'

'I remember your speaking of him when I was here before. Didn't he write *Little Shamus and the Leprechaun of Peace*? I remember the title very well; you were all rehearsing it at Christmas.'

'*Little Frimdl and the Peace Reindeer*,' his daughter corrected him, '*Little Shamus* was another of his that we did at the time of the Irish troubles in the 'twenties, Father. I knew and admired Gustav's work long before I actually met him.'

'Ah. Has he got any money?'

'Really, Father, I don't know. I have never heard him mention money.'

'Probably has plenty, then,' said Mr Fielding in a satisfied tone. 'Yes, I knew it was Little Somebody and the Something. And he's a bachelor, you say?'

'A widower, Father. Mrs Stocke died last year.' Miss Fielding, seeing that an embarrassing train of thought was revolving in her parent's mind, sought to change the subject, but before she could do so, Miss Burton looked up from her task with a flushed face and exclaimed archly:

'Guess who is engaged, Uncle Eustace!'

'Constance!' cried Mr Fielding, with a cheerful laugh, and Miss Fielding looked pained, but not so pained as she would have two months ago and Miss Burton thought that she detected some complacency.

'Alicia Arkwright—you remember her?—to Richard Marten,' continued Miss Burton.

'Betty's boy? No! Why, when I was here before he couldn't look at anybody but little whosit—the girl you had helping in the house. Where is she, by the way?'

'Oh, she has left; refugees never stay long anywhere,' said Miss Fielding carelessly. 'They are going to be married at the end of April.'

'Good thing; very good thing,' said Mr Fielding, filling his mouth with hot scone. 'Two young things like that—how old is he—twenty-six? and she can't be much more—settle down together like a couple of puppies in the same basket; their bones are still soft, you see, and they'll find it easy to fit into each other's ways. Now when people in their forties and fifties start getting married, that's a very different matter. They're set in their ways and they want the basket to themselves! Another scone, please, Frances,' and he darted a sparkling glance at the conscious face of his daughter. It's too bad of Uncle Eustace, thought Miss Burton. Father is *not* chastened, thought Miss Fielding. Ah, thank goodness, there is Gustav's knock.

It was one of Dr Stocke's merits—if such a quality can be

STELLA GIBBONS

regarded as a merit—that he was hardly ever discomposed. He had a cast-iron social manner that could deal with any eventuality or human type and he was never surprised. Miss Fielding had been slightly uneasy at the prospect of his meeting her eccentric and erring father, but she soon found that she need not have worried. Dr Stocke came in looking enormous and exuding a breath of cold spring air from his excellent American clothes, bowed with exactly the right mixture of attentive courtesy to an old gentleman and flattering interest in a new social acquaintance; and in a few minutes they were talking animatedly about America, a country which both knew well, while Dr Stocke cleared the scone dish. Miss Burton took out one of her hopeless pieces of knitting and Miss Fielding her embroidery, and both worked in pleasant silence and listened to the gentlemen until it was time, alas, to begin cooking dinner.

In the kitchen garden, Kenneth was wandering up and down in the rain and making an absent-minded inspection of the broccoli sown last year and the turnip tops. He had returned from the office unobserved, for he did not feel like conversation, and was now doing what he had been looking forward to doing all day. But the garden was not having its usual soothing effect, for the work was much behindhand owing to his absence in London, and the beds, to his experienced eye, looked idle and desolate. The jobbing gardener whom he sometimes employed had dug and prepared them for the busy gardening months of March and April, but he had not planted much, for his employer had hoped to be back in time to do most of the work himself; and Kenneth knew that if he wanted the garden to produce as much this year as it usually did, he would have to work exceedingly hard for the next six weeks. Usually such a prospect would have exhilarated him, but this evening it only made him feel tired and depressed. He had a touch of rheumatism in one shoulder and he could not give his full attention to the garden because of his distress about Vartouhi. Until he came home and found her gone he had not realized how much he had been looking forward to seeing her. In his case he had a necklace of gilt shells, the sort of gay trinket she loved, and he had wanted to see her fasten it round her neck and hear her excited thanks. The house seemed desolate without her; and apart from his own disappointment, he felt so sorry for the poor little girl, going off without any tea into the rain. Suppose she had lost her temper and spat? Shocking, of course, but she was only a child and a foreign child at that, alone in a strange country. Anything might have happened to her.

He went across the garden and opened the door of the old greenhouse. Rain was streaming down its glass panes and in one or two places dripping steadily onto the floor. A faint smell of mould and moss hung in the air. But it was warmer, as usual, in there than it was outside, and Kenneth sat down on a bench and began to pack his pipe. He glanced across at an outsize flowerpot, turned upside down, which stood immediately opposite the bench. It was still covered by the sack he had put there for her to sit on during their last conversation in the greenhouse a month ago. He could remember her quaint remarks and particularly a long account of the appearance and temperament of 'my nice, Medora,' who was a favourite with her aunt; and the memory of the little figure sitting there was so painfully vivid that he stopped packing his pipe for a while, and sat staring at the ground and feeling unhappier than he had felt for years.

32

He intended to go up to London the next day and make further
inquiries at Tekla House and also to find the headquarters of
the League of Free Bairamians in Great Britain and try to trace
her through them. But on the Friday morning his father awoke
feverish and weak and the doctor had to be sent for, and when
Kenneth got to the office, much later than was his habit, he
found Mr Gaunt anxious to secure his full attention for a
complicated case presented by some wealthy clients whose affairs
had been in the firm's hands since his grandfather's day. It was
clearly impossible to go to London; and it remained impossible
for the rest of the week; and by the end of the week, although
he still missed Vartouhi and fully intended to go to London to
make inquiries at the earliest opportunity, his sense of loss and
his intention of finding her had both receded a little into the
background of his life. Habit is so strong in middle-aged people,
and so soothing; it works hand in hand with Time in the task
of softening grief and helping them to endure the pain which
their ageing systems are ill-fitted to support; it is terribly
powerful, and the young do well to mistrust it until their own
nerves and feelings are ready for the anodyne it can supply.
Miss Burton reminded Kenneth at intervals that it was now ten
days—a fortnight—three weeks—since Vartouhi had gone, and
there had been no word from her, and at each reminder he felt
a pang and answered impatiently, because he was unhappy. But
old Mr Fielding was slow to recover from the heavy cold
which succeeded his illness and demanded much of his son's
time and attention, and the case of Masterman *v.* Burtwright,
Sampson and Company continued to present delicate problems

and to require his constant presence at the office; and the days slipped past, and still he did not go to London to look for Vartouhi.

So far as he was concerned, life at Sunglades became more bearable with the departure of Dr Stocke a week after Kenneth's own return. The good doctor went off as cheerful and busy as ever, having warmly thanked the Fieldings for their hospitality and assured Miss Fielding how deeply he felt the parting from her and how much he would miss their long talks, and promised that he would write a journal of his Argentinian travels for her which should reach her (U-boats permitting) every few weeks. She said good-bye to him with loud expressions of regret and vowed more than once that the house would be an intellectual desert without him. He made her promise that she would keep up the study of his native tongue which she had begun under his instruction, and said playfully that in six weeks he would write her a letter in it, and she must swear to read it without the help of a dictionary.

'Oh dear, how tantalizing—I'm sure I shan't be able to!' said Miss Fielding despondently; she felt extremely low and made no attempt to conceal her feelings.

'You will find the gramophone records most helpful,' said Dr Stocke.

'It will not be the same as having you to practise with.'

'Naturally; but you will make progress, Constance, and when we next meet I shall be able to talk fluently with you in my own tongue. It will be very pleasant.'

'Yes; well, I hope so, Gustav. Have you your thermos? I saw it last on the hall table.'

'I have everything, thank you. And now, good-bye, my dear friend,' and he took her two hands in his and shook them firmly, ending up with a kiss on her forehead. Then he hurried into the taxi and was driven away.

Miss Fielding turned back to the house, her mood a mixture

of maidenly confusion and exaltation. No man had ever kissed her on the forehead before; no man, in fact, had ever dared (or wanted) to kiss her at all since the occasion when that horrid Bargle boy had forgotten himself beneath the mistletoe. A kiss on the forehead! What a beautiful symbol of their lofty friendship. She was so moved that she was not annoyed by hearing Kenneth whistling with unusual loudness and cheerfulness on his way to the vegetable garden.

Old Mr Fielding was sitting by the drawing-room fire with the *Tatler* and regretting that Dr Stocke had gone. If a man could talk cheerfully and had a store of anecdotes about interesting places and people, Mr Fielding did not notice if his personality were oppressive and his perceptions limited; and he thought that the house would be noticeably duller without Dr Stocke, who had beguiled the evenings for him during the last week. Mr Fielding had been relying on Betty for conversation and entertainment, after the slight embarrassment of their first meeting had worn off, but in fact he saw very little of her. Every evening she had some engagement or business on hand to help Richard and Alicia with their approaching marriage, and she did not return to Sunglades until late at night.

There is always a vast amount of pleasant business and buying and fuss involved in getting married in peace-time, but it is nothing compared with the amount of exhausting business and failure to buy because there isn't anything to be had, and fuss, bound up with a marriage in war-time. But Richard and Alicia were fortunate: the five weeks of their engagement were not spoiled by fretting about cups and carpets and leases. Richard's mother had been married in war-time and known the happiest days of her life in two cheaply furnished rooms, and hence she concentrated on the realities rather than the inessentials of the married state, and her mood and that of the engaged pair harmonized perfectly. Richard and Alicia both disliked fuss. Richard avoided it because it wasted his precious energy, and Alicia avoided it because it was a bore.

So Richard brought his many books and his telescope out of store, and Alicia asked her father if she might have the contents of her bedroom as a wedding present, and on this, with a few additions, they proposed to set up house. Poor Mr Arkwright had been looking forward to a 'do,' with as elaborate a breakfast as the times would permit, and a huge cheque for the bride, and was so sadly disappointed that Alicia gave way and said that he was a lamb and she would adore a reception and that he might buy them a table to have their meals on.

Richard forbade her to accept the huge cheque. She might accept fifty pounds if she liked; they must not be cranky, and unkind to her father; and they would put it into a nest-egg for emergencies such as illness or a baby. But five hundred pounds would throw the sparse elegant pattern that they had drawn up for their early married life all out of proportion. He would have his salary from the European Reconstruction Council and she would have her wages from the factory and her hundred pounds a year, and as a concession to his bride he permitted himself to take fifty pounds a year from the income left to him by his aunt. Altogether they would have about eight pounds a week. 'Riches!' said Richard decidedly, when Betty had found them two small sunny rooms with the bath in the tiny kitchen in a pre-Regency house in St Alberics. The rent, owing to another stroke of luck which need not be detailed here, was only thirty shillings a week, a bargain in a Home Counties town in war-time.

The house was clean and the little rooms were decorated in blue-green distemper. Alicia found it difficult to concentrate on her work at the factory because her thoughts were busy with a colour scheme of white and blue-green and dark raspberry red. They bought two little gilt antique cups and saucers smothered in delicate blue and pink flowers; and a white utility teapot

which was a good shape although it did drip, and when Richard
took it back and courteously requested another one which did
not drip, he was given one. Alicia was clever at sewing and she
made white net curtains and two pairs of dark red ones out of
the brocade ones in her room, which also provided a tiny dark
red cushion each for herself and Richard. It was a happy and
exciting time for them both, as the two little rooms and the
kitchen-bathroom began to look elegant and homelike and
the weeks passed.

'When you start the baby, darling, you won't be able to get
into the kitchen,' said Richard.

'I shan't take up more room than the telescope,' retorted his
bride. 'But all that brass looks heaven against the bluey-green
walls. Need we have any pictures?'

He shook his head.

'I'm good at doing flowers,' she murmured. 'This summer
we'll have white peonies. I adore them.'

Richard put his head out of the window into the sunny
evening and surveyed the busy square below and murmured, 'All
this is very pleasant. Aren't you glad I caught you?'

'Oh Rick, I am. Only——'

'What?' He turned his head to look at her, still with his hands
on the window-sill.

'It's just a little feeling.'

'Well—what?'

'It's about my asking you to live with me.'

'Well?' he said again, beginning to smile and taking his hands
from the sill.

'I wish—I don't know. I either wish I hadn't asked you or
you hadn't said "no"—I feel——'

He waited, leaning against the window and watching her. She
was standing by the little basket-shaped grate, into which she had
temporarily put a bunch of jonquils that she was taking home.
The double white flowers against the jet-black ironwork matched

352

her clothes, for she wore a black skirt and an elegant plain white blouse. Late sunshine covered all this black and white with a golden light.

He went over to her and put his arms round her.

'Well—you did ask me and I did say no, so we can't get over that. But do you know why I said no?'

She shook her head.

'The conventional situation is reversed in our case, you see. I am more anxious to marry you than you are to marry me.'

'Rick!'

'It's true; you think it over. Who's the frightened one? Who said *Marriage is so permanent*? who talked about their freedom? Not me. I am ready and eager to settle down.'

As usual, he was making her laugh, although she also looked a little ashamed.

'But you do really want to belong to me, don't you?' he went on.

'Of *course*, angel birdbrain!'

'Well, suppose you belonged to me before we were married and then you got a fit of fright about getting married and rushed off, where should I be?'

'Yes—I see——' she said, thinking this over. 'You want to be sure of having me for keeps?'

He nodded, smiling.

'And the only way I can be sure of getting you for keeps is to make you marry me first.'

'I think it's awful!' burst out Alicia. 'You make me sound like some old Victorian rake!' and she struggled to get away from him but the explanation ended in uproarious laughter and many kisses.

But secretly she thought it sweet that he should want her 'for keeps' so strongly that he could submit her to some humiliation and himself to self-denial. It deepened her love for him and made her feel less afraid of the responsibilities she was undertaking. She found out other things about him, of course, during the next five weeks; that he disliked obvious care being taken about his health but appreciated it if the care were unobtrusive; that his dislike of admitting himself to be in the wrong was so strong that a real effort of will was necessary every time he did so. On his side he found out that she was literally unable to get through her day efficiently without some alcohol, and that she did not care whether she was in a poor place or an expensive one so long as she was enjoying the occasion, and she enjoyed easily. This seemed to him as good a characteristic as the necessity for alcohol seemed a bad one. The latter, he decided, would have to be cured by very gradual degrees. He saw nothing unusual, of course, in people drinking alcohol several times a day but it seemed to him serious when anyone, a man or a woman, could not get through their day's work properly without it. She smoked very little because she disliked the smell lingering in her hair and clothes. Her elegance and coolness was a never-failing refreshment to him. He told her that it was like being engaged to a water-iris. Their friendship, apart from their love, grew stronger with each day, and to Miss Burton, who took great pleasure in seeing them together, it seemed that they were fortunate enough to be '*attracted by the indefinable essence, apart from all qualities, that constitutes the self,*' as Charlotte Yonge admirably wrote of two other lovers who were dissimilar in tastes and habits: such unions are the most lasting known to earth.

Richard sometimes thought of Vartouhi in the weeks preceding his marriage; and it slightly shocked him that he did not care what had become of her. She had made him suffer as painfully as a well-balanced and rational young man could, and there was nothing left in his feelings towards her but resentment and dislike. There was also a little fear, but he was not conscious of that, although he should have been warned of it by his hope that he and she would never meet again.

His relations were all very pleased at the engagement and at once began making arrangements to come to Hertfordshire for the wedding. The elderly uncles and aunts could arrange to leave their war-time activities in the Devon village for a day and a night, and they all agreed that this journey, to witness the first marriage among the young cousins, was really necessary; but many of the young cousins themselves were in the Services and their leaves did not coincide with the date of the wedding. However, Alicia's friend Crys found that she had a seven-days due, and could be the only bridesmaid; the schoolboy brother would have started his Easter holidays, and it was hoped that Alicia's sister would have a forty-eight hours about that time, and perhaps it could be arranged to include the date of Alicia's wedding. The talk was all of possibilities and plans, and some of the pleasant excitement spread through Betty to Sunglades, which intended to go to the wedding in a body. Miss Fielding had never been accused of lacking the hospitable instinct and she offered to put up a great-uncle and aunt and an old friend. The offer was gratefully accepted and everyone was looking forward to the 30th of April.

Ten days before the wedding Kenneth had to go to London on business.

It was a very wet morning, not of the dramatic spring sort with sudden showers of rain and broad sheets of wet blue sky and then the clouds again, but a downpour, soaking and grey. The trees were almost fully out now, and as Kenneth was driven to the station the countryside looked rich yet delicate, with that dimming of brown among the dazzling new green that comes from bud-sheaths not yet cast to the ground and trunks and branches not yet completely veiled by leaves. Kenneth was distressed to realize that almost a month had passed since Vartouhi's departure and decided that he would go to Tekla House and make some inquiries and thence on to the League of Free Bairamians in Great Britain, *if* Tekla House could supply the address. But his strongest feeling was sadness at losing her; he could not feel any real hope that he would find her. He was not yet resigned to his loss but he was half-way towards resignation. The three weeks' delay had inevitably, at his age, made a difference to the intensity of his feelings. Vartouhi was in process of becoming a memory.

London looked ruinously shabby and it was difficult getting about because of the crowds and the pouring rain. He transacted his affairs in the City, and then made his way back towards the West End, intending to lunch there and go on to Tekla House in Bloomsbury. While stepping into the taxi he had hailed, he paused to buy a paper from a man who had just received his supply of lunch-time copies, and then gave the direction to the driver; he would lunch as usual at an old-fashioned and expensive grill room in Piccadilly where passable food was still to be had.

He thrust the paper into his pocket, and leant back, enjoying the comparative comfort and the solitude after the streaming rain and hurrying crowds in the streets. Poor old London, how hideous it looks, he reflected, as space after bombed space glided past, each one tidy and desolate and boarded off from the public. The livid grey ruins streamed with darker patches of running rain but in more than one place he saw green wild plants and seedling trees springing up.

The waiter found him his usual table, recognizing him with a murmured 'Good morning, sir; very wet to-day,' and he gave his order and settled himself to await its arrival. Although it was only twelve o'clock the handsomely furnished Edwardian dining-room, with its palms and heavily moulded ceiling and columns, was already full. A not unpleasant smell of former lunches and wine lingered on the warm air. Kenneth unfolded his newspaper.

The first headline he saw was this:

'R.A.F. BOMB SER'

The name meant nothing to him at first. He read on.

'Ser, capital of Bairamia, was the target of Middle-East based bombers last night. This is the first time the city has been attacked by the R.A.F. The airfield outside the city was heavily bombed and fires were started in the hangars. One of our aircraft is missing.'

There followed a note:

'Bairamia, tiny country of 700,000 inhabitants whose chief occupation is fruit-growing, was invaded by the Italians in 1938 and is the smallest of the occupied European countries. It is practically inaccessible except by air, as the mountains run down steeply into the sea along its only strip of coastline, which is not more than five miles long. Bairamia lies opposite the British island naval base of Santa Cipriano.'

At the foot of the paragraph was another note:

'*Bairamians in London rejoice at the news*. Story on page 3.'

He turned with growing eagerness to page 3, and there, smiling at him from a good clear photograph with some other smiling girls in white aprons in the background, was Vartouhi.

Kenneth's first feeling was one of indignation. He had missed her painfully during the last month, and in the press of his legal responsibilities and his attendance on his ailing father, he had imagined her working in some depressing place and longing to be back at Sunglades, to which happy position he would restore her as soon as he should have the time. And here she was,

apparently well and happy and grinning all over her face because
the capital of her country had been strafed by the R.A.F. Just
how she would take it, he thought, remembering various unchris-
tian remarks she had made from time to time and her attack on
the Italian prisoners. Little devil! He began to read:

'Miss Vartou Anamatta ("Peggy" to you) is one of the
happiest girls in London this morning.

'She is one of the five or six Bairamians in Great Britain,
and last night Ser, the capital of her country, was bombed
by the R.A.F.

'Miss Anamatta is employed at a London milk bar, and
when I called on her this morning she was all smiles.

'"It is a very good thing," she said, when I asked her
what she thought of the news. "I hope the Italians were
frightened."

'Miss Anamatta has been in England nearly four years.
Her father owns a large fruit farm in the famous Khar-el-
Nadoon, or Vale of Apricots, which is Bairamia's richest
fruit-growing district. He sent her to England in 1938 just
before the Italians invaded Bairamia.

'"I suppose he had a hunch something was going to
happen," said Peggy, who speaks perfect English with a
charming accent. "I'm very glad he did."

'"I love England and everybody here has been very kind
to me. I would like to go back to my own country for a
visit after the war to see my family but I hope to make
my home in Canada. My fiancé is a French-Canadian."

'Miss Anamatta's Christian name is Vartou but her fellow-
workers have christened her Peggy because it is easier to
pronounce.'

Kenneth read this three times in much confusion, while his
soup cooled. The photograph was certainly Vartouhi; the braids

of hair and long smiling eyes were unmistakable. But since when had she spoken perfect English? and why was her Christian name first truncated of its final syllable and then changed into Peggy? Who at Sunglades had ever heard Vartouhi say 'hunch'? and, most startling of all, who was this French-Canadian fiancé with whom she hoped to make her home after the war? The account made her into the sort of jolly little refugee who does get interviewed by the newspapers, while the more natural kind only appears in those brief paragraphs recording that Mr Woolsack refrained from inflicting a heavier penalty because the accused was a foreigner and did not yet understand English customs. The only faint echo of *his* Vartouhi in the report was in the remark, 'It is a very good thing. I hope the Italians were frightened.' But his Vartouhi would have said, 'Is a varry good thing. Will frighten the Italian dogs, I hope, too also.'

Completely bewildered, he pushed the paper aside at last and turned to his tepid soup. But as he drank it he glanced more than once at the photograph and gradually his anger faded and all he wanted was to see her again and find out if she really were engaged to this fellow, and happy. It might be true. It probably was. A month was a long time in these rushing days of war and Vartouhi was attractive enough to make any man fall madly in love with her in a very short time.

French-Canadian. H'm. He did not quite like the sound of that. They were a wild lot who showed their finest qualities when they were fighting—and some of them, if the rumours were true, found continued inaction in England a trial to their fiery spirits.

But this fellow of Vartouhi's was all right, no doubt.

All the same, while he was drinking his coffee he decided to go to the newspaper's offices and get the address of the milk bar where she was working. There could be no harm in his seeing her and wishing her happiness—and it would give *him* so much happiness just to see her again, perhaps for the last time.

He finished his coffee and paid the bill and went out into the rain. Keeping the newspaper carefully in his pocket, he went by taxi to its offices.

The newspaper, of course, courteously but finally refused to give him Miss Annamatta's address. It was a rule of the paper and could not be broken. The paper was regretful but adamant, and Kenneth stalked off its premises in a rage.

He stood in the shelter of a doorway to escape the steadily falling rain, and glanced hopelessly up and down the street. It was about a quarter to two in the afternoon, a quiet time in this district of newspaper offices and cheap little cafés where linotype operators and reporters on space rates and the minor men of Fleet Street came for their hasty meals. There was a little sandwich bar immediately opposite the doorway where he was sheltering, and it occurred to him to go over and ask the girls who worked in it if they knew where *this* girl—showing them the photograph—worked. It was a very forlorn hope indeed, but he felt that he must do something.

He went across the road and entered the little place, which was less stuffy than it might have been because it was open to the rainy air. There were two soldiers at the counter but otherwise it was empty and the blonde girl in charge was washing glasses as she joked with the men.

All three glanced up as Kenneth came in.

He raised his hat. As he did so it struck him that his inquiries might have a distinctly ribald flavour to low minds, and he became crosser than ever.

'Good afternoon,' he began, 'I am trying to trace a young lady—*this* young lady,' and he held out the photograph—'and I wondered if you might be able to help me.'

The sentence was romantic, and it fell upon sympathetic ears. The respect for an appearance of wealth, and for good clothes, has dwindled almost to vanishing point in England since the Nazi War, but it has been replaced by a simple friendliness and an immediate interest in the human element of a story, which some people like much better. The blonde and the two soldiers both looked interested and the former said cheerfully:

'Sure I will, if I can. Let's have a look,' while the soldiers stealthily tried to get a glance at the paper, which Kenneth handed across the bar.

'Oh,' she exclaimed at once, 'you're lucky to-day. *I* don't know her myself, but I know where she works. The gentleman who wrote this was in here for a coffee this morning and he told me.'

'Oh—thank you—I'm very much obliged.' Kenneth was unable to keep eagerness out of his voice.

'It's a milk bar in the West End,' said the girl and described a place not far from the restaurant where he had lunched.

'He was ever so pleased they gave it such a good show,' she went on, glancing down with a proprietary air at the paper. 'He's a nice boy. He often comes in here.'

'It's extremely kind of you and I'm very much obliged,' said Kenneth hastily again. 'Er—won't you——' and he pushed a ten-shilling note across the bar at her and hurried away to escape any possible thanks, leaving the three in the bar well provided with material for discussion until the place began to fill up again for cups of tea at half-past three.

He took a taxi back to Piccadilly.

33

The West End milk bar was large and prosperous, and it was crowded with Service people; Polish officers in their distinctive square caps, paratroopers with the breath-catching winged horse on their shoulder-flashes; handsome, sallow, full-faced American privates in the uniform that is so popular with our girls because it resembles that of a British Army officer and suggests the higher rank; the girls themselves with untidy curls on their shoulders and cheap bright clothes, put on anyhow; plump A.T.S. and W.A.A.F.s. with smooth pink cheeks and neat hair, and a few American sailors, whose sinister black pirate-like dress did not match their eager faces. The place was stiflingly hot in spite of the cold rain falling outside and the customers were all talking at the top of their voices. There was a smell of damp clothes and hot food. Between the shoulders of the people crowding along the white bar Kenneth could catch glimpses of the tired painted faces of the girls who did the serving, and see the glasses being filled with bright orange or yellow synthetic fruit drinks. He pushed his way to the bar, keeping a sharp look-out for Vartouhi among the figures in their white coats. But she was not there.

He singled out a middle-aged woman less painted than the rest and succeeded in catching her eye. She jerked her head interrogatively at him as if to inquire what his order was, but he leaned across the counter and said:

'Is a Miss Annamatta working here?'

She stared at him as if she did not understand.

'This young lady——' he held out the newspaper with Vartouhi's photograph—'she is a friend——' he suddenly had an idea and

362

continued almost without a pause—'of my sister's and I've got a message for her. Does she work here?'

The woman, who was not English and seemed unusually stupid, glanced at the paper and suddenly smiled and nodded.

'Peggee! Yes, she works here. But she iss not here thiss afternoon. It iss her afternoon off.'

Kenneth's heart sank. He had hoped that in another moment he would see Vartouhi herself.

'Oh. Er—will she be on duty again this evening?'

The woman shook her head, staring at him so intently that he felt embarrassed.

'I suppose you couldn't tell me where she lives?'

'I do not know where she lives.' She turned away for a few minutes to serve two girls, then once more gave her attention to Kenneth.

'Do you think any of the other girls would know? or the manageress, perhaps?'

She made a gesture as if she had not heard what he said, and indeed the noise of voices and laughter was deafening. The brilliant light struck back from the shiny white-tiled walls and seemed to increase the heat and uproar and smells. The food had the bright colours of an artificial paradise, and the ruby and pink soft drinks gushed from the silver taps like the liquids in a chemist's giant carboys. Kenneth repeated his question in a louder tone and the woman looked doubtful. However, she said something to a younger woman, dark and pretty, who was in supervision of the coffee urn, and in a minute this girl came hurriedly to the counter and leant across it.

'It's 14 Ardley Street, Mornington Crescent,' she said smilingly. She looked more intelligent than the first woman and although she was also a foreigner she spoke much better English. 'I don't expect you know where that is, do you? You can get the tube from Leicester Square to Mornington Crescent station. It's on the Northern line. Ardley Street's near the big cinema on the

corner of Crowndale Road. You from another of the papers?'
she added, pushing her fingers among her black curls and looking
at him with friendly interest.

Kenneth was not one of the people who like the new lack of
deference to a superior appearance in England. He had more than
once said that he was too old a dog to learn new tricks. He replied
politely but stiffly that Miss Annamatta was a friend of his sister's,
and that he had a message for her, raised his hat, and turned away.
As he slowly pressed his way through the crowd he decided that
it was as well that he had not rewarded this informant as he had
the first one. He was getting a little tired of the immediate interest
which his questions aroused, and if he went around scattering
notes in return for fragments of information the interest would
be livelier still. And working on the same theory he decided not
to take a taxi to 14 Ardley Street.

When he came out of Mornington Crescent tube station he
found himself in another world.

London is full of these sudden changes, although the rich
streets and the poor ones are now united in a sisterly shabbiness
that in some mysterious way only intensifies the London quality
of them all. But in the streets where the rents are fabulously
high there are still the signs of money and private enterprise
struggling to free themselves from the nets in which the State
has bound them down, while in the poor ones even the few
humble signs of a decent poverty have vanished, and the very
ruins are uglier. It was a long time since Kenneth had seen a
place so desolate as Ardley Street and its environs in the sweeping
rain of this bleak spring day. It was a row of tall brown brick
houses which had once been the elegant residences of a cheerful
yet chaste Bohemia on the edge of the town, a Chelsea of North
London where artists and writers and engravers had settled with
their families in the eighteen-forties to enjoy the squares planted
with youthful trees and the lovely distant view of the unspoilt
hills of Hampstead and Highgate.

To-day, in the middle of the Nazi War, Ardley Street was half in ruins. A few families still lived behind the windows filled in with black paper, and cultivated the long dreary front gardens from which the protecting iron railings had been taken away for scrap, but most of the fifteen houses were uninhabitable. Three heavy bombs had fallen at the back of the row one night, and where once there had been a row of similar houses with back gardens abutting onto those of Ardley Street, there was now a wide expanse of waste land.

Kenneth turned up his coat collar and set out for Number 14, which he perceived to be right at the end of the row. It was still raining steadily and his rheumatic shoulder ached and he was shocked to find Vartouhi living in such a poor and dirty neighbourhood. If anyone had told him that before the Nazi War Ardley Street had had a frowsty comfort, and, on a soft clear summer's day, even a beauty, of its own, he would not have believed it. There were still standards of a kind in Ardley Street and the strange face of something dimly recognizable as beauty, but such an unstraightforward beauty that only a Sickert or a Verlaine could have perceived it.

Kenneth walked up the long garden of Number 14. There had once been a solid iron gate there, set in solid iron railings, but now there was nothing to protect a row of sturdy spinach from the cupidity of man except the honesty of the people in Ardley Street. Kenneth glanced at it and his heart lifted a little. Whatever sort of creatures lived in this dreadful house they understood how to grow spinach and therefore they could not be so bad.

The front door stood open. The inside of the passage into which he peered was like some black tunnel, greasy and worn with the pressure of bodies and the passing of time. It looked as if people were continually banging against the walls as they hurried in and out. There was not a vestige of furniture in the passage and no covering on the filthy floor and none on the stairs; the only sign that this was not a den inhabited by animals was a dreadful black-out which hung lopsidedly at a landing window half-way up the flight. The centre pane of the window was broken and had been filled up with black paper but at either side there was a row of little panel-pictures in coloured glass; doves intertwined on a bough of myrtle, a wreath of white convolvulus, an urn with ivy escaping from it, and the like, and the sill of the window was shapely and wide. This had once been a solid, comfortable, dignified house.

Kenneth turned to the front door with a snort of disgust and gave the knocker a bang, and the sound echoed flatly in the hall. He thought that no one would come, but he was prepared to wait patiently for some time, and after a long time he thought he heard shuffling noises, and then he was sure that someone was coming; and at last a door at the end of the tunnel opened and a little old woman came creeping along towards him.

She had a black skirt down to her ankles and a night-gown which appeared to be of yellow flannel tucked into it, and over this and her head she had a coarse black dusty shawl. Her grey hair was loose and she peered up at Kenneth from under elflocks. She had no teeth. He removed his hat and opened his mouth to inquire for Vartouhi, but before he could speak she piped:

'Yes? What is it? Oh, I don't expect you want me; I expect you want Mr Perzetti. That's three knocks. I live on the ground floor and that's one knock.'

'I'm sorry to have brought you out——' said Kenneth. The faint sickly odours from the hall and the old woman were very disagreeable.

'Quite all right. I wasn't in bed. Excuse me being not dressed,' and she pulled the yellow flannel closer round her yellow wrinkled neck. 'Just having a cup of tea. It's three knocks for Mr Perzetti,' and she smiled dimly at him, as if she could not quite see him, and turned away.

'Is Mr Perzetti the landlord?' he called after her, not sure that he had heard the name correctly.

'That's right; Mr Perzetti,' said the old woman, and shuffled down to the end of the passage and disappeared through the door.

Kenneth turned to the knocker again, and this time gave three loud bangs. He glanced at his watch while waiting for Mr Perzetti to appear. It was just three o'clock.

Mr Perzetti did not take so long to answer his knocks as the old woman had. Within half a minute there was a bustling step on the landing and down came a stout dark man in the fifties with a red face and dark eyes. He was bald and wore shirt-sleeves and had the racing edition of the *Star* in one hand.

'Yes?' he said sharply, then took a closer look at Kenneth, and said less sharply, 'Did you want to see me? I'm Mr Perzetti. You aren't from the A.R.P., are you? Is it about showing a light last night? We told the warden 'ow it was.'

'Oh no, I've nothing to do with that,' answered Kenneth, feeling that it would be helpful if he could smile but quite unable to because he was so disgusted with the house. 'It's a private matter. Does a Miss Annamatta live here?'

'That's right,' interrupted Mr Perzetti at once, again belligerently. 'She's got my top floor back. No trouble, I 'ope? She's a good, quiet girl. Mrs Perzetti won't have the other sort in the place. This is a respectable 'ouse.'

'Oh—it's nothing of *that* sort,' exclaimed Kenneth, now really horrified at the depths he was plumbing: it was twenty-five years since he had experienced how ugly life can be. 'She's a friend of my sister's and I've brought her a message from her—in fact——'

He hesitated. If the whole situation had not been so repugnant to him he would have found Mr Perzetti's appearance and manner not unpleasant. He was clean (at least, clean compared with his house), his expression was alert and his manner of speech was businesslike. He also had that indefinable quality which we call

367

trustworthiness. Kenneth gave him another scrutiny, and decided to take Mr Perzetti in his confidence.

'I want to see her,' he said, 'because my sister and I are very anxious to persuade her to come back to us. She was with us as—er—mother's help for eight months and we found her very satisfactory. But I had to come to London to be with my father, who was ill, and while I was away some—er—there was a little misunderstanding, and my sister and Miss Annamatta had a few words——'

Mr Perzetti suddenly gave a quick nod, as if to say that he knew what women were. This dismayed rather than encouraged Kenneth, but as it did not seem likely that he could see Vartouhi this afternoon without Mr Perzetti's collaboration, he continued with this distasteful revelation of his private affairs.

'——and my sister—er—dismissed Miss Annamatta. We are most anxious to persuade her to return to her former position. Er—is she in now?'

Mr Perzetti shook his head.

'It's her afternoon off, sir,' he said. The word was not empha-sized, but Kenneth felt more comfortable after he had heard it and better disposed towards Mr Perzetti.

'And I expect she's out with her boy friend,' went on Mr Perzetti. 'Rowl, his name is, and a very good name for him too, if you ask me. He's one of these here *French-Canadians*,' he concluded, in a tone completely lacking in Imperial family feeling.

'And I don't expect she'll be back until black-out,' added Mr Perzetti.

'Oh,' said Kenneth, not knowing quite what to do or say next.

'As a matter of fact, sir,' said Mr Perzetti suddenly, 'she told us about you and your sister (not giving any names, of course; foreigners are a close lot unless they're the sort that tells you all their parst 'istory on top of a bus like Jews), and me and Mrs Perzetti didn't believe it. Thought she was making it up, like girls do. Well, as Mrs Perzetti said, was it likely she'd be working in a milk bar after she'd 'ad a good place in a big 'ouse in the country? Of course, we didn't let on to her we didn't believe her. Didn't want to hurt her feelings.'

Kenneth's own feelings towards Mr Perzetti grew warmer.

'What'll you do, sir?' went on Mr Perzetti, who evidently, like everybody else whose help Kenneth had enlisted, now took a personal interest in the story. 'Wait here till she comes in? Mrs Perzetti could give you a cup of tea——'

Here there was a rather surprising interruption. It took the form of a low cough which seemed to come from the landing. Mr Perzetti pulled himself up in mid-hospitality, and continued in a more subdued tone:

'Well, as a matter of fact, sir, I don't know if we *could* rise to a cup of tea. Mrs Perzetti's very fond of her cup of tea, and you know how it is, the ration doesn't go far when there's only two of you. But——'

'It's very kind of you but I'll get a cup somewhere later,' interrupted Kenneth. 'You say you think Miss Annamatta should be back somewhere round about blackout? That's about seven o'clock, isn't it?'

'Seven-two, sir,' answered Mr Perzetti promptly. 'I'm a taxi driver when I'm working (I'm just out of hospital after six weeks with the pleurisy), and you get into the habit of knowing what time black-out is in my job.'

'That gives me about three hours to fill up,' said Kenneth. 'Let me see—I can telephone my sister—and have a cup of tea somewhere—and perhaps drop in at a cinema—yes, all right, I'll come back about seven.'

'I'm sorry I can't offer you a cup 'ere, sir,' said Mr Perzetti in a lowered tone, and a glance up the stairs. 'But you know 'ow it is. It'll be a good thing when it's all over and we can 'ave a *bath* in tea if we feel like it.'

Kenneth smiled, and agreed that it would.

'Two wars in one life's enough for anybody,' went on Mr Perzetti feelingly. 'I was all through the larst one—Somme, Wipers, all the lot. Four years in France.'

There followed an exchange, interesting to them both, of personal reminiscences of the First World War. By the time they were over, Kenneth and Mr Perzetti were on a different footing.

'Yes, and now it's all got to be done all over again,' concluded Mr Perzetti. 'Cor, sometimes even now I carn't *believe* it; I just carn't *believe* we can 'ave been such blinking, bleeding mugs. Well, sir, you'll want to be getting along. The best thing I can do when you come back about seven is to show you up to 'er room and you can wait for 'er there.'

'Oh—very well—thank you—if you don't think Mrs Perzetti will mind?'

Mr Perzetti made an indescribably lively gesture, perhaps a legacy from some Latin ancestor, which expressed impatience, dismissal, contempt and ribald amusement, though all he said was:

'That'll be all right, sir. You come back about seven and she's almost bound to be here. She's never out after black-out. As a matter of fact, Mrs Perzetti had a talk with her about this here *Rowl*, Peggy (that's what we call her, Peggy) being alone in England. Mrs Perzetti hasn't any of her own and she took quite a fancy to Peggy. And Mrs Perzetti doesn't like this *Rowl* at all,' and Mr Perzetti shook his head.

Kenneth was so painfully interested that he could only look inquiring. He felt that he should not listen to such low opinions and gossip, yet he could not help himself.

'Not at *all*, she doesn't. Mrs Perzetti's a good judge of character, and she says he's nothing but a bad lot.'

'Is—er—Peggy actually engaged to him?'

''E hasn't given her a ring, if that's what you mean, sir. (And never will, if he can get what he wants without, Mrs Perzetti says.) And he doesn't say much, either. He just hangs round here whenever he's got leave, staring at the 'ouse and wandering round the back. He follows Peggy about like a shadow. It gives Mrs Perzetti the creeps. Peggy, she only laughs. Well, you know her way, sir.'

Kenneth knew it too well. He began to feel, as he came away from 14 Ardley Street, that he had arrived just in time. The creatures inhabiting that ruined den of a house had turned out to be human beings, who enjoyed a cup of tea and tried to protect a girl from vague yet ominous dangers; he was not afraid of Vartouhi being with them. But the Perzettis and their kindness could not give her solid protection and safety from poverty, illness, and the dangerous love of wild young men. He began to long to have her by his side, laughing and safe, going home in the train to the peace and comfort of Sunglades.

He telephoned his sisters; to Miss Fielding, ignoring her irritated exclamations, he explained what had happened and warned her that he might have to spend the night at Joan's flat in town, and then he got through to Mrs Miles and said that he would probably want a bed that night; anywhere would do, of course. Oh, that would be all right, said Mrs Miles bluffly; Henry could turn out onto the chesterfield; he had been sleeping so badly lately that it made no difference to him where he slept.

Kenneth had a cup of tea and a roll and margarine in a little café in Camden Town High Street, and then found his way up to Camden Town itself and went to the pictures for an hour or so. He was so worried and disturbed that he hardly noticed the film; the hall was just a place where he could sit still and be quiet and try to think.

When he came out, at a quarter to seven, it was already blue twilight. Rain was still falling steadily.

34

He walked quickly down the High Street, past the ruinous gaping spaces where houses had been and the little shops showing gaudy dresses in a brief brilliant display of colour and light before the black-out came down. Low grey clouds scudded over the sky and the wind was freezing. It was a city of shabbiness and ruins, battered, scarred and dismal beyond belief; and he did not see the honour and pride and courage that covered it like the violet blue veil of the spring dusk. To Kenneth, cheap shops were cheap shops, and ruins were ruins, and a beastly evening was a beastly evening. Except during the 1914 war, his life had been passed in pleasant places and he had never had to look for beauty in the heart of squalor.

Mr Perzetti was in the hall when he arrived and led him upstairs, pausing to adjust the macabre black-out on the landing as they went, and apologizing for the condition of the house. It appeared that they had a landlord who would not do any more repairs than were imperative to keep his property from collapsing, and they had been unlucky since the war in their lodgers, while Mrs Perzetti was not robust and the shopping took up most of the time that might have been spent on house-cleaning.

They looked in on Mrs Perzetti on the way up; she was sitting in an apartment filled to capacity with large bursting sofas and arm-chairs, before a bright fire where supper for two was arranged, and nodded graciously to Kenneth with her mouth full. She was rather pretty, with brown eyes and a fuzzy fringe. The room smelt strongly of warm horsehair from the sofas and arm-chairs, and kippers. Kenneth said 'Good evening,' conscious that he was being judged, and could not help being relieved when her manner remained cordial. A bright cloth covered a birdcage on a corner of the table and he caught a faint sweet 'cheep' from beneath it, as their voices disturbed its occupant. 'Mrs Perzetti's pets,' explained Mr Perzetti indulgently, as he shut the door. He glanced up the stairs. 'This way, sir, please.'

It was not quite dark. Blue light came faintly down the well of the stairs from some window higher up, and cast a sheen on an expanse of wall that bulged unevenly beneath its flowery paper. In the uncertain dusk it seemed to heave slightly, as if something alive were behind it. Kenneth had no doubt that something was; the faint sour smell that drifts out from open doors in French villages was here too; the reek of thick, ground-in, eighty-year-old dirt. He held his breath as they mounted the stairs and answered Mr Perzetti (who was telling him that they had had to paper the staircase and bedroom at their own expense), by nods.

'Here's Peggy's room, sir,' said Mr Perzetti, opening a door. He made a sound of annoyance. 'There! she's left the window open, silly girl. Rain all over the floor.' He went across and shut it. Kenneth was only aware that the room was very small, with a little bed with shabby coverings, and that it smelt fresh. Her few treasures on a table by the window had been blown over and scattered by the wind. Her rucksack was arranged over a chair with a broken seat and the corner of one of her bright scarves hung out of a little chest of drawers with only one castor.

'Eight and sixpence a week, Peggy pays for this,' said Mr Perzetti, 'and it's a bargain, sir. She'd have to pay twelve and six anywhere else, since the war, for a furnished room in a nice position like this—gets all the sun *when* there is any—but me and Mrs Perzetti didn't want to be hard on her. She gets twenty-five shillings a week. It isn't much.'

'No indeed,' muttered Kenneth.

'She'll be in any minute now, sir,' said Mr Perzetti. 'The front

STELLA GIBBONS

door's open, and I'll just pop out and speak to her on her way up and tell her you're here.'

'Thank you,' said Kenneth, and as Mr Perzetti went out of the room he crossed over to the window.

He slid up the shrunken frame and leant out, letting the cold rain beat against his face. Then he looked down.

Very far below, dim in the rising dusk, was a grey waste. It was shut in by dark houses; some towered in gaunt ruin against the sky, others were shapeless masses of masonry without a light or sign of human life. He could make out square pits in the surface filled with weeds, and pools of water where the rain steadily splashed, and mounds of darker bricks, and a pile of square objects which he thought must be the doors of the fifteen houses that had stood here. At one end was a brimming pond, surrounded by a wall, that reflected the dark blue sky, and farther off still there gaped against a pallid expanse where half a house had been torn away, two black caves that must be cellars. The rain pattered lightly against the window where he leant and some tall trees kept up a perpetual sighing. There were no other sounds and the ruins and the weeds were cold and soaked with rain, and the place seemed dead.

Yet violence lingered here. He felt it, even he, who was not imaginative. If the strong passions of human beings can leave ghosts in the place where they were suffered, the strange sighing of blast and the terror of fire and of unbelievable force can leave ghosts too. Here was the place where these powers, blind and made by men, had struck. The place was haunted; it was as haunted as any quiet room in an empty rectory or corridor in an eight-hundred-year-old Scottish castle, and as he drew back into the room Kenneth shivered. His shoulder ached and he was hungry. 'Beastly hole,' he muttered, 'the sooner I get her out of here the better.'

But as he was turning away from the window, something moving by the wall surounding the reservoir caught his attention, and he leant out again to see what it was.

Two figures were approaching the waste land from the path beside the reservoir. They were a man and a woman and Kenneth thought that the man was a soldier. He came first, with a slow yet springing walk, and the woman came after him as if unwillingly; hanging back, and now jumping onto a pile of bricks and waiting until he turned to look at her, then putting her hand up to her mouth—ah, there was only one woman who did that; now holding out her hand as if inviting him to take it. She had something odd on her head. Kenneth thought that it was one of Vartouhi's queer little caps and that the woman was she, and he leant further out of the window into the deepening dusk to see more clearly.

The two were apparently taking no notice of the weather, and there was something about the scene—the loneliness, the sweep of rain through the darkening air, the silent ruins still vibrating with memories of terrible violence—that affected Kenneth very unpleasantly. Nobody should have been there at all, in pouring rain with the black-out coming down; it was not natural. If it is Vartouhi, and she comes in wet through, he thought, I shall give her a real talking to.

Suddenly he heard her voice, clear and indignant, coming up through the twilight. He could not help smiling grimly. She was at her old tricks! ticking the fellow off. She wasn't afraid of anybody or anything. The man stood still, watching her, and she put her hand across her mouth once more as if she were laughing. Then she turned away and ran past him, past the wall surrounding the reservoir, and out of sight. He made no move to follow her. For a little while he stood there looking towards the black cellars; then he turned away and slowly moved off towards the reservoir. Kenneth watched him until he turned the corner that led into the street and disappeared.

It was almost dark. He drew back into the room once more and shut the window and as he did so he heard sudden excited exclamations on the landing below, and recognized Vartouhi's voice. He drew himself up and stood waiting. He heard someone running up the stairs, and the next minute the door was flung open and she stood there, smiling and exclaiming in a voice that rang with delight:

'Is Mr Kenneth!' and holding out her hands to him.

He took them both in his. She had no gloves on, and for the moment all he could say rather gruffly was:

'Well, Vartouhi! Good heavens, how cold your hands are!'

'No, no, I am quite warm. Oh, Mr Kenneth, is a *varry* good thing to see you! How I am glad!' and she gave his hands a gay little swing.

'I'm glad to see you, too, Vartouhi—only I *can't* see you properly,' and he laughed shortly and peered at her through the dimness.

'How are you? Quite well? and—happy, and all that sort of thing, eh?'

'Am varry well, Mr Kenneth, and I am live in this house with good kind people give me a lot to eat and I have a job, too also,' said Vartouhi promptly, and sat down on the chair with no seat and gazed up at him with a beaming smile. He could see the gleam of her white teeth.

'Look here——' he said, glancing round the room, and speaking fussily to conceal his happiness, 'can't we get a light? Doesn't this place rise to a black-out?'

'Is a black-out.' She got up and made some adjustments at the window and the room became quite dark. He heard matches rattling and then a light slowly grew, shining on the smiling face she turned on him. She lit a candle and set it down on the chest of drawers. The feeble yet solemn radiance gave the wretched furnishings of the little room a romantic cast, with odd, quaint shadows, and a mild illumination of quilt and curtain that hid their grime.

'Your clothes are wet,' said Kenneth, severely and anxiously. He had not taken his eyes off her. He thought that she was prettier than ever.

'Is my coat, Mr Kenneth. I am not wet at all. I take him off,' and she did, revealing the familiar costume and white blouse and the red necklace that had been his present. 'You sit down, Mr Kenneth,' she went on. 'Is a chair with no seat but is all right. I sit here on the bed.'

When he had sat down, he felt a little embarrassed. He was acutely conscious of Mr and Mrs Perzetti eating their kippers downstairs with, so to speak, both eyes on the clock. But he did not expect Vartouhi to feel embarrassed because he did not believe that she was capable of that sensation. That was one of the reasons why he, a reserved and conventional man, found her attractive.

'Is your ancient and honoured father well once more?' inquired Vartouhi politely, holding out to him a paper bag. 'Is my sweet ration. Fruit toffee. Is no fruit inside them; is a wicked lie; but you eat them, Mr Kenneth.'

'No, thank you, you eat them, Vartouhi. Yes; my father has been ill again with a bad cold but he is nearly well again now.'

'And that wicked woman, your sister, Mr Kenneth? Oh, how I hope she is been ill! Always I am hoping that!'

Kenneth struggled with his duty for an instant, and then gave way to a shout of laughter. Vartouhi continued to smile and eat fruit toffee, watching him sympathetically.

'You think I say a funny joke, Mr Kenneth, but is true. She send me away because I make you a beautiful prasent. You have seen?'

'Oh, yes—indeed I have, Vartouhi. It's a wonderful present, and you're a dear little girl to think of me. Why, it's—when Miss Burton first showed it to me, I could hardly believe it was real—you must have worked very hard.'

He spoke to her as he always did; as if she were a child. It was only when they laughed together that he felt their ages were more akin, and then his delight was so intense that he simply ignored it; he felt it, but he refused to admit what it must mean.

'Is a pratty thing,' said Vartouhi complacently. 'At first I am making it a prasent for Miss Burton because she give me three hat. Then I think I make it a prasent for *him*, to cheer him up in this house where his sister rules. So I make it for you, Mr Kenneth.'

'Oh,' said Kenneth, blankly. The pretty picture which he had painted to himself of Vartouhi planning his present and diligently executing it in maiden secrecy was not the true one. He had been the recipient of something originally intended for Miss Burton. He felt acutely disappointed.

'Yas,' went on Vartouhi, in a meditative tone, 'Miss Burton tell me about your three medal. Is a very brave thing, Mr Kenneth,' suddenly lifting her eyes to his. 'You are a brave man, as well as good and kind too also. In Bairamia all girls who are not married make bed covers for the brave soldiers. Is a very old thing we do. Is called a *djan*.'

'I see,' said Kenneth, his disappointment replaced by pleasure. So long as none of his family or acquaintances ever found out that he had been honoured in this antique Bairamian fashion, he could enjoy the sensation to the full.

'I do not tell Miss Fielding that,' said Vartouhi, 'because I think she would be angry. But she is angry when I do not tell her. So one day I think perhaps I tell her and make her more angry. Yas, I think so I will.'

'Vartouhi——' he interrupted eagerly, leaning towards her and forcing himself to break a dreamy, unreal sensation that was stealing over him because of the gentle light of the candle and the happiness of being with her again—'that's what I came here to ask you. Will you come back with me to Sunglades?'

'Oh no, Mr Kenneth,' answered Vartouhi, cheerfully and without hesitation. 'Is a wicked thing your sister did to me and I can not, no, I can not. I am angry at you all.'

'Not angry with *me*, I hope? I haven't done anything. When I got back and found you had gone *I* was very angry, I can tell you. I told my sister so, and I said I was going to do my very best to get you back again.'

Vartouhi considered this, looking at him with her head on one side. It was an odd sensation to be studied by such a volatile creature and he wondered very much what she was thinking. At last she said:

'I am not angry at you, Mr Kenneth. And am not angry at Miss Burton. Is a kind good woman. But I am angry at Miss Fielding and am angry at the house. Is a grand rich house, Mr Kenneth, but is old.'

'Old?'

'Yas. Is comfortful but is all old. No funny jokes, no dan-cing, at Sun-glades House. Here in this house is all dirty and not comfortful but is a lot of funny jokes and a manny, manny children in this street making much noise. And I go dan-cing with Raoul.'

(Ah! the fellow's name at last! Now for it.)

'Raoul? Is that your—friend—your boy friend?'

'Is not my friend. Is a bad wicked man,' said Vartouhi haughtily. 'Is always angry at me and does not laugh or say funny jokes.'

'Then why on *earth*,' said Kenneth emphatically and severely, 'do you go about with him?'

'Takes me to dan-cing at the U-ni-ted Na-tions Dance Club,' said Vartouhi, sliding her eyes round so demurely that he had to smile. 'And give me——' She held out her wrist, and jingled a bracelet made of tiny enamelled flags.

'Belonged once to another girl,' explained Vartouhi, 'but he does not love her anny more. She is dad, he says.'

Kenneth could only shake his head. But he was convinced that she was not changed; she was exactly the same as she had been at Sunglades. He was deeply thankful; and he then and there made up his mind not to return to Hertfordshire without her, if it took a month to persuade her to go with him.

'Surely you can't enjoy going about with a fellow who's always sulking?' he exclaimed.

She shook her head. 'Is sad for me at first but when we go dan-cing I am glad because he dance varry nice—so light, so soft. And he likes hold me in his arm, he tells me so.'

Kenneth said nothing. He was bitterly jealous.

'How long have you known him?' he muttered.

'Two week,' she answered. 'I see him one day in the milk bar and he comes home after me. All the girl there are afraid of him, but I laugh. Is so funny! Creep, creep along the street!'

Kenneth did not find it funny. The more he heard the more anxious he became. The room was silent except for the sound of her young voice and he hated the black-out pressing silently against the windows. It was a black veil under which dreadful things could happen. A man who would give a girl a dead girl's bracelet must be an extraordinary sort of customer, capable of anything.

'This is a beastly neighbourhood for you to be in, Vartouhi,' he said, abruptly. He hesitated, then added, 'You're not going to marry this fellow, are you?'

'Oh no, Mr Kenneth,' she said cheerfully. 'Is a bad wicked man and has no money too also.'

'But you told the newspaper that you were!'

'No, no. I say, "Is my boy-friend" (is what all the girl at the milk bar call their man) but the man from the paper said, "No, no, you must say you are going marry him or what will all the reader think?" So I say, "Oh, well, say I am," and so he say it.'

'I see.' He believed what she said, and although he became more determined every moment to get her out of all this, his heart was lighter. She did not care a hang for this chap. That was the main thing.

He glanced round the room. The candle had settled into a steady burning, with its blue and yellow flame so still that it looked as if it were painted on the dusk.

'Vartouhi, let's talk it over—your coming back to Sunglades, I mean. Can you come out to dinner with me?'

'Oh yas, Mr Kenneth!' She was instantly all delight and smiles, and stood up as if ready to set out that moment.

'Somewhere with lots of lights and a band?' he said, smiling in sympathy.

'Would be so nice, Mr Kenneth. Lyon Corner House?'

'Oh—well—I think we can find somewhere better than that. And perhaps we'd better go somewhere quiet too, if we want to talk. You—er—change those wet shoes and I'll go down and see if Mr Perzetti can do anything about a taxi.'

Mr Perzetti was most helpful, and expressed regrets that he could not drive them himself. With his assistance and a visit by Kenneth to the telephone box on the corner, a taxi was obtained, and in a short time Kenneth and Vartouhi were on their way to the West End.

35

He took her to a restaurant run by an ex-Paris hotelier, with fresh narcissi on the tables and the soft pink lights that are eternally romantic. There was no band, and the place had added the expense of war-time to its habitual expensiveness, but every table was taken; for men (most of them in uniform) and women wanted a place where they could sit for an hour or so and look into one another's eyes and talk in murmurs, or be silent and forget.

'Will this do?' he inquired. Their table was in a corner and he had made her sit where she could see the long, softly coloured, subduedly lit room with its quiet guests.

'Is varry pratty,' she said, her voice a little subdued by the general luxury and dimness.

'There's no band. You don't mind?' he smiled.

She shook her head. Her long eyes moved with interest from one table to another, then came back and rested on his face, with a smile slowly growing on her own.

'All these people,' she said almost in a whisper, 'are lov-ers.'

'Well—yes, I suppose they are, Vartouhi. It's—it's a very happy thing to be, you know, even now, when so many of them will have to part later on and won't see each other again for a long time—perhaps never. But we don't want to remember sad things this evening, do we? We're going to enjoy our dinner, and then we're going to arrange about your coming back with me to-morrow to Sunglades.'

The first course had arrived and she was tasting it with childish interest and pleasure and she only smiled in answer, and began to tell him about her job. She earned twenty-five shillings a week and the milk bar supplied her lunches and teas. The Perzettis were very kind, she said, and let her have supper with them almost every evening, and on Sundays Mrs Perzetti would cook sausages for her and had more than once let her share their tiny, precious joint. And when Raoul had leave (he was stationed at Mill Hill, less than an hour's journey from London) he sometimes took her out to supper.

'In places where bad girl are,' confided Vartouhi. 'Manny soldiers too. These girls are varry nicely painted on their face but in the ladyroom I am hearing them,' she leant across the table and lowered her voice, 'say *bish*.'

Kenneth did not know whether to laugh or swear himself. With every moment she was growing dearer to him, and with every moment he realized that she was not unhappy in her new life and that if he tried to persuade her to go back, it would be because he so badly wanted her to.

Yet she was helpless, too; like a child who did not know its own danger. Taking the long view, thought Kenneth, I *ought* to get her back for her own good. What's to happen to her if she gets ill or loses her job?

'Vartouhi,' he said suddenly, as they were drinking their coffee and she brought out her battered turquoise and silver cigarette case, 'have you thought about the future at all? What's to happen to you, I mean?'

'Oh yas, Mr Fielding,' she answered. Smoke was wreathing faintly all about her face. 'I shall go to my sister Yania in America when this war is end.'

'That will cost money. Where will you get it from?' he asked, hating himself for what seemed to him his brutality.

'My sister Yania will send me some, Mr Kenneth. Is going to marry a rich American man.'

'Oh,' he said, and was silent. The news was disagreeable to him and he had to compel himself to add conventionally, 'I'm glad. Er—when is she getting married?'

'When summer begin in May she is getting married. Is a varry good thing.'

Both were silent for a little while. Vartouhi smoked with a dreamy look and he gazed frowningly at the table while his cigar smouldered away. In addition to the news about her sister he remembered that her father was a comparatively wealthy man. If ever she became desperate for money that fact might be of great help to her. It certainly made her less finally dependent upon his, or anyone else's, charity, although for the time being she might not be able to get at her sources of supply. He glanced up at her under his eyebrows. How dear and familiar her face was! and yet he knew next to nothing about the circumstances in which her first twenty years had been spent.

'Why did you come to England?' he asked suddenly.

'My father is hearing the Italians are coming, and I am his favourite one. So he is sending me away to England to live with a English family and learn to speak English varry well and be safe. The Mother at the Convent arrange it all. But when I get to England the father of the family is died and they are all upset and do not want me and then I hear that the Italians have come, so I cannot go back. Is a varry sad thing. So I go and work in a café. Always I am working in cafés. Then I stick the knife in that sailor's lag, like I am telling you, and so I am sent away. And then I come to you at Sunglades, Mr Kenneth,' and she ended the story with a smile that was full of affection.

'So you were only sixteen when you first came to England?' She nodded.

'Poor little girl,' he said. 'You've had a rough time, haven't you?'

'Oh no—no,' said Vartouhi eagerly. 'Was all varry nice. Is so manny house and people here, is all so new. I like it. Only I do not like to sleep in a bed with English girl and I do not like men to touch me and prasently I begin to want my father and

384

mother and sisters and my nice Medora. But is all varry nice, really, Mr Kenneth. I enjoy.'

Insecurity, loneliness, poverty, hard work, exile—she did not notice them. It was of no use offering her safety and comfort; she did not want them. What her youth delighted in were struggle and change; the rough brilliance of life itself. She enjoyed. The two words struck him as if she had dashed a rose across his eyes, all sweetness and sting. I must seem a damned dull fellow to her, he thought; and there began to creep over him a profound loneliness.

It was half-past nine. He glanced at his watch, comparing it with the clock on the wall, and adjusted it a little. Then he said heavily:

'Well, we haven't decided what you're going to do yet, have we? How about it, Vartouhi? You will come home with me to-morrow, won't you?'

She shook her head.

'No, Mr Kenneth. I am too angry still.'

'But my sister's very sorry. I'm sure she is. She'll tell you so. You know she's got a quick temper and says things she doesn't mean.'

'Is a bad thing to do.'

'Of course it is but she can't help it; she's always been like that. And Miss Burton and I would so like to have you back.'

She narrowed her eyes in a teasing smile and shook her head.

'The house is so quiet and dull without you.'

'Is *too* quiet for me, Mr Kenneth. I say so.'

'But—Vartouhi—won't you come back just to please me? I'm so *damned* lonely,' burst out Kenneth, leaning forward and looking at her pleadingly.

She continued to smile as she returned his gaze but gradually the smile lost its mockery.

'I am varry sorry, Mr Kenneth,' said Vartouhi softly. 'Is a bad thing to be lonely. You are so good and kind, too also.'

'I don't feel it. When I think of that chap dancing with you I could wring his neck.'

'You are jalous,' she said, nodding. He could not tell what she was thinking.

'Damned jealous,' he said recklessly, finding a strange relief in making the confession.

'Raoul is jalous too also. He say some day he will kill me,' and she put her hand over her mouth and giggled.

'He probably means it, too,' he said. 'You mustn't take any chances with him, Vartouhi. I don't like the sound of him at all.'

'I am not frightened,' she said, and lit a third little dark yellow cigarette.

At last he realized that she meant what she said; she was not coming back to Sunglades with him; and he became very depressed. He had been so sure she would return that the idea of going back the next day without her had never entered his head, and now that it had he could hardly bear to face it. He grew more and more silent and filled up his glass again and again, although he told Vartouhi with a brief smile that too much of this stuff was not good for little girls and would not let her drink more than two glasses.

She did not mind; she seemed content to sit gazing about the room at the women's clothes and smoking, with a calm expression on her face that increased her Oriental look and made him unhappier because it pointed the differences between them; her race and his own, her youth and his maturity, her casual cheerfulness and his own deepening conviction that his life was half over and had never been a proper life anyway. He kept on thinking bitterly about Connie; how she had bullied and bossed him when he was a child and interfered in all his affairs with women (except a few about which she had never known), when he was older. But he had been a fool to let her. Yes, a fool he thought, staring gloomily at Vartouhi.

'It's nine o'clock, dear,' he said at last rather thickly. 'Time we were getting along, I'm afraid.'

'You call me "dear,"' observed Vartouhi, with a pleased glance.

'Well! D'you mind?'

She shook her head.

The density of the black-out was increased by a slight mist which had accompanied a warmer air following the rain, and he could not persuade or threaten a taxi to take them back to Mornington Crescent. They had to go by tube, and his depression was increased by the glare of the lights and the noisy crowds and the fact that they both had to stand and no one offered Vartouhi a seat. Thank God this *must* be over one day and then one will be able to run a car again and get about like a human being, he thought, looking down at the top of her head as she stood by his side. Upon my word, life isn't worth living nowadays, thanks to that damned house-painting Austrian.

The train stopped at Mornington Crescent.

As they stepped out of the station into the still, damp, silent blackness, he took her arm.

'Is varry dark,' she said in a subdued voice.

'Beastly, isn't it. Never mind, I've got you.'

'I like to see.'

'By Jove, so do I! Never mind,' and the beam of his large and efficient torch suddenly illuminated the blackness, 'we'll soon be home.'

Home! Spoken to her, the word sounded warm and comforting, and suddenly he wished passionately that they *were* going home together; not to Sunglades but to some dear impossible home of their own, where she could have all the rum little hats and beads she wanted and he could potter about the garden and take care of her. (Not that she seemed to need it.) He began to play with the thought as they walked slowly on through the blackness, occasionally pausing while he flashed the torch on a house or wall for her to tell him whether they were in the right road. They would get on like a house on fire, he was sure, and she would make a grand little wife; she was so brave and so sensible too, in her own queer way. She was the dearest little girl he had ever known, and to-morrow he would have to go back to Sunglades without her.

He was tired and unhappy and his brain was confused by what he had had to drink and by their slow dreamlike progress through the thick darkness which pressed in mistily on all sides beyond the ray of the torch. There was a smell of young leaves in the air and once the light flashed on the garden of a bombed house where a scanty old may-tree was covered in green buds. Suppose I asked her to marry me? he thought. By God, I've a good mind to. That *would* give Connie something to think about, and it's the only way I could get her to come back with me tomorrow. The idea was so amazing and new that it sobered him for an instant, and immediately his cautious bachelor habits began to argue against it. But its very strangeness increased the nightmare feeling induced by alcohol and the darkness, and soon the thought began to turn into a definite impulse to then and there propose to her.

'Listen!' said Vartouhi suddenly, and stood still, pressing closer to his side.

'What's the matter, dear? Frightened?' He tightened his hold on her arm.

'Some person is following us, Mr Kenneth, I think.'

He shook his head but they stood for a moment, intently listening. There was not a sound save the traffic, muffled and subdued by distance and the mist. Kenneth sniffed the air distaste-fully and recognized a faint familiar smell. What was it? Wet plaster and charred wood and rubble; yes, but it was more than all those. It was the unmistakable smell, sour and chill and frightening, of bomb-blasted ruins. They must be near the waste land. He put his arm round Vartouhi and held her close.

'It's all right, dear. I'm here.'

They went slowly on. Dense darkness enclosed them on all sides except where the dimmed beam of his torch lit up the damp pavement, and the fresh scent of the coming spring mingled with the strange odour of the ruins. He had never known Vartouhi to be silent for so long and presently he pressed her arm again and asked:

'Still hearing ghosts, eh?'

'Yas, I think so, Mr Kenneth. And I am sleepy, and is easy to kill a large strong man if you come behind him, creep, creep, very quiet and put a knife in his back, high up.'

'By George!' he exclaimed. 'You'll frighten me if you say things like that!'

'Is true, Mr Kenneth. In my country we do that.'

'Well, no one's going to do it here,' he said firmly, but just at that moment he thought he did hear stealthy steps pacing along behind them. He did not pause in his steady walk but listened keenly, and presently he was sure; under the now cheerful tones of Vartouhi's voice as she talked about Bairamia there was the sound of footsteps almost, but not quite, keeping time with their own. His heart began to beat a little faster. They were some way now from the main road and the mist was getting steadily thicker. It would be so easy for someone to strike in the darkness and get away across the waste land before anyone even knew of the blow. It was a damned unpleasant situation and he wondered how much farther they had to go.

'Are we nearly there?' he asked, grasping the torch more firmly.

'I think so we are, Mr Kenneth; I have not been out in the black-out here before.'

'I'm glad to hear it, but how's that? Don't you ever work late at that beastly hole?'

'There was the moon when I did, Mr Kenneth—*oh*!' The sentence ended in a cry, as Kenneth turned quickly round and flashed the torch behind him. A man's dark face, blinking in the glare, stared dazedly out of the mist.

'Anything I can do for you?' demanded Kenneth, taking a step towards him.

'Is Raoul!' exclaimed Vartouhi, beginning to laugh. 'Oh, we thought it was some wicked per-son!'

The man said nothing for a minute. The collar of his khaki overcoat was turned up and his heavy chin was thrust down into it. He did not look more than twenty and his small eyes were dark and dull under thick brows.

'Guess I scared you,' he drawled at last. ''Lo Peggy. Got a light?' to Kenneth. His voice sounded stupid and tired and while he spoke he was peering beyond the circle of light made by the torch as if to try and make out Vartouhi's face. He slowly put his hand in his pocket and brought out a packet of Lucky Strikes from which he took one, putting it clumsily between his lips, while never taking his eyes from the dim shape that was Vartouhi.

'You are out too late,' she said teasingly, from the darkness beyond the torch's light. 'You will be punish again.'

'I've got leave,' he muttered, putting his head down to reach the burning lighter Kenneth was holding out to him. Vartouhi had taken the torch and was idly sweeping its beam across the railings and up to the sky, leaving the two men in darkness except for the tiny flame from the lighter.

'Don't do that, Vartouhi!' said Kenneth sharply.

Raoul drew in his dark cheeks and blew out smoke.

'Are you coming to see me?' Vartouhi went on in the same mocking tone. 'Is late and I can-not talk to you to-night, I am varry sleepy.'

He shook his head with a gesture that hardly moved his smooth massive throat. He was still watching her.

'Good night,' said Kenneth curtly, shutting the lighter and returning it to his pocket. He resumed the torch from Vartouhi, who had ceased to play with it, and took her arm again.

Raoul made a sudden movement, it was hard to see whether of his shoulders or his arms, and Kenneth had such a quick impression of danger that he involuntarily moved forward a pace himself. Then he let the torch shine upwards on the dark, savage young face.

'Good night,' he said again, but the boy took no notice.

'Good night, Peggy,' he said. 'Same time to-morrow, huh?'

Vartouhi shrugged her shoulders. 'I will see.'

'Same time,' he insisted, leaning forward a little.

'I will see, I will see. Do not bother.'

They both ignored Kenneth; he might not have been there.

'Come along, Vartouhi,' he said authoritatively, 'you'll get cold hanging about here,' and he moved quickly away, almost pulling her with him.

The young man did not move. He stood still with the red tip of his cigarette glowing, and let the darkness flow back over him, meeting the darkness in his own mind, in silence. Kenneth could not hear any sound of his footsteps, although he listened intently, and presently he thought that they must have left him behind.

'Was only Raoul,' said Vartouhi, her gaiety entirely restored. 'Is a silly boy.'

Kenneth grunted. A damned dangerous young gangster was how he would have described him; the sort of rebel no amount of Army discipline could tame. A woman-killer if ever there was one, thought Kenneth, so disturbed that his usually sluggish imagination was working. She mustn't see him again.

I'll marry her and take care of her—if she'll have me, his thoughts went on. She can't go on like this, she'll come to a sticky end sooner or later, just because she's such a child in some ways and yet so attractive to men. A nice life of it I'm probably letting myself in for!—she's twenty-eight years younger than I am and a foreigner with a horde of relations. And God knows what Con will say. Still—I'll ask her. The fact is I'm in love with her and want to take care of her and I shan't be happy until I've got the right to. Here goes.

He drew in his breath: but all he said, in a growl, when it came out again, was:

'What on earth does that fellow want, hanging round here?'

'He is always hang round here, Mr Kenneth. He say he likes places where the bombs have been.'

Kenneth said nothing, but awaited further interesting revelations. The argument between his love and his common sense was still going on.

'He likes the black-out too also. Always he is asking me to go in those bomb houses with him in the black-out.'

'Young blackguard! I hope you——'

'He say it would be a good place for us to kiss in.'

'Yes, yes, all right, I don't want to hear about that. Er—do you let him kiss you?'

'Cannot help,' said Vartouhi with a shrug. 'Is varry strong and rude too also.'

'But do you *like* to kiss him?'

'No, no. Make me laugh.'

'Er—is there anyone you do like kissing?'

'I like to kiss my nice Medora,' said Vartouhi promptly. 'But is too much kissing in England.'

'A man, I meant, not a child or your sisters.'

He awaited her reply with uneasiness, but his own conflict was over. His next question to her would be a proposal.

'Oh no, Mr Kenneth. I do not like kiss men at all.'

Kenneth gave a sound between a laugh and a groan and said, stopping short in their walk and looking down at the dim glitter of her hair:

'Vartouhi, will you marry me?'

He could not imagine what she would do or say in answer. She might laugh or refuse to believe he meant it or—anything. She was the most unexpected creature in the world and whatever she did was bound to be surprising. The darkness and the confusion in his head from alcohol and their sinister encounter

with Raoul all made the situation seem so fantastic that he felt
as if he were in a dream, with prudence and common sense
banished to the waking world.

'You ask me *marry* you?' exclaimed Vartouhi, her voice shrill
with surprise, also stopping, and gazing up at him. The light
of the torch shone on her shabby trench coat, with a bunch of
primroses which he had bought for her pulled through one
of the buttonholes, but her face was in shadow.

'Yes,' he said gruffly.

'Yas!' said Vartouhi at once, and he heard a brilliant smile come
into her voice. 'Yas, I will marry you, Mr Kenneth. Is a varry good
thing and I am varry please. So will my father be, and all my
sisters and my mother and my nice Medora. Oh, how please they
will be! You are a good kind rich man with a big house and——'

'Oh Vartouhi,' he exclaimed, interrupting the flow of words
which came with such a strong increase in her accent that they
were almost unintelligible, 'don't talk like that! Don't you—love
me at all?'

Only the darkness gave him courage to ask such a question.
He had never felt lonelier in his life.

'Oh yas, Mr Kenneth,' she answered, more quietly, 'I love you
varry much. You are so kind. I will be good wife to you,' she
ended softly, looking up at him through the mist.

She could not have said a sweeter thing and one that would
have comforted him more. He grasped her arms gently and
stooped his face to hers.

'Dear little girl,' he muttered. 'May I kiss you?'

She nodded, and he took from her an embrace as fresh and
hearty as a child's. He heard her murmur some words to herself
and said, still with his arm about her:

'What's that, darling?'

'Is what we say in Bairamia when we are promise to marry.
*I give you my heart and my honour. Bless be our bridal bed and children
born of you and me.*'

He kissed her again, too moved to speak. His loneliness had gone and suddenly he was very happy. He had vaguely imagined what fun it would be if they were engaged, with Vartouhi delighting him by playing about like a kitten, but he had not hoped for more than that. Now it seemed as if he might gain a wife who could give him the frank and abundant love he had always longed for. At the back of his mind there was the faintest uneasy hope this his sisters might not overhear Vartouhi repeating the Bairamian betrothal vow, but he dismissed the idea. Dammit, it's no worse than the Bible and our Marriage Service, he thought.

'You say it,' said Vartouhi, gently shaking his arm.

'Oh, must I? All right, then. Er—*I give you my heart and my honour*—is that right?—er—*blessed be our bridal bed and the children born of you and me,*' he ended, very quickly and almost in a whisper.

'Now we are engage,' said Vartouhi, with a pleased giggle and took his arm again and resumed their walk. 'We are almost at the house, too also. Mr Kenneth——'

'Kenneth. You can't call me 'mister' now, you know.'

'What shall we do next, Kenneth?' she inquired in a business-like tone. 'When you like me to marry you? Soon or a long time away?'

'Oh—er—soon. Very soon. Would you like that?'

'Yas. I shall tell the people at the milk bar and come away back to Sunglades with you to-morrow morning. Is a good thing?'

'Very good, dear. I'll call for you here at eleven o'clock with a taxi and we'll be home in time for lunch.'

They went on to make those first mutual plans to which a new engagement adds such delightful colouring. He found that she was as sensible as he had always believed, in spite of her odd way of looking at things and the disconcerting frankness of speech that was so startling when once her national reserve had been cast aside. With every moment that passed, the prospect of their future contentment seemed more assured; and when he parted from her, on her own doorstep, after another kiss, if he was still a bewildered man he was also an increasingly happy one.

The names of his sisters had not been mentioned between them.

36

The following morning Miss Fielding was in the little workroom with a dictionary and grammar of Dr Stocke's native tongue, having snatched a moment's respite from her wearisome household duties to pursue her studies, when the telephone bell rang. She exclaimed impatiently as she took off the receiver; she had already been interrupted once by a call from Kenneth announcing that he would be home to lunch and was bringing Vartouhi with him. As if this were not disconcerting enough here was somebody else bothering.

'Constance?' said her sister's urgent voice, 'this is Joan. My dear, *have* you heard from Kenneth? Did he——'

'Yes, he telephoned about twenty minutes ago to say he would be back to lunch, bringing that wretched little creature with him. Why, is anything the matter?'

'Didn't he tell you?'

'No, he didn't tell me anything. Wh——'

'He says he's—they're engaged.'

'What?'

'Engaged—engaged to be married.'

'Nonsense!' exploded Miss Fielding.

'That's what I said at first, but I'm afraid it's true. He——'

'Engaged! To that little—why, she's no better than a servant! I can't——'

'That's exactly what I told him. And a foreigner too. I said——'

'Are you sure he wasn't—was he quite sober?'

'Perfectly sober. As you know, he spent the night here, and I thought something was up because I heard him laughing quite loudly with Henry after I'd gone to bed and you know Henry hardly ever laughs. That's queer, I thought, and then Ken's manner was so extraordinary. He was so cheerful and excited. Whistling all over the flat. And then at breakfast he told me.'

'I can't believe it! It *must* be a mistake! Or perhaps it's his idea of a joke. I never heard——'

'I'm afraid it isn't a joke, Connie. He seems very determined. He was quite rude about it. And Henry actually backed him up. Of course at first I just laughed and said 'Rubbish!' but he took not the slightest notice. I pointed out all the difficulties——'

'But she's a Mohammedan!' Miss Fielding's voice rose to a wail.

'Not quite. Don't they have a sort of modified Greek Orthodoxy? But that's bad enough and I don't know *what* everybody will say. Henry's mother was on the telephone to me this morning.'

'How did *she* come to know about it? Whatever——'

'Henry told her, if you please. She was very much upset. And then there's Great-aunt Dolly——'

'I shouldn't think we'd better tell her for a day or two until we see what's going to happen. It might kill her.'

'That's what I thought. After all, they aren't *married* yet, and perhaps the whole thing will blow over.'

'Oh, I do hope so! I *can't* believe it. Are you *sure*——'

'Of course I'm sure, Constance.' Mrs Miles's voice was very tart. 'I'm in possession of my senses, I suppose. If you had seen Kenneth's face and heard him talk about it you'd be quite sure too. I never saw anyone look so besotted; it was quite repulsive in a man of his age.'

'I don't know how I shall bring myself to speak to her,' said Miss Fielding awfully. 'Of course, she set herself to catch Kenneth from the first. There's no doubt of that now.'

'None at all——'

Pip—pip—pip——

'Thr-r-r-ee minutes, please.'

'Oh—we will have another call, please, don't cut us off,' said Mrs Miles hastily.

After a pause.

'——from the very first minute she saw him,' Miss Fielding was saying, 'and of course when she made that quilt for him she showed her hand *just* a little too plainly. How men can be such fools——'

'Exactly what I said to Henry. Constance, do you think Father could talk to Kenneth and make him see sense?'

'I don't suppose so for a moment. Father's very much aged, you know, in these last few months and Doctor Anderson says he mustn't be agitated. Besides, if I did wait until one of his good days and then told him I'm afraid it's just the sort of mad thing he would enjoy. He has a most peculiar and unfortunate sense of humour as you know.'

'Yes. Yes, I don't suppose he'd be much good. I really don't know who to suggest. He wouldn't listen to Frankie, I suppose?'

'Oh I'm sure he wouldn't. Besides, Frankie is fond of Vartouhi; she always has been.'

'Well, then, I'm sure I don't know who to suggest. There doesn't seem *anything* to be done, does there?'

'I will talk to him,' said Miss Fielding, more confidently than she felt. 'I dare say I can knock some sense into him.'

'Well, I'm sure I wish you joy of the task, my dear,' said Mrs Miles. 'I talked to him for an hour this morning (I was so late at the Ministry that I'm all in arrears with my day's schedule) and it had no more effect than if he'd been stone-deaf and blind into the bargain. He's completely infatuated.'

'Dreadful,' said Miss Fielding deeply, shaking her head down the telephone.

'I say, Constance, I suppose you don't think—how about appealing to *her*?'

Miss Fielding's reply to this suggestion took the form of a snort; she did not think it worth while to answer in words. But Mrs Miles persisted.

'You don't think if we told her that she'd be dragging him

down and upsetting all his friends and relations—that sort of thing—eh?'

'No I don't, Joan. *You* don't know her, you see. I do. She doesn't behave or reason like an ordinary person at all. She——'

'Dear me, I hope she isn't wrong in the head, on the top of everything else?'

'Oh no, far from it. She's very cunning. But you can never get *at* her! *I* have never been able to, anyway. And——'

Pip—pip—pip.

'Thrrrree minutes, please.'

This time the sisters did ring off, having made hasty arrangements for Miss Fielding to telephone later on in the day after she had seen Kenneth.

Having replaced the receiver, Miss Fielding strode out into the hall and shouted up the stairs:

'Frankie, Frankie, can you come down? Oh no—perhaps I'd better come up——' for she suddenly recollected that her father, though dozing beside the drawing-room fire, would be sure to overhear an excited colloquy in the hall.

She hurried up to Miss Burton's apartments and found her cousin doing some mending before the fire. She looked up and said, 'Surely it isn't half-past eleven yet? I was just coming down to help you with lunch.'

'Frankie, what *do* you think—isn't it dreadful—Joan has just telephoned to say that Kenneth is engaged to Vartouhi!'

'How splendid! Oh, I am so glad!' exclaimed Miss Burton.

'Glad! How can you, Frances? A paid companion—a sort of servant—and a foreigner——'

'*You* oughtn't to mind *that*, anyway, Constance,' drawled The Usurper. 'But tell me all about it. What happened? What did Joan say?'

'She said he told her they were engaged. He seemed quite besotted and behaved very queerly, laughing with Henry and so on. *He* telephoned here only a few minutes before to say he'll

399

be home to lunch but he never said a word to *me* about being engaged.'

'Is he bringing Vartouhi with him?'

'Yes, he said so. Oh dear——'

'Oh, how delightful!' cried Miss Burton. 'Now, Connie, you will open one of those six bottles of champagne, won't you?'

'Indeed, I shall do nothing of the kind, Frances. You don't seem to understand. It's been a terrible shock to me and I don't know whether I'm on my head or my heels. I simply can't believe it. Of course, Kenneth has always been a fool over a pretty face——'

'There you *go* again, Connie!' exclaimed Miss Burton, dashing down the mending and sitting very upright and staring indignantly at her cousin, 'it's that sort of remark that's driven Kenneth into getting engaged to Vartouhi. Not that he doesn't love her, dear little thing, I expect he's devoted to her and who wouldn't be—but you don't seem to understand that it's natural for men to like pretty faces and they don't like being called fools when they do. For years you've been dinning it into him that he's a fool about women and now I expect he thought: "Oh well, what does it matter if I am? Better a fool and happy than a miserable half-starved old bachelor!"'

'Kenneth is not half-starved, Frances. I don't know what——'

'Starved for love, starved for love, I mean,' said Miss Burton crossly. 'It isn't a happy state to be in, Connie, you know, although unfortunately it's a chronic one for many people. Why, even you've been much nicer since you've had Doctor Stocke.'

'*Frances!*'

'Well, since you've been writing to him or whatever it is you do—I don't know.' Miss Burton was now thoroughly worked up and determined to have her say. 'Yes, much nicer. And why? Because you're happier.'

'I think that's a very extraordinary remark to make, Frances. And how you can compare a purely intellectual and spiritual friendship, such as I have for Gustav, with a mere vulgar flirtation——'

'Intellectual and spiritual fiddlesticks. You're in love with him,' said Miss Burton, snatching up the mending again and furiously examining it for holes.

'You have a low mind, Frances,' said Miss Fielding, after a pause in which she had gone crimson. 'I am very sorry to say so, but you have.'

'Oh rot,' answered Miss Burton, getting up and flinging the mending aside. 'Of course you're in love with him and so is he with you—in a peculiar sort of way, but it's love all right.'

'Well, really.' Words failed Miss Fielding and she took refuge in lofty amusement.

'Yes, really,' mimicked Miss Burton, sweeping past her and out of the door. 'Why don't you come off your high horse and admit it and be nice to Ken and Vartouhi when they come? I think it's all perfectly delightful and I only hope they'll get married almost at once. What are we going to have for lunch?'

'Tinned herrings.' Miss Fielding followed her out of the room and down the stairs, 'I suppose you realize that this may mean you can't live here any longer?'

'Oh, I quite expected that,' said Miss Burton airily, although she had not realized it and her heart sank. 'They won't want an old thing like me around, especially when the children begin to come.'

'Children!' Miss Fielding gave a sort of shriek. 'Oh dear, oh dear, I hadn't thought of that! I *hope* there won't be any.'

'That's simply wicked, Constance,' said Miss Burton flatly. 'I don't like children myself, to be candid, but a marriage is all the better for having them. That's what marriages are for, you know.'

'Dreadful little Bairamian nephews and nieces with yellow faces! Mohammedans! I believe this will kill Great-aunt Dolly.'

'Then don't tell her,' said Miss Burton. 'Shall we have the potatoes in their jackets? It saves work.'

'If you like. Mashed go better with tinned herrings. I think I had better tell her. It would look so odd if she found out.'

'Why should she? She's eighty-seven and bedridden.'

'Joan writes to her every month, regularly.'

'All the same I don't see why she should know. And if she does find out, what business is it of hers? She's had her life; eighty-seven years of it and eight children. She ought not to grudge other people their share.'

By now they had arrived at the kitchen. It was full of sunlight and a yellow hyacinth was flowering in a pot on the windowsill. Miss Burton flung open the window and let in the soft spring air.

'Delicious,' she said, leaning out.

'I don't know where *I* shall go, or what will become of *me*,' said Miss Fielding sombrely, beginning to assemble the luncheon.

'No. She won't want you here, either.'

'Our Mother's home!' said Miss Fielding tragically. 'Is this lettuce too far gone, do you think?'

'Perhaps she won't want to live here herself. They won't notice what they're eating. I'll mix some batter for pancakes, shall I?'

'Do, if you will. I suppose she won't do any work when she comes back, either.'

'Oh I don't know. You never can tell what Vartouhi's going to do.'

'She'll loll about all day like a duchess and we shall be worse off than ever.'

'Are you going to tell Uncle Eustace?' asked Miss Burton, dropping milk into her batter.

'Oh dear, I'd quite forgotten Father! No, I can't; I really can't. I shall leave it to Kenneth. Doctor Anderson said Father mustn't be agitated, and I don't think I could trust myself not to break down.' Miss Fielding endeavoured to look as if she were on the verge of breaking down but only succeeded in looking very cross. 'And there's Betty too; but I suppose *she* will be furious.'

'Why should she?'

'Oh, well, it's been quite plain lately, hasn't it, that she'd have Kenneth like a shot herself if he'd ask her?'

'Yes, you were afraid she would get him at one time, weren't you? What a pity she didn't—*she* wouldn't have given you yellow nephews and nieces.'

'Well, Betty would certainly have been better than Vartouhi—anything—*anyone* would have been better than that!'

And Miss Fielding went on with her preparations, reflecting bitterly that all her efforts to steer Kenneth clear of entanglements with Betty, with the Palgrave girl, and Alicia, and Una Maltravers, had only ended in this, the worst, the most hopelessly unexpected and undesirable entanglement of them all.

Miss Burton took it upon herself to break the news to old Mr Fielding. He was sitting by the fire with the newspaper and his correspondence, which was so extensive and cosmopolitan that his daughter sarcastically said he ought to have a secretary. He looked very small and old and frail but cheerful, and received Miss Burton with a smile.

'Guess what, Uncle Eustace?'

'I have no idea, Frances. You are always asking me to guess what and it's usually something pleasant. What is it this time?'

'Kenneth telephoned this morning. He will be here to luncheon and who do you think he is bringing with him?'

Mr Fielding smilingly shook his head. Loud voices and long conversations and bright lights tired him so much nowadays that he often wished people would go away.

'Vartouhi. And—this will be a big surprise to you—they're engaged to be married!'

'No, good heavens!' exclaimed Mr Fielding, dropping his glasses, and sitting upright. 'Really? Are you sure? How astounding!'

'Yes, isn't it? But splendid news. Kenneth ought to have been married years ago and she will make him a fine little wife.'

'I can't recall her face at all,' said Mr Fielding confusedly.

'Well, they'll soon be here and you'll see her again. And I must go and get on with toast for their lunch. Of course——' but she checked herself and only smiled at him as she went out of the room, saying, 'I thought you would like to hear the news.'

'Thank you, my dear, very good of you. I say—Frances—what's Connie got to say to it, eh?'

'Not very pleased,' said Miss Burton, smiling and shaking her head, and shut the door. She had been going to say that of course this would mean changes at Sunglades and probably old Mr Fielding and herself would have to seek new quarters, but thought it wiser not to worry him yet.

The morning drew on. About half-past twelve Miss Fielding went upstairs and arrayed herself in a dark dress with gloomy brown embroidery and came down with slightly reddened eyelids. I don't care; she should have thought of that before, all those years when she was snubbing Ken and telling him no one would ever fall in love with him, thought Miss Burton. It's nothing but wounded vanity and paddy-whack because her nose has been put out of joint; and she went out into the garden with a walking-stick and pulled down and broke off a branch of double cherry blossom and put it, bridal and opulent, on the luncheon table.

'Was that necessary, Frances?' inquired Miss Fielding, pointing.

'I thought so, Connie. Since you won't open anything to drink and you don't seem very pleased——'

'*Pleased!* Good heavens!'

'——we must do something to welcome them.'

'Frances! Connie! Here they are!' cried Mr Fielding from the hall where he had been pottering about for the last ten minutes, and Miss Burton hurried out to the front door.

Miss Fielding followed more slowly. 'Father, please, remember Doctor Anderson said you weren't to excite yourself. We don't want you ill again, on the top of everything else,' she said irritably.

Kenneth came out first. He was smiling, but immediately

404

glanced beyond his father and Miss Burton to where his sister stood silently in the hall. Miss Fielding's expression was stony, and his smile became uneasy.

The interior of the taxi was dark. There was no sign at first of Vartouhi. Then suddenly a little hand appeared, grasping the window frame, and giving the group on the steps an excellent view of the large single ruby flashing on its fourth finger, and a moment later the door was opened and she appeared, smiling yet dignified, and dressed exactly as she had been when she left Sunglades a month ago.

'Why, she's charming,' muttered Mr Fielding, 'of course I remember her now.'

'My dear!' cried Miss Burton, running down the steps, 'I am so glad to see you!'

But Vartouhi did not take her outstretched hand. She made a low curtsy and said:

'Honoured cousin, I am glad to see you.'

'Oh—of course! I forgot,' said Miss Burton, smiling and colouring faintly and glancing at Kenneth. 'We're going to be cousins. How queer it seems but very delightful. Well, can I kiss my future cousin?'

'Is too much kissing in England,' said Vartouhi decidedly, 'all the time it is nothing but kissing. In Bairamia we put your hand on my heart. Is better,' and she did so, then lifted it to her forehead, bowing twice. 'Am pleased to be back at Sunglades, honoured cousin,' said Vartouhi in conclusion.

This ceremony had to be repeated more elaborately with old Mr Fielding while Kenneth paid the taxi-driver. Vartouhi knelt on the doorstep to receive his blessing, to his extreme embarrassment, as he had never blessed anyone in his life before and could not think of anything to say except, 'Er—bless you, my dear. I hope you will be very happy and I'm—er—sure you will.'

All this time Miss Fielding had remained standing silently in the background and Vartouhi had taken no notice of her. In answer to Kenneth's hearty greeting she slightly inclined her head. Really, I'd no idea Con could be so nasty, thought her brother. I hope to heaven there won't be a row.

Rising from her knees, Vartouhi went across the threshold of Sunglades once more, and found herself face to face with Miss Fielding. Everybody held their breath.

'Honoured sister,' said Vartouhi very politely, making a low curtsy, 'I say good morning to you.'

'Well, Vartouhi, so you have come back,' was Miss Fielding's unpromising response. 'Lunch is on the table, Kenneth,' and she turned away and walked into the dining-room.

Lunch passed off more pleasantly than everyone expected. Miss Fielding ate in silence, with downcast eyes and compressed lips, only saying, 'Very handsome' when Vartouhi courteously held out the ruby ring for inspection, and taking no part in the discussion of wedding plans.

Towards the end of the meal two red spots appeared on her cheeks which Kenneth saw with dismay. By Jove, Connie is in a rage, he thought, and decided to turn Vartouhi over to Frankie after lunch and slip away to the office until the storm had passed.

They were to be married early in May, which gave Vartouhi about five weeks in which to prepare a trousseau.

'How exciting,' said Miss Burton; and there followed an awkward pause. No one liked to break it by asking if the bridal pair intended to live at Sunglades but that was what everybody wanted to know. Three people's futures would be affected by their decision.

It was Vartouhi herself who spoke at last. Placing one hand upon that of Miss Burton and the other on that of Mr Fielding as she sat between them, she said, with a new graciousness and looking indescribably foreign:

'When we are married we shall live here first of all, at Sunglades. Honoured second-father, honoured cousin, will you live here with us? I will look after you in your old age, my second-father; and you, my cousin, too also.'

'Yes, that's a splendid plan,' said Kenneth heartily. 'No, Frankie, no "buts." Father, that will suit you, won't it?'

'Well, it's a wonderful idea, Ken; I should hate to leave Sunglades after all these years——' said Miss Burton, greatly relieved. 'It's more than kind of you both.'

'That will suit me perfectly,' said Mr Fielding quietly. All this excitement should have been pleasant, but he felt so tired and confused that he could not enjoy it.

'Are sixteen people in my father's—first-father's—house,' said Vartouhi. 'My first-father, my mother, me (when I was live there), my sisters, Yania, Yilg, Djura, K'ussa, my nice Medora, my sister husband, two cousin varry old and poor, my mother's three sisters not married, and my first-father's brother, is varry rich and drink too much. Then we have ten servants too also. I like that. To have manny, manny people in a house is a happy thing. So you stay here, both you, and we all be happy together.'

Everyone laughed except Miss Fielding. No one dared to look at her.

As soon as lunch was over Miss Burton said that she would go and telephone the news to Betty, who would be so pleased; would Vartouhi come too?

'No, I clear away lunch. Honoured sister, will you go and rest?' said Vartouhi, inclining her head towards Miss Fielding.

'Oh—er—thank you. You had better——'

But here Miss Fielding's feelings, which had been choking her throughout lunch, at the spectacle of Vartouhi full of fresh airs and graces and queening it over them all, became too much for her. She had been going to say, 'Call me Constance,' but it was no use; she could not bring the words out, the sight of Vartouhi folding the tablecloth with that proprietary air was the final straw, and she rushed from the room.

'Is feeling bad,' said Vartouhi to Kenneth, who had lingered behind the others.

'Poor old Con, yes, I'm afraid she is. After all, it's pretty hard on her. And it's going to be rather complicated too. The house is one-third hers.'

'I do not understand.'

Kenneth explained.

'Buy that bit from her,' said Vartouhi, 'then she can use the money to get a husband.'

'I don't think she wants one, dear.'

'Avvrybody wants a husband. But she is so old. I cannot have her live here, Ken-neth. Would be fighting all day. The wife must rule in the house.'

'Yes, I quite see that. Poor old Con. Well, I suppose I'll have to talk to her, and then I must get along to the office. I'll see you later, dear.'

Vartouhi finished clearing away, then wheeled the dumbwaiter out to the kitchen and began to wash up, first carefully hanging the ruby ring on a hook on the dresser. She sang as she worked and the yellow hyacinth gave out its sweet smell to the sunlight. Afterwards, she went upstairs on affairs of her own.

Kenneth, in his outdoor clothes, went cautiously to the door of the little morning room that had been his mother's and knocked. A muffled voice told him to 'come in,' and he obeyed.

His sister sat there at his mother's desk, with her eyes full of angry tears and a damp handkerchief clenched in one hand.

'Now, Con . . . now, old girl,' he said, and tried to pat her shoulder.

Miss Fielding jerked away from him.

'I am not upset for myself, Kenneth. I am upset for you.'

'Me! I'm as happy as a sandboy—haven't felt so good for years.'

'Yes, that's what worries me. You are so *blind*. You have been entrapped——'

'Now, Connie, steady on, you know.'

'You have, Kenneth. Entrapped by a greedy, calculating,

baby-faced little—little——' Miss Fielding retired into the handkerchief again.

'You've never liked her,' said Kenneth, helplessly, too upset himself to feel angry (poor old Con, her bark was always worse than her bite), 'that's the trouble.'

'Because I've always seen through her. She's been after you from the moment she set eyes on you——'

'Yes, she told me so,' said Kenneth.

'*What! Told* you so? Of all the barefaced, brazen, calculating——'

'I think it's rather flattering and it's damned funny too, the way she tells it—I wish you could have heard her——' said the infatuated man, laughing at the memory. (Miss Fielding gave a dismal trumpet into the handkerchief.) 'She says it's time she had a husband, having reached the impressive age of twenty, and as I hadn't got a wife (she can't make out why, by the way) and I've got a "large rich house" and plenty of money, she thought I would fill the bill nicely.'

'How you can be so—so—materialistic—so unspiritual—you *admit* she's marrying you for your money——'

'Oh, we shall get on all right,' said Kenneth. Not for worlds would he have betrayed the tenderness that linked him with his quaint little love. If Con liked to think he was a fool and Vartouhi was a gold-digger, let her.

'I hope you will, but I very much doubt it.'

'Dammit, Connie, you aren't very encouraging, are you?'

'I am sorry, Kenneth. I do not feel encouraging. I have never regarded you as the right type to make a good husband and I see no reason to change my opinion now.'

'Well, really, Connie——' Words failed him for the moment.

'That is why I have always discouraged your silly flirtations and infatuations,' said Miss Fielding. 'Often at considerable trouble to myself.'

Kenneth said, 'Good God Almighty,' in a meditative tone, and his sister winced.

'There is no need to blaspheme, Kenneth.'

'Sorry. May I ask who you do think is the right type?'

'Well—Henry. Henry is the only person I can think of at the moment, though of course he is not good enough for Joan.'

'No, of course not, poor b-blighter,' said Kenneth feelingly. 'And that's your idea of a happy marriage, is it? with the wife wearing the trousers and the husband going round looking permanently browned off? It isn't mine.'

Miss Fielding shut her eyes.

'The fact is,' said Kenneth, as if to himself, 'most people just don't know what happiness is.' He continued to look at his sister's tear-stained, long-suffering face, and shook his head. 'Just don't know what it is,' he said again. 'But I know. I've always known, only I've been a fool and haven't gone the right way to get it.'

'I shall go and stay with Joan for a time,' said Miss Fielding faintly into the handkerchief.

'That's a very good idea, Connie. It'll give things time to settle down a bit. But you'll come to the wedding, won't you, old girl?'

'Oh I don't know, Kenneth. It's too soon—don't ask me yet. I shall have to see how I feel.'

'Just as you like, of course, old girl. But I think Vartouhi would like you to come and I know I should.'

He waited for an answer, but none came. His sister continued to sit behind the handkerchief in silence, and presently he went out of the room and left her to it. He thought that he would go and take a peep at Vartouhi before he went down to the office; and ran upstairs two at a time, whistling. But at the top of the stairs he stopped. The door of the large linen-cupboard on the landing was open, and its lavender-scented and snowy contents were disposed in neat piles on newspaper upon the floor. Among them knelt the future mistress of Sunglades. She was counting sheets.

★

Some months later Betty Marten was taking a short holiday at her family's home in Devonshire. Among her morning letters was one from her daughter-in-law which she opened with anticipations of amusement, for Alicia's letters although curt as a man's were always entertaining. After reading half a page she gave a slight shriek.

'What's the matter?' inquired her sole companion at the breakfast table (who was none other than the successfully sublimated gardening aunt), without looking up from *The Times*.

'*Who* do you think is getting married now?'

'Goodness knows. There seems to be an epidemic of it in that part of the world.'

'Constance Fielding! I thought I should never get over Ken and that little savage, but this is more amazing still.'

'Good gracious me. That really *is* a surprise,' said the gardening-aunt calmly. 'Who to?'

'Doctor Stocke—at last. Frankie and I always hoped they would. It appears that he sent her a letter in his own language and when she translated it, it turned out to be a proposal.'

'How romantic,' said the aunt. She got up and crossed to the window and stood looking out at the garden where the splendour of another June was beginning.

'They're going to travel about, lecturing on peace,' continued Betty, turning over a page, 'at least, for the present.'

'Let us hope that they will be listened to,' said the aunt. 'Elizabeth, this honeysuckle has forty-seven flowers on it. I've just counted.'

'How delicious, darling. I'll come and smell it in a minute. Alicia and Rick do sound happy.'

'Bless them.'

'Alicia says, *This marriage is like a Mainbocher suit; you don't get tired of it and it will wear for ever.* Oh—when Rick heard about Kenneth's engagement, he said *they would naturally gravitate towards each other because they were the only two*

*pure barbarians in the neighbourhood, Kenneth being the more
amenable barbarian of the two.* That's all. Just her love to us.'

She got up and came over to the window. The delicious scent
of the honeysuckle, rich with the zenith of summer, was strong
on the warm air. The outsides of the long honey-coloured horns
were dark crimson.

'Heavenly,' murmured Betty.

'There's something a little absurd in someone getting
married at that age, don't you think?' said the aunt presently.
'And it's a risk too. They're both set in their ways and too old
to change.'

'Oh, I don't know,' said Betty, bending forward once more to
sniff the honeysuckle and expressing the feeling of most of the
human race, 'I think it's always nice to hear of someone getting
married.'

Chapter The Last

In summer the mighty beech trees cast their shade on the foothills of the mountains of Bairamia, and the dark green leaves above the hoar silver trunks rustle in the wind from the sea. Through the coolness and shadow of evening; along the narrow track that wolves had begun a thousand years ago; down the side of the mountain from her convent where the nuns looked up to the Roman citadel on the height; past the shattered tiles and stones of that citadel mingled with the yellow scree of the slopes; down through the airy shade of the lilac thickets; along by the icy stream where the red tulips grew, rode the Reverend Mother of the Convent of Santa Cipriana on her high sloping Circassian saddle. She rode on an old white horse and before her plodded an old man carrying a carbine. The water made a rushing rippling sound and the air was beginning to smell of lilac. Four black birds flew in the gulf of clear air below the travellers and the sunset shone through the tips of their wing feathers and made them transparent. The eyes of the Reverend Mother and the old man followed their flight.

'Sleep-When-The-Sun-Sleeps is going to his nest,' said the old man. 'We shall not be in the Khar-el-Nadoon before dusk, Holy One. You will have to sleep the night there at the house of Gyges. It is well?'

'It is well,' said the Reverend Mother placidly. She was about sixty years old and dressed in coarse bright blue linen that framed her wrinkled and clever face in severe folds.

They went steadily on. The shadows grew longer and the air cooler. The Reverend Mother glanced down at the brilliant grass, and first she saw the small yellow daisies shut, and then the globe-flowers, and then the tulips. She moved her fingers over her worn dark wooden beads and said the Prayer of Evening and the old man muttered it too. The sun went down behind the mountains and the rose colour faded out of the sky. They reached the Khar-el-Nadoon as the first stars came out.

The family of Gyges was seated at supper in the long, low living-room with its whitewashed walls hung with rich red and blue carpets. Lamps burned in the four corners with a brilliant smoky light and the smell of hot oil mingled with the steam from the whole lamb, piled about with rice and herbs, that smoked in a huge painted dish in the midst of the circle of people. The servants stood against the walls, ready to attend the family with bowls of water and towels for their greasy hands after they had taken food from the communal dish.

The light played over the white and yellow robes, the fair hair under square white caps, the long laughing eyes and smiling faces of Vartouhi's people. Outside the stone house, in the clear blue night, the fruit was setting well on the trees, and in the small meadows, as thick with flowers as with grass, the sheep and goats were being milked under the olives. The nearest Italian soldiers were two miles away in the village, homesick and frightened. The family of Gyges plunged their hands into the lamb stew and ate with the appetite of people who trust in God and know that their country will soon be free from the invader. Presently, at a signal from the old man Gyges, a servant turned the knob of a large battered wireless cabinet and Turkish music rang out on the air; a thrilling and melancholy refrain of eight bars endlessly repeated, sonorous yet shrill. They ate and smiled and listened, the family likeness playing over their faces, and outside the door a crowd gradually gathered to listen to the music; poor fruit-pickers and workers who lived in hovels among the orchards, and people from the village a mile or two away, and one or two of the itinerant beggars whom a progressive Government had forbidden to beg and who hid in the woods by day and only came out at night to steal. A steady murmur of conversation and comment floated into the room on the cool night wind and the light of the lamps played now on a solemn exhausted face under a linen cap stiff with dirt and age, and now on a young face, wild and smiling. All were listening intently and some of them moved their heads and clapped their hands in time to the music.

Presently there was a commotion among the crowd and the old man with the carbine pushed his way through them and past the servants standing at the door and made his way into the room. The meal itself was over, and the family was drinking the thick, sweet syrupy coffee that had just been poured for them by Yilg, the eldest unmarried daughter now at home.

Gyges looked up with dignity as the old man entered and waited for him to speak.

'The blessing of God be with you and on your house, honoured father of five daughters,' said the old man, putting the carbine carefully on the floor and then bowing and touching his brow, his lips and his heart. 'The Reverend Mother of the Convent of the Holy Cipriana is outside and wishes to see you because she has a message from your daughter, who is now in the Country of Ships.'

This had been the Bairamian peasants' name for England since the days of Elizabeth. From their bald mountain slopes of scree where the snow could find no permanent foothold they watched the ships going along the dark dazzling sea in the straits below, and for four hundred years most of the ships had been English. Twice in England's history they had heard how she had been saved by her great fleets and her sailors and now she was being saved by them once again. The soldiers from England who had come to fight the Italians and free Bairamia in the old days had come in ships from England, and scaled the shaly cliffs with ropes and ladders while the guns of the ships kept watch below. Nowadays, of course, the music-and-talking-that-danced-along-the-air told them things about England—and about their own country too—in their own language, and lately the English aeroplanes had taken to flying over Bairamia and dropping packets of chocolate and good advice, and there was an English flying boy, a mere child who seemed half-asleep yet laughed as often as one of themselves, in the Italian prison camp at Ser. But they still thought of England as the Country of Ships.

When the family heard what the old man said an excited buzz of conversation began.

'Beg of the Holy One to enter our poor house at once,' said Gyges, and ordered fresh coffee to be made and sent for some dishes of sticky sweetmeats rolled in finely powdered sugar.

The Reverend Mother came in through the low door. There was a crowd of sallow interested faces peering over her shoulders and her blue robes were the colour of the summer night sky. The old man came after her, carrying saddle-bags full of food and wine.

'I brought these,' said the Reverend Mother presently, with her mouth full of cold mountain guinea-fowl and indicating her provisions with its leg, 'as it is said in our village that there is no food in the Khar-el-Nadoon, honoured Gyges.'

'It is a lie,' said Gyges tranquilly. 'No doubt the black-hearted sons of the she-dogs, the Italians, set it about to cast shame on the name of our valley and to fill the hearts of other villages with despair.'

'Yes, yes, no doubt,' murmured all the aunts and cousins and the young women and the servants and the crowd of faces at the door, eagerly nodding, and one or two of them spat.

'Never have we known hunger in this valley, Holy One,' spoke up a large, plump male cousin.

'It is well. My heart is light.' The Reverend Mother wiped her fingers upon an embroidered towel held to her by a servant and drank some wine. Then she said:

'There is a letter from thy Vartouhi, honoured Gyges. I have it in my girdle. It came——' and she pointed up to the ceiling and smiled. A murmur of laughter ran round the room and spread to the crowd outside, and everyone nodded. 'Sister B'fera was working in the garden and one of the flying men came over in his flying-machine, so low, so low, that she feared for our roofs. She summoned me and we all ran out, praying him to spare us, and he waved his hand to us, laughing. I myself saw his face and had no fear, although he was young and therefore heedless. Then he sent forth a little white thing shaped like a globeflower and it came down, down, down so slowly and lodged in a high beech tree on the path up to the ancient ruins. I sent Hussein to climb the tree, and he brought down the white globeflower-thing, which was made of fine silk and very fair to see, and lo! it was carrying a little packet with sweet dark food and some sayings of those two wise men in the Land of Ships and Am-erica——'

Here there were murmurs of 'Ch—ch'l' and 'Ros'vl' from everybody and more nods and smiles. Only the faces of the beggars, who crouched outside the circle of light and gnawed the bones of the lamb which the servants had thrown out to them, remained exhausted and grave, as if they did not understand.

'——and this letter from thy Vartouhi, honoured Gyges, which I will now read to thee.'

She took a leather bag, which was attached to her hemp girdle, from the folds of her robe and brought out a letter and began to read, in the midst of an attentive hush. Gyges had made an imperious gesture and the wireless had been silenced.

★

Honoured Father, honoured Mother, and my dear sisters,

In the name of God the All–Merciful and All–Wise,
greetings. Blessed be the house, and all that dwell therein,
and all who are far away. I am well, and my heart is light.
I am to be married in the Month of Setting Fruit to a
rich English man. Thou wilt remember, my sisters Djura
and K'ussa and Yilg, how our sister Yania and I, thy sister
Vartouhi, would sit when we were all little maids on the
wall above the stream and talk of what we would do when
we wore the folded cap of womanhood. Thou rememberest?
Yania and I vowed that we would marry rich lords. Now
we are both to do as we said. Yania's lord is an American
and my lord is English. Thou wilt remember, honoured
father and honoured mother, that in the house where I
worked as a servant there was a large and comely man,
Kenneth Fielding, whose sister ruled him in all things.
From the first I looked upon him with kindness and I
thought, I will wed this man. And he looked upon me
with kindness also. But his wicked sister drove me away
because I made for him a *djan* for his bed, after our custom
towards a warrior when we wish to show him that we
would marry him should he ask. (He is a soldier, this man;
a captain.) My heart was angry and I went away, thinking,
there are other rich lords in England and I will find one
for myself, and I will think no more about Kenneth
Fielding. But lo! he came after me and found me, and
now we are to be married.

I ask for thy blessing, honoured father and mother.

Kenneth Fielding's aged and honourable father will live
in our house (couldst thou but see it! with the gardens
for fruit and the gardens for vegetables and the little house
where the food lives, where snow is made all the year
round!). His aged and honourable cousin will also live in
our house. The wicked sister I have sent away, but she

too is to be married, although she is an old, old woman of fifty-three years. She is to marry an old, old man of fifty-eight years. They will have no children. But I shall have many children and when this war is ended and all the wicked Germans and Italians and Japanese are dead I and my husband and my children will come on a visit to the Khar-el-Nadoon and hold thine honoured hands against our hearts.

Farewell, honoured father and mother and farewell to you, dear sisters. I will call my firstborn daughter in the name of my niece Medora.

In the name of God the All-Merciful and All-Wise, blessings on the house, and all that dwell therein, and all who are far away.

Thy daughter,
VARTOUHI.

A babel of voices broke out as the Reverend Mother ceased to read. The letter was passed from hand to hand and Medora, now a slender maiden of ten who had been allowed to return from Turkey, insisted upon having the reference to herself read out to her a second time. She listened shyly, with her thick plaits of fair hair decorated with gold coins falling against her cheeks.

'Ah, soon it will be thy turn!' cried her grandmother, glancing at Djura and Yilg, who at fifteen and seventeen were not yet betrothed. 'If *thou* art not betrothed by thy fourteenth year, come not to me for thy bridal linen!' Medora put her hand over her mouth and her long eyes danced in laughter as she ran away to a far corner of the room.

'But indeed,' continued Fayet, 'is there not hope for all maidens, however old, when a maiden fifty-three years old can be married?'

There was a murmur of astonishment and assent.

'And in spite of this woman's great age and her barrenness,

419

it is well,' concluded Vartouhi's mother authoritatively, taking a sweet rolled in powdered sugar and glancing about the room. 'Young or old, fair or ugly, man or woman (unless of course they be vowed to God like thyself, Holy One), it is well to be married.'

THE END

www.vintage-classics.info